PRAISE FOR THE SUNL

Matt Mikalatos has built a compelling fantasy world with humor and heart.

GENE LUEN YANG, creator of *American Born Chinese* and *Boxers & Saints*

Matt Mikalatos has penned a tale straight out of today's headlines that will tug at your heartstrings. *The Crescent Stone* is a compelling story that will get under your skin and worm its way into your heart.

TOSCA LEE, *New York Times* bestselling author of *Iscariot* and *The Legend of Sheba*

The Crescent Stone hooked me from the first page! With the rich characterization of John Green and the magical escapism of Narnia, this book is a must read for all fantasy fans!

LORIE LANGDON, author of *Olivia Twist* and the Doon series

This is what sets Mikalatos's epic world apart from so many other fantasy realms: the characters feel real, their lives are genuine and complicated, and their choices are far from binary. Mikalatos's creativity and originality are on full display in this epic tale for adults and young readers alike.

SHAWN SMUCKER, author of *The Day the Angels Fell*

The Crescent Stone blends . . . glitter unicorns, powerful healing tattoos, and an engaging cast of characters into a funny and thoughtful story that examines the true costs of magic and privilege.

TINA CONNOLLY, author of *Seriously Wicked*

The twists keep coming in *The Crescent Stone*, a fabulous young adult fantasy with a great cast of characters. I particularly loved Jason, whose humor, logic, and honesty will make readers eager to follow him into a sequel. I found the Sunlit Lands a fantastically engaging place to visit and grew ever more delighted as I discovered more about each culture, their knotted histories, and how the magic worked. Fantasy fans will devour it and ask for seconds.

JILL WILLIAMSON, Christy Award–winning author of *By Darkness Hid* and *Captives*

From C. S. Lewis to J. K. Rowling, the secret magical place that lives alongside our own mundane world has a rich history in fantasy literature, and *The Crescent Stone* is a delightful tale that is a more-than-worthy continuation of that tradition. Matt Mikalatos weaves a rich tapestry that is equal parts wonder, thoughtfulness, and excitement, while being that most wonderful of things—a joyful and fun story. From the first page, you can't help but root for Madeline as she stumbles about trying to navigate a future that is uncertain and fraught with pain. The beauty of Madeline as a character is that her journey is both all too familiar and yet entirely contemporary—the magical land that is her salvation is so much more. I don't know where this series will go. All I know is that I don't ever want it to end.

JAKE KERR, author of the Tommy Black series and a nominee for the Nebula Award, the Theodore Sturgeon Memorial Award, and the storySouth Million Writers Award

The Crescent Stone inspires thought on matters of compassion and privilege in a breathtaking and fun fantasy setting. This is a book that will leave readers empowered—not by magic, but by the potential within their own hearts.

BETH CATO, author of *The Clockwork Dagger*

ALSO IN THE SUNLIT LANDS SERIES

NOVELS

The Crescent Stone

The Heartwood Crown

SHORT STORIES

"Our Last Christmas Together"

"Jason Wu and the Kidnapped Stories"

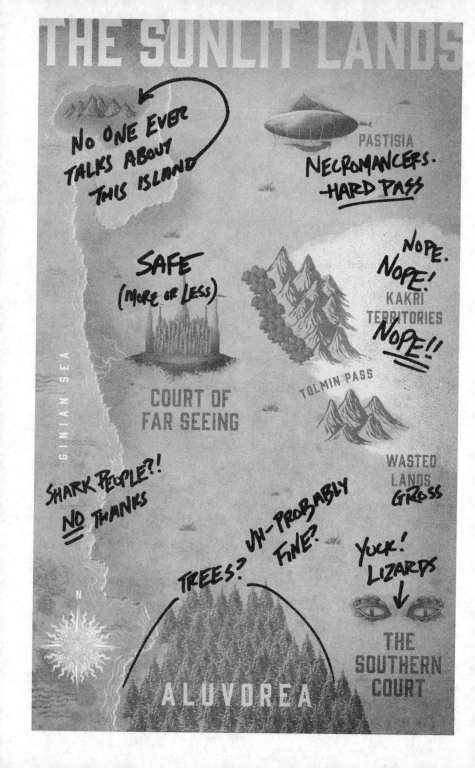

THE SUNLIT LANDS

BOOK THREE

THE STORY KING

MATT MIKALATOS

wander™
An imprint of
Tyndale House
Publishers

Visit Tyndale online at tyndale.com.

Visit the author's website at thesunlitlands.com.

TYNDALE and Tyndale's quill logo are registered trademarks of Tyndale House Ministries. *Wander* and the Wander logo are trademarks of Tyndale House Ministries. Wander is an imprint of Tyndale House Publishers, Carol Stream, Illinois.

The Story King

Designed by Dean H. Renninger

Edited by Sarah Rubio

The author is represented by Ambassador Literary Agency, Nashville, TN.

The Story King is a work of fiction. Where real people, events, establishments, organizations, or locales appear, they are used fictitiously. All other elements of the novel are drawn from the author's imagination.

For information about special discounts for bulk purchases, please contact Tyndale House Publishers at csresponse@tyndale.com, or call 1-855-277-9400.

Library of Congress Cataloging-in-Publication Data

Names: Mikalatos, Matt, author.
Title: The Story King / Matt Mikalatos.
Description: Carol Stream, Illinois : Wander, an imprint of Tyndale House
  Publishers, Inc., [2021] | Series: The Sunlit Lands ; book 3 | Summary:
  "The magic of the Sunlit Lands has been reset, but that doesn't mean all
  is well. Unrest and discord are growing by the day, and Hanali is
  positioning himself as ruler of the Sunlit Lands. But, in order for
  Hanali to seize control, there must be a sacrifice, one that very few
  are willing to make. Jason, Shula, Baileya, and others must work
  together to save the lives of those Hanali would sacrifice for his own
  gain"— Provided by publisher.
Identifiers: LCCN 2021006452 (print) | LCCN 2021006453 (ebook) | ISBN
  9781496447852 (hardcover) | ISBN 9781496447869 (trade paperback) | ISBN
  9781496447876 (kindle edition) | ISBN 9781496447883 (epub) | ISBN
  9781496447890 (epub)
Subjects: CYAC: Fantasy.
Classification: LCC PZ7.1.M5535 St 2021 (print) | LCC PZ7.1.M5535 (ebook)
  | DDC [Fic]—dc23
LC record available at https://lccn.loc.gov/2021006452
LC ebook record available at https://lccn.loc.gov/2021006453

Printed in the United States of America

27   26   25   24   23   22   21
 7   6   5   4   3   2   1

To JR. and Amanda Forasteros,
who teach the world about hospitality, friendship, and love.
They are heroes in every story told about them.

CAST OF CHARACTERS

AMIRA—Shula's younger sister

ARAKAM—a prophetic dragon

ARCHON THENODY—the former chief magistrate and supreme ruler of the Elenil

BAILEYA—a Kakri warrior and Jason's former fiancée

BEZAED—a Kakri warrior; one of Baileya's brothers

BLACK SKULLS—the elite fighting force of the Scim; there are three known members, one of whom is Darius

BOULOS—Shula's older brother

BREAK BONES—a Scim warrior once imprisoned by the Elenil, now Jason's ally

CLAWDIA—a Kharobem with the appearance of a lion cub

CUMBERLAND ARMSTRONG WALKER—Darius's "grandfather"

CRUKIBAL—a prince of the Maegrom

DARIUS WALKER—an American human allied with the Scim; Madeline's ex-boyfriend; a Black Skull

DAVID GLENN—an American human; close friends with Kekoa and Jason

DAY SONG—a "civilized" Scim man who serves Gilenyia

DELIGHTFUL GLITTER LADY (DEE, DGL)—Jason's unicorn; can change size

EVERNU—a gallant white stag who works alongside Rondelo

FANTOK—a sovereign of the Kharobem

FATHER TONY—a Catholic priest

FERNANDA ISABELA FLORES DE CASTILLA—Lady of Westwind; the Knight of the Mirror's beloved

GILENYIA—an influential Elenil; Hanali's cousin

HANALI—an influential Elenil who has recruited many humans to the Sunlit Lands

IAN—king of Pastisia

JASON WU (WU SONG)—an American human who has spent a year in the desert attempting to become Kakri; always tells the truth

JENNY WU—Jason's sister

JORDAN WALKER—Darius's father

KEKOA KAHANANUI—an American human who was sent to the Zhanin by the Knight of the Mirror

KNIGHT OF THE MIRROR—a human who eschews magic; onetime servant of the Elenil

KYLE OLIVER—Madeline's father

LELISE—ruler of the Southern Court

MADELINE OLIVER—an American human formerly in the service of the Elenil

MAJESTIC ONE—the Elenil name for the magician who founded the Sunlit Lands

MALGWIN—ruler of the Sea Beneath

MORIARTY—a brucok (gigantic bird from the Kakri territories)

MOTHER CROW—a Kakri matriarch

MRS. RAYMOND (MARY PATRICIA WALL)—an English human woman who runs the Transition House for humans in the Sunlit Lands; wife of King Ian

NEW DAWN—a "civilized" Scim woman who works for Gilenyia

NIGHTFALL—a Scim child thought to have been killed by the Elenil, but in actuality "reeducated" by Archon Thenody

PEASANT KING—the figure from Scim legend who founded the Sunlit Lands

PATRA KOJA—the antlered spirit of a Maduvorean marsh

RANA—a storyteller

REMI—the Guardian of the Wind

RICARDO SÁNCHEZ—a human servant of Gilenyia

RONDELO—the Elenil captain of the guard in the Court of Far Seeing

RUTH MBEWE—a young Zambian human

SHULA BISHARA—a Syrian human; adoptive mother to Yenil

SOCHAR—an Elenil guard known for his violent treatment of the Scim

VASILISA "VASYA" MARKOVA—a friend of Shula's family

WENDY OLIVER—Madeline's mother

YENIL—a young Scim girl

PART 1

THE BEGINNING

---

*There is a being called the Story King. If there is a more
vast and ancient being, I know not of him. His attention
roves to and fro throughout the universe, and if one seeks—
as I do—power for personal gain, one would be wise to
avoid his gaze. I invest great energy in disguising my small
endeavor here upon the plantation, for if he knew of it,
surely he would confound my every effort. He cannot be
defended against, for a story slips past all defenses. He
cannot be defeated, only stalled. He cannot be destroyed,
for it is said that he has died and yet he lives. And
his servants are living Stories, sent to do his bidding.*

FROM *THE MAGICIAN'S GRIMOIRE*

1
THE KAKRI TERRITORIES

I know this story. I feel I have heard it, many years ago.

THE KNIGHT OF THE MIRROR

✦

I can tell you a story that will change the world." The old woman said these words without looking at Jason Wu. She poked the fire with a stick, and a burst of sparks rose toward the stars, which shone far brighter here in the Kakri territories than Jason had ever seen on Earth.

In the last year, Jason had learned many things. How to drink water from the gourd of a tree called the pentex (or, as Jason liked to call it, the Knife-Bladed Widow-Maker. He was pretty sure he would have scars). How to track the canny wylna to its lair and trap it inside. How to hide in the sand if something was hunting you. How to survive a sandstorm, how to start a fire, and how to sleep despite the cold when fires were impossible. He had made friends with a Maegrom, and he had broken an ancient curse. He had freed a Kharobem—a living story—from slavery. But he had never figured out how to tell when Mother Crow was joking.

He thought she was serious. She didn't make jokes when bargaining with a story. Stories were the cornerstone of the Kakri economy, and several Kakri sayings put stories at the same level as breath and water and food. Story was life. Life was story.

This was how a bargain started. The storyteller told you what sort of story she would tell you. It could be something useful like "I can tell you a story about what is good to eat in the desert." Or it could be something entertaining: "I can tell you a story that will make the listeners laugh every time they think of it." Jason grinned remembering that one. A story could be described any number of ways. The story of how the Peasant King made the crystal spheres. The story of how Mother Crow got her name. Learning the right way to pitch a story to your audience, that was part of the bargain.

For instance, Jason had successfully pitched "Little Red Riding Hood" to Mother Crow by saying, "I can tell you the story of a girl eaten by a wolf." Mother Crow's eyes had lit up at that. She loved survival stories, as did most of the Kakri. Stories that helped you navigate the world were gold, and Mother Crow said the oldest stories were things like "I saw a scorpion near the water hole today." Stories that warned you of danger or prepared you for the risks ahead. She had, to Jason's surprise, loved "Little Red Riding Hood" and said it was about obeying your mother. Jason told her it was about not getting too close to your grandmother, and Mother Crow had laughed and laughed at that. Sometimes she called him Little Red now, which he didn't love, but it made her happy.

She had never offered a story like this. One that would change the world. As the potential receiver of the tale, Jason could ask a few questions. You weren't allowed to ask questions that gave away too much of the story, because she wouldn't share it for free. The last question the recipient asked was the price. But first it was important to know what you were buying. "A story that will change the world," Jason said, trying to act indifferent. "Change it for the better or make it worse?"

Mother Crow smiled at him, pleased with the question. "Better for some, worse for others. It will throw down kings and raise up cities. It will destroy governments and create worlds."

"I thought it was a story, not a riddle."

Mother Crow thought that was particularly funny. "A riddle is only a story you do not yet understand."

"Uh-huh." Jason threw some twigs into the fire and watched them turn bright orange before twisting away into ash. "I hate riddles."

"Remember Nian. He was a puzzle to me. That story was a riddle."

Two days ago Jason had told her the story of the monster Nian, who came down into the village to hunt people. A wise old man in the village suggested that the people band together and make a lot of noise, so they beat drums and lit firecrackers, and the monster was so terrified he ran in circles until he exhausted himself and the people caught and killed him.

Mother Crow had sensed there was something more to the story, and Jason had decided to make her guess instead of telling her straight out. She had pestered him and guessed and clapped her hands in his face, and he had enjoyed having a few hours of power over her for once. She had said, "You've only given me a piece of the tale."

"You bought a story," he said. "And I gave it to you."

So she had bought another story from him. The story of Nian's name. Jason was pleased because he got a really great Kakri story in exchange—the story of the gigantic stone creatures out in the Kakri territories that moved so slowly you almost couldn't tell that they moved at all. He and his former fianceé, Baileya (long story), had passed them when they were on the run from her brothers, who were trying to kill Jason (an even longer story). These creatures, it turned out, had been sent to destroy the Sunlit Lands. They were going to break the entire world apart, or so it was said. Mother Crow said, "This is a true prophecy and a true story." Many years ago a powerful magician had cast a spell on them that made them move so slowly, they were no danger to anyone. "But one day, it is said, they will destroy the Sunlit Lands." It was an interesting story, and he had definitely gotten the better part of the bargain.

Mother Crow had told him the story of the living stone creatures, and he had told her about Nian. How the monster's name was also the Chinese word for "year." That's why the New Year celebration included fireworks and the beating of drums.

Mother Crow had complimented him on the canny deal and said, "A single word can hold a thousand stories." Which, honestly, had sounded like another riddle.

He could ask more questions, but Mother Crow had pitched the story just right. He knew he wanted it. Of course, he could always ask for it another night, but what if she didn't feel like it then? She said there were seasons for some stories—special times, perfect moments. Some stories might come and go. You could pass on a story today and never have the opportunity to hear it again. So he could ask questions, but there was only one question that mattered.

"How much does it cost?"

Mother Crow's eyes sparkled. She stirred the fire with her stick. She knew he wanted the story. He should have asked more questions. He had set himself up for a terrible bargain. He wasn't ready for what Mother Crow said next, though. She settled on the stone she used as a chair and put her hands on her knees. She watched the stars for a moment as if adding all the costs in her head.

"It costs your entire life," she said at last. "Only your entire life."

"That seems a little steep," Jason said.

"To hear it is free," Mother Crow said. "But to tell it requires a lifetime of practice."

"All I want is to hear it."

Mother Crow said nothing to this. She watched the fire, a smile on her face. She knew he wanted the story, but she wasn't going to give him the hard sell. She just waited for him to bite again.

"So it must be a rare story," he said, "to be worth so much."

"It is common." Mother Crow paused and looked into the darkness beyond the fire. She listened for a long moment as if tracking something that had made a small sound and then fallen silent. At last she turned her attention back to Jason. "It is common and a well-known story among the Kakri. Every child knows this story."

"Then it's worthless."

The old woman sighed. "Have you learned so little, Wu Song? It is common, but it is precious. As common and precious as air. Would you rather have air or a diamond? Would you prefer water or emeralds?"

"Could I have a little of both?"

As they spoke, a lion cub limped into the circle of light. Mother Crow leaned back from the fire, one eye squinted, studying the little beast. It settled down between them. "She knows you," Mother Crow said.

Yeah, she did. She wasn't actually a lion cub at all—she was one of the Kharobem, shape-shifting creatures of the desert whom the Kakri claimed were "made of story," whatever that meant. This one, though, wasn't like the one he had released from captivity a while back. This one Jason had saved from a pack of wylna, and she had hidden him and Baileya in a sandstorm. Later a whole bunch of Kharobem had appeared when he and Madeline had confronted the archon in one of the towers of Far Seeing.

"Maybe she wants to hear the story," Jason suggested.

"I think not, Little Red. The Kharobem often come to watch some momentous occasion, some turning point in the history of the Sunlit Lands. They came when we left the city of Ezerbin, and they watched when the Sunlit Lands were being fashioned." She appeared to hear a sound outside the ring of firelight. Her eyes tracked something in the distant darkness.

"Why don't we ask her?"

"The Kharobem do not answer such questions."

"Ha, shows what you know." Jason addressed the lion cub. "Hey, what's going on?"

The lion cub settled onto her haunches. "Many years ago," she said, speaking with the voice of a young child, "there was a shepherd who desired the people of his village to join him in searching for and killing the wolves in the hills. But none would go. 'The wolves have not bothered our sheep in four seasons,' they said. 'Let us leave them alone.' The man grew angry, and when the villagers left the meadow, he killed ten of his own sheep. He made it look as if a great wolf had done it, and he said, "Every five seasons the wolves come and eat all the sheep." This was not true, and none could remember it, but as he told the villagers of the monstrous size of the wolf that had done this horrible thing—it had not even eaten the sheep, just destroyed them—the villagers were filled with fear. 'Do not be afraid,' he said, 'but rather get your swords, your bows, your knives, and your hunting dogs.' They set out and killed all the wolves they could find, and when it was done, the shepherd had lost only ten sheep."

Jason rolled his eyes. "Ugh. More riddles."

Mother Crow stared at the Kharobem, her eyes wide. "Wu Song—" she began, but then the arrow sank into her chest and she listed to the side, sliding into the sand. Jason didn't even know it was an arrow at first. He thought some black bird—a raven—had flown at her, and he was about to say something about how strange it was when she raised her arm, eyes wide, and he saw the shaft of the arrow. Jason ran over and fell on his knees beside her.

"Come close," she gasped. "For one last story."

And when he leaned near her, trying to hold back his tears, she told him the story that would change the world. She lifted her hand and brushed his hair back tenderly, like a mother with her child. He put his hand over hers. She closed her eyes and breathed, ragged and tender.

"You're going to be okay," Jason said. He had promised never to tell a lie again, but he said this more out of hope than anything else. He didn't know anything about arrow wounds. He would need to try to get her to the other Kakri as quickly as possible. Was it safe to move her? He wasn't sure. But safer, surely, than staying here.

Jason recognized the fletching on the arrow. It was from the Scim. He almost stumbled into the fire when he rose. He clenched his fists and stood at the edge of the firelight. "Who did this? Show yourself! Cowards!" But there was no answer. His head, his chest felt tight, felt like he had been wedged into a crack of stone. He could barely pull a breath, and his jaws had clamped shut. He couldn't speak, couldn't shout. Sobs forced themselves through his teeth. He fell beside Mother Crow, cradling her head in his arms.

The lion cub gave him a pitying look with her large, dark eyes, then slipped away into the darkness. Mother Crow had fallen onto the carpet they set out between the tents. Whoever had shot that arrow was still out there—he knew that much—but he also knew he needed to get her out of the open. He dragged the carpet toward one of the tents, then pulled her the rest of the way by her arms.

She was still breathing but felt terribly cold. He put a blanket over her, carefully draping it so it wouldn't disturb the arrow. There was very little blood, which concerned him more than buckets of it would have. He pulled the flaps of the tent shut, so that no one could get a clear shot at her, and propped her up a bit, hoping it would help her breathing.

Jason crouched at the tent door and slipped a long, curved knife into his hand. He had been practicing with various weapons in the Kakri way, and though he still wasn't an expert, he was far, far better than he had been a year ago. This knife was Mother Crow's. She called it her "tent knife." She had a tent knife, a cooking knife, a hunting knife, a blanket knife, a cape knife, and a ceremonial knife. No doubt she had more, but Jason had finally told her he didn't want to know about any others.

A shadow moved beyond the fire. The stranger had a hood over his face, a quiver of arrows on his back, and an arrow nocked on his bowstring. He didn't seem to know where Jason and Mother Crow were. He must have been distracted somehow after shooting her. The hooded stranger moved around the fire to the place where the carpet had been. The sand didn't leave much to the imagination about what had happened, and he followed the tracks easily to the tent. He was thin and about Jason's height. He set his bow and arrow aside, crouched down, and studied the blood on the carpet.

Jason flew from the tent, tackling the stranger. There was a brief skirmish, but a year in the desert had made Jason strong and wiry, and two quick punches—one to the kidneys and a second to the face—took most of the fight out of the man who had tried to kill Mother Crow.

The tent knife appeared at the stranger's throat. Jason wanted to say something about how he was going to kill the guy, but he had taken an oath a long time ago not to tell lies. So instead he said, "Knives are sharp, and people get hurt by them every day. Usually by cutting but also sometimes by stabbing. This is a knife I am holding to your neck right now."

The stranger fell extremely still. "Wu Song," he said. "You are making a terrible mistake."

Jason hesitated. How had this guy known his real name? He tore the stranger's hood away. "No," Jason said. "That's not possible."

"And yet you see me with your own eyes." The man grinned at him. "Surprise."

2
PORTLAND, OREGON

It started in deep grief.

THE PEASANT KING

✢

"Where do you think you're going?"

Darius paused, his hand on the doorknob. "I'm going out, Mama. Just out."

His mom was slender, a full foot shorter than him, her grey-streaked hair done in a twist out, but when she put her hands on her hips, he knew he was in for it. "Darius. I know you've been through some trouble this last year. But you can't be running around without telling me where you're going. I worry. I need to know what's going on."

"I got my phone, Mama. You need me, you text, you call. You know I'm coming home."

"Is there some reason I can't know where you're going?"

Darius pursed his lips and ran his hand over his hair. "Ma. You wouldn't like it."

"Well, if you know your mama isn't going to like it, Son, why are you going there? You want me to follow you in my car?"

"Ma, no. Can't you just trust me?"

"And you say you'll be coming home if I text. You don't remember when you disappeared for months? You don't remember showing up at home one day crying and saying you can't tell me where you've been?"

"Ma."

Her eyes softened. "You don't remember telling me Madeline was gone, Darius? Gone and no body for her parents? Now her mama is gone too, and no one has seen her in close to a year. The police coming around here asking questions, Mr. Oliver calling and trying to talk to you. Then you want me to be okay when you go out? What am I supposed to do next time you don't come home? Leave a candle in the window?"

Darius couldn't bear to look at her. He stared at his Nikes. He tried to get a full breath but couldn't. "Mama. I can't tell you. I would if I could. I don't want to hurt you, but I got to do what I'm doing. That's all."

His mom took his hand. Her hands were warm. "Darius. Son. There's nothing you *got* to do. Only what you *choose* to do."

Darius pulled his hand away, then put both hands on his mom's shoulders. "You and I both know that's not true." Then he was out the front door and halfway to his car.

His mom called, "Dinner's at five o'clock, Darius. If you aren't here, I'm calling your father."

Darius didn't say anything to that, just slung himself into his beat-up Mustang and pulled into the street. He loved his dad, but he hadn't seen him much this year. He only came running when Mom called. Dad was more like the lecture machine, showing up to correct Darius's behavior from time to time, and it built a hard place in Darius's heart. Made it harder to hear what his dad had to say, even if it was good advice. Not that he had any advice for Darius's actual problems. Not really. *My girlfriend died in a fantasy world, and now I'm trying to get back there. What advice you have for that, Pops?*

A pile of fantasy novels covered his passenger seat. Meselia, Narnia, Andelain, Red London, Wonderland, Oz. He had studied them all. How did you get there? Magic rings, paintings, wardrobes. Tornadoes and hot-air balloons. Fever dreams, fatal illnesses, cupboards, and doors only children could see. Try as he might, Darius couldn't find a way to the Sunlit Lands using any of those things, and he wasn't sure they would work for him if he did find them. Hanali, one of the leaders of the people there, had told Darius he was in charge of who could enter the Sunlit Lands, and he was the one who had banished Darius after framing him for murder. So getting permission from Hanali . . . that seemed unlikely. But maybe there was another way.

He turned into Madeline's old neighborhood. The streets were wider here, the lots bigger. Her dad, Mr. Oliver, wouldn't talk to Darius. Wouldn't let him in the house, wouldn't let him anywhere near Madeline's things. Even if she did have a magic ring or belt or sword or bell, he wouldn't know about it. He thought if he saw something from the Sunlit Lands, he'd recognize it, but it didn't matter if Mr. Oliver wouldn't even let him through the front door.

Darius had exhausted every other thing he could think to try. He had even driven up to Seattle to see a traveling C. S. Lewis exhibit that claimed to have the original wardrobe. He had climbed over the barrier, gotten inside the wardrobe, pulled it shut . . . and nothing. Nothing except for being tossed out of the Museum of Pop Culture after a lecture and threats to call the cops. If the wardrobe had somehow opened a portal to another world, he wasn't sure what good it would have done him. Narnia wasn't the same as the Sunlit Lands. But maybe there was an easier way through from there.

He shook his head. This was how it messed with you, going to a real fantasy world. It made you think that maybe all those other stories were real too. Or maybe some part of them, at least. It didn't help that he had met Mary Patricia Wall, the author of the Meselia books, and she had admitted that her books were a thinly disguised version of her own adventures in the Sunlit Lands. C. S. Lewis had written his books, yes, but that was no guarantee he had walked into a painting and met Aslan. He might have just made it all up. Who knew anymore?

The Meselia stories didn't help much, either. In the first book the main characters got into Meselia by following a gryphon into a swirling portal of colors beneath some stairs. In one of the later books a kid got into Meselia from London by hiding in a dumbwaiter. Darius didn't even know a house that had a dumbwaiter, and he suspected he was too big to fit in one. And gryphons were as scarce around here as owls with invitations to study at magic school.

The Oliver house was two stories, with big windows out front. Mr. Oliver shouldn't be home now . . . he was hardly ever around and had rarely been home when Madeline was alive, either. Darius had only seen him a handful of times. He parked at the curb, not in the driveway. A quick knock on the door went unanswered. He looked over his shoulder. It was a quiet, upscale neighborhood. The kind of place where people kept to themselves. But also the kind of place where people called the cops if they saw a Black kid jumping a fence, which is what he was about to do.

It wasn't a low fence, either. It was a wooden board fence, nearly as tall as Darius himself. He put his left hand at the top of the rounded gate, pushed one foot hard against the boards, and hurled himself upward. He flipped one leg over and swung to the ground. He paused, listening for any cry from the neighbors, but there was nothing. He waited for his heartbeat to return to normal, then moved into the backyard.

Mrs. Oliver had kept an enormous, manicured garden. There was a hedge around the yard, a path that led past a bench and a tree, and a small pond with artfully placed bursts of flowers and a mouse-sized village of sticks and rocks that looked as if a clever child had built it. It had always looked just this side of wild, but now it had crossed over. Not just weeds—there were some of those—but even the flowers had spread from their proper places, the grass was too high and was growing into the path, and the hedges had begun to stretch out of their carefully manicured boxy shapes. The Olivers had hired help once upon a time, but Mr. Oliver must have let them all go after Mrs. Oliver and Madeline disappeared. Or maybe he had just stopped paying them and they had eventually drifted away.

Darius felt safer in the backyard, as the neighbors wouldn't easily be able to see him within the perimeter of that hedge. He sat on the wrought iron bench and thought of Madeline. She and Darius had sat there more than once, her head in his lap, as he read to her from one fantasy novel or another. Most often it was *The Gryphon under the Stairs*, her favorite. His eyes unfocused, and he tried to bring the exact sensations of one of those moments to mind. All he could remember was how uncomfortable wrought iron benches were—but when Madeline was with him, he didn't care.

A bright-green hummingbird zipped in front of him. He sat back, surprised, and the bird hovered there, right at eye level, for so long that he almost felt like it was trying to tell him something. But, of course, this wasn't the Sunlit Lands, and after a moment the bird zoomed away with the sound of a hundred wings. *Madeline would have loved that.*

A sharp, high-pitched whistle came from across the lawn. A calico cat stalked some prey along the back of the yard. Darius stood to get a better view. It was a robin, its feathers fluffed out so far it was nearly the size of a baseball. As the cat slunk nearer, the robin panicked, flapping its wings, but one of them must have been broken because it couldn't get off the ground. Darius could have sworn the bird was looking at him, trying to catch his eye, as if asking for help. He glanced back at the house, which was still quiet. He knew Mr. Oliver could come home at any moment.

It would only take a second to help the bird, though. For some reason that seemed like the right thing to do. Darius flipped a rock from the path toward the cat. It bounced near him, and the cat shot a quick look toward Darius but immediately turned its attention back to the robin. Darius took a step in that direction, and the cat's ear turned toward him. It moved faster toward the bird.

"Hey," Darius said, and sprinted across the lawn. The cat ran too, and the bird flapped its useless wings, popping off the ground for a brief moment before falling again. The cat pounced, and the robin burst into a distressed chirping. Darius grabbed the cat by the scruff and yanked it away, the cat yowling and contorting itself, trying to bite Darius's hand. He dropped the cat, standing between it and the bird. The cat gave him a disgusted look, moved away about ten feet, settled in, and stared at Darius with some mixture of anger and hatred.

Darius kept an eye on the cat for a minute before turning to the robin. It wasn't a broken wing at all. The bird had gotten wrapped up in some twine, and one wing was pinned against its body. The bird tried to get away from Darius when he crouched beside it, but he gently put his hands around its body, trying to calm it. He thought of his giant owl, Bubo, in the Sunlit Lands. Darius had often ridden him through the night sky, back when he was the leader of the Black Skulls. It seemed like another life.

He lifted the robin in his cupped hands. He could feel its heartbeat, then the thrash of its wings as it began to panic. He carefully set it among the branches of the hedge, and with a moment's work was able to unwind the twine from the bird's wing, then slowly remove it from the rest of the robin's body. He pulled his hands out of the hedge and stepped away. The bird cocked its head at him, looked at the cat, tried its wing experimentally, and flew away.

The cat shot him a disapproving glare and disappeared into the hedge. Darius shrugged. "I guess that's my good deed for the day." Madeline would have been pleased, though she probably would have brought the cat a bowl of milk as an apology for stealing its bird.

The house was still quiet. Darius moved to the living room window and took a quick look inside. He didn't see anyone. There was a key to the kitchen door that Mrs. Oliver kept in a fake rock. No one but family was supposed to know it was there, but of course Madeline had told him about it one of the first times they'd been in the backyard together. He found the rock, slid it open, and dropped the key into his palm. He reached for the doorknob but stopped just short of grabbing it. The door was already open slightly. Maybe an inch of space. A small pane of glass was broken right above the knob. Just enough for someone to reach in and unlock the door.

Darius dropped the key in his pocket and slipped the door open with his foot. He stepped into the house, silent. Could it be that Mr. Oliver had forgotten his key and come back into the house this way? It seemed unlikely. Wouldn't he have closed and locked the door once he got inside? Wouldn't he have fixed the broken windowpane?

The kitchen drawers were open.

He moved into the living room. The television had been taken from the wall and sat propped against the fireplace. How had he missed that when he looked through the window? The front door was to his left, and it still appeared to be locked. There was a bathroom in the hallway ahead, and if he turned to the right, Madeline's room would be the first one he came to. Mr. and Mrs. Oliver's room was at the end of the hall.

Now that he was closer and listening more carefully, Darius could hear some little shuffling noises coming from down the hall. He poked his head around the corner. A shadow moved in the back bedroom, and he heard drawers opening. Someone was going through the Olivers' room. Madeline's door was closed—the Olivers had moved her downstairs when her breathing had worsened.

Darius moved as quietly as he could—pretty easy on the thick carpet—until he was at the threshold of the Olivers' room. He peeked his head around the corner and saw a skinny teenage boy with blond hair and blood-shot eyes moving methodically through the room, filling a pillowcase with whatever appeared to be of value. Darius's first thought was, *He better not have taken anything of Madeline's.*

There was a sound from the front door. Keys in the lock. Darius froze, and so did the other kid. Then a flurry of noise as the kid swept up his sack of stuff and headed for the door. Darius punched him in the face as he came out of the room, and the kid fell hard, the sack spilling onto the floor.

Some silverware, a couple picture frames, a few pieces of jewelry. And something strange: a dagger in a silver sheath with oak leaves engraved along the sides. Darius recognized it immediately as Elenil work. He snatched it up and slipped it into his jacket pocket.

"Mr. Oliver," he called. "It's Darius. There's a thief back here. I caught him."

He heard a surprised sound. Then Mr. Oliver appeared in the hallway, followed by a priest. "Darius, what's going on here?"

The kid spoke up first, his hand over his nose. "I saw this guy break into your house—"

"You saw what?" Darius glared at the newcomer. Like Mr. Oliver was going to fall for that.

But the kid kept talking. "He said he wanted to steal something from you, so I came in after him to stop him."

Mr. Oliver's eyes widened. "What would Darius possibly want to steal from me?" His eyes narrowed. "Are you trying to take some of Madeline's things?"

"No, that's not even what happened—"

"It was a dagger," the kid said. "A silver dagger with leaves all over it."

He grinned at Darius, who turned just in time to see Mr. Oliver hurrying toward him.

Madeline's dad grabbed him by the jacket. "Is this true, Darius? Give it to me. Give it back to me now."

Darius tried to step away, and as he did, the dagger fell from his pocket and onto the floor. Mr. Oliver saw it, and his face went bright red before he took a swing at Darius.

3
FAR SEEING

Once upon a time, there was a group of magicians.
Powerful and wise, talented and gifted and proud.

FROM "THE BALLAD OF WU SONG," A KAKRI TALE

✛

Something was wrong. Gilenyia could feel it in her bones.

Not just one thing—no, many things were wrong. The Elenil were rebuilding after a time of massive failure of the entire magical system. Old alliances had to be restored. Old agreements reforged. Power reconnected, recollected. Walls, literal and metaphorical, needed to be mended. Too many Scim had rejected their old agreements, insisting on better terms. Some had refused to be restored at all. The magical economy was in danger of collapse.

"Mistress," New Dawn said. "Mistress, I come with a message." New Dawn was her servant, a civilized Scim. She had not left when magic collapsed. Nor had Day Song, nor many of her human servants. Gilenyia had always been a generous employer.

"What is it, New Dawn?" She tried not to lose her train of thought but to give sufficient attention to her servant.

New Dawn curtsied, or tried to. The Scim woman had never perfected such dainty movements. Clumsy and slow, built like a beast of burden and not a creature of the court . . . like the rest of her kind. "Mistress, the archon demands your presence."

Gilenyia laughed at that and leaned back on her divan, spreading her silver dress over her legs. "Oh, he does, does he? Then he should dig his way out of his grave and tell me himself."

New Dawn shuffled nervously, her grey face knotted in worry. "Mistress?"

"I won't ask you to say that to *him*," Gilenyia said. "Though you've known him long enough to speak as you please." She sighed. "Go and inspect the dinner servants. I will think on your message."

The *archon*. She would never think of Hanali that way. He had always been the fop, the fool, the forgotten cousin. They had grown up together, and though he had been tiresome at times, he had been the one to tell her that he would be archon one day. Gilenyia didn't see why she should scrape and bow. She had never required that of him when she had been the one with the power. Curious how he came to be archon too. Alone in a room with a Black Skull and Archon Thenody, and the archon murdered with the Sword of Years. Hanali, in a rage, banishing the human back to his own world.

A convenient story, and one that too many Elenil accepted without thinking. All of the magic was crumbling around them, and they wanted someone who seemed to know what was happening, someone with a plan. The ridiculous party-going Hanali had managed to convince them of what Gilenyia had long known: he always had a plan. The death of his father, Vivi, only worked to his advantage, as there were some who, astonished by the loss of an Elenil to violence, clamored for Hanali's ascension to archon out of loyalty to his father.

But to call himself archon? He was no such thing, though the magistrates had installed him—on a provisional basis—to do some of the work of archon.

Gilenyia took a deep breath. A bird lit on the head of the divan, no doubt a messenger from Hanali. Before it could even speak, she said, "Tell my cousin that I am in the midst of an important task and cannot come to him at this time."

The bird cocked its head. "But, lady, you are only lying on your chair."

"Yes. Tell him that as well." She shooed the bird away.

The city of Far Seeing was rebuilding with admirable speed. Many walked across the city square and through the markets as if they were back in the golden age of a year ago or two. They would continue to do so unless the Pastisians saw some need to fly their craft within sight of the city. The memory of the astonishing Pastisian attack on Far Seeing still shook the residents whenever they saw one of the necromancers' dirigibles on the horizon. Hanali had supposedly worked some deal with the Pastisians to keep them away, the details of which he refused to divulge even to her. Perhaps there was no deal. She had heard only Hanali speak of it.

These were problems that were known by all, or nearly all. But there was something else, something deeper. Ever since she had been healed by Madeline Oliver, Gilenyia had felt a change in the core of her being, nagging at her like a splinter beneath a fingernail. She couldn't see it, couldn't find it, wasn't sure how it had come to be where it was, but something was not in the right place. And when she dreamed . . . she dreamed of another life. Strange faces, people she did not know, could not place.

A cool breeze blew through the open window. She moved to it and studied the city below. Hanali had offered her quarters in what remained of the tower, nearer to him, where she would be more readily available when he had questions or needed a favor. The white towers shone in the constant sunshine, but now workers scurried around them, shoring up the places that were still broken. King Ian of the necromancers had said he was going to tear down the tower, stone by stone. Hanali claimed that it had been a metaphor. In any case, Gilenyia preferred her small compound here, the little mansion a short distance away.

A gravelly voice came from the doorway. "Mistress."

Gilenyia didn't move to look at her. "What is it, New Dawn?"

"One of the traitors has been seen entering the city."

She raised an eyebrow and turned. "Truly? Which one?" All reports claimed that Madeline Oliver was dead, and Gilenyia could easily believe it, though she hadn't seen the body herself. She had set a watch for Shula Bishara, Madeline's fast friend and companion, as well as Jason Wu, who was about as much a fool as Hanali. Which was to say, perhaps no fool at all. Though it would be foolish indeed for him to set foot in Far Seeing, for Hanali had announced a sentence of death if any of the traitor humans came into the city. He had no choice, really, after the events of a year ago. The Elenil demanded swift justice when one of their own had been harmed, and the death of Archon Thenody by violence so soon after the death of Vivi . . . well, Hanali should have sent every soldier under his command to seek the human children. Simply threatening to execute them upon arrival might well be seen as an act of friendship when viewed in the correct light.

"It is the boy," New Dawn said.

"Jason Wu?"

"The same."

Gilenyia touched her gloved fingertips to her lips. "Curious," she murmured. She didn't take him to be particularly brave unless his friends were directly threatened. When his friends were in danger, however, he was so brave as to be stupid. "Has Hanali captured one of Jason's friends, I wonder?"

"Not that I know of, mistress."

She tugged her long gloves higher on her arms, then smoothed her dress. What was going on here? "And what of the other information I sent you to gather?"

New Dawn shuffled nervously. "I do not have much, mistress."

Gilenyia crossed to the Scim and patted her arm gently. "The news of Jason Wu pleases me, New Dawn. Now what of the other matter?"

She cleared her throat. "They will not let me see him unless I join their cult or make a profession of a clear desire to do so. I am not certain they will release me again if I do."

"Then you have chosen wisely. But surely you have learned something."

"Yes, mistress. He calls himself 'the Herald of Mysteries.' He claims that he speaks for the Majestic One himself and that he is a sign that the Majestic One is soon to return to the Sunlit Lands."

Gilenyia lifted her chin, deep in thought. "This message is popular among the Scim? Does he claim that the Majestic One will free them, or something along these lines?"

New Dawn shook her head. "His message is along other lines completely, mistress. He says the Scim must return to their labor, for the Elenil were put in their place by the Majestic One. Who are the Scim to complain about their lot? Their reward, he says, will be greater than the Elenil's upon the return of the Majestic One."

"So the Scim do not tolerate his message."

"Tolerate it? No, mistress, they flock to it."

She pressed her lips together. "They . . . flock to it."

"Some of them, at least. Though the words of the herald are hard, they are clear. Many Scim struggle against the uncertainty of the current situation, and they prefer the old ways when they were bound to the Elenil. At least then they knew their lot and could plan their lives accordingly. The Elenil, too, adore this herald. It is said that when they come to hear him, the Scim and Elenil enter together through the same doors and stand shoulder to shoulder. He has said to them many times, 'Just because one is called to serve does not mean that one is lesser. We are all equal but called to different roles.'"

Gilenyia blinked. This could hardly be true. "And the Scim enter this subservient role willingly?"

"Nay, mistress. Say rather 'joyfully.' For they do not see it as subservience."

Hmm. This would be useful for her cousin, and useful to her if she were the first to tell him of it. "Well done, New Dawn. I would crave more knowledge of this herald. I wonder if he would join me here for a meal? Do you think such a thing could be arranged?"

New Dawn bowed. "As always, mistress, your slightest wish is my deepest desire. I will seek out an influential acolyte of the herald and see what enticements may be offered."

"Where is the human boy?"

"He was seen last at the eastern gate, or so I am told, coming from the direction of the Kakri territories."

Of course he was, and no doubt headed to Westwind, the strange castle of the Knight of the Mirror. She smiled to herself. She had her spies there now, and she knew that the knight had been scarce and slow to help the Elenil in recent days, doing only the bare minimum of what was expected of him. He was a man of honor, which meant that there was some trouble there, though she did not know what it might be. Hanali surely must have realized this as well if he stopped to consider it, but it could be that more pressing matters held his attention. "Where is Ricardo?" she asked.

"Nearby, I think, mistress."

"I wish to see him."

New Dawn bowed and exited without another word. She was the best kind of servant, and Gilenyia congratulated herself again on how well she chose and trained her people. She summoned another bird while she waited for Ricardo. He was a young human whom she had healed when he was nearly dead after a battle with the Scim. He was also intensely loyal and could not bear to be near someone who insulted Gilenyia.

Ricardo's footsteps echoed in the hallway. He was not quite running, but Gilenyia smiled to herself. Another servant who took her wishes seriously and moved swiftly when her desires were known. She arranged herself by the window, and when he entered, she did not turn. "Mr. Sánchez," she said.

"My lady Gilenyia," he responded, and there was a hint of heat in his voice. Not anger, but a scarcely disguised passion. She was hundreds of years his senior, of course, and Elenil, not human. It had been common, once upon a time, for knights to fall in love with the ladies to whom they owed allegiance. She did not mind it, so long as he continued to treat her with the proper respect and do her bidding.

She moved to a pair of chairs, a small, round table covered with intricate carvings between them. A simple nod of the head invited Ricardo to sit, and she lowered herself into the chair across from him, smoothing her dress. She set her hands, palms down, in her lap. "Do you have all you need, Mr. Sánchez?"

"You've provided for all my needs, lady," he said. He was young—sometimes she forgot how young—and his dark cheeks colored for some reason that escaped her. He had begun to grow a struggling mustache, which amused her, but otherwise he looked every inch an example of the strange fusion of human and Elenil fashion popular among the human servants. His green shirt was long and loose, tied about the waist with a thick belt, and loosely laced shut at the neck. The sleeves billowed around his upper arms with cuffs that hugged the forearms, also tied tight. He wore jeans beneath, an Earth style that was hard to break among teens these last few years and had become an acceptable fashion accessory for human servants. Heavy black boots fit for fighting were on his feet.

Gilenyia leaned back in her chair. "What news from Westwind?"

"There has been an increase in humans moving onto the castle grounds," Ricardo said.

She raised an eyebrow. "Building an army?"

Ricardo shrugged. "Lady, the entire Elenil army loves him. If he wanted an army, he wouldn't have to build a new one—he'd just take yours."

"All the more reason we should strive to keep him happy. What is his mood in these trying times?"

"Distant, my lady. Preoccupied. He disappears into his solar, sometimes for days at a time. When I see him, he's deep in thought, unaware of the things around him. He eats when a plate is put in his hands, but it's mechanical. It's rare these days that someone catches his attention."

"And to what do you attribute this mood?"

Ricardo shifted uncomfortably. "There are competing rumors, and the knight won't allow any discussion of it. But it seems to me that it has to do with his missing love."

Missing? The Knight's beloved was trapped in a dimension of mirrors. This was not common knowledge, and the knight did not reveal it to many, but among the Elenil at least it was well known. It was they, after all, who had imprisoned her there. It was strange, though, that when the magic had broken she was not released from her cell. Gilenyia knew for a fact that at the Festival of the Turning she was let free for a day, so why would she still be trapped now? Unless . . . could it be that when he said "missing," he meant precisely that? Had she ceased appearing to her beloved in the mirror? "Missing, Mr. Sánchez? What do you mean by this?"

Ricardo leaned forward, looking at her intently. "I had been under the impression she had died long ago. But the rumor among the people of the castle is that she had always been there somewhere, that he kept her locked away, and that she has somehow escaped."

"Curious," Gilenyia said. And so interesting that the humans would fall to thinking that the knight was the sort of man to imprison his beloved. But humans were often gullible, and they lacked imagination in situations such as these. Nevertheless, she had made up her mind. "Tell the knight that I am coming to meet with him."

Ricardo jumped to his feet, recognizing a command when he heard it. "When, lady? He will wish to make preparations. Next week? The week after?"

She looked out the window, examining the position of the sun. The golden light of morning shone on the buildings of Far Seeing. Of course, in the Sunlit Lands that meant little, as the sun never fully set. She could march to Westwind in pale sunlight in the middle of the night. "An hour, perhaps. No more than two."

The young man bowed hastily and hurried for the door without so much as a goodbye.

So, something was wrong with the knight as well. The whole of the Sunlit Lands seemed to be in an uproar. And still, there was something deeper. Something strange. She looked at herself in the mirror, at her flawless skin, her red lips and high cheekbones, her bright-silver hair. She was the model of the beauty of the Elenil, a paragon of genteel elegance.

But what was this? One dull hair, tucked in among the bright. She separated it out carefully with her fingers, leaned close to the mirror. She was too young, far too young, for grey hair, and this one was so dull and dark as to be noticeable. She knew Elenil of four centuries who had not seen one yet. One swift yank and a moment's sharp discomfort pulled it loose, and it lay in the palm of her hand, curled like a serpent.

Something was wrong. Something deep, something in the very nature of who she was. She could feel it, though she did not know what it could be. Another moment of reflection, and then she threw the hair into the parlor fire, disgusted. It was time to dress for her visit to Westwind, and she did not have time to spend considering trivialities.

4

THE SHORE
OF THE GINIAN SEA

We choose what we remember, and that is a powerful sort of magic.

FROM *THE ANNALS OF THE HISTORIAN*

+

Every morning when the sun rose, Shula Bishara gently slipped from the bed she shared with little Yenil and made her way toward the cliff outside their cottage. She sat with her legs hanging over the edge, toes pointed toward the sea, a thick shawl over her shoulders, her breath visible in the morning air, and made a list of every good thing in her life.

It wasn't that she was a particularly thankful person, but this simple practice helped her ride the wave of grief that too often came upon her before day's end. She didn't need a list of things to grieve—those were as close as her breath. A list of good things sometimes took more work.

The goats bleated softly from their pen. Mrs. Oliver liked to milk them in the mornings and again before bed. They never wanted for milk and soft cheese, and the regular dairy was making Yenil strong. Shula couldn't believe how much she had grown since they had settled here! They never lacked vegetables or fruit either, as Aluvoreans came to them once every two weeks loaded down with edible gifts. In fact, Shula and Mrs. Oliver had bartered their surplus in a local village to get the goats, two chickens, flour, and a thick yellow butter that Yenil prized and wanted to eat on everything.

The new sunlight turned the Ginian Sea a deep greenish blue, and seabirds sat on the undulating surface, riding the waves without moving. There were no dolphins this morning. She had seen a large pod swimming south yesterday, and last week she had seen a Zhanin boat, like a great turtle that swam with its head above the surface, stroking north. The crisp, salty smell of the sea blended with the smell of fresh eggs frying in the kitchen.

She hadn't made her thankful list yet today, but she loved to see Yenil wake in the mornings, and if Shula could smell those eggs cooking, then it wouldn't be long. She pulled the shawl close. She was thankful for the cottage, for the abundance of food, for Mrs. Oliver and Yenil, for the beauty of the ocean greeting her each day.

The cottage door was wide, made for an adult Scim. Mrs. Oliver stood by the stove, watching the eggs, and she smiled as Shula passed her, heading for the bedroom. Shula squeezed her shoulder in greeting. She and Madeline's mother had become closer as the year had passed along. Shula had wondered, at first, if their parallel griefs would keep them from knowing each other well, but instead the older woman had welcomed Shula into her life as a sort of surrogate daughter.

In the tiny bedroom Shula and Yenil shared, Yenil lay on her side, a smile on her face. Her hair had grown thick and long in the last year and was a lustrous black now. Her grey skin had taken on an almost sparkling quality, and with the regular food and exercise her thin frame had filled out. One arm was thrown across a dog-sized rhinoceros, who was supposed to sleep on the floor but always snuck into the bed the moment Shula got up. The rhino opened one black eye, saw Shula standing over them, closed her eye, and cuddled in closer to Yenil.

"It's nice to get up in the morning," Shula said softly.

Yenil's eyes popped open, a giant grin on her face. No doubt Delightful Glitter Lady had already woken her when she scrambled into the bed. "But it's nicer to stay in bed!"

"Breakfast, my little birds," Mrs. Oliver called.

"Race you," Yenil shouted, bursting past Shula, the rhino squealing and chasing her, nearly knocking Shula down. She laughed and followed after them.

Mrs. Oliver had already pulled the round wooden table from the corner and brought it to the center of the room. Shula and Yenil pulled the three stools over, Dee cavorting around their legs the whole time. The three women gathered the dishes and filled the table . . . fresh eggs, warm pita bread, goat cheese, and cucumbers. Not American cucumbers, either, which were too large and had thick skin. These were much more like the cucumbers in Syria. Small, thin-skinned, and easy to eat without cutting or peeling at all. Just a fresh crunch every time you took a bite.

They piled their plates high and discussed the day ahead. Every morning each member of their makeshift family shared their goals and hopes for the day over breakfast, and in the evenings they revisited them.

"I'm going to teach Dee to use the embiggenator on her own today," Yenil said, her mouth full of pita. "That way she can be whatever size she wants without us choosing."

"I choose small," Mrs. Oliver said, cupping Yenil's face in her hand. "We can't have a gigantic runaway rhinoceros tramping through the garden."

"Unicorn," Yenil said.

"Unicorn then," Mrs. Oliver said. "As for me, the beans need picking, and there are more cucumbers to bring in." She raised her eyebrows at Shula. "I do need someone to go into the village and get us more flour."

"Not me," Yenil said. "Dee and I have a full day!"

"Terrorizing the goats," Shula said. She had caught Yenil riding a horse-sized Dee around the goat pen, shouting at them and wearing her war skin. It had all been in fun, but Yenil had been embarrassed. She had thought Shula and Mrs. Oliver were in the village at the time. "I can go into town after I help with the goats and chickens, and the picking."

Mrs. Oliver put another egg on her plate. "We can do all that, can't we, Yenil?"

"Yup!"

The two of them liked having some alone time without Shula a few times a week. Shula didn't know what they got up to when she was gone, but she suspected it involved eating hidden sweets that Shula had not outright forbidden but still wanted to hand out sparingly. She didn't mind, though, because Yenil enjoyed being alone with Mrs. Oliver, which meant Shula got a little time to herself in the day, or the chance to run errands like this one. Shula didn't like leaving Yenil alone, especially since the poor girl had seen her parents killed not so long ago. Anything that left Yenil vulnerable made Shula nervous, but the slow pace of life here made it seem unlikely that something bad could happen to them at home. And Shula had only had a couple of problems on the road, though she had felt unsafe the first few times when she was still getting used to the fact that she had given up her magic. She couldn't burst into flames or walk through fire without being hurt anymore. She had burned herself putting logs in the oven just last week.

"I'll go after breakfast," Shula said. She'd need to take the rucksack and something to trade for the flour.

"We'll never eat all the green beans. Or the strawberries," Mrs. Oliver said.

"We *will* eat all the strawberries," Yenil announced.

Mrs. Oliver patted Yenil's hand and put another warm pita on her plate. "She should probably take Delightful Glitter Lady, don't you think?"

Yenil considered this, mouth full. "But not rhino size. Medium dog size."

Dee's ears perked up. Shula held a cucumber out to her, and she gobbled it up before trotting outside and lying across the threshold. In the mornings Yenil grabbed an armful of dried sweetgrass for her, but Dee's breakfast always came after family breakfast. "You feed Dee while I get ready," Shula said, picking up her plate.

"I'll clean up," Mrs. Oliver said, laughing when Yenil leapt over Dee and ran toward the sweetgrass stockpile. She looked sideways at Shula. "I need more of that fruit as well."

Shula tried to hide her discomfort. "Mrs. Oliver . . ."

Mrs. Oliver's eyes brimmed with tears. "Shula. I need it. To remember."

There was a fruit, a new fruit here in the Sunlit Lands. The berries were wide and bright yellow and smooth-skinned. When juiced, it created a lemon-colored drink that, so Shula was told, caused the drinker to have vivid memories restored. Lost things were found. Things forgotten, remembered.

"It makes you sad," Shula said, and it did. When Mrs. Oliver drank it she became maudlin, depressed, nonresponsive—sometimes for days.

"Madeline being dead makes me sad," Mrs. Oliver said. "The drink helps me remember her better. And . . . other things." Mrs. Oliver claimed that old memories were coming back to her, things from her youth when she had come to the Sunlit Lands with her friends.

"I don't think you should drink so much of it."

"You've never even tried it, Shula."

She didn't want to try it. She was always skeptical of such things. "I have more memories that I want to forget than forgotten things I want to remember."

But Mrs. Oliver was an adult, and it wasn't Shula's place to mother her any more than it was Mrs. Oliver's place to mother Shula, despite the maternal figure she had become in the last year. Shula cared about how the juice changed the dynamic of their quasi family, but she wasn't about to tell the older woman she couldn't drink it.

"They'll bring me some soon," Mrs. Oliver said, almost to herself.

"The Aluvoreans?"

"Maduvoreans," Mrs. Oliver corrected. "They've changed the name of their woods to Maduvorea after my Maddie."

That's right. Shula hadn't meant to forget that, and the Aluvoreans had corrected her politely any time she did forget. And the juice, they called it "Wendy juice." Shula hadn't realized that this was Mrs. Oliver's name for months. The Maduvoreans said the juice was "hers." That it had been left for her by Madeline. Shula didn't know if that was true or if there was some sinister magic trap involved. You could never be sure about such things in the Sunlit Lands, and Shula was wary of any magic that wanted to get into her head and mess with her memories. Maybe irrationally wary of it. But if the fruit had been left behind by Madeline, who was Shula to deny it to Madeline's mother?

"I'll ask at the village and see if they have any," Shula said, but who was she kidding? They always had some in the village. Who wanted Wendy juice when there was addleberry wine? Who wanted to remember when there was a drink that could help you forget? Shula stayed away from them both, but there were days—when the loss of her parents, her little sister, her brother was greatest—that she was tempted to take a swig of addleberry.

Mrs. Oliver pressed a package wrapped in leaves into Shula's hand. Fresh goat cheese. Someone in town would surely want that. Shula threw it in the rucksack, along with a couple days' worth of beans, and headed out. Yenil walked with her and Dee to the head of the trail, then skipped back toward the cliff's edge. Dee trotted alongside Shula happily, still munching on a mouthful of sweetgrass.

The path switched down the cliff face before turning inland near the beach. Mrs. Oliver said that their garden shouldn't do as well as it did in the salt air, but the vegetables and fruit thrived. It must be because they were so close to Alu—Maduvorea. It was like the forest blessed everything that grew near it.

The forest had spread in the last year, too, and faster than Shula would have thought it could. There were new plants, like the Wendy fruit, and something called pudding fruit, which made people speak only truth—or so she was told. She hadn't mentioned it to Mrs. Oliver, who mostly stayed at the shore, but the Wendy fruit had been growing closer and closer to home. It was still more convenient to get it in town, yes, or to wait for the Maduvoreans to bring them some. But on her last trip to town, Shula had noticed a Wendy bush a good half kilometer from the forest's entrance. It had grown faster than any plant Shula had ever heard of.

The path was a pleasant walk, at least. It was mostly downhill from their home, and only a slight incline as she walked toward the forest entrance. She had never seen a guard or sentry on the way in, but she knew there must be—and the occasional hummingbird buzzing by might well be the steed of a faerie, or at the very least the eyes and ears of the forest. She didn't expect they ever thought of her as a threat. She was a friend of Madeline's, for one, and she had lost the one thing that might have made the forest nervous about her: she couldn't light things on fire anymore.

As Shula came closer to the trees, the air turned cooler. It was a welcome relief, as she was sweating a bit from the sunshine and her hike. Delightful Glitter Lady was panting as she trotted alongside. The smell changed, too, from the salty bite of sea air to the pungent, rich smell of fresh-turned soil. They were almost there. The village was a Scim settlement nestled just on the other side of a small section of Maduvorea, a sort of peninsula of forest. The villagers claimed the forest had grown in around them, that it had been an arid stretch of ground a year ago. The wood, new soil, and abundance of edible things growing within an easy walk had made them a new sort of Scim society . . . they had moved away from subsistence living, and that made them feel like royalty. They had everything they needed.

Shula had faced trouble on this path twice before. Once when an Elenil scouting party had been scouring the countryside looking for any human friends of Madeline Oliver and Jason Wu, which she definitely was. It appeared the archon had put a death sentence on her head. She wasn't too worried about it, but she also knew it paid to be cautious. She had seen them on the path and managed to hide and head back to the cottage. The Scim in the village had told her the next day whom the Elenil had been seeking.

The second time it had been a small band of Scim, coming from somewhere that had been harder hit by the collapse of magic. They were desperate for food, weapons, whatever they could get their hands on. She had tried hiding from them as well, but they had found her where she had hidden: dug in beneath the roots of a tree. They had threatened to kill her for whatever was in her bag, but she handed it over and they went away without another word. Her trip to town that day had been for nothing, but better returning home empty-handed than not returning at all.

If it weren't for those two events, she might let Yenil go to town on her own—as long as she was accompanied by a full-grown Delightful Glitter Lady. Shula had been training Yenil in self-defense. Yenil knew full well the dangers of fighting, having been present when her own parents were killed by the Elenil. Shula had talked to her many times about the fact that running or hiding could often be the best defense of all. But she knew, too, that the Scim society focused on teaching all their children to fight. Shula's instruction was a vastly different sort of training than what the Scim did with their children, she knew, but Yenil could handle a blade, and she had practiced fighting from Dee's back. Yenil was shy when she came into town, and she said little to any of the Scim there, but Shula didn't want Yenil to be a complete outsider to her own people.

Delightful Glitter Lady made a low whining noise, snorted, and slowed to a walk. Shula dropped her hand to the dagger she wore on her belt. She scanned the road ahead. Dee stopped completely, staring at a large stone to the left of the path. It took her a moment to see what Dee had already noticed. The stone was smaller than she had thought. Someone was sitting on it, a grey cloak and hood causing them to blend in.

"What do you think, girl?" she asked quietly.

Dee whined.

The figure moved.

"Friend," Shula called. "We're walking through the forest to the Scim town. What's your business?"

"Looking for you," the figure called, throwing back his hood.

She couldn't believe it. After a full year and no word, here he was.

They ran to each other and embraced, laughing. "David!"

"I was asking after you in town, and they told me you'd be out this way."

"Where have you been? Are you okay? Where's Kekoa? Have you seen Jason?"

Delightful Glitter Lady was leaping, trying to get up on him, and David scratched her ears. "Hi there, girl!" He smiled at Shula, and with such affection that it took her a little off guard. "I'll tell you everything, Shula, don't worry! And I want to hear about Yenil and Madeline's mom too." He slung his arm around her shoulder. "Come on, I'll walk with you to town."

"Right!" Shula said, and they walked through the forest, Delightful Glitter Lady sticking close to them. Shula felt at ease, having David with her as they moved into town. But it was strange, wasn't it, that he had come searching for her when he didn't have Jason or Kekoa with him? Those three had always been tight, and to see David here alone . . . Why was he looking for her?

5

THE CAPTIVE

The Kakri are never truly alone in the desert.

FROM *THE WISE SAYINGS OF MOTHER CROW*

+

"Impossible," Jason said again. "I have to be dreaming. Am I dreaming?"

Once, when Jason had a very high fever, he'd experienced hallucinations. Not just any hallucinations, either. Everything had been filled with undeniable menace. He had seen a man with a wolf's face standing at the end of his bed. The man had worn jeans but no shirt, and he had a bodybuilder's physique and, inexplicably, a wolf's head. He didn't say or do anything—he didn't howl or snarl or even move other than breathing. Just stared. And Jason had been filled with a terror so deep he couldn't move. He was trapped, stuck to his bed, sweating through the sheets.

Then a chocolate éclair had marched into the room with tiny legs and arms and a face made out of frosting. In a reedy voice it had said, "And now we will eat *you*, little piggy." Jason had started screaming then. His mother had come running, and when the bedroom door opened, everything else disappeared. He tried to explain it to her, but she kept laughing when he said that a chocolate donut had threatened to eat him, and it had taken a full month before he could eat donuts again.

But this was a whole new level of weird. He had tackled a stranger in their camp—someone who had attacked Mother Crow, shot her with an arrow. Jason had overpowered him and even now had a knife to the bad guy's throat, pointy side down. One wrong move by either of them would skewer the guy.

"You're not dreaming," the stranger—could he really call him that?—said.

"That's exactly what I would expect someone in a dream to say," Jason replied, doing his best to sound like a tough guy.

"After all you've seen—giant birds, unicorns, plant people, and magic battles—is this really so hard to explain away?"

"You're right," Jason said under his breath. "Mother Crow must have drugged me. This is all a hallucination. Oh, man, I hope I don't see any donuts." He shivered. What if there were donut *holes* this time? He wasn't sure he could take it.

"Not a dream," the stranger said. "Not a hoax or an imaginary story. Not a hallucination, Wu Song. This is really happening."

Which was, not to beat the drum incessantly, impossible. Because the guy he had tackled—the guy who had shot Mother Crow—was Jason Wu. Same disheveled black hair, same charming smile (he had to admit it because it was true, and he had promised not to tell lies anymore), same brown eyes that he had seen a hundred million times over the course of his lifetime, looking back at him from mirrors. Jason had captured himself somehow.

"Time travel," Jason said. "In which case, you are the worst, and whatever happened to make me into you is never going to happen now. I know better."

"Time travel," Other Jason said. "Ha! Speaking of things that are actually impossible."

"Mission Impossible, then." Jason grabbed the doppelgänger's chin and pulled on the skin, trying to get the mask off.

"Ow! Hey, watch it. That hurts."

"Twin brother?" Jason leaned back, his grip on the knife loosening a little bit. Another thought came into his head, and he grabbed the knife harder and pushed it so it was in danger of drawing blood. "*Evil* twin brother!"

"Not a disguise, not a twin."

"Well, you got me then. Congratulations, you fooled me. I guess you get the prize."

Other Jason grinned. "Oh yes, I certainly am about to get the prize."

Jason frowned. "What are you—?" He sensed more than saw the person looming up behind him, and he spun in time to see the hilt of a sword racing toward his head, just before the tooth-rattling impact. His eyes rolled back and a stir of cold hit him, like a winter wave at an Oregon beach. Shock spread through his whole body, through every molecule of his being, and then a moment of nausea as he fell into the black void.

A moment of nausea that continued when his eyes opened again. Based on the position of the sun, he must have been unconscious for hours. His hands were tied in front of him. He would never get used to this. It seemed like in the Sunlit Lands people were always catching him and tying him up or putting silver manacles on him or locking him in a room.

He was on his back in a long, open container, almost like a canoe. A quick glance over his shoulder made him dizzy but also revealed a set of ropes that connected his canoe thing to two thickset lizards the size of horses, which were pulling the canoe. Other Jason sat on the back of one of them. And on the second lizard was, presumably, the guy who had knocked Jason out. Which, of course . . . was a third Jason. It was two too many Jasons.

"Now I know what my principal felt like," Jason mumbled.

He took stock of the situation. He had learned a decent amount about the desert and survival from Mother Crow. He knew it was morning, obviously, and from where the sun was he knew they were headed south. He couldn't tell how much distance they had covered. Maybe if he sat up he could see some sort of landmark to give him an idea, but the tender state of his head made that a dicey proposition. He was being transported by two captors, both about his size. Well, exactly his size. Jason had to assume they were about as strong and smart as he was, which meant that the bad guys had basically twice what he had in every way.

He assumed he still had the element of surprise, at least. Well, maybe they had that, too, because he'd definitely been surprised to see himself kidnapping him and hurting Mother Crow. On the other hand, one of his great strengths was doing things that other people didn't expect—even though he often told them what he was about to do before he did it.

They were headed up a rise in the sand. In fact, it was the biggest dune Jason had seen in a long while. He probably would have avoided it if he had been directing the lizards. At least he thought so. The current directors might disagree, and since they appeared to be him, more or less, who knew.

Jason was pleased that they had tied his hands in front of him, which made it easier for him to access that most Kakri of tools: a hidden knife. That's right, yet another lesson from Mother Crow. He always had a hidden knife now. This one was strapped to his calf, and in a matter of seconds he had cut the ropes. He took another quick look at the Jasons. They didn't even know he was awake yet.

The canoe had left a serious wedge in the sand. If he could get away from these jokers, he'd be able to find his way back easily enough—assuming there wasn't a windstorm. He doubted the Jasons had taken care of Mother Crow's wound before they abandoned her. His teeth clenched. Most likely, they had finished her off. He gripped the knife tighter. He'd never been much of a fighter, though his year in the desert had given him some new skills. On the other hand, maybe that meant the other Jasons weren't particularly good fighters, either, and he *had* managed to pin Other Jason pretty quickly. On the other other hand, someone had launched that arrow into Mother Crow without alerting her to his presence, which was not a skill Jason had.

He didn't have time to make a whole plan, so he just did what he did best and rolled with the moment. As the lizards crested the rise in the dune, he popped onto his stomach and ran his knife through the ropes tying his canoe to the lizards. Both Jasons gave a shout of surprise as his canoe slid back the other way.

Jason laughed maniacally. "See you later, Fake Jasons!" He turned around so he was facing the back of the canoe, leaned over the side, and gave a couple of pushes with his hand. That set off the nausea, but the canoe was gaining speed.

This may have been a bad idea. The dune was much steeper than he'd thought. He had that sudden I'm-at-the-top-of-the-roller-coaster feeling. "Uh-oh."

Jason grabbed the sides of the canoe. He could hear the other Jasons scrambling behind him. "Uh-oh!"

The canoe was barreling downward now, sand flying over the sides and into his face. And it wasn't only sand on the side of the dune. Black rocks jutted out from underneath. The kind of rocks you could probably avoid if you were trudging uphill on the back of a mammoth lizard, but which you might have more trouble avoiding if you were sliding downhill without a rudder in an open sand canoe. "UH-OH."

And there it was. A black rock rising like a shark fin in front of him. A hand in the sand might turn the boat, he thought, and he stuck his left hand in, the sand hot and the friction powerfully chafing his skin. "C'mon, c'mon," he grunted, pushing his arm into the sand, trying to get more power. It didn't slow him down, but it did start to turn the canoe. The rock was moving slowly to his right. Too slowly!

The canoe glanced against the rock, and there was a splintering sound as some of the wood exploded away. His boat lifted from the sand for a moment, and Jason let out an involuntary shout as it hit the ground. It was still picking up speed. He glanced back to see the Jasons carefully making their way down the slope. "Hahahaha, suckers," he said, just as the canoe hit another rock head-on, catapulting him into a monstrous parabola skyward and then back toward the sand.

He landed with a teeth-jarring slap, but his body didn't stop moving downhill. Still sliding, he tried to get to his feet, failed, got a mouthful of sand, and scrambled into a run as soon as his momentum allowed. The canoe slid past him, and he ran alongside and leapt into it. He sped to the bottom without further incident and jumped out. The Jasons were closer than he would have liked, about halfway down the slope. He knew how to hide himself in the sand, but he needed to be out of their sight for at least thirty seconds to do it.

An arrow lodged in the sand by his feet. He snatched it up. He shook it at the Jasons. "Ha! Now I have an extra weapon." Another arrow whirred by. "You're just giving me more weapons!" Unless they managed to stick him, of course, in which case they were giving him a new hole in his body, and he was quite satisfied with the number of holes he had.

He studied the dune valley. If he ran west, he thought he might be able to ditch the Jasons by slipping around a smaller hill. Of course, they might still find him, but it would be like looking for a needle in a haystack. Or a person in a gigantic pile of sand. He ran and managed to turn the corner. He risked a look behind him and saw that one of the lizards was loping headfirst down the dune now. It made a high-pitched, keening cry which sounded unnervingly like some sort of hunter's call.

Jason slid around the dune and glanced around for the best spot to dig. He carried a cloth to put over his nose and mouth for just this purpose. By moving his head a certain way and breathing out the way Mother Crow had taught him, he could keep his lungs clear of sand and be nearly silent. It would be quicker if he dove straight into a dune, but the shifting sand might give him away if he didn't do it fast enough.

That strange cry came from behind him again, and he took a deep breath. It wouldn't do to panic now. He picked a spot—at this point searching for a better one would mean less time—and got to work with both hands, digging fast.

A lizard burst over the top of the smaller dune and came sliding down almost beside him. One of the Jasons jumped off its back just as the second lizard came around the corner, a thick sheen of drool falling from its mouth. That was Third Jason, the one with the bow and arrow. He had the arrow pointed right at Jason's heart.

"Drop the knife," Third Jason said.

"And the arrow," Other Jason said.

Jason shrugged and dropped them both. "Listen, OJ, I think we should talk about what's happening here."

"OJ?"

"Other Jason," Jason said. "Although I guess I'm Original Jason, so this could get confusing. So call me Jason, and you're OJ. And he's TJ."

"Third Jason," all three said at once.

Jason grinned despite himself. "Yeah!"

OJ grabbed him and tied his hands, behind his back this time. "I guess I should check him for knives more thoroughly."

Jason said, "Maybe I'd go with you if you told me where you're taking me."

They both chuckled but didn't respond.

Jason frowned. "Did you kill Mother Crow?"

TJ shrugged. "Maybe."

So they weren't exactly like him. There was no way he'd be so cavalier about someone's life, even if the person were a stranger. And definitely not about Mother Crow, who was his friend. "Listen, if we go back and make sure she's okay, then I'll come with you wherever you're going."

The Jasons exchanged looks. "I don't think you'd come with us unless we made you. Your friends didn't want to come, either."

His *friends*? "Wait, you have some of my friends? Who? Which ones?"

OJ said, "We were sent for you. Others were sent for them."

"Others who? Them who?"

"Others like us," TJ said.

"More Jasons?" His stomach dropped into his feet. "Where did you get that Scim bow and arrow, anyway?"

They shoved him, got him walking back toward the canoe. TJ was retying it to the lizards. OJ carefully checked him for knives. "We took it from your friend Break Bones. He was watching over you in the desert. He was keeping it a secret from you." He smiled. "But not from us."

"Is he . . . okay?" But Jason knew the answer to that. Break Bones would never let someone get away with his weapons—even a weapon he rarely used, like a bow and arrow. One of them must have snuck up on him, used Jason's face to get his guard down.

The fake Jasons were on their lizards again, and Jason was back in the canoe. They were getting ready to climb the large dune and be on their way. Jason tried to figure out who these guys could be. He couldn't narrow it down just by thinking about who in the Sunlit Lands was trying to hurt him. The Elenil wanted him dead. The Zhanin had been trying to kill him last he knew. At least some of the Kakri, though that was supposed to be on hold. For that matter, there were still Scim who didn't love him. He hadn't heard about a whole people group of Jasons, though, and he had no idea why they'd try to kidnap him or his friends.

"My friends," Jason said. "You're not gathering them to hurt them, are you?"

Both Jasons threw back their heads and laughed at that, and TJ shook his reins. The lizards trudged forward. "He is funny," TJ said. "They said he was funny, but I wasn't sure he would be."

Jason fell back in the canoe and watched the sky as the fake Jasons took him to his uncertain future. He could tell they were still moving south, but that's all he knew. He was nowhere near as comfortable now that his hands were behind his back, and his head still hurt. He had the strange sensation that he should know these guys. Something about their weird sense of humor seemed familiar.

A bright flash of color caught his attention. A red streak in the sky, small and quick. It zipped forward, disappearing for a few seconds before hovering directly over his face. A hummingbird. Jason had been visited nearly every day by a variety of hummingbirds since the day he set foot in the Kakri desert. In recent weeks, though, they had thinned out. Some days he didn't see one at all. This one he recognized—a beautiful bird with a red head. His name was Rufus. Or, well, that's what Jason called him.

The bird perched on the edge of the canoe and cocked his head at Jason, turning a tiny black eye toward him. Jason leaned forward. "Warn Baileya," he said. "Tell her to check on Mother Crow, then tell her to come find me."

Rufus chirped twice, leapt into the sky, and darted away north. Jason fell onto his side. Baileya was coming. Which meant OJ and TJ were in serious trouble. They weren't even covering their tracks. He grinned to himself, then closed his eyes and tried to get a few minutes of sleep. He needed to be ready for whatever happened next.

PART 2

THE MOUNTAIN WHICH MUST BE CLIMBED

---

*You may have heard of other kings, other forces in the
world, and they are both real and beings of power. They
are of varying moralities and varying motives. The Story
King is more powerful than them all. The question then
becomes why the Story King does not simply enforce his
own will and morality on the lesser forces of the universe.
I, for instance, use my power, such as it is, to tame men
who are my inferior, and to use them for my own gain—an
action the Story King finds repugnant. I can feel his eye
on me. I suspect my spells of camouflage are as effective
as a child hiding his face in his hands. Yet he does not
move against me. I have made a plan which may keep me
safe from him in the future. A sort of pocket universe
apart from his all-seeing eye. The pieces are nearly in
place. For though he has not moved against me, just the
weight of his disapproval is a tyranny I cannot abide.*

FROM *THE MAGICIAN'S GRIMOIRE*

6

THE DAGGER PERILOUS

Get your swords, your bows, your knives, and your hunting dogs.

FROM "THE SHEPHERD WHO KILLED HIS SHEEP," A KHAROBEM STORY

arius was younger, more athletic, and faster than Mr. Oliver. Not to mention that he had been fighting in the Sunlit Lands as a Black Skull for some time. Though some of those fighting abilities had come from magic, they were still skills that belonged to him. He easily stepped under the first two swings from the enraged man. Not wanting to hurt him, Darius placed his palm in the center of Mr. Oliver's chest and pushed, sending him stumbling into the priest.

Then there was the thief, still behind Darius and now desperate for an exit. One quick throw of an elbow was all it took to drop him. The thief hit the ground hard, his nose bloodied, both hands covering his mouth. His initial shout of surprised pain gave way to sustained moaning.

The priest held Mr. Oliver back when he tried to come for Darius again, and Darius raised a single finger in warning, turned sideways so he could still see the crumpled form of the thief. "Mr. Oliver," he said. "I can explain."

"What are you doing in my house? Get out! Get out and take your friend with you."

The priest cleared his throat. "It might be good to hear their story."

"Their story, Tony? They're thieves, common thieves come to cause me pain." His eyes turned on Darius. "Where are they, Darius? Where are my wife and daughter?"

Darius deflated, letting his guard down. He had tried to have this conversation more than once, but it was like oil and water. Every time he explained, it slipped away, as if Mr. Oliver hadn't even heard him. Texts, phone calls—it didn't matter. Any way he said it left the man in the same place and asking the same questions.

"Are you going to call the police?" Darius didn't know what else to say.

"The dagger," Mr. Oliver said. "Give it back to me."

The thief stirred. "I told you! That kid was stealing it. I saw him break in here, and I was trying to stop him."

Mr. Oliver paused as if he had heard the words from a thousand miles away. "You live here in the neighborhood. I've seen you."

He nodded vigorously. "Josh, yeah, I live here. I even—" Darius read the look on Josh's face in his pause. He was debating a calculated risk. "I know your kids."

Mr. Oliver's attention snapped back to Josh. "My kids?"

Josh stood, rearranging himself, and sneered at Darius, obviously thinking the tables had turned. Darius thought he might be right. "The blonde girl and the dark-haired one and that super ugly kid."

Madeline's dad hesitated, turned half away as if he had heard his name called from elsewhere in the house. He put the palm of his hand on the back of his neck. "But I only have one child, and she's—"

The priest put a hand on Mr. Oliver's shoulder and guided him back toward the living room. "Shula and Yenil," the priest said. "He's talking about Madeline, and Shula, and little Yenil."

Josh brushed past Darius, giving him a shove as he went by. "Josh from the neighborhood," Darius said. "I have a guess the cops know 'Josh from the neighborhood.' Don't try to walk out of here with a single thing, or you'll be getting to know me a lot better."

Josh glared at him, then dashed through the living room, the kitchen, and out the back door. He jumped a fence and was gone.

The priest and Mr. Oliver were sitting on the couch. Darius picked up the dagger and crouched down in front of them. Mr. Oliver still looked like he was in another place.

"He okay?"

The priest nodded. "He will be." He held out his hand. "May I see the dagger?"

Darius put it in his palm. "Sure. It's not mine."

Mr. Oliver's eyes went to it, but he didn't reach toward the silver-sheathed weapon.

A long sigh escaped from the priest's lips. "I didn't know he had this. No doubt it has caused its share of grief."

"What is it?" Darius asked. The old man seemed to know more than Darius would have expected.

"I'm Father Tony," the priest said. "I assume you are Madeline's boy-friend, Darius. Maybe Madeline or Shula mentioned me?"

Darius shrugged. "No."

"Ah. I was in the Sunlit Lands once, many years ago. With Madeline's mother and father."

Darius raised his eyebrows. He hadn't seen Madeline, had only briefly connected with her since they had worked together to topple the Crescent Stone. She had gone back to Earth, and he had stayed in the Sunlit Lands, and then, when she returned, he had gone to find her too late. She had already . . . well, he didn't want to think about that. Their only communica-tion had been brief and via intermediaries, and now his chance was gone. Did she know about her parents going to the Sunlit Lands? Was that why she was invited to join the Elenil? "So you've been there. Years ago, you say. Did you meet a young Elenil named Hanali?"

Father Tony closed his eyes. "I knew him well. Hanali, son of Vivi."

Darius couldn't believe it. A weight lifted off him like a cord had been cut and some great burden rolled from his shoulders. Someone else who knew about the Sunlit Lands, who would understand and believe his story. "Madeline's dead," he said.

Father Tony nodded. "I suspected as much."

Mr. Oliver didn't even move, didn't look up or make a sound.

"What of Shula and Yenil?"

"Alive, so far as I know. Jason, too, I think."

"Alive is good," Father Tony said. "I hope alive and well."

"That I don't know. Archon Thenody is dead."

"No great loss."

"Killed by Hanali."

The priest's eyes widened. "So he has finally made his move. He's calling himself archon now, I suppose. He figured out a way."

"He banished me from the Sunlit Lands and said he was going to frame me for the murder." Now the Sunlit Lands were closed to him. Once before he had found his way in, found a back door in a dome of darkness, but now every path he tried was blocked or destroyed. He couldn't find his way to the Sunlit Lands any more than he could climb a ladder to the moon.

The silver dagger glinted in Father Tony's hand. "You are safe now, Darius. Are you so foolish as to seek another way to the Sunlit Lands?"

"Yeah. I am." He didn't say anything more.

"Hmm." Father Tony walked to the window, clasped his hands behind his back. He stared at the garden for a long time. "Why do you want to go back there? Madeline is gone. You have been framed for murder by the one who is theoretically the most powerful person in the Sunlit Lands. What use is it for you to return? Stay here and build a peaceful life."

Darius clenched his jaw. "No."

"But why? What do you want in the Sunlit Lands?"

"None of your business," he said, but even as the words came out of his mouth, he knew the real answer was that he didn't know. He kept telling himself he had a reason, but the fact was he wasn't sure. The first time he had gone to the Sunlit Lands, it made sense. Madeline was there, and would be for a year, so he wanted to be there too.

He had, thanks to the strange magics of the place, arrived before her and become an integral part of the Scim defense against the Elenil. He had been the one to show her how the magic worked, how her breathing was coming as a result of Yenil losing hers. Maybe if he hadn't been in the Sunlit Lands, Madeline wouldn't have figured it out. Maybe she would have gone through the whole year unaware of how she was stealing some kid's life away, and she'd be here with him now, none the wiser. Healed. Healthy. Happy. His jaw tightened.

When Madeline came home and Darius chose to stay, his reason to remain in the Sunlit Lands was flimsier. Madeline didn't have long to live, that much was clear, but instead of staying with her, he had chosen to bring justice for the Scim. She had supported his decision to stay. At the time it had seemed noble, good, beautiful even.

But Madeline had also broken up with him just because she thought his pain would be less if she started making the transition away from him before she died. She hadn't really let him be part of that decision, and he knew that was well-intentioned but also wasn't fair. And then at the end she had asked him to stay in the Sunlit Lands. It was what he wanted, it felt right, but in hindsight he wished he had gone home with her.

Then, when Madeline returned to the Sunlit Lands, Darius didn't see her because he was in a hurry to bring justice for the Scim. When he discovered she was there, he was so close to getting revenge, so close to finishing off the archon, that he decided to complete the job before going to her. But she had died too soon. And Hanali had ejected him from the Sunlit Lands before he could even visit her body or get the details on what had happened. She was gone, that was all. No final conversation, no saying goodbye, no closure, nothing.

So why did he want to go back now?

He didn't know. Some part of him hoped she was still alive, somehow. Magic was strange and did unexpected, even impossible things. Or maybe, if she wasn't alive, she could be brought back. It happened often enough in the fantasy books the two of them had read together. Resurrection wasn't out of the question, was it? And there was Hanali to deal with. And this nagging feeling that Darius had unfinished business there. That he belonged there in some way.

"Danger," Mr. Oliver said. "Danger and suffering. Every path from this room only leads to the same two places." He wasn't looking at either of them, just staring at the knife.

"The Dagger Perilous," Father Tony said. "We used it in the Sunlit Lands. It can tell you which paths lead to danger, and which to safety."

"What does he mean, every path leads to danger and suffering?"

The priest hefted the dagger in his hand, then passed it to Darius. "He could always use it better than the rest of us. He said he saw our paths like bright lines, telling him which ways to go—which were safe, which were foolish. I don't know how he escaped the Sunlit Lands with it—it was considered a weapon of considerable importance to the Elenil. They always loved tools that told the future."

"I stole it," Mr. Oliver said, and for the first time his eyes lit with some glimmer of life. "Stole it, and once I had it, the dagger told me how to avoid being caught. They thought I might have it, but they couldn't find it. It's the one thing I took from them. From . . ." His eyes lost focus again, and he stared out the window.

"There's a curse on him," Father Tony said. "On Madeline's mother, too. They can't really remember our time in the Sunlit Lands, and when something reminds them, it causes unnecessary pain and confusion. They never remember for more than a few minutes at a time."

Darius held the dagger tight, and he did feel something. Some low-level sensation of dread that came over him when he thought about the Sunlit Lands. "How could you stand to hold this thing? It's making me feel horrible."

"It kept them safe," Mr. Oliver snapped. "Kept us all safe."

Madeline had always said that her father was distant and cold, worked too hard, and was often absent. Maybe this knife had been to blame, though. Darius could imagine Mr. Oliver holding it before leaving work, and the dagger telling him the traffic would be too dangerous if he left now. That if he waited a few hours more, the roads would be safer. "Does it tell you what *will* happen or what *could* happen?"

"How would we ever know the answer to that?" Father Tony said, sounding like the most tired man in the world. "Trying to uncover the inner workings of magic is like trying to see the wind. You might think you understand how it operates. You might even be able to predict certain things about it. But you won't ever see it, not really."

"I need to find my way back," Darius said. "I came here looking for something that might help. Listen, Father, if you know some way back, I need you to tell me."

A look of deep sadness came over the priest's face, and Darius could tell it was a look he wore often. His face settled into the sorrowful wrinkles without a bit of trouble. "Human children can only come to the Sunlit Lands if they are in danger. With this dagger . . . the person who wields it could use it to avoid danger, to choose the safest paths. Or he could use it to chase danger. To find the most perilous, the most deadly paths forward."

The thought gave Darius a thrill of joy. If he followed the most dangerous paths, the worst possibilities—if he put himself into harm's way—maybe a door to the Sunlit Lands would open for him. Even as he thought it, the dagger burned a terrifying warning into his palm. The danger was increasing with every moment he held it.

"Mr. Oliver," Darius said, "can I take the Dagger Perilous? Even if you just let me borrow it for a little while . . ."

"Take it," Mr. Oliver said. "It hardly matters now. Every path is only grief and suffering from this room to the end of my life." He left for the hallway, headed toward his bedroom, and didn't lift his head or say goodbye.

Father Tony clicked his tongue. "Young man, I don't know if this dagger tells the truth or teaches its owner to fear everything. Be careful with it."

The dagger shook in his hand. "Father Tony," he said, "I plan to do the exact opposite."

7
RUMORS OF HOME

"I will never forget you" is the great lie of the human race.

FROM *THE ANNALS OF THE HISTORIAN*

✦

The forest path was cool and inviting during the day, and the birds flitted overhead like quick little paintbrushes dipped in color. Shula always enjoyed this part of the walk. It was cooler by the ocean, but the winding path down from the cliff baked in the sun. The tree canopy was a welcome relief.

David seemed distracted, though happy to see her. He had stuck to small talk, something he had never done much of. He was quiet, yes, but when he spoke, his words almost always had a deeper significance than most. He deflected her questions about Kekoa, saying that he would fill her in later. She asked about Jason, and he said he hadn't seen him . . . except for a strange interaction in Far Seeing. "He said hello, but said he was too busy to talk."

"That doesn't sound like Jason at all."

"That's what I thought. And he seemed unconcerned that the Elenil had a price on his head."

"That doesn't sound like Jason, either."

David shook his head. "No, the Jason I know would be shouting about being in danger every five minutes."

Shula paused. They were in sight of the village now, but she couldn't shake the unsettling feeling that something was wrong. It wasn't David, but it was something he had brought. He looked the same . . . his black hair pulled back in a ponytail, his thin, muscular frame a little harder, maybe, than it had been a year ago. But he had been living on the road, or so it seemed.

"There's something you're not telling me," she said at last.

David's eyes clouded over for a moment. "Yes. I thought we should finish your errands first. I . . . I suspect you won't want to do them after our conversation."

She took his hands and looked him in the eye. "David. We've been friends for a long while now. Is what you need to tell me more important than flour?"

His dark eyes looked sad. "Yes."

"Is someone in danger?"

He didn't seem to know how to answer that. At last he said, "Someone is always in danger, Shula."

She nodded, then turned back toward the cottage. David fell in beside her. "Yenil will be happy to see you," she said, and at the mention of Yenil's name, Delightful Glitter Lady did a happy jump and ran ahead a short way.

"What about your flour?"

"Oh, we aren't completely out yet. It can wait. Death's Head has some set aside for me, I'm sure. But it always takes a couple hours to do the shopping, even when it's simple." Shula had done her best to make inroads with the Scim community, but they all still kept their war skins on when she was there, and of course never shared a name other than their intimidating war skin names. She always laughed when she was haggling over cheese with someone named Rend Flesh. But still, the Scim were a highly community-oriented people, and you couldn't just swoop in and haggle. There was a sort of informal expectation of conversation, a drink, talking about life for a while before business could be politely commenced. Shula didn't want to wait that long to talk with David. Mrs. Oliver would be disappointed that she returned without Wendy juice, but Shula had mixed feelings about that anyway.

"Do you want to talk about it as we walk?" David asked.

Shula considered that. There was dread in the pit of her stomach. She feared what he was going to say for some reason, and she wanted to keep her normal life for a few minutes more. "Let's sit down together after we get home. It can wait a half hour or so?"

"Of course."

So they turned their attention to other things. David had always had a quiet sincerity to him, and he enjoyed looking at the natural beauty of the world around him. He mentioned the view as they climbed, noting with particular pleasure the way the distant crystal sphere of the sky arced into the far horizon, imagining what it might look like where the crystal met the sea. Shula found herself glad for his company. It had been a long while since she had been around someone close to her age, and human, too.

When they were within sight of the cottage, Delightful Glitter Lady took off running, honking for Yenil the whole way. This was nothing new—it was what she always did. No question, Yenil was the favored one in the family. Yenil burst out of the cottage and raced to the tiny rhino, and soon the two of them were wrestling and playing in the grass.

"I see you've been in the sugar," Shula said, smiling.

Yenil didn't even stop wrestling, just said, "That's why we need more flour! We used the rest to make cinnamon rolls!"

Then she noticed that Shula wasn't alone.

"DAVID!" Yenil shouted and raced to him. He swept her into the air and tossed her high, to much delighted shrieking.

Shula stepped into the cottage just as Mrs. Oliver was putting the rolls into the oven. "That was a quick trip," she said.

"I had an unexpected visitor."

Mrs. Oliver's eyes widened. "Trouble with the Scim?"

"No, it was David. You met him before."

"Oh yes," Mrs. Oliver said, but her voice was brittle. "Maddie's friend."

"Right. He came looking for me. He said he has some sort of news. But I'm feeling nervous about it."

Mrs. Oliver knocked the flour from her hands and wrapped her arms around Shula. "Whatever comes, dear, we'll be here together, right?"

Shula put her head on the older woman's shoulder. After the loss of her own mother, Shula hadn't thought another woman would ever move into that space. And she hadn't, not really. But it was nice to have someone who cared about her, and Yenil, too. During this year of grief, just loving and losing Madeline had bound them.

David walked in, Yenil hanging on his leg, and Dee doing her best to trip him. He had a grin on his face. "What smells so delicious?"

Mrs. Oliver went to him and gave him a brief hug. "Welcome, David."

"Thanks, Mrs. Oliver."

"Come, have a seat. What have you been doing this last year?"

David managed to maneuver himself into a chair, and Yenil immediately transitioned from his leg to his lap. He laughed and set her aside, and she grabbed hold of one of his arms. He tousled her hair. "My friend Kekoa was missing. He sent some birds asking for help, so I set out to find him. He was with the Zhanin, or so the messages said."

"The Zhanin," Mrs. Oliver said. "We've seen them less and less this year." When they had first moved into the cottage, they would see Zhanin moving up and down the coast now and then, maybe two or three times a week. But they hadn't seen one in a couple months now. The Scim said the Zhanin migrated. So it was probably just that they were gone for a season. Not that the Sunlit Lands had traditional seasons.

"Their islands move," David said. "There are great trees on them called sail trees that catch the wind. And depending on the time of year, the Zhanin and their living boats are to be found in different places." He shrugged. "I couldn't find them."

Mrs. Oliver frowned, concentrating. "I remember them. When I was young. We went to . . . what was it? My friends and I lived among them for a time."

David looked between her and Shula. "You probably remember," Shula said, "that Mrs. Oliver came to the Sunlit Lands when she was our age. But the Elenil took her memory of that time."

David's eyebrows raised in interest. "Mrs. Oliver . . . when you lost your memory, did you *know* you had lost it?"

"I didn't *lose* it," she said carefully. "I had come to the Sunlit Lands with five other people. Some of them survived. A few of us returned to Earth. I remember . . ." She paused, squinted. "I remember some things clearer than others now. When I left this place, my memories of my time here were wiped clean, along with a sort of maintenance spell from the Elenil to keep me from remembering. I've been remembering more every day. Madeline left the Wendy juice for me, and that's helping."

David looked at Shula, and she could see him considering something. She had no idea what, but the way he looked at her . . . it was as if there was something sad about her. What that might be, she didn't know.

"I'm going out to play," Yenil said. "C'mon, Dee!" They ran out, and then Yenil stuck her head back in. "Call me when the cinnamon rolls are done."

David sighed, and his face relaxed. "A year ago, after everything that happened in Aluvorea—"

"Maduvorea now," Mrs. Oliver said.

David nodded. "After everything that happened in Maduvorea, I decided it was time to look into what was going on with Kekoa. I knew that if he had been caught in some situation he couldn't control, I needed to be wise in how I chose to approach it. So I went back to Far Seeing."

"What was it like?" Shula asked. "I've heard rumors."

"It was a mess. The Pastisians were still there, with their great necromancer blimps, and the Palace of a Thousand Years was being dismantled. The Elenil were in disarray, shocked by what had happened. I went to find Hanali, but . . . something had changed there."

Mrs. Oliver leaned forward, strangely interested. "Changed how? Did he seem less certain? Troubled by something?"

David watched Mrs. Oliver with the same quiet attention he often gave Shula, as if weighing her words, trying to understand what might be beneath them. "No. More certain of himself. Less playful, less goofy. I don't know, maybe it's because Jason wasn't around. But when I talked to him about Kekoa, he barely listened. Told me if I needed to go to the Zhanin, he would provide me a boat, but that's it. No help other than that, and no information about the Zhanin themselves."

"Was he archon by then?" Shula asked. "Maybe he was just busy."

"He was busy, of course. That's what I thought too. So I figured I would go talk to a storyteller. See if they might be able to tell me something helpful." David shifted uncomfortably.

Mrs. Oliver took the cinnamon rolls out of the oven, and they all fell to small talk for a moment as she passed out the plates and scooped beautiful, steaming rolls onto each one. Shula shouted for Yenil, who was chasing a chicken with Dee. Yenil shouted back and said she'd come in later.

"Which storyteller did you go to?"

David glanced at her, and Shula finally recognized what the lurking emotion was in his eyes: guilt. He felt bad about something.

"In the tower quarter there's a woman who lives in a wall of ivy," he said.

Shula frowned. "That's the one Hanali took Madeline to."

"Right. So I asked her for a story. She asked which story, and I—I told her I wanted whatever story she thought would be best for me."

"You can do that?" Shula asked. She had been to the storytellers a lot of times, and usually you had to tell them which story you wanted, and even which version of the story. Most often people asked for the Elenil version.

"She said it didn't happen often, but it's allowed. So she told me a story. About someone called the Historian."

Mrs. Oliver had a strange look on her face now too. "The Historian," she repeated in a faraway voice, almost as if she was remembering something.

"I don't understand," Shula said. "Who's that?"

"The easy answer might be that he's a sort of magician. He works for the Elenil—or maybe *with* the Elenil, I couldn't get a straight answer to that. Sometimes she said one thing, sometimes another. A lot of her answers about him were like that. He lives beneath the city of Far Seeing, she said once. Another time she said that he built it, even. But she also said he lives on an island far to the northwest, an island that people are afraid to name or even mention."

"What? I've never heard of this," Shula said.

"Yeah," David said. "Me neither. So I waited until the next time I was with Hanali. The necromancers had just left the city. We were at the base of the tower, which had been torn down to the foundation. Hanali was convincing the magistrates that it should be rebuilt. After the conversation he looked at me, and I said, like it was a joke, *If they had kept going, they would have dug all the way down to the Historian.* And Hanali . . . he grabbed me by the arms and said, 'Where did you hear that name?' I shook loose and I asked, 'Doesn't everyone know about the Historian?' Then Hanali called for a bird and whispered in its ear."

Shula found herself unaccountably nervous. Why would Hanali be trying to keep a message secret in this moment? "What happened?"

"Hanali tried to keep talking normally, like nothing was going on. But I watched the bird, and it flew directly to one of the Elenil guards. I saw him talking to some of the others, and he looked over at us . . . at me."

Mrs. Oliver said, "Eat your cinnamon rolls. There's plenty of time to talk, and we're safe here."

David took a bite, but that didn't stop him from continuing. "Hanali saw that I saw what was happening. He leaned over to grab me, but I ran. I knew something important was going on. I hid in the city for the next five weeks, and every day I found a way to sneak into the storyteller's room and pay her to tell me another story about the Historian, a branching network of stories that radiated out from him. She kept telling me stories that had something to do with me. Somehow, one way or another, every story of the Historian came back to me or someone I knew. Like Mrs. Oliver—"

Shula shuddered and lifted her palm toward him. "Don't say it, David."

He looked at his plate and then, without raising his head, turned his eyes to Shula. "And you."

"Me?" Shula pushed her chair back from the table in surprise. "But I've never heard of him."

David hesitated. "You've not only heard of him. You've met him."

"What do you mean? When? Who is he?"

"Like I said, some sort of magician. He specializes in editing people's memories."

Shula's stomach fell away from her as if she had jumped off a cliff. "But . . . no one has edited my memories."

David held her gaze, and there was intense sadness in his eyes when he spoke. "You had a brother once, right?"

"Boulos," she said, confused. "But he's dead." Burned to death in the fire at her apartment a million years ago. Along with her mother, her father,

her little sister. Leaving her alone in the world, fending for herself. Which is why she had ended up here, in the Sunlit Lands.

"Boulos is alive," David said. "That's one of the last stories the story-teller told me. Boulos is alive, and he's being held captive by the Historian."

Shula grabbed the lip of the table. She felt light-headed from shock. She heard David talking to her, but from a long, long way off. Mrs. Oliver was expressing concern, was coming around the table to her, and all Shula could hear was the voice in her head that repeated, over and over, *My brother is dead, he is dead, Boulos is dead.*

8

TEA FOR THREE

The Elenil play the tune.

THE KNIGHT OF THE MIRROR

✛

ilenyia did not like to be told no, and she did not like to be kept waiting, two things this human guard seemed intent on making her experience. Ricardo stood at her elbow, and she could feel him bristling with indignation.

"Lady Gilenyia demands entrance," he said, his hand on the hilt of his sword.

The guardswoman looked unconcerned. She lazily glanced at his hand, then his face, then turned her attention back to Gilenyia. "She's not the lady of Westwind, though, is she?"

Gilenyia cleared her throat. "What is your name, young woman?"

"Thuy," the guard said. "Why, you gonna report me to my boss?"

"Your 'boss'? I presume you refer to the Knight of the Mirror, the lord of this castle."

The girl had the audacity to shrug. "Sure."

Insufferable. Gilenyia rearranged the stole on her shoulders and looked back to her carriage. New Dawn sat obediently within it. The guard had stopped them at the drawbridge, and now she would not let them pass. "Is your lord on his way here to make sense of this offensive action you have taken?"

The girl didn't look behind her. "Do you see him behind me? Is he walking up on me right now?"

"No," Ricardo said through gritted teeth.

She shrugged. Again. "Let me know if you see him."

Ricardo pulled on his sword, and the girl gave him her full attention for the first time. "Try it," she said. Ricardo let the steel fall back into its sheath. "I didn't think so."

Gilenyia pursed her lips. The castle of Westwind fell into a grey area as far as jurisdiction went here in the city. Though it fell within the limits of the Court of Far Seeing, it had come to the Sunlit Lands together with the knight, and what happened on its property was his to control and command. This was part of the bargain made to ensure his service to the Elenil. It was an enormous concession on the part of the person who had made the deal, a sure sign of how important the knight was to the Elenil, and of the power he wielded. He had been a loyal follower who had worked with all his strength for their cause, even when he had been asked to do things that were difficult, dangerous, or against his own self-interest. It was strange indeed that he had not been responding to Hanali, and stranger still that he would leave instructions for his guards to keep an influential Elenil like Gilenyia from entering the castle.

A lumbering purple beast of burden dragging a wagon of hay came up behind the carriage, and a human called out, "Hey, get out of the way. I have to get this to the stables."

"Wait your turn," Ricardo snapped.

Gilenyia felt certain the guard, Thuy, smirked at that. "Pull it around, pal," Thuy said to Gilenyia's driver. "You're gonna have to pull that carriage back to make room. Go ahead there. That's right."

A great deal of jostling and neighing and complaining later, the human was pushing past them over the drawbridge, his beast of burden and the burden itself so large that Gilenyia—who had not had the foresight to evacuate the bridge—was being pushed toward the edge, precariously balanced over the moat.

"Apologies, lady," the human said as he pushed past, tipping his hat toward her. But he didn't look sorry at all. Not even a bit.

The cart rumbled across, and Thuy took her place at the center of the castle gate again, relaxed and immovable. Hay had fallen on Gilenyia. She picked it off her stole. Ricardo reached up and pulled some from her hair. She swatted his hand away. Yes, something was wrong here in the Sunlit Lands. Something was happening, but she couldn't put her finger on it.

And then the Knight of the Mirror was before them. He looked haggard. He was unshaven, his hair unkempt, his face more worn and lined than she remembered. "My lady Gilenyia," he said, and inclined his head. He did not bow, she noticed.

"Sir Knight," she said politely. "Your servant here will not grant me entrance."

The knight's eyebrows raised slightly. "Miss Nguyen? Then she does her job admirably, though she is no servant of mine."

Thuy grinned. "I volunteer for this position. I could do it all day. It's fun."

The knight raised his hands when Gilenyia moved to object. "As you know, I allow no magic in Westwind, whether for healing or war. Gilenyia, you must agree to this before you can cross the threshold."

No *Lady* Gilenyia this time. So there was some trouble here, some issue she was unaware of. "Sir Knight, I know your rules well, and never have I broken them."

"Very well then," the knight said, and stood aside, indicating that she could enter.

She glided past him, but when Ricardo stepped behind her, the guard blocked his way. "Where are you going, Ricardo?"

"With my lady," he said.

Thuy pointed at the tattoo on his left arm. She was right to notice it, as it was a particularly complicated one that went from his wrist up nearly to his shoulder. He sometimes went bare-armed to display it, an act of strange loyalty and braggadocio that also felt unsettling to the Elenil, who preferred to cover as much skin as possible. "That's a lot of ink, Ric. You able to walk in here without using any magic?"

Which, of course, he could not. Nor could many humans in this place. Nearly all of them had made a deal with the Elenil that bound them here, and that meant magic to bind them as well as reward them. And although magic had been reset, Gilenyia had been surprised that most of the humans came back into their previous agreements with precious little bargaining. Hanali had been surprised by her surprise. "I promised their heart's desire," he said. "Who wouldn't want that?"

Ricardo cleared his throat. "No. Not really."

"Then break your oath to the Elenil or remain outside," the knight said.

Gilenyia was shocked. The fact that the knight said it made it clear that this was not something to be questioned. It was his castle, and therefore he was the ultimate authority. Gilenyia objected. "I know beyond doubt that you have often allowed people with magic in your gates. Did you require Madeline Oliver to stop breathing when she entered? Did you force Shula Bishara to forswear her oaths?"

"Apologies, Gilenyia, but those were not your servants, and so long ago that it feels to me another era, not only another year. Much has changed since those days." He waited, but she was struck silent with wonder. When she did not respond, he said, "We could speak in your carriage if it would make you more comfortable?"

But of course it would not. She had significant magic of her own, and the protection of someone like Ricardo was largely ornamental. She had, like all Elenil, been trained in war for more than a century and could fight off a battalion of humans with little more than a stick and some high ground. But the sheer insulting cheek of the knight to insist that no one with magic be allowed in—but to let Gilenyia herself in, not to mention his own people—was astonishing. She did her best to make herself sound aloof and unconcerned. "Of course, dear knight. It is your home, let us follow your rules. Where shall we refresh ourselves?"

She said that on purpose, *refresh ourselves*. If he were going to treat her as an honored guest, there would certainly be food and drink awaiting them, and comfortable seats in which to recline, and perhaps some light entertainment. But the knight took her to a room that was plain, unornamented, and filled only with a simple wooden table and three wooden chairs, a large mirror with a sheet over it, and little else but dust. The knight was a man of honor, so he pulled out her chair before sitting, but to suggest it was the least he could do would not be incorrect.

"Sir Knight," she said, trying to keep her anger to herself. How dare he treat her with such incivility? "Perhaps something has changed and I am unaware of it. But I feel as if you and I are at odds, and I have not yet shared with you the reason for my visit."

The knight, too, was barely concealing his anger. "It must be of great import, for you gave us no warning at all, nor any choice in the matter."

She rearranged herself, but it was no use trying to find a comfortable position on this chair. "I am not accustomed to this being a problem. What is more, I have noticed your absence in the court. Are you not concerned about what my cousin the magistrate may desire of you?"

"The magistrate, ha! Do you not say 'archon' like your cousin then?"

Gilenyia filed that away. So the knight had also noticed Hanali's usurpation of that term and did not like it. "I do not say things that are not true," she said carefully.

The knight's eyelids dropped halfway, as if he had suddenly fallen nearly asleep or grown so tired he could not continue the conversation. He stood and walked around the table. Gilenyia, despite herself, felt for the knife she kept in her sleeve. But the knight did not come so close. Instead, he paused at the great mirror in the room and uncovered it. He looked into it with great longing, but after a moment turned his back on it and stared at Gilenyia. It was only a moment more before his beloved, Fernanda Isabela Flores de Castilla, appeared in the mirror behind him. It had been many years since Gilenyia had seen more than a brief glimpse of her, though of course all the Elenil knew about her, and it was not uncommon to catch a glimpse of her in one's mirror from time to time.

"Do you note anything strange in my mirror, lady?" the knight asked.

"Strange?" Gilenyia moved to the mirror. Fernanda had always been beautiful, for a human. Dark, luxurious hair. Wide eyes. A bright smile. But she was not smiling now. "Strange, sir knight? Say rather beautiful. I have never found your beloved strange."

The knight searched her eyes, seeking a lie. She did not know what lie he sought. She had, in fact, felt some pity for the man and his beloved over the years. His arrangement with the Elenil had been early in the Elenil's dealing with humans, and though he had been given many magical boons, the price also had been steep.

The knight took his seat, but Gilenyia knew he could leap up at a moment's notice. He watched her like an opponent in a tourney: unwavering, with a thin veneer of courtesy between them and violence. "Do you think it strange, lady, that I would enter again into my magical agreements with the Elenil? I, who will not allow even the barest magic in my domain?"

"Enter again?" Gilenyia said, as if she didn't understand, and yet she knew with a sickening certainty what impossible thing he was implying.

"Yes, lady, again. Or do you not recall that our friend Madeline Oliver broke all magic in the Sunlit Lands and reset every agreement, every bond? It was not so long ago, Gilenyia, when this happened."

She scowled. He was treating her like a petulant child. "I recall it well, Sir Knight. If you have a tune to play, then sing out."

The knight laughed ruefully. "The Elenil play the tune, and the humans dance for their pleasure." He pointed at his lady, who looked both nervous and frightened. "At the Festival of the Turning, I am given one day with this lady, one glorious day each year, because the Elenil magic has been put on hold. Yet why, when all of magic was reset, did my lady not fly forth from the mirror in a shower of glass?"

"Truly, I know not."

"Then, when the archon himself dies—the very Elenil who has caught me in this devil's bargain—still, my love remains ensnared. Why?"

"Sir Knight, I promise you—"

He interrupted, face red and voice raised in a way no one had spoken to Gilenyia in fifty years. "The promises of the Elenil, I care not for them. Give me something true."

"You forget yourself, sir!"

"Would that I could," he snapped. "Magic was broken, but my bonds were not. All these years the archon has played his flute and I have danced, for he told me when the song ended we would be free. Now I learn, Gilenyia, that perhaps all these promised freedoms were not in his power to give. So what use my loyalty and obedience then?"

Something came unstuck inside her. This was worse, far worse than anything she had imagined. She thought perhaps the knight had grown unhappy, was wanting to bargain for more control or a shorter term of service. But of course she had not thought about it carefully enough. If his agreement with the Elenil had been broken, he would have left the Sunlit Lands, gladly and with all speed. He would leave behind his castle, his horse, his people, his history here, all of it, so long as his lady went with him. He'd live in a hovel as a beggar with her at his side.

Gilenyia reached across the table toward him, but he moved away. "Sir Knight, I promise you, I do not know the meaning of this. Now that my cousin is . . . in a position of power, surely we can find an answer. You need not be so combative."

The knight had always been a keen student of the people around him, and he had an uncanny ability to discern when someone told him the truth. Or so she had thought. Perhaps he had been fooled all those years ago by some member of the Elenil and entered into a dishonest pact. "I believe you, Lady Gilenyia," he said at last. He stared into the mirror. "Seven days. I will wait seven days for you to bring me word from Hanali." His eyes shifted to hers. "After that, I have no reason to serve the Elenil. I have, rather, reason to destroy them in the hope that my curse will be broken."

Gilenyia breathed in deep. They could not afford an enemy like the knight, not at this time. He could hold his own against an Elenil warrior, was likely better than some of them, and many of the human soldiers were loyal to him. The Elenil had thought his loyalty was unshakable, and thus it was no problem that the soldiers followed him. Now that was thrown into doubt. "I hear your words and will do all I can to find answers, Sir Knight." She nodded toward the mirror. "And for your sake, too, dear lady."

The knight relaxed. "I thank you, Lady Gilenyia." He called into the hall. "Where are our refreshments? Would you leave the lady waiting?" He touched his fingers to the mirror, and his lady reached for them from the inside. Then she turned and drifted away, like a ghost. He covered the mirror. "What business brings you to Westwind, lady?"

"I have heard a rumor," she said. "One I can scarce believe to be true. I have heard that one of the traitor humans has come to Westwind seeking safety and that you have provided it, despite the clear instructions from

Hanali that those children are to be immediately turned over to the Elenil, dead or alive."

There was a knock at the door, and a servant backed into the room, pulling a cart of treats and hot tea. He turned, teapot in hand, and grinned at Gilenyia. "What can I interest you in? Coffee, tea? Complete overthrow of the Elenil empire?"

"Jason Wu," she said, scarcely able to believe it.

He swept into a low bow. "At your service." He straightened, set the teapot on the table. "Well, not actually at your service. That's more of a metaphor." He grinned wider. "The menu, though, that I'm serious about." He poured three cups of tea and took his seat.

9
VAIN BOYS

Every child knows this story.

FROM *THE WISE SAYINGS OF MOTHER CROW*

✦

Darius had taken the Dagger Perilous and gone home. His mother, surprised to see him so early, was suspicious. She was right to be, as he was only here to say goodbye. He had every intention of leaving early in the morning while she slept and then finding his way into the Sunlit Lands. Either that or he'd be, as his mother would say, "dead in a ditch somewhere."

She watched him carefully all evening, and he did everything he could to seem normal, recovered, at peace. He ate dinner with good cheer, even sat with her and watched the news, something she loved and he hated. He played some video games after the news, right there in the living room, and acted like he didn't want to stop when she asked him to clean the dishes.

He waited a full hour after she went to bed before packing his bag. He knew she could still be awake, looking at her phone or watching a show. He threw a change of clothes and a couple things he thought might be of use in his school backpack: a flashlight, the dagger, his charger. He shoved the whole mess under his bed and set his alarm for 4 a.m.

The house was completely still when Darius woke. He put his pillow under the blanket. He didn't know if that trick ever really worked, but he figured it was better than nothing. He slipped his window open, grabbed his bag, and then it was out and over. He opened the car door as quietly as he could, then put the Mustang in neutral and coasted down the driveway. When it stopped, he started the car and drove away, pulling the driver's-side door closed. He looked in the rearview mirror, but his mom's light was still off.

The dagger pulled Darius toward downtown. There weren't many people around, just a few homeless folks loitering. He found a parking spot and took a nap in the driver's seat. Woke up again just before seven, the city stretching and waking all around him. He bought a cinnamon roll at a bakery attached to a hotel and ate it while he walked.

He could tell where danger was even with the dagger in his backpack. It was strange. There was a frightening-looking homeless man on the sidewalk at one point, and the dagger didn't so much as buzz. Darius walked by him, and the guy just nodded and said hello. It gave him a surge of confidence that the thing worked. It wasn't quite right to say the dagger was pulling him, he realized. The dagger was just letting him know which direction was the riskiest. He could easily choose to go away from the danger, and the dagger wouldn't care. Its job was to identify danger, not take him toward it or away from it.

A police officer walked toward him, and the dagger pinged. Darius got the impression maybe the officer wasn't a danger, but he was an indication of some other hazard elsewhere. Darius's father had trained him what to do when he saw a police officer. He put his hands where the officer could see them, relaxed to make it clear he wasn't nervous, and was careful to neither look the officer in the eye nor to look away. From the corner of his eye he could see the officer watching him as he passed, like he was debating saying something. Darius just kept walking.

"Hey, kid," the officer said.

Darius looked back, slowed his walk, said, "Yes, sir?"

"Listen, you probably shouldn't go that way."

The dagger was telling him the same thing. It wouldn't hurt to have more information, though. He stopped. "What's the problem, officer?"

"No problem. Not to speak of. But there's a protest scheduled for this morning. Probably not the kind of people you want to be around. There are plenty of officers, so we're going to keep them under control. To be on the safe side, though."

"What kind of protest?" The dagger buzzed harder when he thought about finding the protesters.

"Called the Vain Boys. They come to town, hold their little parade."

"So what's the deal, they don't like teenagers or something?" Darius knew about these guys, so he was asking the question to let the officer be the expert. The Vain Boys held protests here once or twice a year. Most of them came to the city from elsewhere—it was an internet association. They were racist in the most old-school KKK sense. Said they were "Western chauvinists," but what they meant was that they were white supremacists.

"It's not your age they'll have a problem with," the officer said.

Darius lifted his eyebrows, like he had just figured it out. "Thanks for letting me know."

"Be safe," the officer said, and continued on his way.

Darius waited a minute just in case the officer turned back, and then he headed toward the protest. He had fought the Elenil from the back of a gigantic flying owl. He wasn't worried about a crowd of racists. He had read up on the Vain Boys for a civics paper he wrote last year. They were loud, obnoxious, and leaned toward violence, but they also weren't the smartest. That probably made them more dangerous, not less—but that's what he was looking for, after all.

When Darius found them at the square downtown, they were still getting their parade ready. It was a motley collection of men (almost all men), a little younger than he thought they would be. All the stereotypical images Darius had in his mind were represented: big burly biker types, careful lawyer types who "aren't racist, just want white people to be celebrated," and even one guy in Klan robes, minus the hood. He didn't see any swastikas, at least, so that was something. In fact, their logo was an eagle wearing a top hat, a beer bottle in one claw and a machine gun in the other. Many of them were wearing yellow shirts with the Vain Boys logo in black. There seemed to be some sort of hierarchy, with "officers" wearing black collared shirts with yellow stripes on the shoulders. Weirdly, there was at least one Asian American man in the mob. Darius would be interested in asking that guy some questions.

There were counterprotesters, too, in a dizzying array of unplanned chaos. The members of one group were wearing handkerchiefs as masks, and others were dressed as unicorns, complete with rainbow wigs and silver horns. He wasn't sure what that was about. He noticed the counterprotesters were nearly all white. Maybe most of the people of color knew enough to stay away today.

The knife was trying to warn him now. He might have been wrong about its neutrality, because it clearly wanted him to leave. He felt a steady magical pressure building that seemed to be pressing on his skull from the inside.

Darius walked a full circle around the protest first. He wasn't as interested in the protesters as he was in finding an entrance to the Sunlit Lands. He kept an eye out for unusual doors, sewer grates a human might be able to squeeze through, trees with strange wounds that could pull open and create a doorway. Of course, when he had found his way in before, it had been through a tent-sized dome of darkness in the middle of the day. He felt like that would be pretty obvious if it popped up, though.

He had to embrace the reality that there might not be an entrance. If Hanali really had the power to control who came into the Sunlit Lands, it was entirely possible that there wasn't a door or a window or a crack he could use, in which case he'd have to start thinking of a backup plan. Maybe he could find other people who were likely to be recruited, fill them in on the situation, and ask them to find a way to bring him across.

The whole "filling them in on the situation" thing might be tricky, though. *"There's a magical world full of magical people, and I can't get there, but if you happen to go, please tell the Scim (you'll think they're the evil bad guys) or the necromancers (don't worry, they're fine) that I need help to get back."* People would think it was some sort of prank or that he was on drugs. He would have thought the same thing before he went into the Sunlit Lands.

Protesters were massing now. Police with bullhorns were letting them know when they spread out too far, and the police were also keeping the counterprotesters at a distance. They obviously thought there was a decent chance of a fight breaking out. It had happened last year.

The chants didn't make a lot of sense. As the parade began its journey, the Vain Boys were still bunched in place as their police escort started them down the approved path. Their first chant was a pro-police thing. Maybe to try to get the cops on their side if something happened? Darius wasn't sure. As the last of the Vain Boys started walking, Darius fell in step behind them, along with the counterprotesters. There were about ten feet and six cops between them. Now they were chanting, "Vain Boys maim toys," and Darius had no idea what that meant. He assumed it was some sort of coded message, but he had to admit it could just be dumb nonsense.

He checked his phone. Six texts from his mom, asking where he was. He shot one back, telling her he was okay. He thought twice, then sent her another one saying that he loved her. He regretted it almost instantly, as his mom replied, What's going on? Is something wrong? and telling him that if she didn't hear from him, she'd be calling the cell phone company to track him. He texted back, telling her everything was fine, and then he turned the phone off. He should have left it in the car—it wouldn't even work in the Sunlit Lands.

Although the dagger assured him he was in danger, he didn't see much to prove it. He wandered behind the Vain Boys for about half an hour, and nothing happened aside from his increased certainty that the Vain Boys was a drinking club of unrepentant racists who were tired of being told that they were, well, unrepentant racists. There was some "White lives matter" chanting, then some "You will not replace us," and a couple of anti-Semitic chants. They were shifting into "If you don't like it here, go home" when someone sidled up alongside him. It was the kid from the Oliver house.

"What are you doing here?" the kid asked. What was his name? Josh. The thief.

Darius gave him a hard look and a once-over. He could definitely take this kid. Darius had actual battle experience, and Josh looked like he had been in a few scraps, sure, but when it came down to it, Darius didn't pull punches. "Free country," he said.

"Yeah, you should be thankful we brought you here," Josh said.

Darius nodded. So it was like that. "Weren't free when we got here, though, were we?"

"You are now. You should be falling on your knees, thankful to Western society. We lifted you up out of your grass hut. I don't know what slum you live in now, but it's no grass hut."

"I take it you're not a counterprotester," Darius said. The dagger was sending piercing warnings into his head now.

Josh showed him his elbow. Along his forearm was a tattoo spelling out the words *VAIN BOY*. "What do you think about that?"

Darius shrugged. "Seems accurate."

Josh sneered at him. "You don't know what you're talking about."

"Why aren't you up there with your people, Josh? Why you hanging around back here with the smart people?"

"You'll see," Josh said. "I'm here to make sure things go the way they're supposed to. We need to make some noise if we're going to get any media attention."

"Oh yeah? You boys here to get coverage?"

"Don't be stupid. Of course that's why we're here. When did some dumb parade ever change anything?"

Darius squinted at him, trying to see if he was joking. "Didn't pay much attention in history class, huh?"

"Shut up." Josh pulled his jacket open, revealing a bottle of booze.

"You're a little young for that."

Josh cackled. "I don't waste my time drinking. This is for the protest. Look closer." There was a handkerchief shoved in the neck of the bottle, soaked in the alcohol.

Darius didn't need the dagger to tell him that was trouble. He had no interest in being lit up like a torch to help the Vain Boys get on the news. Josh wasn't on guard—again, Darius could tell these guys were amateurs— so it took the kid by surprise when Darius grabbed him by the jacket with his left hand and drove his right fist into his face. At the same time, Darius yelled, "Officers, help, this kid has a gun!" It wasn't a gun, no, but Darius suspected it would be easier to get the attention of the police by shouting *gun*. And he wasn't wrong.

The police whirled in time to see Josh wiping the blood from his face and popping a lighter from his pocket. An officer was two steps from Josh when he lit the Molotov cocktail and sent it arcing over his head into the mass of Vain Boys. The officer pushed him to the ground, and then the explosion came. The Vain Boys let out a howl of rage and scattered in all directions in a response that was so rehearsed as to be laughable.

Darius walked, fast, away from Josh, cutting across the parade path. Vain Boys were flooding backward now, dodging police and hitting the counterprotesters. Darius tried to stay out of their way, looking for any evidence of a door to the Sunlit Lands. He could hear Josh yelling that the Black kid was the one who punched him. Of course he used stronger language than "the Black kid." Darius knew better than to stick around. Sure, one cop had seen Josh use a Molotov cocktail, but on the other hand, Josh was white. Cops were people too, and you just needed one bigot to turn things the wrong way.

Two burly Vain Boys had a counterprotester on the ground. They had stripped her sign out of her hands, and now they were kicking her. She was one of the unicorn crowd, and now she was curled in a ball, trying to protect herself from their attack. Darius debated helping her, but there were more pressing matters. If he was ever going to find his way back to the Sunlit Lands, it would be somewhere like this. He couldn't stop to help every person who needed it along the way.

Ah, who was he kidding. He couldn't not help, either. He punched the first guy in the kidneys without any warning. No reason to call their attention to him when he had the element of surprise. The guy folded easier than he'd thought. The second man turned. This one wore a collared shirt and a whistle around his neck. One of the officers or whatever. Maybe a coach? His eyes widened when he saw Darius. "I'd think your kind would know better than that by now."

"Right back at you," Darius said, fists ready.

"She your girlfriend?" the bruiser asked, disgust in his voice.

"Just an everyday, ordinary unicorn." Darius shook his head. "If beating up a unicorn didn't give you a clue you were the bad guy, I don't know what would."

The Vain Boy curled his lip at that. Instead of advancing on Darius, though, he blew the whistle.

"I don't understand," Darius said. "Am I supposed to run laps or something?"

He dropped the whistle and grinned. "If I were you, I'd definitely run."

Darius took a quick glance and saw that about six Vain Boys were headed their way. Of course. Because the whistle was a predetermined sign of some kind. Like "Come help me beat up this guy." The dagger was piercing his brain. Undulating waves of warning pounded him. Maybe it would be good to get a little farther from the center of the danger. But he was worried about the unicorn girl.

"I always like to get some work with the dumbbells first," Darius said, and drove his fist into the guy's neck, then followed it up with a sideways elbow to his face. The guy fell to his knees, choking, and Darius shoved him so he fell on his side. He helped Unicorn Girl to her feet. The Vain Boys were almost on them. Darius was a great fighter, but six on one . . . he would definitely lose. And he had the feeling losing here would mean a trip to the hospital instead of the Sunlit Lands.

He dragged the girl over to the side. She seemed okay, just shell-shocked and probably bruised. There was a coffee shop half a block down. "Can you make it into that shop?" he asked her.

She nodded. "Thank you."

"I'm going to get those Vain Boys to chase me," Darius said. "You go in that shop and stay there until it's safe. Text your friends, tell them where you are. If the cops ask if you want to press charges, the answer is yes."

"But I don't know which ones did it."

"Tell them to look for the guy with the bruised trachea."

She hugged him quickly, and he gave her a little push toward the coffee shop before he ran. He had only made it about a block before the first of the Vain Boys caught up to him.

10
WENDY JUICE

To say "a single memory" is no different from calling a leaf a tree.

FROM *THE ANNALS OF THE HISTORIAN*

✦

Shula slowly came to herself, like a swimmer rising from the deep. Mrs. Oliver was rubbing her back. David crouched nearby with a cup of water. She sipped from it. No one asked her anything, but Mrs. Oliver squeezed her shoulder, and David watched her with careful concern. She should feel happy. More than happy—she should feel elated, she should feel excited and eager for more details. Her brother, Boulos—whom she'd thought dead!—was alive. Or so David said. But she felt none of those things. Instead she felt a deep, undeniable dread. Anger. Defensiveness.

"I don't understand," she said at last. "He died. He died back in Syria."

David waited a moment before speaking, as if weighing his words carefully. He did that often, Shula noticed. "Did you see his body?"

Had she? She thought back to that night. The apartment building burning. The assault. She had seen the bodies of her parents, her little sister.

Had been about to look in her brother's room, but someone—Hanali—had told her she wouldn't want to see that. And she hadn't. Why pile grief on top of grief? But now she wondered. What might she have seen if she had opened that door?

Mrs. Oliver sat next to her and squeezed her hand. "Shula . . . I have had my share of forgetting. I have dealt with layers of false memory. I'm still working through it all."

Shula shook her head. "Are you saying I used to know that he was alive? That I somehow forgot? How is that even possible?"

"Maybe," David said. "Memory is a strange thing." He shook his head, as if trying to get rid of a memory himself.

Mrs. Oliver glanced out the window, and Shula turned to look. Yenil was chasing Dee, screaming with delight as she charged after the chickens. Mrs. Oliver turned back to Shula, put the palm of her hand against Shula's cheek. "Dear girl. There is a way to know for sure. To have some idea if you're forgetting something. You could drink some Wendy juice."

Shula flinched at the thought, and a sting of guilt resonated inside her. She hadn't wanted to get more Wendy juice for Mrs. Oliver, and she had come home with David without even trying to find it. "I didn't get any more, Mrs. Oliver," she said.

Mrs. Oliver smiled. "I know, Shula. And I've told you more than once to call me Wendy now. I still have a bit." She moved to one of the larger pots—one they really only used in the winter for making long-standing stews that they would tend for days, adding more scraps as the days went by. She reached inside and pulled out a clear glass bottle, handing it to Shula. The bright liquid inside could have been lemonade. Shula took the cork out and smelled it. Sweet and bright, like a summer afternoon. Like it held the promise of bringing back the best days of your childhood. But Shula knew that even the best days were surrounded by other days, dark days, difficult times.

"What's it like? When you drink it?"

Mrs. Oliver looked away. "Is there something you've forgotten, Shula? Are you sure you've forgotten something, or just thinking it's a possibility?"

"I don't know. I'm . . . confused."

Mrs. Oliver sighed, took her apron off, and sat down at the table. "Have you ever been with an old friend, and they bring up something from a long time ago, but you don't remember it? Then, maybe they pull out an old photograph or a letter, and you look at it and realize you were there after all?"

Shula shook her head.

"Of course not. I forget how young you are. What could you have forgotten in such a short life?" She drummed the tabletop with her fingers. "At first you think to yourself, no, that can't be. I have no memory of that. But your friend keeps telling you the details, reminding you of different parts of it. 'Remember, we went to the boardwalk,' they say. 'We rode on the bumper cars, and you knocked Sammy so hard and he complained about his neck hurting the rest of the day.' Sammy complaining, that sounds familiar. The more you think about it, it starts to come back. You were buying cotton candy, and he was rubbing his neck, or he complained that he had to sit in the front seat on the way home because he had been hurt. Little by little, these tiny memories come in, like leaks in a dam, and when there are enough of them, the memories break through until you can remember everything—things you never knew you had forgotten. But it takes work. If you want to keep forgetting, you can do that, too. You could even remember some little bit of it, then decide it's too much and lock the rest away. I don't remember everything about my first trip to the Sunlit Lands, but there are some small things coming back to me."

Shula turned the bottle in her hand. She could drink the Wendy juice, see if it brought back any memories. If it didn't, she might sink into grief about the loss of her family again. She hated the small glimmer of hope she felt about her brother being alive when she knew he was dead. It had been a long time since he had died, and she had dealt with it as much as she was able. There was a weight of grief she would always carry for her parents, her brother, her little sister, and yes, for Madeline. If she could lay a portion of that burden down, if any of her birth family were somehow still alive, she wanted to know.

Another thought occurred to her. What if she hadn't chosen to give up her memory? Just because that's what happened to Mrs. Oliver didn't mean it happened to her. What if someone—someone powerful—had wanted Shula to lose her memories? What if they were protecting something?

Could she be waking some power, drawing attention to herself or even to Yenil? To Mrs. Oliver? She couldn't shake a vague feeling that someone powerful was involved. She kept seeing Hanali's face in her little apartment in Syria. *"You don't want to see that."* Isn't that what he had said? Well, what if she chose to see it anyway? Her fingers trembled against the smooth glass of the bottle.

"I might be putting you and Yenil in danger," Shula said. "I might have to leave for a little while."

"You don't," Mrs. Oliver said. "Even if we're in danger, we've been there before. You don't have to leave."

Shula reached for her hand. "Mrs. Oliver, promise me that if I drink this and say that you're in danger, that you will take Yenil and go. Back to Earth, or to the Scim, or wherever will be safe."

"I will promise to keep Yenil safe," Mrs. Oliver said. "I won't promise to leave you."

It would have to do. She held the bottle in her shaking hands. There was no going back once she took a swallow. No way to know what memories might return. "Does the juice make you sad?"

"The *memories* make me sad, Shula, and I know that's hard on you and Yenil, and I'm sorry." Mrs. Oliver stood and squeezed Shula's shoulder. "I'll go check on her."

Shula took a deep breath, trying to center herself.

"Do you want privacy?" David asked.

She shook her head. "I want you to stay. Will you?"

He looked genuinely surprised. "Of course. If that's what you want."

"It is."

Shula breathed deeply again and lifted the bottle to her lips. She took a small sip and held it in her mouth. She didn't feel any different. No memories flooded her mind. She downed the entire bottle, placed it back on the table, and felt a rush of regret. But there was no going back now.

Everything flashed brighter for a moment. She could feel the grain of the wood in the table, could hear Mrs. Oliver talking to Yenil and the bleating of the goats. She cast her mind back, searching for any change. A new memory, an edited one. A clue, an idea, a possibility.

A flash of bright remembrance came to her. It was her family: her mother and father, Amira, Boulos, all at the breakfast table. They were laughing, all laughing. Boulos was not in his regular seat. Instead, Father had pulled up a red metal stool, so tall that her brother's knees rose above the table. A woman with dark hair was in Boulos's usual seat, her blue eyes lit with joy. She leaned against his legs, thumping him on the thigh with her fist, as if he was too much, simply too much, and the source of all this hilarity.

Vasilisa. That's the name that came to Shula when she saw the woman's face.

She was wearing a green collared shirt, sprinkled with camouflage black and yellow and shades of green—the colors of a Russian soldier on the street. Military police? Medic? Shula couldn't tell, but on Vasilisa's left arm, the arm facing Shula, there was a small bloom of color. The Russian flag. And around her neck, a silver cross, not unlike Shula's own.

Anger burned in her chest, wrapped in a dull cocoon of confusion. She recognized it not only as her emotion at the time of the memory but her emotion now. How could they let this woman share their breakfast, let her share their table? Shula's father was a pastor, yes, and so often he let people into their home who made Shula wince. But a Russian?

Vasilisa turned to Shula in the memory, smiling, but Shula could tell that the woman had noted Shula's own mood in that moment because her smile dimmed, her eyes took on a note of concern. She reached her hand toward Shula's, but Shula pulled away, and as she stood from the table, taking her dish to the sink, the memory faded and Shula was at her own table in the cottage overlooking the Ginian Sea.

She had no other memory of this Vasilisa. Some friend of her family? And something more to Boulos. How could she have forgotten this, and what else had she lost? It was like Mrs. Oliver described: as if this memory were a thread, and if she pulled it, some fictive universe would come unraveled, revealing something else beneath it. Something that Shula must have put significant effort into covering.

"What is it?" David asked. "What did you see?"

"I remembered something. Someone. A friend of my brother's." She shook her head. It made no sense. Why would she have forgotten Vasilisa? How would this woman be in any way associated with the Sunlit Lands or whether or not Shula's brother was alive or dead?

"Your brother? Anything about him?"

"Nothing." She sighed, leaned away from the table, rubbed her face with her hands.

"What do you want to do?"

Shula glanced outside, then back to David. She didn't need to think about it, didn't need time to figure it out. If her brother was alive—if there was even a chance—her course of action was clear. "I need to go see the storyteller in Far Seeing."

He nodded. "I'll go with you. Leave now? Just the two of us, or . . . ?"

"It might be dangerous," she said quietly. "It would be best if we went alone."

"AHA!" Yenil shouted, marching into the cottage. She put her hands on her hips and glared at Mrs. Oliver, who came in close behind her. "I told you something was going on in here." She pointed at Shula. "And if you're going to Far Seeing, I am going too."

David grinned at the girl. Shula looked to him for help, and he shrugged. "It's hard to say what's safest in the Sunlit Lands," he said.

Mrs. Oliver jumped on that. "The two of you together are a lot more protection than staying here in the cottage, just me and Yenil."

That might be true, of course. Shula pictured the young Russian woman again. Vasilisa. Another memory tugged at her mind. A nickname. Vasya? Why didn't she remember anything else about her? Was she there the night Shula's family was killed?

"You can come," she said at last.

Yenil cheered and jumped on David, hugging him around the neck and knocking him backward. He wrestled his way upright, still grinning.

"On one condition," Shula said loudly. "You do what I say, no questions asked."

"Sure," Yenil said, much too quickly. She thought for a moment. "And my condition is, don't tell me to do things I don't want to do."

David laughed at that, but Shula felt a deep foreboding. And another memory, just beneath the surface, and beneath that one a hundred more, a thousand more.

11
ELENIL HISTORY FOR DUMMIES

*I declare ye, Ele and Nala, lords of light
and guardians of the wide world.*

FROM "THE ORDERING OF THE WORLD," AN ELENIL STORY

✦

The smirk on the boy's face. Gilenyia would have liked to slap him, but she was still reeling from her conversation with the Knight of the Mirror. She wasn't sure what was happening, and though she was only a few centuries old, she knew better than to act in a situation when she had not taken its full measure. "Overthrow of the Elenil empire," she said carefully. "That sounds a great deal like insurrection."

Jason took a sip of tea. "Well, I've never been a member of the Elenil empire," he said, and something about this struck him as funny. He started to laugh. "So think of it more as foreign aid."

"Sir Knight, are you a part of this rebellion?"

The knight inclined his head. "Mr. Wu perhaps exaggerates our cause."

"It seems to me," Jason said, "that the Elenil have lied to the people of the Sunlit Lands—not least of all themselves—in order to maintain their power. I'm of the opinion that truth should out. I'm thinking if we just let people know the truth of what's going on, there won't be any need for an insurrection as such. The Elenil will simply lose their power."

Now it was Gilenyia's turn to laugh. "I don't know what you think you know, Jason, but if you believe revealing it will cause the Elenil to simply step aside from their authority—authority entrusted to them by the Majestic One himself—you are either foolish or naive."

"That doesn't seem like an 'either/or.' I could be both."

This child. She could see why Hanali found him so difficult. "What is this explosive truth you intend to share with the people of the Sunlit Lands?"

Jason's eyes lit up. "Do you already know it?"

She sighed. "Know what, child? How can I know what you are referring to unless you speak plainly?"

The boy looked uncertain now. He glanced at the knight. "Does she know?"

The knight shook his head. "She has never spoken of it to me or in my presence. Neither Hanali nor the magistrates have, either. Perhaps none of them know. Or perhaps they knew many centuries ago and have forgotten."

Many centuries ago? Then they were speaking of some old truth. Something that had been hidden for generations. Well. Not Elenil generations, but generations of the Sunlit Lands. What could they possibly be referring to? She wasn't aware of any devastating secret that would shake the foundations of the world.

Jason put his hand over his teacup and stared at a corner of the room for a long moment. Was it her imagination, or was there something like compassion in his eyes when he turned back to her? "With magic, things are not always as they seem. We all know that, don't we?"

Something about the way he spoke. It lacked the careless abandon of the Wu child. She narrowed her eyes, studied him more closely. "Indeed," she said. "There are secrets and false truths, and illusions as well as assumptions that prevent the casual viewer from seeking the truth."

Jason leaned forward across the table. "Yes, but we can feel it, can't we? When we don't know the truth? When the world has been pulled over our eyes? A sense that something is wrong, that something is not the way it should be?"

Gilenyia moved uncomfortably. This was too close to her own thought process of late. But the child could be correct. Perhaps there was a truth she had suppressed or forgotten or avoided. "I know this feeling," she admitted. "Have felt it more than once."

"Then you know that there are ways we protect magic and protect the status quo. The way we arrange things. The stories we tell." He raised his eyebrows as if this were some revelation. "The stories," he said. "They tell us a lot. Do you know the story of Ele and Nala?"

Of course she did. Every Elenil knew the story. In fact, every newcomer in service to the Elenil learned the story in their first day or two in the Sunlit Lands: Ele and Nala, the first servants of the Majestic One. When other peoples fought the great magician, Ele and Nala and their children stood by his side. All peoples were given their place in the world, and this included the children of Ele and Nala—or, as they came to be known, the Elenil. They were put in the highest seat of honor in the Sunlit Lands and made the rulers and caretakers of it.

"Imagine that I have heard it," Gilenyia said drily.

The boy grinned widely, as if it were a great joke. "It's just that the story doesn't make much sense, does it?"

"It makes perfect sense," Gilenyia said.

"Don't you see any problems with it?" Jason asked the knight.

The knight crossed his arms. "I am no historian of the Elenil."

Jason laughed outright at that. "It's not history at all, you dummies. It's *mythology*. And someone is using that story like a sword to hold all of the Sunlit Lands in their grip." The boy laughed even harder, as if his strange theory—or perhaps the telling of it—brought him enormous joy. "Who are the Elenil?" he asked at last.

"This is ridiculous," Gilenyia said. "I thank you for the tea, but—"

"Who are the Elenil?"

"A simple question from a simple child."

"So answer it then."

Perhaps this would silence him, though experience said nothing did. "The children of Ele and Nala, of course."

"But the Elenil don't have children," Jason said.

"Nonsense. I am a child of the Elenil."

"And how many are in your generation? Fifty? A hundred?"

Probably less, few enough that it was common practice to call one another cousin. She did not see where this was going. "Elenil birth is complicated, of course. We can only become pregnant . . ." She paused. Thoughts began to whir in her head. "Can only become pregnant on . . ."

Jason jumped up. "Yes! Exactly! So they've told us. Do you see it, lady? Do you see the unplucked thread in the story? If so, take hold and let us unravel it together."

The Elenil could only become pregnant on one day of the year. The Festival of the Turning. Or so it was said. "If we can only have children at the Festival of the Turning, then it must be that somehow our magic is preventing Elenil pregnancies."

"Most certainly," Jason said. "And another question . . . have you ever seen an Elenil baby?"

"No," she said idly, not even really listening to Jason. Her mind was seeking answers to so many other questions, exploring strange new rooms that had opened up within her.

"And why is that, do you think?"

"Why is what?"

"Why haven't you seen a single Elenil child?"

"Because I am of one of the most recent generations. Hanali and I and our cousins. Perhaps I saw an infant once upon a time, but I have no memory of it."

Jason clapped his hands. "So in the several centuries since you became Elenil, only a handful of others have entered into your society? Only a handful of Elenil children conceived on the Day of Turning. That seems strange."

"Since you became Elenil," he had said. Not *"since you were born."* She struggled to understand what he was saying, and her mind wanted so badly to take her away from here, to go somewhere else. She was supposed to be here straightening out the knight, who was sitting at the table with his

arms crossed, a look of concern and resignation on his face. She had a flash of memory—someone called the Historian. She recalled his thin face, the dark paths he traveled . . . and then it was gone.

The boy leapt to his feet. "Let's go for a walk," he said. "I'm feeling cramped in here."

She did not want to have this conversation in the open, where others could hear. Already she could feel the questions the boy was asking and her own fears that something was wrong aligning, snapping into place, and she could not allow that. The potential price of such a thing. The ramifications for her own life. But the boy was already outside, the knight standing at the door, waiting for her, as a gentleman should.

She followed them into the castle's courtyard. "This whole castle was brought over from Earth," Jason said. "Hard to believe. Moving everything stone by stone would be an impressive feat. But the Elenil did it with magic."

"The Elenil are not stonemasons," she said dismissively. "How else would you have us do it?"

"What else in the Sunlit Lands comes from Earth?" Jason asked innocently.

"The humans, of course," Gilenyia said.

"That's in the story, even," Jason said. "The humans are cast out of the Sunlit Lands and sent to 'another earth' where they won't have magic or anything."

"So the storytellers say," Gilenyia replied. She was losing patience with this whole charade. "If you have something to say, say it."

"Okay," Jason said. "Since it's about a story, I'll tell you a story."

"Is there nothing you can do to cause this fool to speak plainly?" she said to the knight.

"Believe me, lady, better men than I and more powerful people than your ladyship have tried."

There was a small wooden stage in the center of the courtyard, and Jason leapt onto it, indicating that Gilenyia could take a seat on the wooden benches if she chose to do so. She swept over one with a gloved hand, smoothed her skirts, and took a seat.

"Once upon a time," he said, "there was a group of magicians. Powerful and wise, talented and gifted and proud. They looked at all the world and said to themselves, 'This is not so great a world. For with our own magic we could make trees to grow and animals to walk upon the earth and even make stars and moons and suns and oceans.' For they were very wise indeed. 'We are not only magicians,' they said, 'but gods. For who but the gods could make all of creation in their own image?'"

"What story is this, and whose? What gods are being referred to, and what magicians are these? Should I know who you mean to tell me these people are?"

Jason held up one finger, his eyebrows high. "But God heard the wicked magicians—for though they were powerful, they were also quite wicked to think they were gods—and came to them and said, 'Let us have a competition, God versus the magician gods, to see who is the wisest, the most powerful. And if I am the champion, so be it—the whole universe knows this already. But if you are the champions, I will make known in all the universe the power of your works. And if you fail, you will receive the punishments due to you for saying, 'We are like gods.''"

"I know this story," the knight said. "I feel I have heard it, many years ago."

"Maybe so," Jason said. "Maybe so. It's not my story, I didn't invent it. So the magicians say to God, 'What will our challenge be?' God doesn't hesitate for a moment. 'Let us make human beings,' he said. 'Each in our own image.' The magicians trembled and said, 'Let us confer among ourselves for a short time, to be certain we can do such a thing.' God agreed, and for seven years and seven months and seven weeks and seven days they deliberated, and then they returned to God and said, 'We have spent these years reflecting, and we know now how to make human life.' So God created two marble tables and said to them, 'I will make life on this table, and you on yours.' The magicians assented, and after a few minutes of discussion they began to pile dirt upon their table and shape it into the form of a human. And God watched them for a moment and then said, 'I thought you were going to make something." And they said, 'Yes, we will make dirt into a human and breathe life into it.' And God said, 'Get your own dirt.'"

The boy erupted in peals of laughter. "Get your own dirt," he said again, falling to a sitting position and wiping his eyes. The knight was not laughing, but he did smile, whether at the story or the boy Gilenyia could not tell.

Gilenyia stood, straightening her gloves. "This is you speaking plainly, Wu Song? Then I fear I must be on my way."

The laughter evaporated immediately. "The Elenil are the magicians, lady. They are wise and powerful, but everything they have ever made, they took from someone else. They are creatures of great riches, which they've created by impoverishing everyone they touch. They cannot bear children, for they have stolen even from themselves."

"You speak in riddles and nonsense. I ask you one more time, child, speak plainly."

Jason slipped from the stage and came close to her, much closer than one such as he should dare. He took her hands, as if about to deliver news that he knew to be painful. "Elenil are not born, they are made. Human beings are the dirt, the raw stuff of it. And there is a price to your longevity. A great and terrible price. The Elenil live for centuries by giving up their right to have children. Such is the cost of your magic."

Gilenyia snatched her hand away and stalked toward the castle drawbridge. She did not have to listen to such drivel. Did not have to listen as an Earth child prattled on, questioning stories that had been told by his betters for literal centuries. The Elenil were not humans. They were superior to them in every way. Stronger. More beautiful. More learned. Longer lived. Humans were less than dirt to the Elenil. They were garbage. They were fertilizer.

"There is more," Jason called. But she would not listen to more.

The boy had the audacity to grab her forearm and swing her around. "Do. Not. Touch. Me," Gilenyia hissed through her teeth and snatched her hand away.

"Something is wrong," he said. "Ever since the human girl healed you. Something is wrong and you feel it in your bones."

She stared at him, aghast. What magic was this? Could he see even her innermost thoughts? "The girl is dead," she said. "The Elenil are rebuilding. One little human won't stand in our way. We have time as an ally, Wu Song, and all that has been taken from us will be restored. In time."

The boy didn't respond to her barb about Madeline being dead. Again, so strange for Wu Song. He must have grown in this last year, must have somehow changed. "A grey hair," he said at last. "You're not supposed to mention it, but there it is."

He was pointing at her own head. Her own hair. But the Elenil didn't go grey, did they? Not so young. And she had removed her grey hair just this morning. Her hand wandered toward the place he pointed. "But how?" she asked. She knew he wasn't lying about something being wrong.

He leaned close. "Because," he said. "When she healed you, Gilenyia. When she healed you, she took away your curse. She unbound you from the Elenil. She undid the bargain that made you live for so many years. Why do you think, all these centuries, it has been called the Festival of the Turning? It's right there in the name. When Madeline healed you, she made you—"

But Gilenyia put her hand over his mouth before he could say another word, drawing him even closer with her other arm. "Enough," she said savagely. "Say no more, Wu Song." She stared at him, at the surprise in his eyes, and only when she felt certain he was scared, possibly terrified, did she remove her hand.

"Human," he said, as if he couldn't help himself, as if the sentence had to be finished and the threat of mortal violence were no impediment to the inevitable pressure of the word that had built up behind her hand like a dam.

Gilenyia was an Elenil who liked to plan. Not like her cousin Hanali, perhaps, with his soothsayers and prophets. Nevertheless, she plotted her actions, her words, made careful decisions, and carried out her plans with flawless precision. So Jason Wu was not the only one surprised to find a silver dagger in Gilenyia's hand, the blade in his belly. She yanked upward, watched his eyes widen as she pulled it to a stop at his breastbone.

Then she fled to her waiting carriage, the boy crumpling to the ground. Ricardo said nothing about the blood, and she did not speak to him or anyone else, but kept her hands folded in her lap to prevent them from shaking.

12

THE STREET FIGHTER

It was a weariness to the world.

THE PEASANT KING

✦

Darius shook the first of the Vain Boys off. He had been in track and field for years, and he knew how to run. He settled into a comfortable pace even with the Boys behind him. Drawing them away from the girl was the main thing. He wasn't trying to get out of trouble. On the contrary, he needed all the trouble he could find. He was having some doubts about whether this whole thing was going to work, but he wasn't about to give up.

It didn't occur to him that the Vain Boys might be communicating with each other. Or that some of them might have transportation of some sort. Or that they might have allies who weren't in the parade, who were waiting around for a signal. But all those thoughts occurred to him at once when a white pickup truck pulled across his path and five men jumped out of the bed. They had handkerchiefs covering the lower halves of their faces, and all five wore heavy boots, probably steel-toed. Two of them held baseball bats, a third had a length of iron pipe. One of them—a guy in sunglasses—carried a rifle and had a pistol in his belt, but he stood in the back, not moving toward Darius. The last one had a knife.

There were more men coming from behind him, Darius reminded himself, and the longer this took to clean up, the sooner they would all be on top of him. Darius took a quick mental inventory. He had his backpack, a change of clothes, a flashlight, and of course the Dagger Perilous, which was still screaming at him. It was a sharp object and, he assumed, could be used for cutting things or, you know, people.

Not that he had time to get it out.

These guys were random dudes who had grabbed weapons but obviously had no experience. They weren't soldiers or even fighters. The iron pipe was just a third bat, really. The guy with the knife was more concerning. The first and safest thing to do when fighting someone with a bat, he knew, was to stay out of his range, but that option was quickly shrinking away. The second-best thing was to get as close to him as possible so he couldn't get a good swing in.

One guy was already planting his feet for a two-handed swing, which was the best possible approach for Darius. One-handed swings were less predictable . . . which way he would swing, which angle, and so on. But the two-handed version was more or less always the same, at least here in the States: some guy thinking he's about to hit a baseball.

Darius leapt in close, and by the time the guy swung, Darius was already grabbing hold of his elbows, pushing him off balance. A glancing blow hit Darius's shoulder, but it had lost nearly all its power. Darius snatched the bat from the astonished man and rapped him in the kneecap as hard as he could. That should keep him out of the way. He swung hard at the second guy with a bat, aiming for his hand and managing to catch him in the knuckles. Sounded like he might have broken a couple, and that was batter number two out. The iron pipe and knife men stepped back, having learned that rushing Darius might not be the best idea.

"I don't want to hurt you," Darius said. He could hear the footsteps behind him now, the guys he had ditched before catching up. The two batters were groaning on the ground.

"Well, we do want to hur—"

Darius threw his bat, and it flew in a pleasing cartwheel to catch the knife man in the jaw. Another one down. Leaving him with only the iron pipe, the guy with the gun, and, of course, the crowd following behind him. He ran up on the iron pipe guy, but he wasn't fast enough. He was inside the swing radius but not close enough to avoid being hit. The man had been taken off guard—Darius was always surprised at how often he could catch someone off guard in battle by doing the exact same thing he had done a few seconds before—so it wasn't a full-strength swing. Darius twisted hard so his backpack would take the brunt of the impact, and it did. Darius threw his left arm over the man's swinging arm and locked it in place, then drove his fist into the guy's face, twice.

He glared at the man with the gun, panting. "You gonna shoot at me? Should bring every cop in the city over to take a look."

The man pursed his lips. "Maybe I'll follow you home to your little shanty in the ghetto and do it after all the cops have gone home."

Darius shrugged. "I'm not the kind to put things off when I enjoy them." He stepped forward and punched the guy in the face, breaking his sunglasses. The man stumbled backward against his truck and fell on the sidewalk. Darius kicked the rifle out of his hand and under the truck.

The man had real hatred on his face now. The glasses had shattered, leaving fine cuts around his eyes. "I'm going to kill you now," he said. He reached behind his back, but Darius kneed him in the face, yanked his hand back out, and stomped on his trigger finger. While the man yowled, Darius rolled him onto his stomach and pulled the pistol out of his belt, then slid that under the truck too.

Adrenaline was coursing through him. The dagger was alerting him of danger, but all he felt was the pure burn of his anger and an endorphin-fueled joy at putting these five men on the ground. When he had been the leader of the Black Skulls back in the Sunlit Lands, the battles had made him buzz with excitement, and to beat an enemy was a high like nothing else.

Darius didn't even hear the next guy coming. Must have been one more in the truck or maybe the driver, but he sucker punched Darius in the back of the head. He stumbled, reeling, ears ringing. He turned in time to catch another blow, this one hitting him on the right cheek. Darius tried to move away from the guy. He knew he needed to block all the emergency messages coming from his body, telling him that he was in pain, so that he could think clearly and move. But another punch landed, then another. Darius knew some of the guys he had dropped might be recovering any moment. He caught a fist in the stomach, doubled over, and knocked against the truck. Then his feet were swept from under him, and he hit the pavement hard.

"Help me get him in the back," a gruff voice said, and then he was being lifted and slung into the bed of the truck.

A weight crashed down on his back. Someone twisted his arms behind him, and when Darius tried to buck, they shook him and knocked him hard against the metal bed. He heard the zip and then felt the bite of the ties on his wrists. "Keep him low so no one sees him," the voice said. "Will, you drive. The rest of you, head for the meeting point. Drive slow, drive legal."

"He broke my hand," someone said.

"You're going to do a lot worse than that to him," came the reply. Then the weight again—someone was in the truck bed, with his knee on Darius's shoulder—and the truck started to drive.

What was he going to do? The dagger was sending up every warning flare it knew how to give, and Darius was starting to think it might catch fire, that it might slice through the backpack and attack him itself.

"Just sit tight," someone said. "We got to get out a ways, where the cops won't notice us. Don't you worry, though. They're busy with the protest."

"You could just let me go," Darius said. "No reason to put yourself at risk of being arrested."

The man chuckled. "I've been there before, boy. No, you shouldn't have embarrassed my men like that. I gotta admit, that was some fine fighting. Of course, we have to expect that you are gonna be a little scrappier, raised on the streets. Have some better instincts when it comes to fighting."

Now wasn't the time to say anything, but this comment set off a spark of anger in Darius. That old assumption that he had been raised "on the streets." What did that even mean? He had grown up here in the city, in a little house that cost more than a mansion in some parts of the United States. He had a mother and a father who cared about him, and friends. He'd attended a private high school and had some of the best grades in his class. But, of course, this yokel only saw him as the Black savage who grew up in the hood. "Or maybe your men are spectacularly incompetent," Darius shot back.

The man laughed at that. "Or could be a little of both. Me, I'm a military man. I know a good fighter when I see one, and I know how to assess a situation. Standing back a minute so I could take you off guard was worth it."

The truck stopped. "Don't go anywhere," the man said with a laugh, and the truck rocked as he jumped out. "No, no, leave him there until the others get here."

Darius's mind raced. There weren't a lot of options. He was on his stomach and couldn't see where they were . . . other than outside. If he could get the knife into his hands, he could use it to cut the zip ties. Maybe. But he couldn't get access to the knife. Maybe the way into the Sunlit Lands had opened up. "If you can hear me, Hanali," he said under his breath, "open the doorway and bring me back."

Nothing.

Other cars were arriving, people whooping and laughing about the parade. About how well it had worked. How many reporters had been there, who had gotten in a fight with whom, how stupid the antiprotesters were, and various disparaging comments about the cops.

"Stow that talk," the gruff voice said.

A few of the men came over to the truck to get a look at Darius. One threw a half-empty beer can at him.

He pulled his hands back and forth, seeing if he could feel even the slightest give in the zip ties, but no luck. They were tight, and he could feel the chafing as the edged plastic dug deeper into his wrists.

"How are we going to do this, boss?" someone asked. "He's pretty tough."

"That was one against five," the gruff voice replied. "This will be one on twenty. We'll put him in the middle of a circle of us, have someone untie him. Maybe even give him a stick or a knife, so if the cops find out any of us were here, we can say it was in self-defense."

Maybe he would have a chance, Darius thought. If they let him have the Dagger Perilous, it might give him enough of an advantage to counterbalance being in the center of the circle. He wouldn't have to look behind himself with the dagger giving him warning, which meant that he could focus on picking them off one by one. And maybe the cops would come in time. But that might be too much to hope for.

"Cut his backpack off him. I want to see what's in it."

Someone leapt up in the back of the truck and knelt over him, grabbing the backpack and pulling him up by it. This gave Darius enough of a view to see more of where he was. Looked like an abandoned parking lot with a chain-link fence around it. He didn't see a restaurant or business nearby. No passersby to rely on, no one to call for help. The poor idiot trying to cut him out of the backpack had literally straddled Darius. A second guy jumped in the truck bed and started sawing at the straps while the first guy held Darius up.

"Keep him still," the second guy said, and the first yanked him onto his knees and leaned over him.

"Don't move," he said, right in Darius's ear, probably not thinking about how that put him directly next to Darius's head.

Darius headbutted the guy as hard as he could and ignored the sharp crack and throbbing in his own head that came in response. The guy started to lose his balance, grabbed his buddy for stability, and Darius twisted toward them, pushing against them to give himself the leverage he needed to pop to his feet. One of them fell over the side of the truck, and Darius kicked the second as hard as he was able.

There were more than twenty of them. Closer to thirty. Not much he'd be able to do with his hands behind his back, but he had no intention of letting them hurt him without a fight. Now that he could see the whole lot, he had a better idea of what he was dealing with. The lot wasn't giant—maybe a third the size of a football field. They were partially under an overpass, and there were a few buildings nearby—looked like construction-type places, maybe? No people he could see. A gate was pulled shut and locked where they had driven in, and in addition to the truck there were a handful of cars and a couple motorcycles. And thirtyish guys, all of them furious.

Except one, who was laughing. The man who had ridden beside him in the back of the truck, from the sound of his voice. He was a thickset man, maybe forty. The kind of guy, Darius knew, that you could punch in the gut more than once before he started to feel it. Looked like he was mostly muscle and bone. His hair was shaved low, his face smooth. His smile didn't touch his eyes. "I'm starting to like you, kid."

"Wish I could say the same."

The man turned to his followers. "If you poor idiots can't get that boy on the ground and get his legs zipped and a blindfold on him, I'm turning you all in to the cops and starting over."

He didn't wait for them to move on him. Now that he was sturdier on his feet, Darius gave the guy still in the truck bed a more convincing kick, high on his torso. When the guy leaned back to avoid the kick, he went over the side. Darius slid onto the top of the cab, jumped on the hood and then to the ground. He didn't have his arms, but he could still run. There was a chance—a slight chance—that he could squeeze between the gate and the fence where it was chained shut. He wouldn't be able to climb it with his hands behind his back, that was for sure.

Darius was fast. The men kept making the same mistake, clumping together because they all ran toward him instead of spreading out. There were only so many directions he could go, and if they used their heads, they would have him in a second. As it was, their insistence on going straight at him made them easier to avoid. He spun past one of them, feinted like he was going to push into another, then broke for the fence. They were shouting, threatening, cursing at him the whole time.

He slammed into the fence, not wanting to slow down even for a moment. The chain was at waist height. He kicked the gate, which was on wheels, to try to get it to open farther, but it was going to be tight. He crouched down, swung his head under the chain, and started to wedge himself through. His backpack, though. That was going to be a problem. It was caught. He should have let them take it off!

Two men jumped the fence, trying to get in front of him, and strong arms grabbed him, yanked him back into the abandoned lot. He struggled and kicked, but they had him on the ground quickly enough. Someone sat on his legs while someone else zip-tied his ankles and then his knees. Not gently. And definitely too tight. Another pair of hands tied a stinking handkerchief around his eyes. They pulled him away from the fence and hurled him into the bed of the truck like a sack of trash.

"Good job, men. You see, we always win over his kind. We're smarter, stronger, better organized. He has a certain animal cunning, I'll give him that. But what do we do with animals?" The leader waited. No one answered. "We break them. Tame them. Slaughter them. Eat them. Use them. We do what we want with animals."

Another voice, this one quieter, self-assured. "He's no animal. And you're going to let him go."

That laugh again. "You have a lot of nerve, boy. Didn't you see what we just did to that kid? You think we're going to be gentler on you?"

"Last warning," the quiet voice said.

"Tie him up and put him with the other one."

There was a loud bang, like the backfire of a car, and then a flash of light so bright that Darius could see it through his blindfold. The sound of crunching metal and the shouts of men. Not angry, though. Terrified. The truck rocked as a body slammed into the side of it. "Stay away from me," someone shouted, and then the sound of something breaking.

"You don't want to do that. You do that, and I'll make you regret it," the calm voice said, and then Darius heard the sharp crack of a rifle, the hot smell of the ammo. The calm man laughed. "I always keep my word," he said. "The rest of you had best remember that."

Men were shouting and running away. Someone must have jumped on the fence—the metal was shaking and vibrating like a bell as he climbed. "No," the calm voice said, and someone screamed. The fence fell silent.

The gruff voice—the military guy who had ridden with Darius—he was talking now. "Please, sir. Please don't hurt me."

"You go get that boy out of the truck. Go on now."

"Are you going to kill me?"

"Don't make me say it again."

Big hands took hold of Darius, pulled him up to sitting, slid him to the end of the bed. The gate was down now. "What do you want me to do?"

"Cut him loose," the voice said. "What do you think? Use your head."

A knife sawed through the zip ties, and then a hand pulled off his blindfold. The military man was standing in front of him, and Darius couldn't see the stranger.

"He's cut loose," the big man said. "I did what you said."

"I think an apology is in order, don't you?"

The man fell to his knees. "Forgive me. I shouldn't have done that. I'm sorry."

But Darius wasn't interested in this guy. He looked over the big man's head. A thin Black man was standing a few feet away, not appearing the least bit concerned or worried. He tapped a cigarette into his hand, hung it on his lip, lit it.

"Not the best apology," he said. "No clarity on what the wrong was. And no restitution offered. How do we know you won't do it again?"

The big guy was crying now. Every other man in the lot was sprawled on the ground—many of them bleeding, all of them still. Moans and soft crying filled the air. Two of the cars were crushed, and black smoke poured out.

"Heya, Darius," the calm man said.

Darius struggled to find his voice, trying to locate the right words to say. He rubbed his wrists, staring in shock at the devastation around him. Finally he managed to speak. Nothing profound, nothing witty or insightful. Just a simple, surprised two words.

"Hey, Dad."

13

THE RESCUE

Then he said to the desert,
"Thou sands, cover them, and slow them even more."
FROM "THE TRIUMPH OF THE PEASANT KING," A SCIM LEGEND

✦

Where are you taking me?" Jason asked.

"South," TJ said.

"Stop asking," OJ said.

"I've only asked 217 times," Jason said, still on his side, watching the desert go by.

"Plus asking to use 'the bathroom,'" OJ said bitterly.

"Then complaining, 'I can't just go on the side of a dune,'" TJ added.

"Then all the questions about whether we can build something to shade your face, and who we are, and why we're doing this."

"In my defense," Jason said, "you don't give very compelling answers. Like 'South' isn't really an answer to my question. I assume you're referring to the direction, but then wouldn't you say 'southward'? Unless we're going to the South Pole, but I'm not sure there is a pole in the Sunlit Lands. I'm pretty sure it's not even a round planet. Not that there's actually a South Pole on Earth, either. Did you know someone put a pole—like an actual pole—at the North Pole on Earth?"

"Please," OJ said. "Please, just stop saying things."

"What's interesting is that your compass, you know, it doesn't point to the North Pole—it points to *magnetic* north. So you could get to the North Pole and look at your compass, and it wouldn't even be pointing at the pole you were standing by. Weird, right?"

"So weird," TJ said, looking right at him so Jason could see him roll his eyes.

"Oh. People have told me that's annoying, but it actually *is* annoying," Jason said. "Note to self. Note to selves?"

"Do we have a gag?" OJ asked.

"We could make one," TJ said.

But Jason suddenly fell silent all on his own because he saw a little flicker of red in the sky above him. It was Rufus the hummingbird! Rufus zipped down and perched on the side of the canoe thing Jason was in and chirped twice.

TJ looked back, frowning. "We've noticed there are hummingbirds around you all the time. Why is that?"

"I honestly don't know," Jason said. It was true. They had started following him all over the place right around the time Madeline died. He wasn't sure what the deal was exactly, but he liked to think that maybe, somehow, it was a message from his old friend. Maybe a way to say that she was okay in the world after this one, or that she was looking out for him. Another possibility was that he was sweet as nectar and hummingbirds couldn't help but watch him and lick their long beaks, but that seemed less likely.

Today, though, he suspected he knew exactly what it meant that Rufus was here. It meant that he had flown for help, just like Jason had asked, and that he had told Baileya to go check on Mother Crow and then come find and help him! He wasn't sure what that would look like, but whatever happened, he knew there was no way that two Jasons were a match for Baileya. She'd wipe the floor with them. Or, well, wipe the sand with them—floors were few and far between in the Kakri desert.

"We made it to the Passage," OJ said.

Jason tried to prop himself up. "Can I see?"

"Finally," TJ said. "Do you think they left us some faster transportation on the other side?"

"Hey guys, can I see?"

"I hope so," OJ said.

"Guys, I'm not from the Sunlit Lands—can I see the Passage? What is it? Is it like a door in the world or something? Is it a tunnel? Is it just a sign that says "The Passage"? Guys? Hey, guys, it's me, Jason. Original Jason. Hello?"

"He won't stop until we let him," TJ said with a sigh.

"It's fine," OJ said. "We can probably untie him at this point. What is he going to do? Run away?" Both Jasons laughed at that, and they pulled their giant lizards to a stop and dismounted.

"Good idea," Jason said. "It would be stupid to run away."

The Jasons exchanged glances. "He's right, you know," OJ said. "And he is really prone to doing stupid things."

"Good point. Let's keep him tied up."

"Wait, what? Are you guys kidding? You're kidding, right? I promise not to do anything stupid. I hate being tied up! Every time I go on an adventure, someone is shackling me or tying me up, and is it too much to ask that you just threaten me with violence if I run away? I mean, I am very sensitive to threats."

OJ yanked him up so he could see. Ahead of them were jutting shelves of stone, black against the sky. They formed a narrow mountain range, and a path went through the center. "That's the Passage."

"I see," Jason said. "So the naming conventions in this part of the world are pretty straightforward."

Both Jasons laughed. "He really is quite funny."

"Agreed, agreed." TJ clapped his hands and brushed some sand off his pants. "Well, let's keep going. I'll be glad when we finally get—"

OJ interrupted him. "South. When we finally get South."

Jason moaned and fell back in his canoe. "Aw, c'mon guys. I'm going to figure it out when we get there. You might as well tell me now."

"Surprises are more fun," TJ said.

"I do like surprises," Jason said sulkily.

The fake Jasons jumped on their lizards and moved forward into the Passage. Jason was relieved. The stones were high enough that they shaded the ground, and it was a relief not to have the sun beating down on him. In fact, he felt a little cold now. "Can I get a blanket?"

The other Jasons groaned in frustration.

Rufus buzzed in Jason's face, then shot toward the wall of the Passage. Jason watched as the little bird zipped behind a pile of rocks. That was weird. But looking more carefully, he saw . . . was that a hand? A hand coming up from behind the rock? It was soon followed by a head, completely wrapped in long cloths, in the Kakri style. All Jason could see within the cloths were the glowing eyes of a Kakri warrior. Which meant he was about to be saved! He didn't know which Kakri it could be, but whoever it was, it would be a relief to be back with the Kakri, living a Spartan life in the desert instead of the life of a trussed-up roast in the bottom of a sand canoe. He had to be quiet so he wouldn't draw any attention to the Kakri. Didn't want the Jasons getting warned now, did he?

The Kakri pointed at Jason, then made a shushing motion with his finger. Jason made his best *Duh, I know* face and rolled his eyes. Oh yeah, annoying, right. He was going to have to try to stop doing that. The Kakri slowly unwrapped the cloths until his face was completely bare. Oh no. Jason knew this particular warrior.

It was the worst possible person.

It was Baileya's brother Bezaed. The most talented Kakri warrior Jason had ever met (except Baileya), and he had a specific plan in mind: kill Jason. There was a whole cultural subplot about this. Kakri brothers always tried to kill the men who got engaged to their sisters. Jason had been engaged to Baileya, and therefore Bezaed vowed to try to kill him for a year. But then Baileya had ended their engagement, and Bezaed said he'd let Jason become Kakri before he tried to kill him again. It was all a big mess. But they had a truce! It really would not be fair of Bezaed to kill Jason while he was tied up. Would it?

"I thought we had a truce," Jason said loudly, trying to sound conversational and as if he were talking to no one in particular.

"What are you talking about?" OJ said.

Bezaed's eyes went wide, and he signed again for Jason to be quiet.

"Yup, it would be breaking your word to kill me now," Jason said. "And when I'm so helpless."

"We're not going to kill you," TJ said. "We already would have done so if that was the plan. You think we're dragging you through the desert for no reason? We're not stupid."

"I've thought about it," OJ said. "Not gonna lie." Then the fake Jasons laughed. A little too hard, it seemed to Jason.

"If you were to kill him, you would face my wrath," a deep voice boomed. "But then again, people who shoot me with arrows are likely to experience sixty years of captivity and torture."

Jason would know that violent, deep, gravelly voice anywhere. "Break Bones! I thought they killed you."

"So did they," Break Bones said. Jason couldn't see him—he must be standing in front of them, blocking the path.

"We really did," TJ said.

"This is the worst possible way to find out we were wrong," OJ said.

"Let Wu Song go," Break Bones said. "And I may allow you to escape this encounter with one or more teeth."

"Yikes," Jason said. "Really upping the creepy threat game, BB. Good for you!"

Bezaed was creeping down from the rocks now, a curved Kakri dagger in one hand. He slipped toward Jason. The fact that he was here with Break Bones made Jason think he was probably part of a rescue mission, not here to murder his ex–future brother-in-law.

"The Scim is wounded," TJ said. "No real threat to us."

Jason couldn't help it. That made him laugh. OJ looked back and spotted Bezaed, who froze like a kid with his hand halfway into the cookie jar. That made Jason laugh too. But then it was all knives and shouting as the two Jasons cut the ropes holding Jason's canoe and spurred their lizards into battle.

"How did he—?" OJ said.

"I thought you liked surprises!" Jason said, delighted.

Jason mostly heard what happened next, as he was still tied up. There was a great deal of shouting. Some hissing from the lizards. The sound of metal on metal.

When it was all done, Break Bones appeared, his great grey head looming over Jason, a wide smile on his frog-like face. "Greetings, Wu Song."

"Greetings yourself, Break Bones. Any chance you could help a brother out of his bonds?"

"My pleasure," Break Bones said, and he started to laugh. Then Jason was laughing too, and he sighed with relief as the ropes came off his wrists.

"Ugh, being tied up is the worst!"

"I've never experienced it," Break Bones said.

"Ha! You were chained to a wall the first time I saw you!"

"No simple rope could hold me," Break Bones said. "Chains are another matter. But I thank you, Wu Song, for releasing me from my chains, once upon a time."

Bezaed walked over to them, wiping the blade of his knife on the strips of cloth on his chest. "Enough laughter and banter," he said. "This is a serious time."

"I did get kidnapped and almost taken all the way to the South," Jason said seriously. "And where am I? I mean the other me's? Did you guys, uh, kill me?"

Bezaed grinned this time. "Don't think you will get away from me so easily. I know if I were to kill one of them, you would use it as an excuse to say I had already killed you for trying to marry my sister."

Oh. That was a good idea that had not occurred to him. "Would that work?"

"We shall never know."

TJ was tied very tightly with a thin series of cloths that wrapped around his chest many times before knotting his hands together behind his back. Both the lizards were dead. OJ was missing.

"One got away," Jason said.

"Someone drew attention to me before I was ready," Bezaed said.

"A poor excuse," Break Bones chortled. "I captured mine easily enough."

Bezaed scowled. But he did that a lot, so Jason wasn't too worried. Rufus zipped over and landed on Jason's shoulder, and he was suddenly reminded of what happened before he left camp. "Did you find Mother Crow? Is she okay?"

Bezaed dropped his head and, after a moment, looked back up at Jason.

"Mother Crow will live. Or so the healer says." Bezaed was hiding something or not telling the whole truth in some way. Jason didn't know what it was, but he assumed it would come to light eventually.

"Did you find a healer too?" Jason asked Break Bones. "The fake Jasons seemed to think they had killed you."

"A strategic decision," Break Bones said. "I was wounded but not badly hurt. Though if I had realized they meant to harm Mother Crow, I would have tried another strategy."

"Mother Crow *and* Wu Song," Jason said. "You wouldn't want me to get hurt, either."

Break Bones clapped him on the back. "How I have missed you this year, Wu Song. Your strange, big mouth that always speaks exactly what you are thinking. It is a relief that you have not changed much on your path to becoming a Kakri."

"Hardly changed at all," Bezaed said under his breath.

Break Bones grabbed the other Jason—it was TJ—and shoved him back the way they had come. "Let us move quickly so Mother Crow does not have to travel so far."

"She's coming here?" Jason asked.

"She was concerned for your well-being," Bezaed said, but without the bitterness Jason expected.

They made good time. It felt great to be walking again, and the sun didn't bother him too much. He had Kakri clothes on, after all, and now that his hands were free he could wrap some cloths over his head, keeping the sun off. He might have a sunburn from the day's activities, but it wasn't the worst thing that could have happened. Mother Crow had taken an arrow, after all.

After half an hour, Bezaed handed Jason a skin of water. Jason drank from it gratefully. Break Bones appeared to enjoy having a prisoner and seemed doubly pleased that it was a Jason. It definitely made Jason uncomfortable when Break Bones gave TJ a little shove. "Hey, man, be careful with me," Jason said, and TJ shot him a thankful look.

Another half hour later, Bezaed said they were getting close and that he would go ahead and tell the Kakri to make camp. Jason had no idea how he could tell they were close—nothing had changed in the desert as far as he could see—but the Kakri had a way of knowing these things.

As Jason, Break Bones, and TJ came over the final rise before walking into the Kakri camp, the little crippled lion cub limped up beside him. "Oh, hey," Jason said. "How are ya?" He scratched her behind the ears. This was, he knew, a Kharobem. In their natural form—flying, four-faced creatures—they were respected and treated with awe by the Kakri because, so they said, the Kharobem were "made of story." Mother Crow had said they usually showed up when something momentous was about to happen, as witnesses. But there was nothing momentous about walking into a Kakri camp.

The camp had only been set up ten minutes at the most, but it would look identical if it had been in place for a year. A storytelling circle in the center, with different tents made of animal pelts fanning out in concentric circles from there . . . living tents, food tents, tents for hosting guests, common-area tents, even tents for the animals if a storm came. The largest tents were near the center, with smaller tents radiating out to the edge.

As they approached, Kharobem came hovering in from all sides, appearing out of the desert. Their wings were covered with eyes, something that always creeped Jason out a little bit, though not as much as the fact that each one had four faces: human on one side, lion on another, ox on the third, and eagle on the fourth. "What is going on?" Jason said.

Break Bones shook his head. "Something of great import, or they would not be here to watch."

TJ was in awe. "I have never seen a Kharobem before."

"It's your lucky day," Jason said. "Other than the beating you took from Break Bones."

TJ actually laughed at that.

Bezaed came out to them. "Break Bones, take the prisoner to the center of camp. Someone will show you where we will keep him. Jason, Mother Crow wants to see you immediately."

"I want to see her too."

"Come with me." Most of the Kharobem didn't follow, they just hovered on the outskirts of camp. Only the lion cub went with them. Bezaed led him through camp until they came near the center, just on the edge of the Storyteller's Circle. They stopped in front of a tent larger than many of the others, made of cloth instead of pelts. There were stories painted all along the outside of it.

"This is Mother Crow's tent," Bezaed said. "It has been empty this year while Mother Crow has taught you the way of the Kakri. I still do not understand her decision."

"Yeah, yeah. Can I go in now?"

"Treat her with respect," Bezaed said, in that deadly serious voice again.

"I am so respectful all the time," Jason said, and he pushed the flap aside. The cub limped in beside him. It was dark, even though there were torches lit on the side poles. The tent wasn't crowded with people—it was almost empty. He didn't see any of the pillows or soft furniture that Mother Crow preferred. Jason thought she would have wanted carpets and pillows everywhere. She even had an outdoor carpet at their last camp, but here there was just sand.

Then he noticed one carpet toward the center of the tent, along with a couple of pillows, and even in the dark Jason could make out the unmistakable silhouette of Mother Crow's feathered cape. She stood. Was she taller? Did getting shot with arrows make people taller? And thinner, too?

"The Elenil have all but declared war, Wu Song," Mother Crow said. "The Kakri are sharpening their blades." She stepped forward. Jason's eyes were still adjusting to the torchlight, but even if it were pitch black, he would know that voice. But . . . there was no way that could be true. It was even less likely than being kidnapped by two Jasons.

"Baileya? Is that you?"

14

PREPARATIONS FOR THE JOURNEY

*They need no magic to forget. They need only
time, or distraction, or force of will.*

FROM *THE ANNALS OF THE HISTORIAN*

+

Mrs. Oliver wanted to go to town, to ask one of the Scim to care for their animals while they were gone. David went with her. No reason not to be careful, he said. So Shula and Yenil had set out to do all the chores for the day and make sure everything was set for the morning. Mrs. Oliver and David should be back by late afternoon, and they would eat a light dinner and sleep before leaving for Far Seeing. Not that Shula would be able to sleep. Not with the thought pulsating in her head that her brother was alive out there. Not with the questions about this new woman, Vasya, and the tantalizing feeling that if she could just think about it the right way, she could maybe remember something more about her, and about what had happened when she had come to the Sunlit Lands.

By early afternoon, Shula was exhausted and ready for a break. She'd finished mucking out the goats' pen and decided she wanted a dip in the ocean before David got back. A swim would be refreshing, and Yenil would love it too. She was a good kid. Serious when she needed to be, and a creature of unfettered mirth when "serious" wasn't in demand. Yenil was under strict commands never to go down to the water by herself. The path was a little treacherous, for one, and in addition to the danger of drowning, there were various sea creatures and magical beings she might come across.

Shula found the girl in their room, packing a small waterproof rucksack that Shula had given her a few months ago. Yenil quickly threw the flap closed when Shula came in. Shula smiled to herself. No doubt Yenil had snuck some sugary treat from the kitchen into her sack. Delightful Glitter Lady was sleeping on the floor beside Yenil, and one ear twitched toward Shula when she cleared her throat.

"I was packing," Yenil said.

"Great," Shula said. "Can I check what you have in your bag? Make sure you got it all?"

Yenil frowned. "I'm not a baby."

"You can double-check mine, too."

Yenil crossed her arms. "Fine."

A change of clothes. "Good." A bit of chocolate, wrapped in oilcloth. Shula smiled. "This might melt. Maybe we should eat it in the morning before we go."

Yenil didn't perk up the way Shula hoped for when she said that. "Okay. Thanks for checking my bag. You found it."

That was strange. Shula concentrated on the girl, who definitely looked nervous. She pushed deeper into the bag, and her hand closed around something hard. A handle. She pulled it out. "Yenil, why do you have this?" It was a kitchen knife, a sharp one.

The girl shoved her lower lip out and crossed her arms. "You said it might be dangerous."

"David and I will be with you, though. You don't need this."

Her face hardened further. "Adults can't always protect you."

Which was true. Terribly true. Shula knew this too well. And she knew about the night that Yenil's parents had been killed. Madeline had told her about it, had laid out all the details. Madeline had been there, in their home, with the Sword of Years. The Sword of Tears, Yenil's parents had called it. Elenil soldiers had come, looking for Madeline or the sword or both. Yenil's parents had tried to protect the girls. Her mother had told Madeline to dig a hole beneath the back of the hut so she and Yenil could escape. The Elenil had killed both parents in retaliation.

It made perfect sense that this wouldn't feel like protection to Yenil. Even though, in a true sense, it had been. But her parents were dead now. And was it very different from Shula's own experience? Her parents, burned to death in their apartment, leaving Shula to fend for herself in the Sunlit Lands? Not really.

Shula put the knife back in Yenil's sack. "We'll discuss this later," she said. Yenil's eyes lowered, and she looked side to side in a quick movement that seemed designed to help her find a way out. No doubt she was surprised to be able to keep the knife and worried it would be taken from her. Shula touched her shoulder. "Do you two want to go swimming?"

Dee's ears perked up and she got halfway to her feet, looking to Yenil for a cue. Yenil pursed her lips, looked at Shula for a long moment, then shrugged. "I guess."

"Cool," Shula said, smiling to herself.

A couple minutes later they were hiking down the steep cliff trail, the cool ocean air rising to greet them. Shula loved the smell of the salt, the touch of the spray on her face. In the distance, the crystal sphere of the sky rose from the far horizon. Something vast and dark moved in the waves—too far to be any trouble while they were swimming, but a good reminder that this wasn't the Blue Beach or any shore from back home. She kept an eye out for a Zhanin "boat" . . . living creatures with flat, turtle-like shells on their backs where the sailors stood. The Zhanin had never given them trouble before, but Shula knew it was hard to keep track of the shifting alliances of the Sunlit Lands from a hut on a cliff at the edge of the world.

When they reached the sand, Yenil ran about twenty meters toward the waves before looking back. She knew not to get in the water until Shula gave her the all clear. "Go!" Shula said, laughing, and Yenil shrieked with delight. Yenil dialed Delightful Glitter Lady to her full size—she always liked the rhino to make the biggest possible splash—and the two of them barreled toward the water.

Shula dove in after them, letting the cool water sluice away the sweat and grime. Her own worries and fears washed away with them. She hadn't grown up by the sea but had come to love it. Even in the Sunlit Lands, where she could see the termination of the world in the shape of the crystal sphere, the sea felt larger than her. Wild and broad, an expanse of untamed water that left her with a swelling sensation, a lifting feeling in her chest . . . that if something like this could exist, then maybe there was a way for her to be free of all the troubles in her own mind, in her own world. She could forget for a moment. Or at least know that in the scale of the universe, her own troubles were so small as to be unremarkable.

Dee waded into deeper water, and the waves crashed against her side. She chortled in rhino glee. At her largest, she was bigger than an elephant. Yenil swam toward her, patted her on the nose, then wrapped her arms around the rhino's horn. "Fling!" she shouted.

Dee dipped her face into the water, waited for a wave to pass, then flung her head high. Yenil soared ten meters in the air, screaming with glee, her arms pinwheeling all the way until she hit the water. Shula held her breath for a moment—the impact had made a flat slapping sound that sounded like it hurt—but Yenil burst from the water with a triumphant shout and swam to Dee for another toss.

Sixteen throws later, Yenil had exhausted herself, and she and Dee pulled themselves onto the shore. Dee flopped on her side, and Yenil draped herself over the wet rhino, letting the sun bake them both dry. Shula dropped into the sand beside them, and the cool sea breeze combined with the heat of the sun made her feel warm, contented, and drowsy.

After a few minutes, Yenil, eyes still closed, said, "They didn't fight for me."

Pushing onto her elbows, Shula asked, "Who?"

"My parents. They should have fought. They were Scim, but instead of fighting they made me run. They died because they didn't fight."

"Yenil . . . I wasn't there, but that's not how Madeline told the story."

Yenil didn't open her eyes, didn't seem particularly upset when she said, "Madeline didn't fight, either."

"That's not true. She's the one who brought all this change. She's the reason that the Sunlit Lands have a chance of getting out from underneath the Elenil. She reset magic, and she set us free." Shula got to her feet, rubbed her wrist absently where the magic bracelet had sat beneath her skin once. But now it was gone, and that was thanks to Madeline. Yenil's words troubled her, but she knew the girl meant no harm . . . knew that she was reaching out, trying to share how she saw the world.

"You're not fighting," Yenil said, opening her eyes a sliver. "You used to, but now you live with me, far away from the fight."

Shula paced on the sand. Took a deep breath. She came close to Yenil and leaned up against Dee, who let out a long, contented sigh. "Yenil, do you feel unsafe?"

She gave a half-hearted shrug. "I know that because you don't fight, I will have to someday."

"Here's the thing, Yenil." She tried to say it gently. "You're a child. Madeline didn't want anyone to fight. Your parents, it sounds like they didn't want anyone to fight either. But when the time comes, when someone has to fight, it shouldn't be children. That's why I don't want you to take that knife. I don't want you to fight."

"I cut off the archon's hand," she said. Matter-of-fact.

Shula's heart dropped in her chest. "I wish you didn't have to do that."

Yenil pulled her feet up, wrapping her arms around her knees. "I'm Scim, and you're human. Maybe that's the problem."

Shula frowned. "How is that a problem?"

"You don't understand. We're trained our whole life to fight. To be ready for it. Because we know one day it will happen to us, whether we like it or not."

"But your parents didn't want that for you. They died so you could get away from the Elenil."

"They sold my breath to the Elenil so Madeline could have it."

That was true. "They did what they thought was best. And yes, the Scim fight, but not because that's what it means to be Scim. It's not right that the Elenil have shaped your people into this. When you fight, that's the Scim being controlled by the Elenil just as surely as if they had chains on you."

"You used to fight the Scim," Yenil said, and it was half question.

"That's before I knew," Shula said simply. "I was angry, and I was fighting because it was the only thing I could do to feel human at the end of the day. It was the only way to let some of the anger slip away before I got into bed. I didn't know anything else. It was Madeline who showed me that there might be other ways to do things, that there might be other solutions."

"What if I am angry?" Yenil asked. "What if I need to fight to sleep?"

"Then you can fight with me," Shula said. "That would be okay. But I don't want you to fight with a knife. I don't want you to ride into battle."

Yenil frowned, thinking things through. "Will you still love me if I fight? If I chop off more hands? If I kill?" A tear slipped down her face.

Shula clambered up the side of the rhino and sat down next to Yenil. She waited until the girl looked her in the eye. "I will always love you, Yenil. Always, always. And because I love you . . . I don't want you to ever have to fight someone. I don't want you to chop off hands. I don't want you to live with the pain of killing someone. It's a heavy weight to bear. But whatever comes—even if the sky fell in—I would love you. No question."

Yenil flung her arms around Shula and squeezed. Shula squeezed her back. "Can I keep the knife? Just in case?"

"If you promise to only use it with my permission or if you're in real danger of being hurt."

"Deal." Yenil stood and peered out toward the horizon. "Look, boats!"

Shula stood beside her, and together they watched. Zhanin boats—you could tell by their long necks, their heavy heads turning this way and that as they swam—moving fast. On one of the decks, someone raised a hand toward them. Shula hesitated, then raised her own in greeting.

"My father didn't believe in fighting," Shula said. "He was a pastor."

"I don't know what that is."

"A . . . a sort of holy person. Someone who tries to teach other people how to follow God and how to do the right thing, even when it's hard." She fingered the cross that hung around her neck. She showed it to Yenil. "Have you seen this before?"

Yenil nodded. "Mrs. Oliver calls it your cross."

"Right. That's what it's called. A cross. It's a reminder that sometimes, to do the right thing, you don't need to fight. But you have to be willing to die for people you love. Like your parents did."

"Hmm." Yenil stared at it for a moment longer, shrugged, and said, "You should try getting flung by Dee."

Shula laughed. Yenil did that sometimes. Just decided she was done with a conversation and jumped to another without warning. She looked toward home. There was no telltale silhouette of Mrs. Oliver or David on the cliff. They probably had at least an hour before they'd be back. "I don't know, Yenil."

"I'll trade you. You let Dee throw you, I'll give you the knife back."

"Deal."

They swam out into the surf, Dee thrilled to be back in the water. Yenil swam onto Dee's back and pointed to the rhino's horn. "Hold on tight, right there."

Shula grabbed onto the horn, and Dee exhaled through her nostrils, salt spray flying up around them both. "On the count of three?"

"Yes!"

"When do I let go?"

Yenil laughed and pounded the rhino on the side. "Don't let go. Try to keep holding on. Dee will do the rest. One—"

"I'm not sure about this, Yen—"

"Two!"

Shula redoubled her grip. Was Dee laughing at her? The rhino was shifting from side to side, clearly happy to be here with her and Yenil. How high was she going to fly?

"THREE—FLING!"

It wasn't unexpected, but that didn't mean she was prepared. Dee's head dipped for a moment, then swung upward. Shula tried to hold on, but her hands slid across Dee's face, and she lifted into the air. She was still facing Dee and Yenil, and she could see the joy in the little girl's face as she shouted and cheered for Shula's liftoff. The girl and the rhino dwindled below her, and Shula felt the shift as gravity tried to bring her back down. There was a moment when she wasn't moving up or down but just hovering in midair, and then she was plummeting back toward the water, and a giddy scream tore out of her body just before she slammed into the waves.

She sank for a moment, got knocked forward by a wave, but when her head broke into the air she gasped a deep breath before shouting, "Let's do that again!"

Yenil cheered and met her at Dee's nose. They both wrapped their arms around the slick face of their rhino friend. Yenil's eyes were bright as stars when she grinned at Shula and shouted, "Fling!"

Then they were flying and laughing together as they journeyed into the sky.

15
THE GRIEF OF KINGS

Sorrow so deep you didn't think you could plumb it.

THE PEASANT KING

✛

His father took a drag from his cigarette, held it in for a while, watching Darius, weighing him with his eyes. He blew the smoke out, gave him a tight smile. "Walk with me, Son."

Dad didn't wait for an answer, he just walked toward the gate. It had been locked before, but now it was twisted and splayed inward, the lock and chain nowhere to be seen, a gap large enough to drive a truck between the stretches of chain-link fence.

Darius couldn't believe it. The men on the ground, the crushed cars, and now this destroyed gate. "How . . . What did you do?"

No answer from his father, who was walking down the street now, apparently unconcerned. "Your mama tells me she's having trouble with you, Darius."

"No, sir. No trouble."

A piercing look from Dad. "You calling your mama a liar?"

Darius put his hands in his pockets. "Just saying there's no trouble, Dad. She doesn't like me being out without telling her exactly where and with who and when I'm getting back. I like having a little freedom, that's all."

"I understand that. And *you* understand that when you disappear for the better part of a year, maybe your mom gets a little nervous when you don't show up for dinner."

"Yeah, I get it. But there's no trouble, that's all I'm saying. I love Mom. I'm trying to do right by her."

"Uh-huh. So you told her you were gonna go poking white supremacists with a stick this morning?"

"Not exactly."

"You didn't sneak out the house through your window and leave a pillow under your blanket in some sort of sophomoric attempt to make it look like you were sleeping?"

"I might have done that."

"Might have. Mm-hmm. I see." They were walking back toward the protest, the exact opposite of the direction Darius thought they should be walking. There was a small park there—really just a concrete square that had been set apart by the city planners, with some benches built into the ground and a handful of trees and shrubs, a little hut for a bathroom, and a scattering of pigeons and solar-powered garbage compactors. "Take a seat, Son. It's time for us to have a talk."

Darius hated having talks with his father. It wasn't that he didn't respect the man, because he did. More than he knew how to express. It was just that whenever his dad gave him advice, there was this temptation, this constant temptation, to say, *Well, why aren't you around more then?* But it's not like his dad was absent, not at all. Darius saw him all the time. But why wasn't he with his mom? It's not like Darius was missing strong male figures in his life. His mom's brother had lived with them for three years after Dad moved out, some of the men at church played basketball with him every week, and it was a strange week if he didn't see his dad three, four times even. Not as much this last year, but when he was growing up. There were always walks, long talks, trips to the movies, staying over at his apartment, grabbing drinks at the convenience store.

Darius slung his backpack on the ground and sat. "What do you want to talk about, Dad?"

His dad nodded, like this was a wise and insightful question. "I think it's time for us to talk about what's been going on with you the last year. We've been giving you some space, but now that space is turning into trouble."

"That's what you want to talk about? How about the fact that you just laid out thirty racists and blew up their trucks?"

His dad shrugged. "You can't blow up all the racists. Can't even blow up all the white supremacists. Plenty of time to talk about that. I'm interested in you, Son. What's going on in there?" He pushed, hard, on Darius's breastbone. "What's making you act the way you're acting?"

A hot flash of anger burned through him. It was a stupid question, and just the thought of laying it all out made him even angrier. "My girlfriend died a year ago," he snapped. "I don't know if you heard."

His dad didn't react. Didn't look offended that his kid was just one tone short of yelling at him. Didn't look offended that Darius had made it sound like he was so out of touch that he might not have known. His dad just kept staring at him. Took another drag. "I did hear that. Go on."

"You did hear that?" Darius shouted, getting to his feet.

His dad was perfectly calm. Maybe more calm now. "Yeah, I heard. Your mom and I, we both loved that girl. Sweet Madeline. Good kid. So odd how she and her mom disappeared. Her dad so strange about the whole thing. The cops sort of dropping it with no answers. You saying she's dead but can't tell us anything about what happened. Strange that the police never even talked to you about it."

"Ha. Yeah, that is strange, isn't it? Can you think of any other strange things about it, Dad?"

"Sure. Plenty. You and Madeline disappeared at the same time as another one of your classmates, and you turn up alone. Distraught. Saying she's dead, but can't say how you know. Can't lead anyone to a body. Won't talk, really. That seems a bit out of the ordinary."

"A bit—" Darius threw his hands in the air, started to leave, turned around to yell at his dad, couldn't find the words.

"There you go," his dad said. "I can tell you have something to say, but you just don't trust me. Can't say it, can you? You can't trust your own people. Won't talk to me, won't talk to Mom. Just keeping it all to yourself. And when you finally go looking for help, you go ask a bunch of white dudes who don't know anything instead of going to your own dad."

"What? What are you even talking about?"

His dad raised an eyebrow. "You're acting like you don't know what I mean. But you do." He pointed at the backpack. "You gonna tell me there's not a silver dagger from Madeline's house in this sack?"

How could he know that? Had Mr. Oliver called him? Darius didn't know how that could be—they had never even talked before that he knew of. The Oliver family had never shown much interest in meeting the Walkers. They barely tolerated Darius, or at least that's how it had always felt to him. "He called you?"

"Nobody called me, Son. You think I don't keep tabs on you?"

"You're following me? Spying on me? What are you saying?" He pulled his cell phone out, looked at it. "You have an app on here or something?" But that didn't make any sense. How would he know about the dagger just by knowing Darius had been to the Oliver house? This had to be something different, something else. "How did you knock out all those guys?"

"We're not talking about me right now, Darius. We're talking about you. You're trying to change the subject. Is it so hard for you to share how you're feeling about Madeline? It's time for you to speak up. Your mom and I can't help you if you keep shutting us out, acting like we can't understand."

"You *can't* understand!" How could he explain this to them? His girl-friend had been lured to a magical world where she had been healed, had rejected the healing, had come home again, had gone back, had died by letting a magic tree use her as the seed for resetting all of magic? They would be calling the pastor for an exorcism or sending Darius to a work camp.

"Try me."

"Try you. And what if I try and you don't understand, what then?"

His father held his palms up. "Then I let you do what you want, and tell your mom to back off. You're a grown man, Darius. We're trying to help. Nobody wants to barricade you in your room. But whatever happened, Son, *whatever happened* . . . you can trust me."

The way he said it, Darius got the feeling his dad was thinking about something specific. "There's a lot of rumors out there," Darius said. He didn't even talk to the kids from high school anymore. Last year he had walked through the hallways like a ghost. But he had still heard the other kids. He knew what they said.

"Sure."

"You know about any of them?"

"A few."

"Any of them sound like something I would do?"

His dad crushed his cigarette out. "A couple."

"Like what?"

"I heard someone say that Madeline was dying, didn't like the idea of going out slow and in pain, and convinced you and that other kid to take her off somewhere quiet. Help her OD in peace somewhere."

"And you think I would do that?"

"I don't think you *did*. But it's a story that makes sense, at least."

"What if my story doesn't make sense?"

His dad shrugged. "The whole world doesn't make sense, Darius. Why would I be surprised by that?" He leaned back. "Seems to me the girl would have left a note, though, if that's what happened. And the other boy, he would have come back too, then, right? Besides, people seem to forget that Madeline didn't just disappear once. She disappeared from the hospital. Then she came back. Then she disappeared again."

"I can't tell you what happened."

"I think you're misunderstanding me, Son. I don't need to know what happened. I'm wanting to understand how you *feel*."

Darius shrank away from the thought. How he felt. He felt like someone had taken a red-hot syringe and injected acid into his bloodstream, and that it had burned through every branching vein. Where the acid touched, there was intense anger and pain . . . at first. Then it burned away and left nothing but scars and an empty place where life used to flow through him. The thought of Madeline made his chest hurt. When he was reminded of her, his eyes backed up with tears. "I'm struggling," he said. "I'm sinking in a deep pool. I can see the light, but I can't reach it. I have a weight on me, but I can't get it off."

"You can't get it off, or you don't want to get it off?"

Darius thought about that. "I don't want to. Because all tied up in that weight are my memories of Madeline. If I throw it off so I can get a breath, I can't get them back. I don't want to lose all that. And I don't know what I'm going to do about it, so I'm thrashing around under the water."

His dad stood, walked over to him, set his hands on Darius's shoulders. "Your mom and I, we're putting our hands into the water, Son. Let us help pull you out."

Darius tried to find his voice, but he couldn't speak. A tear spilled onto his cheek. His heart felt like it was contracting, moving away from his dad, away from everything, and leaving behind an endless void in his chest. "I don't know how."

Then his father was hugging him tight. Darius couldn't get his arms up, didn't have the emotional strength even to return the hug, and his father pulled him in even tighter until Darius's chest started to heave, and then he was sobbing while his father just held him. In the back of his head, Darius remembered they were here in a public park, and he felt awkward, but his father didn't pull away.

The tears stopped eventually. Darius didn't know how—they just did—and his dad stepped away from him, cupped Darius's cheek with his palm. "We're not going anywhere, Son. You can tell us anything."

"Yeah. Thanks, Dad."

"It's on a clock. Grief, I mean. It won't ever go away, but it gets easier to carry. There will be good days and hard days. Days you can't get out of bed, and days you can't sleep in one. It's all normal, Darius. All human."

Darius nodded and wiped his eyes with the backs of his hands. He slung his backpack onto his shoulder. "I guess I should call Mom."

"I told her I'd call tonight. She knows you're with me. Let's go find your car."

They walked a ways. Dad stopped at a convenience store and bought them each a soda and a bag of chips. Darius held his cold drink against his face. He had a large bruise forming around his left eye. "Think the cops are looking for us?"

His dad grinned. "Unless I'm much mistaken, those aren't the kind of guys to call the cops and say they got beat up by two skinny Black men."

"Can we talk about what happened back there?"

His dad nodded seriously. "Okay. But I'm gonna start. Son, you haven't been living up to your name."

"What?"

"What's your name mean? What have I always told you?"

"Darius means 'kingly.' You always told me you named me that because I'm a king."

"Yeah. And does a king go picking a fight with street trash?" Darius started to answer, but his dad just kept talking. "Nah. Definitely not. Maybe you send a couple of your soldiers to take care of it or something. But a king doesn't dirty his hands on something so small. Not if he can take care of it another way. But then again, you weren't there because you were trying to teach some white supremacists a lesson, were you?"

"No."

"And that's the problem, you know. That's what I was getting at earlier. You're not able or willing to tell me and your mom what the problem is, but you're running off to two old men who you think might have a solution. They don't know you, don't know your history, and you're asking them questions like you don't already know the answer. Just like you're asking me, 'How did you destroy those thirty men?' as if you don't already know."

"But I don't know," Darius objected.

His father snatched Darius's backpack, unzipped it in a fury, and pulled out the dagger. "You *do* know, Son. I've been telling you your whole life you're a king, and here you are using the Dagger Perilous like you're some commoner. Trying to 'find trouble' as if every Black man in the US doesn't know how to find it already. Asking old men to tell you how to get back to the Sunlit Lands when *you're a king*, Darius. A king doesn't need permission to enter—a king has his own authority."

Darius stumbled backward, shocked. His heart was pounding, his mouth wide open. "You know about the Sunlit Lands?"

His dad's anger deflated, like air escaping a balloon. He dropped the dagger. "This must be my fault, Son. If you know so little. Of course I know about the Sunlit Lands. Me and your mom both."

"Why didn't you ever say anything?"

"Good question," his dad said. "Why didn't *you* ever say anything?"

And there it was. His dad was right. Darius had never mentioned it, either. Had worked hard to cover any path that might lead to bringing it up. He had kept it a secret, hidden it, protected it, never imagining that his own parents already knew all about it, might even have some insights to share.

"C'mon," Dad said, walking toward Darius's car. "It's time for you to meet your grandfather."

"My grandfather? I already know—"

"You want answers, Darius? Get in the car and drive where I tell you."

PART 3

THE SOUND OF A VOICE, LIKE MANY BIRDS

I had suspected the Story King knew my plans and opposed them, but today he made it abundantly clear. I entered my workroom to discover a monstrous creature of enormous size. Ten feet tall at the minimum, it floated in the center of the room. Six-winged, four-faced, hooved feet, muscular arms of a man, and eyes enough for several choirs. It did not speak, but I recognized it at once: a Kharobem, a living story in service to the Story King. A shiver ran down my spine. Not for the unnatural number of faces, but rather the eyes, which covered the beast like scales cover a fish. Unlike a human's, they did not blink in tandem, but in a chaotic whirl that left me with the uncomfortable sensation of being completely exposed and totally known.

I yelled at the creature, cursed at it, demanded that it leave at once. It floated, unmoved, two of its great wings sufficient to keep it aloft. I began to pelt it with objects from my study, but again, it did not stir from its place. It was only when I threw one of my crystals that it evidenced some aversion. Though it did not turn, it floated away from me, its accursed eyes watching all the while. It moved through the wall of the house like a man moves through the water, and I raced to the window to watch as it glided across my property. It paused for a moment beside the slave quarters, and then—never taking its eyes from me—shot into the sky with such speed and velocity that one might have mistaken it for a bolt of lightning. Now I find myself shaking and unable to focus upon my work. Look at my letters upon the page! See the trembling of my hand!

FROM *THE MAGICIAN'S GRIMOIRE*

16

MUCH TUMULT

Go and do Death's bidding if you must.

FROM "THE TRIUMPH OF THE PEASANT KING," A SCIM LEGEND

+

Gilenyia's hands would not stop shaking. Not because of the death. She had seen death many times. She had seen, for that matter, Jason Wu himself near death. It was not her practice to insert the knife herself, and she had been astonished and shocked at how angry she had been, at how easily the knife had parted skin and muscle and how happily she had yanked it upward until the breastbone stopped it. But her hands were not shaking because of the death, or the murder, or the blood.

It was Jason's words. She could not get them out of her head, could not stop hearing his voice as he said them, like it was the most obvious thing in the world. *Something is wrong and you feel it in your bones,* he had said, and she could not deny it. *A grey hair,* he had said, and she could not help but see it herself. *She made you human.* This sentence pierced her like a sword, and she could not dislodge it.

"Can I bring you anything, lady?"

It was Ricardo. She had forgotten he was here, in her chamber, sitting against the wall in a chair and watching over her. She could not bear to have him here. A *human*. She hated them, the ugly little things with their short lives and uncultured world. "Tell Day Song to bring me tea," she said.

"Of course, lady." He paused by the door. "What kind of tea?"

She knew what he was asking. Addleberry tea, to help you forget whatever has upset you? Had she known about being human before and forgotten it? She did not think so, but then, that was the point of addleberries. "Mint tea," she said at last. "Have Day Song bring it. You are excused until I call for you."

Ricardo had a look of pain on his face, but he bowed his head in assent and went to fetch Day Song. Gilenyia swept to the window and watched the people below, all going about their business. What was to be done? It wasn't just that she was a human, as horrific as the thought was. It was that Jason's point seemed to be—must have been—that other Elenil were human too. Somehow. She looked out at the wonder that was the Court of Far Seeing. Could humans have made this? The soaring arches? The beautiful white towers, the crimson flags, the singing fountains? Perhaps. But she thought not.

A bit of calm came over her at that. The Wu boy had always been known for causing disruption. Surely by now that was clear. This was the perfect story to seed into the Elenil society to cause trouble. By responding to it as if it were true, she was playing into his hands. She was giving him ammunition. And if she mentioned it to someone else, if she even tried to look into it, she would be doing the exact thing he most desired: spreading his ridiculous story. Her hands began to calm. She peeled off her gloves and studied the intricate tattoo patterns on her hands, the lines of magic in her skin. Humans often said Elenil were illiterate, but she could read these patterns. She looked at them closely, searching for any indication that she had *become* Elenil, but there was nothing. She used far more magic than many Elenil did . . . the tattoos even whirled across her fingernails. But nothing, nothing that suggested what Jason Wu had said.

She almost felt bad for killing the boy. It was an overreaction to his words, which could give the story more power than it deserved. If the knight spread the story that Gilenyia had heard those words and then killed Jason, it might be whispered that she had done it because she was hiding something. But that was not the case. She had been filled with a righteous fury, that was all.

A knock at her chamber door. She slid the gloves back on and called for Day Song to enter. He bowed carefully, then set the tea on the side table beside her receiving furniture. She noted that there were two cups.

"I do not intend to entertain today, Day Song," she said.

"Yes, mistress. And yet you have a visitor. Shall I send him away?"

"Don't be coy. Who is it?"

"Your cousin, mistress."

Her cousin always had the worst timing. "Send him in, of course," she said, pouring tea into her own cup. She had no convincing reason to turn him away, but she wouldn't be waiting for him to get here before she drank her tea. The hot liquid, the bite of the mint—both calmed her. She felt her muscles unwind. This whole thing had been an overreaction. Of course she wasn't a human. She was hundreds of years old. She was taller, thinner, more beautiful than a human. She was of the proud line of the Elenil, a descendant of Ele and Nala. She was one of the caretakers of the Sunlit Lands, and all the other races—*all of them*—were under her care. Under her authority. Including the humans.

I will need to think of a brave punishment for the boy, she thought to herself. But then she remembered the knife. He was dead already, no doubt. She felt a stab of disappointment. The wording made her smile to herself. *Less than the stab of disappointment he felt*. It was possible, however, that here in the Sunlit Lands there was a healer who could have brought him back from the brink. The thought warmed her because that meant she could find him and punish him in a more creative and lengthy way.

The chamber door opened, and Day Song announced, "Hanali, son of Vivi." The Scim bowed and removed himself. Hanali wore a headpiece that rose to a tapered end, like some sort of tropical flower that had grown to outrageous size. His robes had shoulder pads that stretched a good foot from his shoulders on both sides, like great red thorns. The top layer of his robes cascaded down his back like a white cape, the gold fringe thick but short. The next layer was crimson, and he wore a wide golden belt. Gilenyia could not see his feet, though she suspected he wore platforms, and she felt certain they were gaudy and overblown. Something strange happened when she saw him this day. His entire outfit—the overblown foppishness of it—seemed somehow wrong. She pictured him stockier, swarthy, younger, and in simple clothes. Like a human. And she was disturbed to realize that it somehow felt . . . correct?

Hanali's face lit up at the sight of her, and she had to admit this simple thing caused some of her hostility to fade. They had grown up together, after all, and he had spent many years at her family's estate. "Gilenyia," he said. "It has been too long."

Was there a mild rebuke there? Hanali wasn't known for his subtlety. But just because he wasn't known for it didn't mean he wasn't capable of it. She knew that well enough. After all, what other Elenil at his age had moved within striking distance of being a magistrate, let alone the archon? None. "It certainly has," she said. "A pleasure to see you, Cousin."

He smiled at her. "No need to remind me we are family, I know that full well." That was a definite echo of something she had said to him once, when their positions were reversed and she had all the power, and he had been orbiting her in the hope of table scraps. Nevertheless, she smiled. This had the feeling of a childhood gibe, not a rebuke.

"Sit, Cousin," she said, a slight emphasis on the *Cousin*. "If you are able to do so in that trendsetting outfit."

His smile widened. It was like old times. "You didn't wait for me," he said, pouting. He poured himself a cup of tea, took a small sip. "Archon Thenody has an exquisite selection of teas," he said. "I will send some to you today, the moment I return to the tower. There is no excuse for a cousin of mine to be sipping water steeped in ivy."

"Mint, Hanali," she said, taking another sip herself. "The aroma calms me."

He raised an eyebrow. "Are you feeling tumultuous, Cousin?"

"There is much tumult in these days. Who among us has not felt it?"

"Indeed." He set his cup down and relaxed his body, turning sideways to look out the window. "Those people out there. They have no idea the difficult decisions leaders like you and me make to keep them safe. To keep the Sunlit Lands well and running. No doubt they would be horrified if they knew."

"These are complicated times," she said, inviting him to share more if he wanted to do so. It had been a long time since they had talked like this, like equals. He said nothing for a stretch. Finally she said, "Are you well?"

It was as if he didn't hear her at first, or as if he had wandered down a long path and it took him some time to find his way back to this room, this conversation. "The death of the girl shook me," he said at last.

"Madeline?"

He nodded. "You know me, Gilenyia. How many prophets and soothsayers and oracles do I consult for something simple, like a party?"

She laughed. "A score at least."

"A score! For a small party!" His smile faded. "I admit I have been dishonest in the past about some of the prophecies. I have exaggerated here and there what was said. Have fabricated new and enticing prophecies from whole cloth, in fact, if it suited me."

She knew this, of course. But to hear him say it shocked her. "We are speaking frankly, Cousin."

"Indeed we are." He sighed. He lifted his cup, held it to the light, studying it. "Does this tea truly calm you? Mayhap I shall have some mint grown in the terrace garden."

"Are *you* feeling tumultuous, Cousin?"

The left side of his mouth twitched upward. "Do you know how many of the prophets and soothsayers and oracles told me that Madeline would die? And that she would die in Aluvorea, destroying the magical dam which allows the pooling of power the Elenil require to maintain the authority given us by the Majestic One?"

"By your agitation, I suspect the number is low."

"The number is low because it does not exist. Not one. None of them said anything of the kind. The best of them said they saw nothing."

"Soothsayers are vague at the best of times, Hanali. It need not mean the world is out of place."

Hanali sniffed. "Would that my problem were so simple. I've never fully believed the prophets, or why would I so readily twist their words or invent new ones? Their failure with Madeline only reinforces to me that they are most useful as tools." He shrugged, a complicated gesture given his headpiece and shoulder pads. "My favorites were always the ones who specialized in fashion. They gave me an excuse for my more outrageous styles. And when I visited with five of them, or ten, I would know what outfit every Elenil in the city was wearing. They are gossips, nothing more."

"Then why so upset about the Oliver girl?"

He leaned toward her. "Because I believed in her, Gilenyia. You saw the things she could do. How like the Elenil she was in so many ways, but better than us. Do not you think? Better than us in her heart. I have seen the injustices put upon the Scim and worked to end them. I have been working toward it with Mrs. Raymond. But this was not enough for her. She wanted to burn the entire city to the ground in the hope that it might provide some modicum more of justice. How strange she was. How passionate and strong."

This unexpected transparency took Gilenyia off guard. "Speak on, Cousin. You have come for frank conversation, so tell me plainly, what do you need?"

"I need you in my inner circle," he said. "The days of trolling the soothsayers for fashion advice are long behind us. The game is more complicated and far more dire. Things are spinning out of my control. I need another set of hands I can trust working for the same goal."

She ran a gloved finger around the rim of her cup. "What goal is that, Hanali?"

"Peace in the Sunlit Lands," he said, his voice full of wonder that she did not already know this.

"With you as archon."

"I do not see another path to achieving a full peace, do you?"

She wasn't sure it could be accomplished even with him as archon. "How close are we, Hanali, to achieving 'full peace'?"

"The Scim remain a problem. The Maegrom are our allies, of course. The Pastisians are uneasy, and I would not say they trust me. King Ian continues to ask where Darius Walker is, and I continue to tell him the truth: on Earth. But he is skeptical of my answers, probably in no small part because of my work to rebuild the Palace of a Thousand Years. The Zhanin no longer respond to my messengers, but when last I spoke with them, a human child—a friend of Jason Wu's—had somehow become their ruler. I have had no word from the Kakri or the Southern Court. It is a conflicting mash of confusion. I can see, however, a thread. If I pull on this thread, I sense that it will all come together, that it will all be made right. Do you see the thread?"

The similarity to Jason's words took her off guard, and she struggled for a moment. Was it only a similar figure of speech? The thread Jason had referred to had been, of course, the Elenil's human ancestry. But surely that was not Hanali's intention? "I do not," Gilenyia said, astonished. "I haven't the faintest idea what thread you mean."

Hanali smiled serenely. "Ah. Come, Cousin, I know you see it."

But she did not. She ran through his list in her mind. He had not mentioned all the peoples of the Sunlit Lands. "The humans?" she asked.

"The humans," he echoed. "Madeline Oliver and her strange crusade for justice. Darius Walker and his strange compulsion to murder the archon. Jason Wu and his . . ." Hanali laughed. "Jason Wu and his *strange.*"

Her throat tightened. Hanali would not be pleased to know she had murdered one of his pets. "There is something you should know."

Hanali waved a hand at her. "I have his corpse in the waiting room."

She dropped her cup, and it shattered. "You *what?*"

"Oh dear," Hanali said. "Clumsy."

"Do not play games with me, Cousin. Of whom do you speak?"

"Jason Wu. His corpse is out there with your servants. The human one—what's his name?"

"Ricardo."

"Yes, Ricardo. He seemed quite surprised. Ricardo is, as you know, another human. The knight is not pleased with you, by the way. And there he is, the knight, yet another human."

Her mind raced. "What are you suggesting? What is the thread that you will pull?"

"I have been thinking how much better my life has been since sending Darius Walker out of the Sunlit Lands. I have been considering how the authority, the permission to be in the Sunlit Lands lies with me. And I've been wondering how much easier it would be to unite the people of the Sunlit Lands if we had a convenient group of people—some foreigners, some outsiders—to blame for our various troubles." He stood, swept his hands behind his back, and moved toward the window. "It's not even a lie, Gilenyia. Every problem we have can be traced back to them, you know. Our own stories say that they were meant to go to another earth and to come here only in dire need. Our mistake has not been the way we treat the Scim, but the laxness of our policies that allow the humans entrance."

Gilenyia got to her feet as well. "You have brought more humans into the Sunlit Lands over the last hundred years than anyone. More than many other Elenil combined."

He gave her a pitying look, as if she were five or six steps behind him in a chess game. "All the more reason that everyone in the Sunlit Lands will believe it. There will be significant cost for me, personally and politically, to speak up."

The pieces began to click into place. The careful planning that Hanali did, the audacity of his schemes. Had there been another Elenil like him in the last five hundred years? She could see what he meant to do now. How his humility, his insistence that he be punished, and the fact that it was his own fault the humans had been brought here in such numbers, would make people like him more, not less. He was just being honest, even though it put his own political life at risk.

"How can you speak of Madeline the way you did and then suggest the humans be your scapegoats?"

"There is no other scapegoat that will do," he replied calmly. Some doubt flickered in his eyes. But he seemed to push it down, his face becoming resolute. "She is gone, Gilenyia. No need to dwell on such things. And the Elenil need to see my strong hand at work."

He had, she realized, already cleared every obstacle from his path. "You will be archon within three months," Gilenyia said.

"Three weeks," Hanali said mildly. "I have another advantage. Have you heard of the Herald of Mysteries?"

"I have," she said. "In fact, I have my servants trying to infiltrate his cult even now. What of him?"

Hanali took her hand, something he had not done in ages. "Gilenyia, his entire message is about the Scim taking their proper place, because the Majestic One is returning, and the Elenil must be in *their* proper place of authority. He is encouraging the Scim to take on their magical debts again as an act of fealty to their Peasant King, and many of them are doing so."

"Is he yours, then? One of your false prophets you've created to say what you need said among the people?"

His eyes lit up. "Even better, my dear Gilenyia. There was no need to write words for him, as he truly believes what he says. Not only that, but—" Hanali stopped himself midsentence. "No, it's too delicious. You must meet him for yourself. I'll tell you no more. I'll set up an audience instead, so you can meet this Herald of Mysteries."

"I would be very interested to hear him speak."

Hanali patted her hand with affection and looked out over the city. "Within a month every human in the Sunlit Lands will be dead or banished." He squeezed her hand. "Gilenyia. I should like very much for you to be at my side when I officially ascend to become archon."

She stiffened. Was this an offer of marriage? They were cousins only in the Elenil sense that they were from the same generation of children. There was no barrier to marriage. His words were vague enough that they didn't require a response, but the doors they opened . . . Hanali still managed to surprise her. *Every human in the Sunlit Lands will be dead or banished.* Before she could stop herself, one hand rose to her head, seeking a grey hair.

I am Elenil, she said to herself. *Not human.*

She repeated it a second time.

"Did you say something?" Hanali asked.

Her heart beat faster. "No," she said, but her hands were shaking again.

17

MOUNTAINS LIKE MEN

*Death sent forth his servants, great hillocks of stone, and told
them to destroy all the works of the Peasant King.*

FROM "THE TRIUMPH OF THE PEASANT KING," A SCIM LEGEND

✦

Baileya!"

It was her, it was really her. He hadn't seen her in months.
Mother Crow had said that although he "left behind all" to follow
her into the desert and learn how to be a Kakri, that didn't mean
he shouldn't occasionally see his friends, and she wanted him to
participate in the normal festival days and holidays of the Kakri. So he had
seen Baileya a few times over the past year. His favorite time had been on
Watch Day when he and Mother Crow had walked through the desert to
an isolated town that had been trapped in some sort of curse. Jason and
Baileya had broken the curse, and he'd even met some of her extended
family . . . who didn't want to kill him! Who even kind of liked him! It had
been the best day and a half of his time with Mother Crow. Speaking of
which, where was Mother Crow?

"Wu Song," Baileya said, and took his hands in hers. "My heart warms to see you in this troubled time."

He squeezed her hands. "Baileya, I can't even say how happy I am to see you." He wanted to talk to her more, to tell her everything he felt about her, to spill all the thoughts he'd had since they had last seen each other. But the thought of Mother Crow dead—is that what happened if Baileya was being called Mother now?—weighed on him too heavily. "Is she okay?"

Baileya knew exactly who he meant. "She is in dire health," Baileya said. "But she is strong, Wu Song. Our healers think she will recover with time."

Jason dropped Baileya's hands and pulled her into a hug. He held her tight, and she laughed at his sudden burst of affection. She had teased him in the past about how slow he was to be fully open about his feelings for her. She returned the hug for a moment, then pulled away. "There is much to discuss and not much time, my love. Strange things are happening in the Kakri territories."

"You're Mother Crow now," Jason said. "How did that happen?"

"We cannot go to war without a Mother. She chose me."

"I'm sorry I missed the ceremony."

She smiled down at him. "We did not have a ceremony, though in better times we would have. It had to be done with speed so that certain decisions could be made."

"Makes sense."

"Come with me," she said, and grabbed his hand.

He would go with her anywhere, he really would. There was still this nagging voice in the back of his head reminding him how she had broken up with him. After they had (accidentally) gotten engaged, she had told him that she couldn't marry him because he couldn't accept her love. Because he didn't love himself. He hadn't known what to say to that. Baileya had gone back to the Kakri, and he had gone with Mother Crow into the desert to learn to be a Kakri.

She took him outside the tent. The sun was setting, and the stars were rising on the crystal sphere of night. A literal crystal sphere, which is how it worked in the Sunlit Lands. The temperature would drop fast, but Jason was used to it now. Baileya led him to two brucoks—giant birds sort of like ostriches—and Jason recognized one of them immediately. Moriarty. He was Baileya's brother's bird. They had stolen it from him once and used it to escape her brothers when they were trying to murder Jason. Which was great and everything except that the bird was always trying to bite him.

"My old nemesis," Jason said under his breath.

Baileya had already mounted the other brucok. He was clearly meant to ride Moriarty. Something thumped against the side of his leg, and he looked down to see the little lion cub. He scooped her up into his right arm, grabbed the reins with his left hand, and jumped onto Moriarty's back. The bird turned one eye on him as if to say, *Ah, it is you, my frenemy*, and Jason could swear he had a smile on his beak. But Moriarty hopped into a canter when he snapped the reins.

The crow cape spread out behind Baileya—Mother Crow—and it really looked like she was flying. With a pang of regret, Jason remembered that in the past they had ridden on one brucok together. That was out of necessity, but still . . . his arms ached to be around her waist again as she led them through the desert, not following on Moriar—

Jason flew into the air, landing in a pile of sand. Moriarty gave a great honking victory cry. So that's the way it was going to be. Jason had managed to keep the cub safe in his arm even during his ride to the ground, a definite testimony to his training in the desert.

"Listen," he hissed at Moriarty. "You are embarrassing me in front of my girlfriend."

The bird turned its head, keeping one beady black eye on him. It honked again.

"Are you well, Wu Song?"

He turned back to Baileya and beamed the brightest smile he could. "Oh, I'm great. I'll be along in a moment."

"I may not have made this clear, but time is short."

He turned back to the bird, yanked the reins to bring its face close to his own. "Listen, birdie, unless you want to become part of the biggest bucket of KFC that this world has ever seen, you better shape up. There's already a bunch of evil Jasons out there, and that says to me that I have the potential to be one too. So watch it." He swung onto its back. He'd have to be careful not to get distracted again.

The rest of the journey passed quickly. The last bit of sun had just descended into the west when Baileya swung off her brucok and walked into the center of a long, flat field of sand. Jason jumped off and walked beside her. She slipped her arm through his. "Wu Song. I am afraid."

Jason shuddered. He had never heard her say anything like this. He couldn't imagine her being scared. She was the bravest, strongest person he knew. He had seen her fight enemies twice her size. In the first fight he had seen her in, she had broken a spear *and her leg* fighting a possum the size of a horse. "I'm here," he said. He had been afraid. He knew that saying "There's nothing to be afraid of" was so often a lie. And he knew that when you told someone else you were scared, what you really wanted deep down was just to know that you weren't alone.

He could see her smile in the starlight. "You are a wise man," she said. "I am glad you are here with me during this time."

Out in the field of sand he could see what looked like small hills, but with strange protrusions. He looked at them closer. They were *moving*. Slow, yes, but definitely moving, and not like something swaying in a breeze. Moving with purpose. He had a sudden sense of déjà vu, like he had been here before. The big shapes blocked out the starlight, leaving only silhouettes. They almost looked like people.

"Do you remember this place?" Baileya asked. "We passed it when we ran from my brothers. Long ago."

"Maybe in the daylight," he said.

"Let's move closer," she said, and they started walking toward one of the shapes. "They are statues," she said, and it all came back to him. When they had been running from her brothers, they had camped here overnight once. They had sheltered behind one of the great statues, and in the morning when they woke, Jason had realized that the statues had moved. They weren't in the exact places they had been the night before.

"Statues don't move. That's kind of the definition of *statue*."

She laughed. "You said the same thing when last we were here. So you do remember?"

"I do, yeah."

The lion cub scrambled down from his arms, and when she had moved far enough away, she took on the shape of a young girl in a simple white dress. Jason had seen this before, but it always startled him. He had saved her from some predators in the desert, not knowing she was one of the Kharobem, the supernatural creatures who were "made of story." She had never spoken to him plainly—she had only ever told him stories.

The three of them came near one of the statues. It was shaped roughly like a human, but only its upper torso was out of the sand. Its hands were both palm-down on the sand, and it appeared to be levering itself out. It was a little unsettling, seeing the top half of a man who had to be at least eight stories tall, attempting to emerge from the sand. Pushing upward, slowly falling back in, pushing up again. There was a sound of sand on sand, like at a beach. If he closed his eyes and pretended he was on a beach, it might be better, but watching a giant stone man trying to pry himself loose from the sand was less relaxing. The statue was bare-chested, wearing some sort of vest, and it had a strange headdress and a long goatee that stuck out from its chin.

"They are moving faster now," Baileya said. "Do you remember, last time you only knew they were moving when we had camped beside them for a night?"

"What does that mean?" Jason asked. "Why are they speeding up?"

The young girl took his hand. "They came at last to the great Enemy, who stood taller than a hill. He had no flesh but was only darkness in the shape of a giant. He wore a pale crown set with seven shining stars and carried an iron sword which wept blood. The Peasant King told the gardener she must now say farewell, for he must battle his foe."

Jason knew this story. He had learned it from Mother Crow. The old one. "This is a Scim story," he said. "About the Peasant King fighting death. But she told me only the Scim know the whole thing. She's never heard it all. Do you know the whole story, Baileya?"

She shook her head. "I know a bit more. The Peasant King has no sword and no horse, and the woman—the gardener—tells him not to fight, and he says that before morning comes he will ride in Death's chariot."

"Right," Jason said. "And she tells him that if he just stops being king, he won't have to fight. But he says he has to fight. I remember this part—he turns toward Death, and 'the sun shone upon his face as he stepped forward.' That was all that Mother Crow knew of the story."

The Kharobem nodded her head slowly. "Death sent forth his servants, great hillocks of stone, and told them to destroy all the works of the Peasant King. 'Tear down the crystal spheres of the sky,' said he, 'and drain the Sea Beneath the world. Cause the islands to flee and the land to tremble.' The Peasant King tried to turn this curse away, but Death is strong, and the curse could not be broken. Death is strong, yes, but the Peasant King had built the Sunlit Lands from his own heart and with his own two hands, and he also was strong. He said to the mountains that walked like men, 'Go and do Death's bidding if you must, but do it wondrous slow. Let the people wonder if you move at all.' Then he said to the desert, 'Thou sands, cover them, and slow them even more.' And he said to the people of the desert, 'Keep watch over them, for in the day they climb free, they will destroy all things. And none can stop them.'"

Jason shivered. "So you're saying these statues are going to destroy the Sunlit Lands." No one said anything. He thought about it for a little while. "Baileya, we have to get back to Earth. We have these things called wrecking balls. We'll break these big boys into tiny little boys and then see what happens."

"Mother Crow is wounded," Baileya said. "The great stones are moving faster than the Kakri have ever seen. The Elenil have declared war. You were kidnapped by strangers wearing your own face. Now I am Mother Crow, Wu Song, and during a time of such upheaval as we have not seen in my entire life."

"That's why you're scared," Jason said.

She looked away from him, and in the starlight he saw the glint of a teardrop fall from her eye. "I am not afraid of death, or war, or of taking on the mantle of the Crow. I am afraid, dear man, that it means we will never be together, you and I."

"What?" Jason said. "Why would you say that? Baileya, I will marry you right now. Here. With these stone dum-dums as our witnesses and this little girl as the minister. Let's do it."

She laughed, and another tear fell. "Oh, Wu Song. If only it could be. Mother Crow cannot marry during a time of war. She is a Warbird and must take care of the tribe. She does not have time for a husband then." She put her arm around his shoulders. "I do not fear the battle, Wu Song, and I do not fear death."

"You said that already."

"I fear that the world's end has come. Which means we will not be together, my love, for there will be no land to stand upon when all is done."

"So you brought me here to show me." He waved at the monster statues. "To show me what the end of the world looks like."

She kissed his cheek. "I brought you here to say goodbye. The Warbird does not take time for lovers or parents or brothers or sisters or cousins."

"Just to be clear," Jason said, "if I save the world, you're going to be my girlfriend again, right?"

Baileya laughed and hugged him. "We will always be something more than that. You are in my heart, as I am in yours."

Jason took the Kharobem's hands and put them over her eyes. "Keep 'em shut, kid, because I'm about to give Mother Crow here the biggest kiss ever." He reached up to kiss her, then paused. "Hold on." He pulled the girl's hands away. "I want to try that again, because I'm too creeped out after calling her Mother Crow. I can't kiss her if I think of her that way. Mother Crow is an old woman." He put the Kharobem's hands over her eyes again. "Eyes closed, et cetera, kisses for Baileya may now commence."

He wrapped his arms around her neck and kissed her. It was comfortable, and amazing, and sad and exciting and beautiful. He could taste the salt of her tears on his lips when they pulled away from each other. She rested her forehead on his.

"Mother Crow," someone called. "Your council is waiting."

She put her palm on his cheek. "I have ordered Bezaed to fight by your side and keep you safe."

"WHAT? Bezaed your brother who is trying to kill me?"

She grinned at him. "To be fair, Wu Song, so many people are trying to kill you that you really limit my choices of protectors."

"That is a fair point," he conceded.

"I'm off to the war council," she said.

"And I'm off to save the world so we can date," Jason said.

She kissed him, quick this time. "Please do." Then she was on her brucok and disappeared into the night.

Jason took the Kharobem's hand and walked with her to his brucok. Moriarty hissed at him. "Oh, go on, you big grump," Jason said. He lifted the girl onto the bird, then climbed up behind her. "I sure hope Moriarty knows the way back to camp," he said.

He would start by checking in on Mother Crow, he thought. The original. Then touch base with Break Bones, who would be a great save-the-world companion. It might be good to interrogate himself, he thought. He still wasn't clear how his doppelgänger played into this whole mess.

As Moriarty trotted toward camp, the Kharobem girl started to speak again. "Your people have all deserted you," she said. "Throw down your holly crown. Toss away your oaken rod. If you are not king, you need not fight this evil."

"That's what the woman says to the Peasant King in the story," Jason said.

The girl nodded, then turned halfway around so she could look him in the eye. "Death said to the Peasant King, 'Will you truly travel into my kingdom? Will you die to save these people who have rejected and despised you?' The great king replied, 'I would die a hundred times to save a hundred of my subjects, and I would die a thousand times to save one person whom I love.'"

Jason searched her face for a clue. He still didn't understand the way the Kharobem communicated. He got the distinct feeling, though, that whatever her message was, she meant it for Jason Wu and no one else.

18

THE LOVE OF LIBERTY BROUGHT US HERE

What story is this, and whose? What gods are being referred to, and what magicians are these?

FROM "THE BALLAD OF WU SONG," A KAKRI TALE

✦

arius took the turns his dad directed, following a road that wound into a forest within the city limits. There were a lot of houses for the wealthy here, and Darius still didn't understand where they were going or who they were going to see. His dad had said "your grandfather," but Darius had known both of his grandfathers, and neither of them had lived here. They turned, at last, onto a heavily wooded drive that was just wide enough for the Mustang. Darius drove slowly, his palms sweating. He wasn't sure why this place made him so nervous, but it did.

A tall, wrought iron fence barred the path. Darius rolled to a stop beside an intercom on a post. He rolled his window down to say something, but the gates slid open before he could speak.

"Go on," his dad said.

The Mustang inched forward. The road wound through a strange topiary garden, the bushes overly large and shaped like heroic statues, almost like Communist propaganda art. A king holding a sword high, high over his head. A crown-wearing monster bearing down on a tiny hero, the monster so large it was almost like a wave about to crash. A unicorn. A mermaid, a great bird whose wings were spread wide, a gigantic salamander. "What is this place?" Darius asked.

His dad snorted. "I'd hate to be the gardener. That's what I always tell the old man."

As they left the garden, a series of evergreens arced over the road, until finally some of them touched, forming a rainbow-shaped tree tunnel for them to drive through. Then all the bushes and trees fell away, the road ended, and a gigantic lawn sprawled before them. At the far end of the lawn stood a great fountain, and then a wide avenue of stairs, and at the top a mansion larger than any Darius had ever seen, with bright windows and wide red double doors and flowers and large plants in tall, tasteful pots around the base of the house.

"I usually drive across the grass and park by the fountain," Dad said. "But he doesn't like that. Let's walk. Bring the dagger."

The sky was blue, and Darius could see so much more of it than he was used to. There wasn't a single plane or even a bird that Darius could see. He didn't bother locking the car door, but he slid the Dagger Perilous beneath his belt. It wasn't warning him of danger. It wasn't doing anything—as if it had been silenced, or maybe had never been magic at all.

"Is it safe, Dad?"

His dad squinted, thinking it over. "Is family always safe?"

"No."

"Well. He's family."

Darius considered that. His hand went to the hilt of the dagger. "Okay," he said.

"That dagger won't do a thing to protect you, though, I'll tell you that for free."

Then why did he have it? The house was so still, and so huge. It gave Darius the unpleasant feeling you might have if you turned around to discover a tarantula sitting on a shelf behind you. The fact that it was watching would be enough to creep you out. It wouldn't matter that it wasn't moving toward you.

The fountain was splashing and bubbling—the only thing making a sound near the house. His dad trailed a finger in the water as he passed. Darius decided not to touch it. They hiked up the stairs, and Dad knocked on the red door.

After a minute they heard something clatter, and then someone walking toward them inside. It was strange that the gate had opened to them without a word, but that no one had been waiting for them at the door. They should have known, shouldn't they, during the drive through the garden, and then the walk across the lawn, that someone was on the way?

The door swung open. The man who stood there had his silver hair cropped short, a thick black beard with grey streaks, and a sparkle in his eyes. He wore tan slacks and a green button-down shirt, with a purple cardigan hanging loosely over the top.

"Darius!" he said, a wide smile on his face. "And Jordan, too. What a pleasure. Come in, boys."

"Thanks, Pops," Dad said, and hugged the man.

The old man held a hand out to Darius. "You probably don't remember me."

"No," Darius said, and took his hand, which was dry and cool. He couldn't help but notice that when the cardigan pulled back from his wrist, the old man had a network of scars there.

"Well, come on in," the man said, pulling the cuff back over his scars. "Hungry?"

"Darius had a cinnamon roll a while back," his dad said, and Darius wondered about that. Had he been following him? *Watching* him this whole day?

"That's no breakfast. Eggs and bacon, some biscuits, gravy. Fresh blackberry jam I've got too, so fresh you can tell which direction the bees came from that pollinized the vines." They followed him through a large open foyer. Stairs wound up to their right, and a hallway branched off to the left, wider than the road they had driven in on. They walked through a dining room that could seat thirty, and the kitchen was large enough that a full staff could have run it. The bacon was already frying. "How you like your eggs, Darius?"

"Scrambled," he said. They weren't even to the back of the house yet. There weren't windows in the kitchen. Three stoves. Two dishwashers, four sinks, a couple full-size refrigerators.

"My name's Cumberland," the old man said. "Cumberland Armstrong Walker."

"Dad says you're my grandpa," Darius said.

The old man laughed at that, raised an eyebrow at Darius's dad. "Simplifies things, sure. Your grandpa Walker called me the same thing when he was a boy. You can just call me Cumberland, if you're more comfortable."

"What kind of name is that?"

Cumberland laughed. "Well, it's not from Africa if that's what you're asking! Next question you're gonna ask is how old I am."

Darius smiled. "Well, I thought that might be rude."

"It's definitely rude!" Cumberland chuckled and threw a biscuit at him. Darius caught it, and the old man slid him a jar of blackberry jam, then a butter knife. The jam was thick and full of seeds. He took a bite, and the natural sweetness of the berries combined with the flaky, buttery biscuits was perfect. The biscuits were still warm.

Dad went around the counter, grabbed his own biscuit, and slathered jam on. "I have to insult you to get a bite?"

"You know everything in this kitchen is fair game to you, Jordan."

"Just bustin' your chops, Grandpa."

"Speaking of busting things, Jordan, you know I don't like to see you using magic for violence."

Darius's dad shrugged. "Well, Pops, it was us or them."

Cumberland raised an eyebrow. "You know, Martin Luther King Jr. used to say, 'Love is the only force capable of transforming an enemy into a friend.'"

"Yeah, well, they killed him, didn't they, Pops? Besides, maybe I don't want those boys as my friends."

"Humph. That's what you always say."

"I'll keep saying it so long as it's true."

Cumberland nodded, almost to himself. Darius could practically see the conversation . . . there were grooves worn into it. They'd had this same talk before plenty of times, maybe using these same words. But that's how people were sometimes. The same things kept coming up, so the same conversation had to be had yet again. Cumberland's face settled, as if to say, *Well, that part's out of the way.*

"Eggs are almost done. Why don't you two set the table?"

"We can eat at the counter," Dad said.

The look Cumberland gave him could have frozen the sun. "I don't get visitors anywhere near often enough. Let an old man eat at the table."

"Okay, okay. Darius, get the plates from that cabinet there."

Darius found three and grabbed them. Cumberland told him those were the small ones, and there was too much food to mess around with small plates. So he put them back, picked up three larger ones, and followed his dad into the dining room. It was strange to set three places at the end of the giant table, but that's what they did.

"Everybody grab some food," Cumberland said, and they did. Darius got the biscuits and jam, his dad a big plate of bacon and fried ham, Cumberland the eggs and a large skillet of corn fritters. When it was all arranged to Cumberland's liking, he said a short, authoritative prayer and then said, "Dish up!"

The three men fell to eating, and there wasn't much talking other than appreciative commentary on the food. Cumberland dished more onto Darius's plate multiple times, and he seemed pleased that Darius ate the food without objection. It was delicious, and hot, and all homemade as near as he could tell.

When they were done, Cumberland leaned back in his chair and patted his belly. "That was just about right. Let it rest for a half hour, and then it'll be time to start cooking up some lunch."

Dad laughed at that. "You always set a full table."

"When I get the chance, when I get the chance. Now. I'm not complaining a bit, but why are we here today?"

"Darius has some questions, that's all."

"Does he now." Cumberland stood, grabbed his dish and the egg pan. "We don't have to clean up, but let's move everything into the sink."

"Where should we do this, Pops?"

"In the garden?"

"Ugh, no. You know I hate the garden."

"The study?"

Darius's dad squinted at him as if making sure he was ready for the study. "Sure, that'll work."

Cumberland led them back toward the front door and then up the stairs. Down another hallway, and then they walked for a long time until they came to a large, open room with windows along one wall and books lining a second. There were several leather couches, a big table with an old-fashioned globe, and a sword on a stand. The windows looked out on forest as far as Darius could see . . . way more trees than he would have expected.

"Quite a view," Darius said.

"It sure is." Cumberland settled into a wide easy chair. "What sort of questions do you have, Darius?"

He wasn't sure, when it came right down to it. He couldn't figure out what was happening here and why his dad had brought him. He was still reeling from the fact that his dad knew about the Sunlit Lands, and his mom somehow did too. Now this old man who didn't look as old as he should was serving them breakfast in a mansion. What was the right question to ask first?

"Start with this," Dad said, and slipped the dagger from Darius's belt, tossing it to Cumberland.

He smiled, held it up, studied the silverwork on it. "The Dagger Perilous. Where has this been, I wonder? Disappeared years ago."

"Kyle Oliver had it, turns out."

"You don't say." He looked at Darius. "And what are you using it for?"

He didn't know why, but he felt uncomfortable and a little foolish. "To try to get back to the Sunlit Lands."

"With this? How?"

Darius shrugged. "Following the warnings to the most dangerous places I could find."

"Doesn't work like that, though," his dad said.

Cumberland chuckled. "You say that, Jordan, but the boy is here now. Seems like it's moving him in the right direction. You should have brought him here when he was first looking for a way in. Or when Hanali pushed him out."

"You know his mother doesn't want him going into the Sunlit Lands again, Pops."

"Well, that egg's already cracked, isn't it."

Darius crossed his arms. "The biggest question I have is how do I get back?"

"We've been trying to keep him out," Dad said. "But he doesn't give up easy."

"I don't suppose he does. The creator of the Black Skulls," Cumberland said, smiling.

"How do you know about that?"

"Oh, I keep an eye on the Sunlit Lands, Darius. That's pretty much all I do." He went to a cupboard installed in the bookcase, unlocked it, and opened it. There were a variety of knives, daggers, and other items inside. He set the Dagger Perilous in there, then closed and locked it again. "How do you get back? The first question is how you got there in the first place. Your parents tried to keep you ignorant, but you got in somehow anyway."

Darius pursed his lips. "My girlfriend—"

"I know all about Madeline and how she and Jason got in. How did *you* get in?"

"Well, I couldn't at first. There was a fence that wouldn't let me go past it. I tried climbing through tunnels and pipes and water drains and all sorts of things but couldn't find an entry. Then one day I saw a possum in the middle of the afternoon, which seemed weird, and I followed it to a . . . a sort of dome of darkness. I went through that, and it took me to the Wasted Lands."

Cumberland was nodding as if this all made perfect sense to him. "Where did that dome of darkness come from? Who created it? How did you find it?"

"I don't know."

"Why don't you go that way again?"

"I haven't seen a dome of darkness lately," Darius said, getting irritated.

"Why don't you make another?"

"I don't know how. I thought I was supposed to be the one asking questions?"

"So ask," Cumberland said.

"How do I get to the Sunlit Lands?"

Cumberland sighed. "You're asking all the wrong questions, Darius. You don't even know what the Sunlit Lands is. You have to know a thing to find it."

"I know what it is. I lived there for—" Well, it had seemed like years, but time was strange in the Sunlit Lands. "—for a long time. I'd recognize it if I saw it."

"He's bullheaded," Dad said.

"It's genetic," Cumberland said, and walked to the wall of windows. "Darius, come here. Look out the window."

He did as he was told. "I didn't know there was so much acreage in the city limits."

"There's not," Cumberland said mildly. "Why do you want to go back to the Sunlit Lands? Madeline is gone, Darius."

"She wasn't my only friend there. The Scim are there. Jason is there. There are others."

"So you want to throw a party, see all your friends?"

Darius shook his head. "No. I want to overthrow the Elenil. They're unjust. They're keeping the Scim in practical slavery. Hanali is setting himself up to lead them, and he's no better than the last guy. Not really."

Cumberland nodded sadly. "So what would you do? If you had the ability?"

It wasn't like he had never thought about this before. "Kick them out of power. Maybe kick them out of the Sunlit Lands."

"What about the ones who won't go?"

Darius scowled and tapped his fingers against the glass. The forest was so vast. Birds flew back and forth between the trees. "I don't know."

"That's not a sufficient answer for people with power," Cumberland said. "Kill them?"

"Maybe."

"Put them in prison?"

"Sure."

"Set aside a camp where they can live, but it's only them?"

"I get it," Darius said. "You're saying it will be complicated, but none of that matters, or it doesn't matter much since I not only don't have the power—I can't even get there."

"He's not ready," Cumberland said. "He's too young."

"How old was I?" His dad shook a cigarette into his hand.

"That was different. And you know I have regrets about that." He grunted. "Put those cigarettes away."

Dad shrugged and dropped them back into his pocket.

Cumberland ran a hand over his hair. "Darius, what do you know about Liberia?"

"Nothing," Darius said. "What does this have to do with the Sunlit Lands?"

"Patience. Strange thing about Liberia. Some white folks started these associations. Groups like the Society for the Colonization of Free People of Color of America. Eventually they were called the ACS, the American Colonization Society. There was something similar in Britain. The idea was, well, all these Black folks have it hard in white society. People are prejudiced against them. What if we made a new country for them in Africa? We could send them down there, they'd have a better life."

"This was after the Civil War?"

"After and before. It was a strange coalition. Quakers and abolitionists, some of them liked the idea because they thought maybe people could be really free if they could just get out of America. Slaveholders liked it because they thought all the freedmen would go and remove all this confusion between free Black people and enslaved ones."

In the forest, a bird much larger than Darius expected leapt from a tree, flapped lazily, and rose into the sky. "What did Black people think about all this?"

"They didn't like it. Most of them, anyway. A few signed on. Some slaves were told they'd be set free if they agreed to go. And the white folks had gone down and sold or leased a big swath of land from old Zolu Duma,

King Peter himself. Stories say one 'negotiator' put a pistol to his head to get the land that became Monrovia, and getting the land for Liberia wasn't much different. Colonizing always requires some . . . hard negotiations."

"I don't understand what any of this has to do with the Sunlit Lands."

"Ha! Because you don't know the Sunlit Lands, that's all. I'll cut the story shorter. You're young. When you're older, you'll have time for a longer story. The colonization societies found a few thousand people to come to Liberia, and they eventually founded a nation there in West Africa. Their motto was 'The love of liberty brought us here.'"

"That's pretty cool," Darius said. "How come I never heard about this in history class?"

"Empires don't spend a lot of time talking about other people's countries, that's why." Cumberland grinned. "At the end of the day, all those folks who went 'back to Africa,' they were American. Grew up here, spoke English—even the ones who had been slaves had a lot of American cultural baggage packed in with them, you see? They started having trouble with the locals. The Africans. And the first people in charge, the people the ACS gave authority to, well, they weren't Black, were they?"

"I'm guessing not," Darius said.

Cumberland shook his head. "Imagine that." He started ticking things off on his fingers. "People were dying from tropical diseases. Armed skirmishes with the native Africans. Black folk being pressured to immigrate. Racism on the rise in the US being used as a way to recruit people to Liberia instead of fixing things in America. Liberia started taking in Africans freed from illegal slaving ships too. Returning everyone home was too difficult, I guess."

"What are you getting at?"

Cumberland took Darius's shoulders. "A lot of those men and women, white and Black, were trying to do something good. Something noble. They thought, *We took these people away from Africa—let's undo what we've done.* Never mind that precious few Black folks wanted to go. Never mind that many of them had been born in the United States and Africa meant little to them. My name, Cumberland, you asked how I got it. My master gave it to me."

"Your . . . what?"

"My master. Mr. Walker. He named me that. Cumberland, that's an Anglo-Saxon name. Walker, that's an English name. That's my slave name."

Darius's jaw fell open. He looked at his dad, who was sitting on the couch, cool as anything, his eyes sparkling with amusement as he watched his son.

"I don't understand."

"This is the part where you ask me how old I am," Cumberland laughed. "But I think you can guess the ballpark."

"How?"

Cumberland laughed harder and harder. "This boy can ride a giant possum, but tell him an old man is a couple hundred years older than he thought, and he's saying, 'How, how, how can it be?'"

"You look good for your age," Dad said.

"I sure do," Cumberland said. "I sure do. But we're off topic."

"We're coming back to this," Darius said.

"The point, Darius, the point is that some of those folks were trying to do what was right, but they were so soaked in the racialized ideals of their time, so wounded by them, that even when trying to do the right thing, they were doing the wrong thing. Talking to themselves all about the solution, not listening to the Black folks who were telling them they didn't like it. Only a couple thousand Black people agreeing to go out of the millions who were in the States at the time. And that's not all! Then from the 1800s until *the 1980s*, Liberia was run by the descendants of the Black *colonists* . . . despite the country being made up mostly of the descendants of the native African folks by that point. The colonists—this is true, Darius—they were never more than 5 percent of the population, and they built a segregated society with themselves at the top, and all their American values and religion and everything else were the signs of civilization. They said that the 'savage' 95 percent could be educated and civilized only if they got a Western education and converted to Christianity. In the 1920s Liberia was investigated for de facto slavery. This is the nation that was founded because 'the love of liberty brought us here.'"

"So the whole thing was wrong? A mistake?"

"That's not my point, Darius. It's that all these problems, this whole pattern of trouble, came because the land was created, was put together by people who had been broken by the corrupted philosophies of colonization and racism. If we don't know our history, how can we know how to repair our present? You want to bust into the Sunlit Lands, but you know almost nothing about it. You don't know who founded it, who brought it into being. You don't know why and how and when."

"The Peasant King," Darius said. He had heard that more than once from the Scim. "He created the world."

"Do you know him?" Cumberland asked. "Have you met him?"

"No," Darius said. "Madeline said she had seen him, but I never have."

"Hmm," Cumberland said. "Okay." He looked at Darius's dad. "I want to take him into the Sunlit Lands."

"Uh-huh. You're going to leave me here to tell his mother, I take it."

"And do the dishes," Cumberland said. "And watch over the house until I get back."

Darius's heart was beating fast. He assumed Cumberland was telling him the truth and could get him into the Sunlit Lands. He was ready to go. "I have a backpack in the car with some things for the journey," he said.

"You won't need it," Cumberland said, dismissing him completely. "I'm going to introduce you to some people. Some folks who know what the Sunlit Lands is. And after that, Darius, I'm going to ask you what you think should be done to the world. And then, son, then I'm going to let you do it. This is the way of it. Each generation, we got to hand it off to the next, see if they can find a better way forward."

"Who are we going to meet?" Darius asked.

"Oh, the Peasant King, and Patra Koja, and Malgwin, and a few others, too."

"How do we get there? When do we leave?"

"Say goodbye to your father, at least."

Right. Darius crossed to his dad, who stood up, grabbed him by the shoulders. "Be safe, Son. But also do the right thing."

"Tell Mom I'm sorry for sneaking out."

"You tell her yourself when you get back. Now I got to go wash those dishes."

Darius grabbed him and hugged him tight. "Thank you," he said. He wasn't even sure why he was thanking his dad. For watching over him? For saving him from those idiots in the parking lot? For taking care of him his whole life, for teaching him how to survive in this world? For helping him get to the Sunlit Lands again? All of that and more.

"Go on now," Dad said. "I don't want those eggs to get stuck to the pan."

"Oh, they're already stuck," Cumberland said. "Don't you scratch my pans!"

"I'm not watering those bush statues out front," Dad said.

Cumberland chuckled at that. "You always were afraid of plants." There was a door in the corner that Darius hadn't noticed before, leading out back. He pushed it open. "Come on then, Darius."

They stepped outside. Since they were on the second floor, Darius expected to walk out onto a balcony, but instead they were in a green meadow overlooking a forest. Darius took a deep breath. No exhaust, no sound of machines, no sulfur or plastic smell in the air. They were in the Sunlit Lands! A thrill of anticipation and triumph went through him. He couldn't believe it. He had made it back!

"I don't understand. We *drove* here."

"Close the door behind you, Darius. Yes, you drove to *my house*. The main level is on Earth, and the upstairs connects to the Sunlit Lands. You're still thinking like someone who has never seen magic."

So it was true. He was really back. "Watch yourself, Hanali," he said under his breath.

"I'd recognize it if I saw it," Cumberland said, teasing. "Come on now, we have a good distance to walk before we rest."

Cumberland started on a well-worn path through the grass, downhill and toward the forest. As Cumberland walked, he started to sing an old spiritual that Darius only half remembered. Darius grinned, his spirits buoyed by the easy entrance to the Sunlit Lands, the bright sky, the flash of color from the flowers in the field. There was a little garden near the path, a square of land full of fresh vegetables. He turned once to see his dad watching from the window of Cumberland's house. Darius raised his hand, and his father did the same, and then Darius was headed down the packed dirt of the path, listening to Cumberland's rich voice as it floated over the grassy field.

That heav'nly home is bright and fair,
Oh yes! Oh yes!
But very few can enter there,
Oh yes! Oh wait 'til I put on my crown
Wait 'til I put on my crown
Wait 'til I put on my crown
Oh yes, oh yes.

19

A STICK? OR A SNAKE?

Sometimes your greatest enemy is yourself.

FROM "THE BALLAD OF WU SONG," A KAKRI TALE

✦

Jason knew what he needed to do. He needed to interrogate himself. Figure out what was going on here. When he got back to camp, it was surrounded by Kharobem, an event that stressed the Kakri out but also filled them with glee. The Kharobem only assembled for truly significant occasions, and if you were fortunate enough to see them, you were about to be in an important story for sure.

"You've never told me your name," Jason said, helping the Kharobem girl down from the brucok.

She nodded, acknowledging what he had said. Okay. Well, so much for that. Still, she followed him wherever he went. He stopped a Kakri warrior. "Hey, where's Mother Crow?"

"In the war council."

Oh yeah. Right. That was Baileya. "Uh, no, where's *old* Mother Crow?"

The warrior had no time for him, was apparently on an assignment of some sort. He just kept walking without answering.

"Wu Song," a gruff voice called.

"Break Bones!" The Scim warrior had been sitting by a campfire, his monstrous form hunched down. Jason had thought he was a stone, to be honest.

"What brave deeds do you seek tonight?"

"Well, to tell you the truth, buddy, I've decided to save the world."

"Even so?"

"Even so. You want in on this?"

Break Bones grinned, showing off his many crooked, sharp teeth. "Nothing would please me more."

Another voice interrupted their conversation. "Mother Crow has put you under my keeping, Wu Song, and 'saving the world' sounds like a task more dangerous than you can survive."

"Ha. Shows what you know, Bezaed. I've been part of saving the world at least twice, depending on how you look at it."

Baileya's brother stepped into the firelight, thin and stern, his arms crossed. Jason knew that even with his arms crossed, both hands were close to the knives he kept at his waist. Not that he expected to get in a fight with the guy now that Baileya Crow had ordered him to take care of Jason.

"How many times have you nearly died?" Bezaed asked.

"Hmm." Jason took a quick mental tally. "Five? I don't know, could be more."

Break Bones chortled. "Did I hear, strong warrior, that thy sister has put thee in charge of this wastrel?"

"Not in charge," Jason said. "He's supposed to protect me."

"Yes," Bezaed said. "In charge of my own future brother-in-law."

"Ex–future brother-in-law," Jason said. "Baileya broke up with me, remember?"

"No memory gives me more pleasure." He flopped by the fire and threw a stone into it. "Now I must follow a child and keep him safe, and tolerate his Scim friend who—it is no small thing to say—is a gifted warrior but a terrible companion."

"Better that than a gifted companion but a terrible warrior," Break Bones said, laughing.

"Let's get one thing clear," Jason said. "You might be my babysitter, but you are not the boss of me."

Bezaed's face contorted in disgust. "Humans sit on babies? Disgusting."

"Ugh, never mind. The point is, I'm the one in charge here."

Break Bones took out a stone and began to sharpen his ax. "I thought you humans liked to put things to a vote. I do not recall voting for you."

"Whose side are you on, anyway? Look, here's the thing. You both know that I am extremely gifted at sneaking away and causing trouble when no one is looking. Agreed?" Break Bones and Bezaed exchanged glances, then nodded. "So maybe I'm not in charge, but I'm going to tell you what I'm doing, and then if you want to go along and make sure I don't get murdered, killed, maimed, or crushed, you can if you want."

"My sister said nothing about preventing maimings."

"Fine," Jason said. "Break Bones, you're in charge of preventing any maimings."

"I happen to enjoy maiming people."

"Okay, right. You're in charge of maimings in general then. You choose who gets them. But not me. No maimings for Wu Song. Get it?"

"Got it."

"Good." Jason pointed at the Kharobem girl. "No maimings for her, either. She already has a bum leg."

"Agreed," Break Bones said. "Now. What is the first order of business?"

"First, I'd like to interrogate myself."

Bezaed perked up a bit. "Can I torture you to help you get answers?"

Jason glared at him. "The *other* me."

"Humph. Less fun," Bezaed said. "And he's under guard with strict orders that no one is allowed to be in the tent other than him."

"That makes sense. We'll have to get Baileya to tell them it's okay."

"She's in the war council, which is where I should be," Bezaed said. "She won't take time out of it for this small matter."

"Small matter? They're just planning a war. We're saving the world. Speaking of which . . . Break Bones, why aren't you in the war council? Don't they want the Scim on their side against the Elenil?"

"I've been away too long," Break Bones said. "I cannot speak for the Scim."

Away for too long meant that he had been watching over Jason in the desert for a while, something Jason hadn't known until recently. He would have felt a lot safer if he had known Break Bones was wandering around out there, keeping an eye on him. "Do you know what tent he's in at least, Bezaed?"

"Indeed, brother, I know where he is being kept."

"So show us the way."

Bezaed led them through camp, Jason close behind him. The girl limped beside him, and Break Bones took up the rear, his great ax over his shoulder. If anyone tried to get past Bezaed or Break Bones, Jason felt sorry for them. He hadn't met two fiercer warriors in the Sunlit Lands. Except Baileya, whom he felt certain could lay them both out flat.

The little Kharobem took his hand. "You need a name," Jason said. "I can't keep calling you 'the girl.'"

She looked up at him with wide brown eyes but said nothing in response.

"Your name is a story, I'm guessing?"

She nodded.

"And it would take a long time to say it to a human?"

More nods.

"Okay. Well. Can I give you a human nickname?"

She smiled.

"I'll take that as a yes. Sometimes you turn into a lioness. So I'm thinking something related to that. It's a unique trait of yours, for sure. How about Toni? Like Tony the Tiger?"

"She's a lion, not a tiger," Break Bones said.

"True. But they're a little lax about animal identification around here."

The girl shook her head.

"Tawny?"

No.

"Nala?"

No.

"MGM? That's like a movie lion. Pretty famous."

More head shaking.

"I don't know. Pawla. Because you have big paws?"

No.

"Clawdia? Because of your claws?"

She grinned and nodded.

"Ha. Okay, Clawdia it is."

"A pleasure to meet you at last," Break Bones said, and she inclined her head toward him.

"Here we are," Bezaed said. Two guards stood outside the tent, both of them lean and muscled in the way Kakri people tended to be, their dark-tan skin shiny and lighter where they were scarred. The Kakri didn't use magic for healing, and they spent a lot of time training with knives and other pointy objects. Scars were pretty typical.

"Hi there," Jason said. "I'm Wu Song. Nice to meet you. I've come to talk to the prisoner."

One of the guards said, "We are under strict orders that until Mother Crow says otherwise, only the prisoner is allowed in the tent."

"A good try, brother," Bezaed said. "Now let's go and drink yak's milk and eat some hare, and then you can sleep until Mother Crow calls for you."

Wait a minute. Jason leaned close to one of the guards. "Did you see the prisoner?"

"Of course."

"And did you notice that he looked . . . similar to anyone here?"

The guards exchanged glances. "We noticed."

"I guess what I'm trying to say is, *I'm* probably allowed to go in there because *I am* the prisoner. Right?"

One of the guards seemed nervous. "We're just trying to follow Mother Crow's orders. Bezaed, what do you say?"

Bezaed looked Jason over carefully, and then a devious smile came onto his face. Jason did not like that devious smile. He did not like it one bit. "I think, friends, that if you are in the desert and think a stick might be a snake, it's unwise to pick it up. If Wu Song says he is the prisoner, then it seems to me he should be tied up and put under guard."

"Uhhh, that's not exactly what I was suggesting," Jason said, backing away.

Break Bones leaned close to his ear. "An ingenious way to get access to the prisoner," he whispered. "Bezaed and I will await your signal out here. You'll be perfectly safe."

And that's how, much faster than Jason would have hoped, and much tighter than he would have requested, Jason ended up bound hand and foot and tossed into the tent, where he landed with a thump on his chest, next to TJ, who was tied to a stake, his hands behind him.

"So they caught you, too?" TJ said.

Jason shook his head. "Nah, it's me, Jason. Your buddy is still out there somewhere." Sigh. Stupid truth telling! He could have tried to trick the guy. Of course, the last time he tried to trick someone had ended with him being tied up and thrown in this tent. There were so many disadvantages to being honest. On the other hand, he never had to keep his stories straight, and he never got caught lying. Perks! "I wish I could lie to you about it, but that's the truth. It's me, the real Jason."

TJ nodded. "Telling the truth is always superior."

"So," Jason said. "You're not me."

"But I am you," TJ replied.

"Uh. So I'm you?"

"No, you are not me. I'm you."

"I'm me."

"And so am I."

"You're really frustrating," Jason said, and there was a cackle of laughter from outside the tent. Break Bones and Bezaed both.

"It's like you just met yourself for the first time," Bezaed said, his voice carrying through the thin walls of the tent.

"Shut up," Jason said. And then, apologetically to TJ, "Not you. Those guys out there."

"I knew what you meant."

"So what's the deal? Why are you me? Is this a time-travel thing? Alternate dimensions? Multiverse? Mass hysteria?"

"Nothing so complicated," TJ replied. "But I'm not allowed to tell you. When you come to my leader, he will explain everything to you. Your friends have already gathered there."

"How do I even know that's true? Break Bones is here, Baileya is here. Even Bezaed is here, so I know you're not going too deep in the friends list."

TJ smiled. Jason couldn't help but feel weird about it, like seeing himself in a mirror, but the mirror was doing something different than he was. He had seen enough horror films to know that when your mirror self started doing something different than you were doing, it was time to make a run for it.

"Shula," TJ said. "Yenil. Kekoa. David. The Knight of the Mirror. Or what about Delightful Glitter Lady? You have been blessed with many friends."

"How do you know so much about me? How do you know who my friends are? And why are you trying to get them all together? What is going on?"

"The end of the world is coming," TJ said. "You might have heard."

"I did hear that, actually, just recently. I'm planning to stop it."

"So you can marry Baileya."

"I mean, obviously."

"Smart," TJ said. "We want to help."

"Oh, I see. So you're the helpful kind of kidnappers."

"Yes!" TJ was so obviously pleased that Jason had figured out that they were helpful kidnappers that he felt bad letting the guy down.

"Helpful people don't kidnap each other," Jason said. "There's a fundamental lack of trust on display when you force someone to go somewhere they don't want to go." He raised his voice so those outside the tent could hear him. "In fact, any time you're tying someone up, that's a pretty fundamental sign that you're not being a very good friend."

Break Bones and Bezaed roared with laughter. Jason could practically see them trying to hold each other up, they were laughing so hard.

"I'm not your friend!" Bezaed called back.

"Are we friends?" TJ asked.

"No! You're driving me crazy. In addition to kidnapping me and dragging me through the desert, I just generally find you annoying, and I'm glad they have you tied up. Which, if you're actually me, makes perfect sense because people are always chasing me, tying me up, trying to kill me, or getting me to say stuff that I probably shouldn't say but I can't help myself because I promised to be honest."

TJ leaned toward him. "Do you want to see something interesting?"

"Ugh. It sounds creepy the way you say it. Is it a card trick? I love card tricks, but it's hard to do them when you're all tied up."

"More like a rope trick," TJ whispered, and in a horrifying motion that seemed to happen way too fast, he dislocated both shoulders, did something behind his back, stood up, and the ropes fell away from him. Before Jason could shout, TJ had jumped over to him and covered his mouth with his hand. Jason tried to shout, but only a muffled fury came out.

"I wish I could get a single answer out of you," TJ said loudly. "But no, you are just sitting there not telling me anything and meanwhile I'm all tied up—" TJ was tying Jason to the pole as he said this. "And there you are, also tied up to that pole."

"How the heck did you do that?" Jason asked, half in wonder and half in disgust. "Guys, guys, you better get in here. Fake me just got untied—hurry!"

TJ's face looked way more evil than Jason thought he could get his own face to look. But, well, he was learning more about himself all the time. TJ picked up the discarded ropes, there was a weird crackling noise like bones shifting against one another, and he fell to the ground, the ropes tied around his hands and feet.

Break Bones, Bezaed, and both guards practically fell over each other coming into the tent. Bezaed scowled. "That was not funny," he said, looking straight at TJ.

Jason realized what had happened in a sudden, horrible rush. "Oh no."

"I wasn't joking," TJ said. "Fake me really did get loose."

Bezaed walked behind Jason, looked at his ropes. "He's tightly bound now." He came back around, squinted at Jason, then told the guards, "Tighten his bonds."

"No," Jason said. "No need for that. Also, I'm the real me. HEY, OW!" Those were very tight. He couldn't feel his fingers.

Bezaed untied TJ, and the fake Jason winked. "Well, I didn't get anything useful out of him," TJ said. "He was just too smart for me."

"He's not," Jason shouted. "He's not too smart and he's a big jerk!"

Break Bones started to say something, looked at TJ for a moment, confused, then looked back to Jason. "He really does look like you, Wu Song."

"Yeah, but he's smarter than me, I have to admit it," TJ said, walking out of the tent. Bezaed and the guards followed.

Break Bones studied Jason for a long moment. "It seems that Wu Song is learning a lot about himself. I am curious how you have learned so much about him to be able to copy him so closely. I assume you are copying him, and not some magical double, or Wu Song's previously unknown twin brother."

"Break Bones, it's me," Jason said. "And I get it, I understand why you might have your doubts, and I'm not asking you to untie me. Unless, you know, you're open to that because these are really tight. You have to watch that guy carefully. And don't let him near Baileya, whatever you do."

"Hmm," Break Bones said. "Very convincing."

Then he ducked under the tent flap and was gone.

20

A TRUE ELENIL

*The one thing I love about the Elenil more than
anything else is how they can't take a joke.*

FROM "THE BALLAD OF WU SONG," A KAKRI TALE

✦

Gilenyia was doing her best to keep her face neutral, here in the
Palace of a Thousand Years: the high seat of the archon, the center
of the Elenil's power. She was here at Hanali's invitation to meet
the Herald of Mysteries, the Scim prophet who had grown such a
large following in recent months.

A completely still face would not be a surprise to Hanali. Gilenyia had
a reputation for coldness, a reputation she embraced with serene calcula-
tion. Those who knew her well—those precious few—understood that the
perceived coldness was not because she lacked emotion, but rather the
opposite. Her emotions raged with such unchecked passion that she feared
giving them the smallest avenue for expression. She needed time to examine
them and had learned to sear herself with white-hot self-control, leaving
only unfeeling scars as far as anyone around her could tell.

What she felt now was fear, overwhelming and all-encompassing. New Dawn could probably sense it, and Ricardo seemed to have some idea what was happening. She tried to find the telltale signs and eliminate them. It wouldn't do to have Hanali notice. She could feel the pulse in her neck, so she wore a high collar. She wanted to whisper her every word—some primitive idea that she wouldn't be noticed if she were quieter—so she made sure to pronounce her words with clarity and proper volume. She found herself holding her breath, then gulping down air, so she adjusted her breathing, making a conscious effort to do it calmly rather than trusting her body to be in control. She flinched at the slightest noise, and the only solution seemed to be that she must let her guard down completely.

The one thing she could not control was the shaking. Hanali had already noted this. He had dismissed it, saying, "My words fill you with a strange excitement. I know. I, too, feel this. A fundamental shift is taking place in the Sunlit Lands. How wonderful that we are at the center of it." She did not know if he was referring to his plan to ascend to become archon or if he was referring to his veiled suggestion that they be married, but both filled her with some measure of terror.

It wasn't that Hanali was wholly objectionable as a mate. She had known him her whole life, and she did have affection for him. But she couldn't avoid the feeling—try as she might—that he desired to marry her in part because she had always been above his station. Because she would bring a certain respectability to his reign as archon. And she feared Hanali saw marriage as a way to *tame* her. She wasn't sure why she felt this to be true, but she had learned that interrogating these sorts of instincts rarely produced answers, just certainty that her feelings were valid. She had done her share of taming things over the years, and she sensed Hanali circling her, as surely as a lion sensed its tamer in the ring.

Gilenyia's fear of Hanali in authority over the Sunlit Lands was more complex. He had always expressed a desire to change certain things. He felt the Scim had been treated unfairly and that young Elenil were looked down on. He had disliked Archon Thenody, though now that the archon had been murdered, Hanali's feelings toward him had softened. This bitterness toward the humans was new, though. Gilenyia tried to trace back the roots of it and thought it may have originated around the same time as

Madeline's death but could have started earlier—like when Hanali's own father, Vivi, was killed in battle at the Festival of the Turning.

If Hanali was building a detailed and intricate plan that turned on the removal or death of all the humans, and he was doing it all while dealing with unresolved grief or anger, what would he be capable of if he were completely aware of his own motivations?

"Not him," Hanali said, and Gilenyia came into the present with a sudden jolt.

She looked around, confused. "Not who, Hanali?"

"The human," he said. "Your Scim servants can come in if you like, but not the human."

"Ricardo? He's completely trustworthy. I'd stake my life on it."

"Nevertheless," Hanali said mildly.

Gilenyia's emotions flared: terror, fury, frustration, pride. But externally she showed only a mild look of inconvenience. "Very well, I'll enter unattended. All three of my servants will await me here."

The three servants bowed their heads, just as she had taught them. The great double doors swung shut, and Hanali escorted her toward the mural room, a large receiving chamber with detailed paintings of the history of the Elenil upon its walls. "You are not unattended," Hanali said. "I am here with you, Cousin."

She put her arm through his. He had called her Cousin again, perhaps a test to see if she was considering his subtle not-quite-proposal. She had not decided what to do, but it would be wise to leave the door open. Or, at least, to make Hanali believe it was open. "Nevertheless, my dear," she said, "we will need some mechanism to decide which humans are to be trusted. Surely you cannot intend to remove every single one of them."

"Perhaps I have been unclear, my lady, but that is precisely my intention."

She studied him. He was less ostentatious today. Almost reserved. He wore a gold and silver brocade jacket with roses worked into it. She thought, in fact, she had seen him wear it before, an almost shocking possibility. A white, high-collared shirt with a silver cravat. Golden trousers and silver boots. No capes or hats, no form-changing accoutrements. She herself wore a high-necked, long-sleeved dress—also silver—that fell to her toes, though the coordination with Hanali's outfit was by happenstance.

Unless Hanali had somehow discovered what she planned to wear, which would not surprise her.

"Ricardo will be disappointed not to meet the Herald of Mysteries. He has been seeking an audience for some time now, on my instructions. I have been curious to learn more about him."

Hanali laughed merrily. "And I have set up an appointment for you with nothing but a few carefully extended invitations and requests. There are some benefits to being in a relationship with the proxy magistrate and future archon."

"Indeed," she said, patting his hand. "Now, before we are face-to-face, tell me what you know of this Herald of Mysteries."

"It will be far more entertaining for you to see for yourself. I have invited many celebrated Elenil to join us and have reserved seats near the front for us, with the magistrates."

Hanali was always true to his word with such promises. Gilenyia found herself seated beside the basileus, Prinel, himself. He was flanked by two of his soldiers, Sochar and Rondelo, both of whom greeted her warmly. Tirius was there as well as the rest of the magistrates and a variety of the most interesting and influential members of Elenil society. Servants mingled with trays of drink and food, all of them, she noted, tame Scim. Not a single human to be found. It was, indeed, a topic of some conversation. It was unlike Hanali to miss an opportunity to platform his little pets from Earth. He begged for Gilenyia's leave to go care for his guests, which she granted readily.

Rondelo walked beside her as she mingled in the crowd. He was younger than she—not many Elenil were—and had distinguished himself often in the war against the Scim. Hanali had suggested more than once that Rondelo might well become the leader of the Elenil army sometime in the next fifty years. It was wise to remain friends with him. This was easy in Gilenyia's opinion. Rondelo was kindhearted, and he made friends easily enough. He had a natural affection for anyone who treated him well, and this included a deep bond with his white stag, Evernu. She had often seen the two of them in the marketplace, patrolling for misdeeds in the streets of Far Seeing.

"Have you seen this herald?" she asked Rondelo.

"No, and not for lack of trying," he replied. "He has caused some trouble for the city guards. His followers are growing, and they look to him as their true authority."

"I've heard he's Scim," Sochar said, spitting out the last word. Gilenyia did not know this guard as well as Rondelo. She had heard he had a temper, and she knew he rode upon some great cat. A lion, perhaps.

"Peace," Rondelo said.

"We will have peace when the Scim are all in their proper places," Sochar said, taking a small roasted apple from a Scim servant and popping it into his mouth. The servant said nothing, only offered the tiny apples to Gilenyia and Rondelo, who waved him away.

"And where is that?" Gilenyia asked. "In the Wasted Lands? Or serving us here?"

"Or a prison. Or a grave. Beyond that, there is no place for them."

"You are too harsh and too quick to anger," Rondelo said. "Again I say, peace, Sochar."

Hanali had been wise to invite these two. Though Sochar was not influential or well-known, she could see that he reflected a certain stratum of Elenil opinion. She decided she would sit with them rather than with the influential Elenil on Hanali's seating chart. "Gentlemen, let us find a seat, that we may best see things when the Herald of Mysteries begins his speech."

"We have seats over here, lady," Rondelo said. "But surely Hanali—"

"Will be too busy hosting to worry about me," she said smoothly, following them to their seats.

Hanali stood upon the stage now, and she had to admit that he looked fine in his silver and gold, with the brightly colored murals behind him and encircling the room. He looked as if he were being painted into Elenil history, but as if the artist were taking extra time in deciding on his colors. Another evidence of Hanali's subtlety and care.

"My dear friends," Hanali said, "and most honored magistrates. It is astonishing to see you all assembled in one room. What a testament to the wisdom of the Majestic One that he would choose a people such as this to rule over all the Sunlit Lands, to care for it and the people whom the Majestic One set aside to live in their places."

She noticed the careful way he spoke. According to the stories, the Majestic One had chosen humans to live upon Earth, not in the Sunlit Lands. Hanali had not played his hand yet, but he had laid the groundwork. She doubted a single person other than herself knew what he meant by this statement, but she saw the way he would be using it in days to come. *The Elenil must care for those whom the Majestic One chose to live in the Sunlit Lands . . . which includes all our people other than the humans.*

"He has always spoken well," Rondelo said.

"Too many words and too little action," Sochar said sulkily.

"I am pleased to welcome among us an influential prophet," Hanali continued. "As you know, I have a particular affinity for oracles and soothsayers."

A wave of mirth passed through the audience. Hanali was known for choosing his outfits for parties based on the advice of fortune-tellers. This statement was carefully crafted as well, Gilenyia noticed. It was self-deprecating but also drew attention to his simpler, more reserved clothing choice for today. This signaled his seriousness and no doubt made more than a few think, *Perhaps the young fop could lead well if he were installed as archon,* as well as lending weight to the message of the herald, whatever it might be.

"But you are not here to listen to me," Hanali said, another modest saying designed to remind them all of the opposite. They were there precisely because he had invited them, because he had told them it would be important. "So allow me to introduce the Herald of Mysteries." He stepped to the side and took a seat upon the stage.

Interesting. She thought Hanali would have insisted on using the herald's true name, to show that the Elenil were peers at the very least with the herald. But he had used the title as if implying that perhaps this office of herald was one with some value.

The Herald of Mysteries entered from behind the curtain. He was not tall for a Scim, and a good bit less muscular than most. Gilenyia leaned forward. It appeared that he was not wearing his war skin. Even tame Scim kept their war skins on in the presence of strangers. To tame them required a great deal of attention and work, including filing down their tusklike teeth. But this young man—and he was young—looked less Scim than most tame ones. His black hair was braided back from his face. He wore simple Elenil clothing, and his expression was placid. If he were not a Scim, she might even have described him as "regal."

"I know him," Sochar said. "I swear it. Does he look familiar to you, Rondelo?"

"There is some familiar line," Rondelo mused.

Yes. There was something familiar to him, though many things were unfamiliar. She had never, in hundreds of years, seen a Scim without their war skin. Not a living one, in any case. She tried to imagine him with a heavier brow, thicker muscles, and more teeth, and a memory tickled the back of her mind. But try as she might, she could not bring it to the fore.

"Poverty," the Scim said, his voice booming through the room. "Poverty and ignorance. Such was my life in the Wasted Lands. I knew nothing and owned less. My elders, who should have taught me the way of the world, taught me only to be a victim. They taught me to cry out and claim the Elenil as the aggressors who had taken the world from me. 'If not for the Elenil,' they said, 'you would be rich. If not for the Elenil,' they claimed, 'you would be well-fed.'"

The entire audience was captivated, as much by the young Scim's hypnotic delivery as by the words. Gilenyia was not, she realized, the only one leaning forward in her seat. She checked herself, bringing her emotions under control, smoothing her face, sitting back, straight, in her chair. An interesting child, she admitted. She could see why Hanali hoped their messages might intersect.

The Herald of Mysteries continued. "It is not their fault. The Scim. They have been deceived. They have misunderstood the Majestic One. How many times have I heard a perverted version of some story of the Majestic One, twisted through a victim's lens? How many times did they call him 'the Peasant King' as if there were some inherent glory to being poor? How many times did they try to convince me that the Majestic One was 'just like us'? How many times did they succeed? A hundred? A thousand? More than that! A million! A hundred million! And so I continued in my poverty. And so I persisted in my ignorance, as my kind has for generations." He paused, choking on emotion. "We even fell so far as to raise our hands against the Elenil, the people chosen by the Majestic One to enact his will in the Sunlit Lands." His face contorted with fury. "And who is responsible for this? At whose doorstep can we lay the blame for this?" He paced the stage as if getting the strength to say what must be said. "You," he thundered at last. "You Elenil, you are to blame!" He whirled on Hanali. "Not least of all Hanali, son of Vivi!"

Hanali's face went pale as an angry murmur shot through the crowd. Sochar was half out of his seat, Rondelo's hand on his forearm, pulling him back down. "Patience," Rondelo said. "Hear all his words."

The herald slumped as if all his energy was gone. Hanali rushed to him, helped him into a chair that had been set at the center of the stage. Was this planned? Had Hanali known about this? Was it rehearsed? Gilenyia of all people knew he was capable of such a thing, but his panic seemed real, the young Scim's collapse authentic. Hanali gave him water, carefully waited on him.

The Scim smiled weakly. "Even now, Hanali, when I have publicly decried you, what do you do? You bring me water. You wait on me as if I am your better." He turned to the audience. "Do you see? You Elenil have forgotten your place. You are here in the Sunlit Lands to rule, not to serve. Too often you coddle us. Too often you listen to our cries and—instead of reminding us of our place—you disobey the very decrees the Majestic One left for us."

"What do you mean?" Hanali asked. "I beg you, though you are a Herald of Mysteries, enlighten us, sir!"

"'Sir'? You *beg* me? So polite. And, forgive me, so misguided. The humans, you know. It was the Elenil who brought them here. The Majestic One was clear. They would live upon another Earth. But the Elenil sought to create a new class of servant. They took the place of the Scim. You should have ridden out among us and brought justice, and instead you brought in another race, an artificial Scim, to serve you. To fight us. And thus you kept us in poverty. Thus you reinforced our ignorance."

Hanali objected. "In times of great need, the humans were allowed to return."

"Great need," the Scim repeated. "What of Wu Song—a human we are both well acquainted with—what great need had he? What great need counterbalances the trouble he brought upon the Sunlit Lands? Is it any surprise that people from every corner of our world seek to kill him?"

Hanali fell back as if he had received a physical blow. "You do not understand," he said.

"No! I do not understand! Explain it to me, O wise Elenil! Speak, I am your servant! Speak, I am listening!"

"The Scim *are* oppressed," Hanali said. "Surely we can agree on this. I am well-known among the Elenil as a spokesperson on their behalf."

"A well-intentioned but poorly reasoned conclusion," the herald said lightly. "Far be it from me to educate my betters. But would you hear more on this topic?"

Hanali appeared conflicted, but several Elenil shouted, "Let him speak!"

"I will tell you my own story," the young Scim said. "Then let you decide the truth. When I was a child, I was orphaned and living in poverty."

"Precisely," Hanali said. "The Scim live in objectionable conditions."

"But why was I orphaned? Because my parents fought the Elenil and lost their lives in battle. What if they had accepted their lot? They would have lived, and I would not be an orphan today. Nevertheless, my siblings and I grew in stature and skills among our people. We were taught to fight, to wear our war skin, to spit at the name *Elenil*."

"I see tattoos on your skin," Hanali interjected. "So you must have accepted some authority of the Elenil."

"I did not serve the Elenil, I bargained with them. 'Give me some bit of bread for this skill or that use of time. Give me a crooked hut, and in exchange I will sift your garbage.' The Majestic One intended us to serve and the Elenil to care for us. But neither was true in my childhood."

Hanali sat, produced a handkerchief, dabbed at his forehead. Gilenyia marveled. If this was an act, he played the part to perfection. Even she worried for him and where this conversation might lead.

"I will be brief. I came—rightly—under suspicion from Elenil peace-keepers. I was helping to hide a criminal. You will object that I was only a child, and that is true. But I did it with full knowledge and full intention to cause harm. An Elenil here in this room arrested me, and I raged against him. I insulted the great Archon Thenody. I spit at him. And one of the Elenil, who sits here even now, pierced me with an arrow."

Rondelo and Sochar were whispering to one another now, with some urgency. "It's him," Sochar said. "I tell you it's him."

"I hold no ill will against him," the herald said. "Sochar knew no better. He struck out at the unnatural state of the world, not at me."

Many eyes turned toward them now. Sochar flushed in embarrassment, but before he could speak, Rondelo again squeezed his forearm. "Be silent, Sochar. Anger now will be regret later."

"I nearly died," the Scim said. "But Archon Thenody sent his own to find me. To bring me back here, to this very palace. They nursed me back to health. The Lady Gilenyia, a true Elenil, saved my life when I did not deserve it. The archon helped me to understand, taught me to see. There is a natural order to the world, and when we turn it upside down it is foolish to complain when the coins fall from our pockets."

Actual conversations were breaking out in the hall now, and Hanali tried to call them back for attention, but it was getting away from him. "I brought humans to help, not harm," Hanali called, and there were angry shouts back to him. They weren't going to install him as archon, they were going to tear him apart.

"One more word," the herald shouted. "I beg you!" The crowd settled and grew silent. "My war skin name, once upon a time, was Nightfall. I have set that name and that skin aside. They are lies, built on deceit, and their foundation is pride and ignorance. Today I am neither poor nor ignorant. To that I owe Rondelo's sense of justice. Sochar's arrow. Gilenyia's mercy. Archon Thenody's instruction. And yes." He smiled. "Even Hanali's tender heart. My message is a simple one. We must rebuild the world according to the Majestic One's instructions. There is a time and a place for my people, and for yours, and for the humans. We are told the Majestic One will return and reward those who serve him, and punish those who do not. And what will he find in the Sunlit Lands when that day comes? As for me," he said, bowing, "my place in that day will be—as it should always have been—as your humble servant." He exited the stage, and the crowd burst into furious discussion.

Hanali sat upon the stage, exhausted. He caught Gilenyia's eye and smiled wearily. The magistrates were already moving to encircle him, hands gesticulating in wild conversation. He held her gaze for a long moment—longer than she expected he would in the presence of the magistrates—then threw his hands in the air and began to defend himself.

Gilenyia tapped her teeth with a gloved finger. Three weeks, Hanali had said, and he would be archon. Now she rather suspected three days. Who better to rid the land of the humans than he who brought them in? She swept out of the reception hall, her mind replaying the speech. *Gilenyia, a true Elenil,* the herald had said. Her heart beat harder, and she put her fingers against the artery in her neck. It felt like it could break, so swift and fierce was the heartbeat there. A true Elenil, he had said. Why did the public pronouncement make her feel less assured?

She found her servants, and they made their way back to her home. She would not hear from Hanali again today, she was certain. She needed time to think. She felt she was on a ledge near a great precipice, and it was crumbling away beneath her feet. It was time to decide whether to go back or push ahead.

21

THE HIGHEST HEAVEN

*The Peasant King had built the Sunlit Lands from
his own heart and with his own two hands.*

FROM "THE TRIUMPH OF THE PEASANT KING," A SCIM LEGEND

✢

"You must have heard stories about the Peasant King," Cumberland said.

Yes, Darius had heard stories. The Peasant King was one of the favorite figures in Scim mythology. He made the world, he solved problems, he showered gifts upon the righteous poor and judgment upon the wicked rich. "A few."

Cumberland paused. "Take in that view." They had hiked through the woods, the trees thinning as they ascended. The rock grew increasingly bare as they moved upward, and now they stood on a mountain of some sort, the whole of the Sunlit Lands spreading below in a view that Darius had only seen before when he was flying one of the Scim's gigantic birds. "Look there, you can see the curve of the crystal spheres above us. To the west there, the Ginian Sea. And that's Maduvorea just over there . . . not the forest we hiked through, but farther north, do you see?"

Darius knew the geography of the Sunlit Lands well enough. He had made it his business to learn it when he was preparing for battle against the Elenil. Knowing where there was a cave to slip into, a ravine with no exit, or a thick copse of trees could be an advantage. Today they were farther south than he typically went, possibly in the Southern Court, even, though he didn't know the name of this mountain, and he had never heard of a wood known as Maduvorea. He took a deep breath. The air tasted of fresh trees and a hint of wild strawberries. It was just cool enough to bring some relief to the heat from walking.

"Have you met him? The Peasant King?"

Darius shook his head. Hadn't he already answered this? "Madeline said she did."

"Do you believe her?"

"Sure," Darius said. "She never lied to me, and she had a way of seeing things I didn't. Sometimes, anyway."

"Right. Because sometimes you saw things that she didn't."

Darius shrugged. "She grew up rich in a white family. Of course there were some things she didn't know because of that."

"Makes sense," Cumberland said. "A wonderful person, though, wasn't she?"

"Yeah," Darius said. "Yeah, I guess Mom and Dad must have told you about her."

"Your parents have given me lots of updates about your life. I'm sorry I wasn't more personally involved. But my responsibilities in the Sunlit Lands keep me busy." Cumberland pointed up the path. Through the sparse trees, Darius could see a glint of gold or copper. "That's where we're headed."

"What is that, a dome or something?"

"Something for sure." Cumberland climbed with renewed energy. "It's strange, isn't it? Hiking in the woods?"

Darius hadn't thought of it like that. "Well, being alone in the woods is not something I love to do for fun if that's what you're getting at."

"Sure. Because you don't know what might happen to you. That's where Black people disappear sometimes."

"Could be, yeah. Not like it's never happened."

"You're right," Cumberland said, and just then they came completely out of the trees and Darius saw the gleaming thing ahead. It was a gigantic birdcage, maybe thirty feet tall. There was a door, open on one side, that was about eight feet tall.

Darius immediately regretted the choices he had made that day. He had left his dad behind, had believed Dad when he said Cumberland could be trusted. He had left the dagger at the gentle insistence of this man he had never met and then hiked with him through isolated hill country. He didn't have weapons or anything else, and now this man had lured him to a gigantic cage far away from anything or anyone.

It wasn't like Darius hadn't fought before. He was sore from this morning's fight, but he thought he still had an advantage over this old man. His fists rose, almost of their own volition, ready to strike.

The old man laughed and laughed, and stepped into the cage. He slapped his knee like some character out of an old-timey cartoon. "It's not a cage, son," he said. "Don't worry, I'm getting in it too. You and me together!"

"I'm not getting in that cage," Darius said. "Why would I?"

"Look at it more closely, Darius. Look at the top."

The bars of the cage met and were welded together, and a thick ring protruded upward, large enough that a man could stand in it and stretch his hands above his head and not touch the top. The ring had deep scoring on it, as if it had been hooked by some giant thing and lifted over and over. "What is that?"

"It's not a cage," Cumberland said again. "Think of it as a gondola."

"Gondola? I thought those were boats."

"Like in the mountains. The little covered cable cars that carry you up the slope."

"Where's the cable?"

"Get in, Darius, and I'll show you."

He hesitated, then stepped up and over the lip of the cage. "Now what?"

"Close the gate."

He did. Nothing happened. The gate didn't have a lock. He relaxed a little. It almost reminded him of the transportation of the Pastisians: they used hooks to connect small rooms to the crystal sphere of the sky. But there were no hooks.

"Cumberland, nothing's happening."

The old man was grinning. He gripped a bar with his left hand. "There's one more thing you have to do, Darius."

"What?"

"Hold on to your hat." He shouted, "Fantok! We're ready."

There was a shriek so loud that Darius jumped and covered his ears. Cumberland was laughing now, thrilled. He pointed toward the sky. An enormous orange and red bird of prey—*enormous* meaning the size of a small plane—was dropping toward them, claws extended. Darius gripped the bars.

The bird plummeted toward them and at the last possible moment flung its wings open, arresting its fall. Its claws grasped the cage ring, and the bird swept forward, the cage tipping and dragging for a moment before its great wings lifted them off the ground and into the air. Cumberland was still laughing, a look of joy on his face. "Amazing, isn't she?"

The wind and the sound of the flapping meant they had to yell to one another. "Is that a roc?"

"No, that's Fantok. She's one of a kind. I'll explain when we get to the meeting place."

They were far above the mountains now. Darius had been this high before—riding his owl, and when he was with the Pastisians. But it never got old, looking down on everything. "There's a Pastisian dirigible," Darius shouted, because there it was, headed south.

"Strange," Cumberland said. "Looks like it's going to the Southern Court! King Ian usually keeps his people closer to home."

"You know Ian?"

Cumberland laughed again. Something about being in the Sunlit Lands made him practically giddy, it seemed to Darius. "I know him, yes, and Queen Mary Patricia as well."

"She doesn't like to be called that."

Cumberland's eyes softened, and he looked sad for a moment. "No, I don't suppose she does."

Darius tucked his questions about the Pastisians away for later. He'd want to return to them. "Where's this meeting place?"

They were so high now. He could see almost the entire circle of the Sunlit Lands. Travel often didn't seem to take long enough in the Sunlit Lands—or sometimes it took too long. There was something wrong with the way time worked here, and it affected the distances, too, it seemed to Darius. From this height, the whole thing looked like a round table. He could see the arc of the sky clearly now . . . could see the crystal. Fantok was skimming along the top of the sphere.

A bit ahead of them, Darius saw the ball of fire that was inserted into the day sphere's surface. The sun was part of the closest sphere, which was why it moved so much faster than other, farther heavenly bodies. Fantok was flying straight toward it. "We're headed for the sun," Darius said.

"Don't worry, the flames won't hurt her," Cumberland replied. He sat down on the floor of the cage and rummaged through his sweater. He pulled out a pipe, loaded it, and tried to light it with a match. But the wind blew it out each time. "I should have known to light this when we were still on the ground."

"What about *us*?" Darius asked.

The great bird was flapping faster, gaining speed as she sought to catch up with the sun. The heat was getting more intense. The old man even took off his sweater. "I wouldn't suggest looking directly at the sun when we get closer," he said, chuckling.

Darius's grip on the bars tightened. He didn't like this feeling of being out of control. There was nothing he could do. Jumping out of the cage would be foolish . . . he would never survive the fall. Attacking the bird would be likewise foolish. His best option was to trust that, whatever was about to happen, it had all been done before, and the magic of the Sunlit Lands would somehow keep them safe.

Fantok banked suddenly, then dropped a good fifty feet. She was almost directly beneath the sun now, flying at a speed that made no scientific sense even for a bird of her enormous size. She let loose another ear-shattering shriek, then shot upward. Despite Cumberland's warning, Darius couldn't help but look at the sun.

The heat went from unpleasant to burning. Darius let go of the metal bars, and the feathers on Fantok's wings and tail caught fire. The bird shrieked again and flapped harder. Then they were in the flames of the sun itself, and Darius could see nothing but light, light all around him. He shouted, and then they were through.

Fantok coasted on the cool breeze above the sun. They were between the sun sphere and the moon sphere now. Smoke trailed behind Fantok, the last remnants of the flames snuffed out. Darius could smell a whiff of smoke on himself, but he was unharmed.

Cumberland sat, a smile on his bearded face, and puffed away merrily on his pipe. He held it up to Darius. "Better than a match any day."

Fantok coasted for a while before making slow, lazy strokes in the air as she moved to catch up with the moon. It didn't take long.

"We're lucky the moon is near the sun now. . . . It could be a long journey otherwise," Cumberland said. They slipped through the hole where the moon was suspended. Fantok flew for only a moment there, searching for something Darius couldn't see at first. "The planetary spheres," Cumberland explained. "They're at different heights but are all set close together, at least. And there are more holes in these spheres than most suspect. In fact, different folks in the Sunlit Lands get the orders of the spheres wrong, and . . . well, sometimes it changes, anyway. It's magic after all. Still, this first climb will be unusual."

The great bird set the cage down on top of the moon sphere, then landed beside it. She had to hunch over, as the distance between the moon and the next planetary sphere was not much. It was bright and warm from the sun sphere beneath them. "Follow me," Cumberland said. He clambered up Fantok's back to his shoulder and stood there, examining the crystal sphere above. Cumberland reached up, letting the crystal slide away beneath his fingers. "This is how the universe should be," Cumberland said. "Not how it is, but how it should be. There's some poetry to it."

Darius put his own hand out and felt the glassy smoothness of the sky as it rolled past. There was a planet gliding toward them, a white hole in the sky. Cumberland waited until it was in front of them, grabbed the lip, and pulled himself through. Darius almost missed it and had to leap backward from the bird's shoulder, his legs kicking in the space between planets and the moon, and then he pulled himself up too. A large feathered wingtip stuck through behind him, and Cumberland grabbed hold of it and yanked. The feather morphed into a hand, and Cumberland pulled a person from the level below . . . a woman with red and orange feathers instead of hair. Fiery wings rose up behind her, folded but aflame. It was strange, Darius thought, that in her bird form she had regular wings, but in her human form she had wings of flame. She wore a loose black shirt, black trousers, and boots.

She bowed and extended her hand. "Fantok," she said.

"Darius."

"You're both too humble," Cumberland said. "Fantok, you already know Darius, yes?"

Fantok nodded once. "I have often heard of him. Have watched him a few times."

"And Darius, this is Fantok, a sovereign of the Kharobem."

"The Kharobem? The beings who are made completely of story?"

Fantok clapped him on the shoulder. "Who isn't?"

There were ladders here, strapped to the upper side of the sphere below them. They unstrapped one and set it up so they could get through the next sphere. Cumberland asked Darius to pull the ladder up behind them. They did this through each of the planetary spheres until they came to the second-to-last one, the star sphere. The stars were almost like gems, cold and small and round. Cumberland got on the ladder and popped one out. The hole was smaller than a manhole cover, but they each managed to wedge their way through. Cumberland pushed the star back into its place.

There was a sumptuous room—or rather, a space like a room, as it had no walls—assembled on top of this sphere: an expensive-looking handwoven carpet, rich leather furniture, a wide oak table, and smaller tables beside the chairs. There was no sky above them, just one more crystal sphere, but far, far above. A soft, diffuse light filled the air. Kharobem flew all around them, like guards, though Darius had no idea what they would be guarding. "This sphere moves slowly," Cumberland said. "You shouldn't even feel it turning beneath us."

He didn't.

Darius noticed a bigger table surrounded by chairs as they moved farther through the "room," and each chair had a name and picture carved into it. The chairs were connected to the table and equidistant from one another. The stories always said the Peasant King's throne was a bale of hay, and where a seventh chair should have been there was, indeed, a bale of golden hay. Strange beings stood around the table: a hideous mermaid thing with sharp teeth, a humanoid creature made completely of stone and nearly twelve feet tall, a man made of leaves and vines, a winged cat, and a gigantic salamander that appeared to have flames licking along its skin.

"This is Malgwin," Cumberland said, gesturing toward the mermaid. "Ruler of the Sea Beneath, and champion of women who have been wronged, of children and especially orphans."

Darius knew enough to bow. "My lady." Malgwin's lip curled up, but she said nothing.

Cumberland continued the introductions. "This is the Stone of a Thousand Worlds. It has many names on many worlds. Some are unpronounceable, some too terrifying for humans to speak."

The stone face smiled. "You may call me Pookie. It is a name a human from your world gave me, once upon a time. I am told it is a name that is not frightening."

Darius bowed. "My pleasure, Pookie."

"He is a polite one," Pookie said, chuckling to itself.

"Patra Koja, the patron of growing things and healing magic."

The plant man nodded to Darius, his branch-like antlers swaying. Darius returned the nod.

"Remi, Guardian of the Wind."

The cat licked its paw and didn't look up. "Yes, yes, Cumberland. This is tedious. We all know each other."

"I am introducing Darius," Cumberland said.

The cat sighed. "You might as well finish, but I don't see why we all need to hear this. You could have informed the boy before you arrived."

"Arakam the dragon, lord of fire, poetry, and the spaces between."

"A pleasure," Darius said, bowing toward the salamander.

"The pleasure is mine," Arakam said, "though we meet in dark times."

"Fantok you've already met. Sovereign of the Kharobem."

Fantok nodded, then said, "In honor of our guest, let us all take on our human forms."

There was a murmuring from around the table, and then a flash of light. Malgwin had become a stunningly beautiful East Indian woman, wrapped in a sari that looked to be all the colors of the sea. The pallu that hung over her shoulder was the deepness of dark water before a storm, the petticoat the bluish green of clear water on a sunlit day. Much of the embroidery was the color of seafoam, and it was all intricately done.

The Stone of a Thousand Worlds was a bald, grey-skinned person, still a good bit too large to be truly human. Patra Koja was a dark-skinned man with a great beard and long locs. Arakam wore Greek robes and a wreath of laurels. He had long, dark hair, delicate features, and dainty hands. Remi looked exactly the same: a flying cat.

"Remi," Fantok said sternly. "Take on a human form. In honor of our guest."

"Pass," Remi said, flipped her tail in Fantok's direction, and leapt onto the table beside her chair, where she curled her tail around her feet. The others took their seats, too, leaving Darius and Cumberland standing.

Fantok looked at the assembly before her. "We wait only for the Peasant King to take his seat, and this council can begin."

"Indeed," Cumberland said, and sat upon the bale of hay. "Let us begin."

22

MOTHERS CROW

*It is common, but it is precious. As common and
precious as air. Would you rather have air or a diamond?
Would you prefer water or emeralds?*

FROM *THE WISE SAYINGS OF MOTHER CROW*

✛

Jason didn't like being tied to a post. He had never been tied to a post before, and he would have guessed he wouldn't like it, but now he was sure. He was too straight up and down, and if he tried to slouch, the ropes dug into his chest. His hands felt numb, which was a worrying sign. Not just because he couldn't feel them now, but that meant pins and needles later. He hated pins and needles. He was thirsty, and he was a little concerned about what would happen when he needed to use the restroom. He didn't imagine the Kakri guards were going to let him have much privacy.

Mother Crow had taught him that the most important part of being a storyteller was learning to tell the difference between what was true and what was not true. That meant you had to learn to listen to the world around you, to hear and see and smell and feel things and to sort it all out, figure out what it meant. When someone said something to you, you had to listen to the words, figure out why that person said them, and know the history in their life that led to the moment they said that thing.

It made sense. Two people could say the exact same words and mean something completely different. Or say things that seemed to be in conflict but actually had the same meaning. Sometimes people said something they didn't mean because they were scared or embarrassed or kind or just big liars. There were a lot of things to consider, a lot of shifting variables that you had to take into account when you were listening to someone tell a story. You did all this to learn from other people's stories so your own stories would be true and clear and make sense. Mother Crow said Jason had an advantage on the truth thing, but that he needed to learn to pay more attention, to gather more facts.

Mother Crow had taught him some exercises. She said he needed to learn to be in the present. Jason pointed out that he lived exclusively in the present, that he often didn't think about what was going to happen if he opened his big mouth. Mother Crow smiled gently and asked him, "Why did you spend so much time focused on your sister, Jenny? That was in the past."

"Yeah," he had said, "But that's an exception, not the rule."

"With Madeline," she said, "you were very worried that she would die. You made Baileya promise that she would watch out for her. That was worry for the future."

"Another exception," Jason said, and he'd rolled his eyes. "I get really worried when people are dying."

Mother Crow had given a fatigued nod as if Jason was losing the argument but she was too tired to run it all down. "I am sure you are right," she said.

"Ha," Jason said. "You're saying that, but you don't mean it."

She'd looked up at him, a twinkle in her eye, and said, "Ah, at last, you are here in the present in our conversation."

Oh, he had been mad after that. She had tricked him into admitting that he struggled to be where he was. "Enjoy the good, and experience the pain," she said. "Don't try to avoid what is bad or fear the loss of what is good, but notice what is happening with both."

The simplest exercise focused on just that— noticing. She taught Jason to stop worrying about everything and pay attention to all the signals his body was sorting through. He tried it now. His body was extremely uncomfortable. There was a burning at the place where he had started to lose feeling in his hands. The ropes had rubbed his wrists raw. His chest hurt where the ropes wrapped around him, his back where he leaned against the pole. His lips were parched, and his tongue was dry. As if it had noticed he was taking stock, his stomach started rumbling. He could feel the pulse in his neck.

He could smell the dry ropes, made from some sort of plant fiber. The tent had a faint smell of cured animal skin. He could smell himself, too long in the desert without a good dunk in a tank of water. He couldn't see much—night was falling. But there was a bright spot against the wall of the tent, which was likely a fire somewhere on the other side. He could see the shadow of the guards outside—which, come on guys, it was a tent. He could dig out the back of the tent. If he were free.

And he could hear. The guards shifting from time to time. The crackling of the fire, which meant it must be relatively close. The sound the sand made when someone walked past.

None of this gave him the sudden ability to get out. None of it gave him any insight into how to free himself. He sighed. Well, he could at least tell this part of the story well if he ever got the chance. "Gather around, children," he said to himself. "And I'll tell you the story of how I ended up getting executed because the Kakri thought I wasn't me."

"Quiet in there," one of the guards said.

"Meh," Jason said.

There was crunching in the sand. A light step, and another, almost dragging step. The guards shuffled, standing straighter, Jason thought. Which meant it must be someone important. Then he heard Baileya's voice, low and quiet, but he couldn't make out the words.

"Baileya!" he shouted. "It's me, Jason! They got the wrong guy tied up."

Baileya threw the flap open, her crow cape billowing behind her. "Silence," she said, furious. "Would you speak with such familiarity to Mother Crow, the leader of the Kakri?"

She sat in front of him, her legs folded, a good two feet away.

"Hi," he said. He had this sudden realization that if he couldn't convince her it was really him, this could be the last time he saw her. He could get executed or thrown in a cell or who knew what terrible thing, and he would never have a chance to say good-bye.

"It is appropriate for you to call me Mother Crow," she said.

"No offense, but I would really prefer to call you Baileya Crow because I feel really weird about the whole calling you Mom thing."

The flap of the tent opened again, and an old woman shuffled in, leaning on a staff.

"Mother Crow!" Jason said.

"No longer," the old woman said. "You may call me—"

"Listen," Jason said. "I'm just going to get your name wrong. You're going to tell me it's Lemaril, and I'm going to call you Lemon. So let's just simplify things and I'll call you Mother Crow and her Baileya Crow, and we'll all know who we're talking about."

Mother Crow leaned on her staff and laughed, a laugh that turned into a rasping cough. "Are we certain this is not the real Wu Song?"

"I am definitely the real Wu Song," he said. "Seriously. I promise. Pinkie swear."

"Do you have the real memories of Wu Song?" Baileya asked.

"Totally."

Baileya frowned. She turned to Mother Crow. "It concerns me that these doubles have his memories. It narrows what sort of magic we can be dealing with, and I need to know what the situation is so I can make plans with the war council."

"Agreed," Mother Crow said. "And I believe your theory is the only one that makes sense."

Baileya turned back to Jason. "I know who you are."

Jason slumped. "Oh, wow. That's a relief. You had me going for a minute there."

"There are only a few possible explanations for all these doubles."

"I'm thinking a cloning machine."

"The one that makes the most sense is that for some reason the people of the Southern Court have seen fit to take Wu Song's likeness."

"Uh, wait, you're talking about me in the third person. I think you mean to say '*your* likeness.' Meaning mine. Right?"

The Mothers Crow looked at one another. The older raised an eyebrow, and Baileya turned back to him, her expression unreadable. "Do you remember the Festival of the Turning?"

"Uh, yeah, of course I do. I had never seen a goat pull a cart before. Then Break Bones tried to murder us. But we escaped. And I jumped into the moat at Westwind, which is to say, I jumped into a medieval sewer."

"Yes," Baileya said. "And do you remember—"

"It was memorable is my point," Jason said. "Medieval sewers are really memorable."

Baileya held up a finger, and he stopped talking. "Do you remember seeing three White Skulls in the crowd?"

Oh yeah. He did. The Black Skulls were the elite fighting force of the Scim. They wore black skulls and boots and gloves with white clothing. But that night there had been three people in the crowd wearing black robes with white skulls, gloves, clothing. And when they got close, it turned out to be members of the Southern Court. Who were . . . *shape-shifters.*

Jason's jaw fell open. "So you think—"

"I know," Baileya said. "When you kidnapped Jason, you took him toward the South. We stopped you just before you passed into territories belonging to the Southern Court. That was my first thought. But we are preparing for war with the Elenil, and that was more pressing for a time. Now I must make a decision about what to do with the Southern Court. Only they have the sort of magic that would allow for this deep a transformation. But I do not understand what you want with Wu Song."

"Oh no," Jason said. "Man, I never did anything to the Southern Court, and now they're trying to kill me too? Is it really that hard for me to make friends?" He shook his head and clucked his tongue. "Well, at least the Maegrom seem to like me."

"I do not understand why you would kidnap Wu Song and take him to the Southern Court. Was it to try to gain power over me? Did you know that I would be Mother Crow? Is that why you harmed my predecessor?"

"That's a pretty good theory," Jason said. "Here's a question, though: If the Southern Court wanted to take my shape, fine, but how would they get my memories? Come on, that's just weird. It's not like I sat around telling them everything about myself."

"It's blood magic," Mother Crow said. "They would have had to take some of your blood somehow."

Baileya pursed her lips. "Mosquitoes?"

"It could be," Mother Crow said slowly. "Wu Song was particularly susceptible to them."

"Gross," he said. "Are you suggesting that members of the Southern Court turned into mosquitoes and sucked my blood so they could use magic to get my memories and take my shape?"

"It seems the most likely explanation," Baileya replied.

"Oh, boy," Jason said. "I'd love to go back and talk to myself in freshman year of high school. I thought I had it rough back then. 'Don't worry, buddy, it's not like a race of lizard people stole your memories and your shape. Not yet, anyway.'"

"Why do you say lizard people?" Baileya said.

"Uh, they are lizard people, right? I mean, they had scales when we saw them at the festival."

"Did they?" Baileya asked.

"I thought they did." Oh, man. He was going to mess this up. He was going to get banished to live with the lizard people. "I hope they don't eat live mice," he said under his breath. "I don't think I could get used to that."

Mother Crow shifted, putting more weight on her staff.

"You are tired," Baileya said to her, concern in her voice.

"Go lie down!" Jason said. "You shouldn't be walking around! Didn't you get a punctured lung or something?"

"You are the one who must learn quietness," Mother Crow said.

"You are the one who needs to stop busting my chops all the time," Jason shot back.

Mother Crow laughed again, a wet, raspy sound. "Are you certain, Mother Crow, that this is not your beloved?" she asked Baileya.

"Go and rest," Baileya said, and she escorted the woman to the exit of the tent and instructed the guards to take her. When they objected, she said, "I can keep watch on our prisoner until you return."

"So," Jason said, "what do we do now?"

"I am going to take you home," Baileya said.

"Wait, what? *Home* home? To see my parents?"

"I am going to return you to the Southern Court. And I am going to do it myself. War with the Elenil, this I know. I understand it. I know what is to be done and how to help my people survive it. But this unknown threat . . . it seems to me because it is unknown it requires the attention of Mother Crow. So I and a small party of my most trusted Kakri will accompany you. Their king and I will bargain. I will return you to them, and in exchange I will learn what I can about their plans."

"I really wish you would give them, uh, Jason instead of me."

Baileya crouched in front of him, slipped her hand in the sleeve of her blouse and pulled out a long, curved knife. He had seen her use this knife to completely disembowel a wylna once, when they were in the desert. She set it on her thigh, the blade balancing perfectly. "I need you to understand something," she said. "Wu Song is important to me."

"You're important to me, too, Baileya. Baileya Crow," he added.

Her face hardened. "Be silent and listen. Wu Song is the one true love of my life. He is my heart's blood. Do you understand?"

Jason felt the heat in his face. "I . . . yes, I understand."

"I am going to bring him with me to your Southern Court. If your people harm him at all, I will be angry in a way that your people have never seen. If Wu Song is hurt, I will use this knife to take your people apart as easily as quartering a chicken. I will turn my entire life and my entire people toward making sure that you never harm anyone ever again. He is something more than family to me, pretender. We are two halves of one soul, and when we found one another, I became complete again. Do you understand?"

Jason's heart was pounding blood through his body three times too fast. He knew that Baileya loved him, and he loved her too. But he had never heard her speak about it with such ferocity and passion. He felt honored and loved and unworthy of it all.

"Baileya—"

"Mother Crow," she said. "You will call me by my title when I speak to you of the future between our two peoples."

He cleared his throat. "Mother Crow. I lo—"

She gripped the knife tighter. "Do not presume to speak for my beloved," she said.

So this was really it. She didn't know it was him. She was taking him to the Southern Court, the same people who had tried to kidnap him, and she was going to deliver him to them, gift wrapped. Unless he could figure a way out. But in the meantime, who knew if he'd get another chance to talk to the most important Kakri leader? It seemed unlikely. He was just a prisoner.

"Mother Crow," he said. "Jason—Wu Song—he would want you to know that he loves you. He loves you so much it scares him. He never wants to be apart from you. He wants to tell you a story you've never heard before. He wants to tell you a new story every day, a story that only you would know." It was, in Kakri terminology, a promise of enormous wealth and generosity. To gift someone with a new story, an original story every day, a bit of wealth that you never shared with the community, was so lavish as to border on selfish. Now it was her turn to blush.

"Enough," Baileya said. She touched the knife so that the point turned toward him. "Remember my words." She crossed to the exit, paused. "We leave at dawn," she said. The guards arrived as she left.

Jason slumped against the pole. "Well, you've really done it this time," he said to himself. "I can't believe I got outsmarted by my own self." He thought of the way the other Jason had snapped his arms around to get in and out of the ropes and realized with an unpleasant shock that the guy had been using his shape-shifting powers. "And here I thought maybe I was double-jointed and just didn't know," he said. "How disappointing."

23
A STORY
OF HER OWN KEEPING

What is truth?

FROM *THE ANNALS OF THE HISTORIAN*

✚

"What is this place?"

Shula glanced back at Mrs. Oliver. They had just come within sight of Far Seeing: the white walls, the colorful buildings that clustered around the clear high point of the city—the Palace of a Thousand Years. Rumor said it had been destroyed a year ago by the Pastisians, but apparently it had been rebuilt. "It's the Court of Far Seeing," Shula said. "The home of the Elenil."

"It's . . . changed. When I was last here it was . . ." She rubbed her hand over her face. "Of course that was a long time ago, even in human years. Who knows how long it has been in the Sunlit Lands?"

Shula wasn't sure either, but her best guess was at least two hundred years. Who knew what this place looked like back then? Well, Mrs. Oliver did. Most of the Elenil, probably. "Is it very different?" Shula asked.

"There was no wall," Mrs. Oliver said slowly. "And far more trees. Most of the homes were in trees along the river or in the caverns, not on the ground. That tower wasn't there either."

David came trotting back toward them. He had gone on ahead, checking for trouble. He smiled at Yenil and Dee, who were jumping back and forth, running ahead of Shula, then falling behind, playing tag, laughing, and enjoying each other. "There are a few guards ahead, but they're scarcely paying attention. Human. I think if we keep cool we won't have any issues." He crouched down to Yenil. "But Dee is going to need to keep quiet. Do you think she'd ride in your bag for a little bit? If you dial her down to her smallest size?"

"Sure," Yenil said. "Dee likes it when we play that game."

"And no war skin," Shula said. "They get nervous about untamed Scim here in Far Seeing."

"Unless there's trouble," Mrs. Oliver said, and took Yenil's hand.

Yenil nodded once. "Unless there's trouble," she agreed.

Shula helped Yenil get the tiny rhino into her backpack. Dee stuck her face out and snorted once, then settled down on top of Yenil's clothes. Should be okay.

David was right, though, so it didn't end up mattering much. They walked past the guards, no trouble. "I thought Hanali was looking out for us," Shula said.

David shrugged. "He was. But things are different now. Everyone's buzzing, but the guards are distracted. I'm not sure what's going on. It's good for us. We can head over to the storyteller's place no problem."

They passed Transition House on their way. It was so strange. Shula could see the window to her room from the road. How long had she lived there? It seemed like a million years ago that she was crashing in that room, waking in the late afternoon and preparing to fight the Scim. Now she had a little Scim girl with her. Back then she had been able to catch on fire, burn her enemies. That had changed too, and that core anger was . . . well, it wasn't gone, but it was less. Burned out in the fires that had destroyed Aluvorea, the fires that had birthed Maduvorea.

"It's all so different," Mrs. Oliver said again. "There are so many *people*."

"Weren't there always a lot of people here?" Yenil hitched her bag up. "And can Dee get out yet?"

"When we get to the storyteller," David said.

Mrs. Oliver pursed her lips. "I said that wrong, Yenil, dear. Not so many *people*—although there were fewer back then—but so many *humans*. The last time I was here, it was only me and my friends. We met . . . oh, maybe three other humans the whole time we were in the Sunlit Lands." Her eyes lost focus, and she walked a little slower. Shula squeezed her hand and moved her forward.

"A long time ago," Shula said. "Are the memories painful?"

Mrs. Oliver smiled at her, and there was something in that smile, like a shared secret between them. "Sometimes. But I'm glad for them, I guess."

And there it was again, that strange itch of memory in Shula's own head. Who was this woman, this Vasya? Why didn't Shula remember more about her, and why, oh why had she forgotten her completely until recently? And how did Vasya relate to the loss of her brother? Or, if David was to be believed, it was not a death at all. It was literally a loss . . . he was missing.

"There it is," David said, pointing out a little two-story home covered in ivy, with a staircase climbing up one side. It was, Shula was almost certain, the same place she had brought Madeline once upon a time.

"Race ya," Yenil said, and took off running. A distressed bleating came from her backpack, and a tiny rhino head poked out of the flap.

"Oh no, you don't," David said, and he was about to run, but then he stopped and looked at Shula. "Think you can beat us?"

She grinned, thankful to be invited in. "I don't know about Yenil, but I know I can beat *you*." She dashed past him, and he gave a surprised shout of mock fury, then pelted after her. Yenil had a significant lead, but when she got to the stairs, Shula gained an advantage. She jumped past Yenil and took the stairs two at a time.

"No fair!" Yenil shouted, then let out a delighted shriek as David scooped her up in his arms and ran behind Shula, right on her heels.

"A tie," he said, as they reached the landing.

"No!" Shula said, laughing. "I was definitely first."

"I was watching," Yenil said, "And it was almost a tie except for one thing. David was holding me in front of him, so I got here first!"

"Ha! Your feet haven't even touched the ground yet," David said, and he lowered her toward the step, then yanked her up again before her shoes hit stone.

They all burst out laughing, and then Shula remembered Mrs. Oliver. She hadn't run. In fact, she had stopped walking. She stood staring at the building, a blank look on her face. It took three seconds to get down the stairs and into the street, and then Shula was beside her. "What is it? What's wrong?"

"This whole place," Mrs. Oliver said. "What happened to it? Is this where Madeline lived when she was here?"

Shula kicked herself mentally. She should have pointed out Transition House. Of course Mrs. Oliver would have liked to see that. "No, this is the storyteller's house."

Mrs. Oliver pressed her lips together, something just short of a frown. "What have the Elenil been up to?" she said to herself. "Let's see this storyteller."

They ascended the staircase together, and David held the door until everyone was in. The room was small, cool, and dark. Shula had been here before and knew what to expect. One wall was covered in ivy. A woman moved forward, also covered, the ivy wound into her hair and across her body. She almost looked like someone from the great forest—a Maduvorean—but her skin wasn't green or blue or the color of any plant.

"So you have returned," she said, "for another story. Brought you a button, or a thimble, or a spool of thread?"

David nodded and drew a button from his pocket. "Not just any button. I took this one from an Elenil a few days past."

The ivy woman nodded eagerly and held her hand out, and David dropped it in her palm. She snaked her hand into the ivy, and when it returned, it was empty. "What story do you desire?"

"Whatever story you think we need to hear," David said, and the storyteller watched them for a moment: Yenil unpacking Dee with Mrs. Oliver; David standing there, tall and almost regal; Shula's attention flitting between them all.

"Each of your stories would be different," the woman pronounced at last. "Shall I tell you the child's story, a tale of much danger in years to come? Shall I tell you the story of Shula's lost memories and of the being known as the Historian? Or the story of Wendy Oliver's foolish bargain, and the losses she has incurred . . . and the losses yet to come?" She turned her eyes toward David. "Your story you already know."

Mrs. Oliver moved toward the storyteller, studying her. She came close, her eyes wide. "Rana? What did they do to you?"

"Hello, Wendy."

Mrs. Oliver tried to reach for her, to hug her, but the woman was covered in ivy. There was no way to get her arms around her. "What happened? The last time I saw you—"

"Yes," the storyteller—Rana?—said. "It was a difficult coronation, and Allison was . . . she—the forest—was not pleased with me when it awoke."

"I don't understand," Shula said. "What are you two talking about?"

Mrs. Oliver grabbed Rana's hand. "When I was here . . . before. My friends and I . . . ." She shook her head as if trying to drive the memories away. "It wasn't a happy trip, Shula. They killed her. Allison. Rana had promised to protect her, but—"

"I failed," Rana said. "So she has been punishing me since. But now things have changed. Maduvorea is a new forest, and it claims it will release me soon. It is still in negotiations with the Aluvorean parts of it that remain."

"I'm so sorry," Mrs. Oliver said. "This whole place . . . the horrible things it does to people."

"Your world is no kinder," Rana said, and Mrs. Oliver gave the storyteller a sad smile.

"I suppose not." She sighed. "Why not tell us all three stories?"

"There is a matter of some urgency," Rana said. "One of your friends is in mortal danger. If you choose to go to him, I can help move you there."

"Jason," Shula and David said simultaneously, because of course it was Jason. Mortal Danger should be his nickname.

"Indeed. But first, choose a story."

"I have plenty of time," Yenil said, sitting on the floor with Dee. "Tell me my story next time."

Rana smiled at her. "You are a generous soul, child, and your stories will always say so."

"We came because of Shula," Mrs. Oliver said. "It should be her story."

"Very well," Rana said.

Shula hesitated. "Is there time? Or should we go to Jason right now?"

"There is always time for one story," Rana said. "This one is of some importance to you. It is a story of my own keeping. I do not tell it lightly. For there are certain forces which have labored hard to remove it from the world. If it were known that I held this story—if it becomes known that *you* hold it—the Elenil would seek to destroy us as vessels of this tale."

David looked protectively to Yenil, but the girl was flat on her stomach, blowing in Delightful Glitter Lady's face, and laughing as the tiny rhino jumped and spun around as if looking for who had touched her.

"Okay," Shula said. "Let's hear it."

Rana deflated a little, and the ivy around her rustled. "Once there was a boy . . ."

✦

Once there was a boy . . . spoiled, rude, and cruel. He was not a prince, though prince-like in many ways. His family was wealthy, and he had never heard the word *no* except from his own lips. His name is lost to time as were, you will see, many other things.

It was on his seventeenth birthday that the boy killed his brother.

Within a year he had entered the village below the family estate and made lavish promises of wealth to any young person who would work for him. But when they arrived at the estate, he kept them in chains. "It's your own fault," he would say to them. When, in time, they came to believe him, he would release them to work for him on the estate, and they would be thankful. Thankful to be kept as his unpaid servants. He would tell them a story about how the people of the village had hated them, how they had been cruel, and he had come to rescue them, and they should be grateful.

For the boy had come to realize that even the most egregious lie would be seen as true if repeated often enough and with enough conviction. There was a kind of magic to it. He learned not to doubt his own lies. He learned not to admit to any wrongdoing or a crack in the way he saw the world, and in time others would—instead of looking at the world and making observations to gain knowledge—look to him to tell them the state of the world.

He grew pleased with his own power and would do cruel things, like asking a servant the color of a dish.

"Yellow, sir," she might say.

"No," he would reply. "It is red." And though the color did not change, the servant would.

"Red, yes, of course it is red," she might say, and in time she found that such questions ("What color is this?") became difficult. For if she found a napkin that was the same color as the dish, she was uncertain if it was red or yellow. So she needed to go to the boy and ask him, "What color is this?" and he, callous and cruel, would mock her and tell her she was stupid before telling her the color of the napkin "which is clear and obvious to any who look upon it."

It was not long before the creator of the Sunlit Lands was made aware of the boy. So it was that the boy woke one morning and sat down to his breakfast, only to discover a man already waiting at the table, seated upon a bale of hay.

"Boy," said he (though he knew the boy's name and used it—I know it not). "Boy," said he, "I have come to ask you, where is your brother?"

For the boy, as I have already told you, killed his brother, though all seemed to have forgotten it.

"I have no brother, nor ever have had one," the boy said.

A deep frown creased the man's face. "Your magic will not work on one such as me," the man said, "for I have lived many centuries, and some of them alone, and I will not allow another man's falsehoods to color reality, not even for a moment."

Then it was that the boy felt real fear, perhaps for the first time in his life. "Who are you?" the boy asked.

"I am the one who wishes to know what became of your brother."

So the boy called in one of his servants and said, "Look, here he is."

And the man took the boy by the scruff of his neck and said, "Here is how one grabs a serpent, so it will not bite," and he carried the boy thus all the way to a cave in the ground, near the place called Far Seeing.

"Here is your home now," he said to the boy, and he put certain wards in place so the boy could not leave. "When you are prepared to speak truth, but say my name and I will come and release you. For the Sunlit Lands cannot stand upon lies and half-truths. Such things always become the tools of men with evil intent."

But the boy said, "Oh, how much nicer this place is than my old mansion, and how grand. Surely people will come from all over the Sunlit Lands and beg to live here, and I shall allow it . . . for a price."

And the man crossed his arms and thought long and hard, but could not think of a punishment both just and fair that would keep his people safe. So instead he sent word to all in the Sunlit Lands to avoid the cave and to never listen to the words of the boy who lived there.

But the boy lived long, and the boy grew in craftiness. And in time he began to call himself the Historian, and with the magics of the Sunlit Lands he changed himself, he grew and shifted and became something Other. He sent out word with his servants (of which he had many in those days) to say, "If you wish to know the secrets of the world, long hidden from you by those in power, come to me." And they came.

So the story goes, and there is more, far more, to say. But of most importance to you is this: the father of the Elenil came to that cave, once upon a time, and promised to build an entire city around the cave if the Historian would give him power. The deal was struck, the promise made, and upon that very ground was built the Palace of a Thousand Years.

And it was there, Shula Bishara, that the Historian used his magic to take away your memories of your brother and of another woman, too. For he feared you would come to know the truth, and a deal was struck to protect you from that truth and thus to keep the power of the Elenil strong. Then you, who should have been the Elenil's great enemy, became instead one of their champions.

✦

Shula took a deep breath and looked at David. "You've heard that one before?"

"No. That one's new."

"So we go to the tower," Shula said. "Is that where Jason is? And we find this Historian, and find my brother."

"It will be a painful journey," Rana said, "when you come to it at last. If you were to choose to go straight there, I would not blame you. Your brother, however, has been safely held there for a long time. And your friend Jason, even now, stands at a crossroads of great trouble."

David and Shula exchanged some sort of conversation through looks. Shula felt a small blush of heat in her cheeks. She had never had such easy communication with a man, but she felt like she knew what he was saying without words. "Jason first, then to my brother?"

"Yes," David said. "Rana . . . you said you could send us there? Wherever that may be?"

"Through the vines, yes. To the Southern Court."

Mrs. Oliver cleared her throat. "And—" Mrs. Oliver paused, thinking. "Is Hanali here? In Far Seeing?"

"He is in the tower even now."

"I promise we'll come straight back here," Shula said. "But we can't leave Jason in danger."

Mrs. Oliver listened calmly. She put her hands on Shula's shoulders. "I have to go speak to Hanali. I should have done it decades ago, but . . . I forgot things that mattered. I can't put it off anymore, Shula. Do you understand?"

Shula put her hands over the older woman's. "I do. We'll meet you at the tower as quickly as we can."

Mrs. Oliver leaned in and kissed her cheek, hugged David. She bent down and said a few quiet words to Yenil and scratched Dee on the head, and then she was out the door and gone. Shula felt a strange emptiness watching her leave. Was it safe for her to go alone?

A rustling came from Rana, and she stepped back into the ivy. "Come," she said.

Yenil picked up Dee, and David picked up Yenil. He held out his hand to Shula. "So we don't get separated."

She gladly took his hand, and they pushed into the wall of ivy.

24
TROUBLE

Beware those who prize truth more than power.
FROM *THE ANNALS OF THE HISTORIAN*

+

ilenyia paced her quarters, her mind in disarray. The Knight of the Mirror, just this side of becoming a traitor. Jason Wu, dead at her own hand, and Hanali unconcerned. Her childhood friend nearly archon now, and a Scim nobody child she had healed raised to the status of prophet to the Scim and now, it seemed, to the Elenil as well. Archon Thenody had insisted she heal the child, claiming he had plans for the Scim. At the time it had seemed like merely one more small task for the archon, but now she wondered. Could he have known his reeducation would be so effective? In the midst of all this, the troubling accusation of Jason Wu echoed in her head: *"She made you human."*

She had always been clear-eyed about difficult truths. Denying them only made you more vulnerable. A surge of rage came upon her, and she swept a vase from the mantel over the fireplace, taking some small pleasure in the sound of it shattering. Ricardo burst into the room, sword drawn. He was clearly taken aback to see her in this state, chest heaving, face flushed, with a fierce satisfaction in the broken shards on the ground.

"My lady, is all well?"

Soon Hanali would be her husband if he had his way. It seemed that he knew how to get his way in all things. His whispered suggestions of marriage were formalities only, courtesies to let her mentally acclimate. She had no doubt that subtle wheels within wheels were already in motion.

"No, all is not well, Ricardo," she said, her anger draining away. Or rather, she walled it off, pushed it away. She had expressed it and now needed to set it aside.

A thought struck her. "What did Hanali do with Jason Wu's body?"

"My lady, he left it here," Ricardo said. "Day Song was unsure what to do with it, and we didn't want to bother you or Hanali, so it's stored in a cold room."

Interesting. She had known Hanali for a long time, and she knew that whatever he said, and whatever reason he had for using the Wu boy—and Madeline for that matter—he had truly cared for them. There was some affection there. But his response to Jason's death had been matter-of-fact. Unconcerned. She knew not to underestimate her cousin's knowledge at any time, and now she wondered about the dead boy. Did Hanali know something she did not?

"Take me there at once," Gilenyia said. "Does Hanali know where the body is?"

"No, lady."

She snatched up her small bag of tools. "Give instructions to the others that if he asks where it is, they are to speak to me before responding. Now lead me to the corpse."

It was rare that Gilenyia would enter the sections of this place reserved for the servants. Scullery maids and cooks scattered at the sight of Ricardo, Gilenyia striding purposefully behind him.

The body was in a cold room, alone, on a slab of stone and covered in a sheet. There was no blood. Odd. "Step into the hall and keep watch," Gilenyia said. "No one is to enter." Ricardo obeyed at once.

With the sheet flipped back, the Wu boy looked peaceful. As if he were sleeping. She slipped a small, round mirror from her bag and held it beneath his nose. She waited a full minute, then looked at it. It was slightly fogged, as she suspected. She went to slide it back into her bag and saw a flash of movement in the glass. She flipped it quickly, in time to see the Knight of the Mirror's beloved lady moving away inside the mirror. She cursed under her breath. This was the sort of mistake Hanali did not make. Not that the knight's lady would know anything for sure, but this gave her an indication, at least, of what Gilenyia suspected. She did not know if the knight had knowledge of this or not, but surely his lady would now give him a clue.

Gilenyia took a deep breath and steadied herself. She removed her left glove and watched the magic pulsing through her golden tattoos. Could a human act as a conduit for so much magic? She thought not. She placed her palm on the boy's face and gently pushed the magic forward.

The connection was cold and quiet, a frozen lake. She tapped on the ice. It was thick, but here in this mind space she could break it. So she did. She dove deeper into the icy water, swimming down many, many leagues until even the sunlight refused to go farther. Still she swam. Until she touched something. A mind. But it was sleeping.

She had seen something like this a few times before. It was a sort of hibernation state. It could be artificially induced with certain drugs or magics, or naturally induced in the right kind of animal. She spoke to the mind, but it did not respond. Too sluggish, too deeply asleep. Satisfied, she rose to the surface again and broke the connection. "Ricardo," she called.

He peered in. "Lady?"

"I have need of your sword."

He unbuckled his entire belt, scabbard and all, and handed it to her without hesitation. Well trained. She yanked the sword free, put some room between herself and the body, and pierced the boy deep in the shoulder.

There was a scream, followed by a thrashing, amorphous thing that took the place of Jason's body. It was human for a moment, then—something else. It settled into a humanoid shape, but reptilian. Scales and yellow eyes, and a mouth too wide. She kept the point of the sword at its chest.

"Hello there," Gilenyia said. "And what might your name be, little troublemaker?"

"Call me what you will," the lizard said.

"Trouble is name enough, I suppose." She glanced at Ricardo. "Watch the door, Mr. Sánchez. From outside."

The lizard watched him leave. "Squeamish about witnesses?"

She regarded it coolly. "Please don't imagine I have any compunctions about killing you again."

It licked its lips with a thin tongue. "Last time you thought I was someone you knew. I know you'll kill me if it's to your advantage."

Her lip curled up on one side. "So. You want me to believe I am human, and meanwhile you are most certainly not human."

Trouble laughed at that. "You don't understand anything about the Sunlit Lands, do you? You Elenil with your long lives and short memories. I suppose in a year or two you'll forget that you killed me in a cold room once upon a time."

"Why do you want me to believe I am human?"

"Lady, surely it is clear by now that I am of the Southern Court. There are a great many of us seeded throughout all the people of the Sunlit Lands. Some of us for generations. We are people who love to collect information, and we love the truth. We can't help but think it's time for us to share some of what we know."

"For your own benefit, no doubt."

"Of course," Trouble said. "We are not overfond of the Elenil."

"It seems that scarcely anyone is these days," Gilenyia replied. "Was this your entire mission here? To introduce doubt about my status as Elenil?"

"No," the lizard boy said reluctantly. "You weren't even my target. When you came to us, I thought it would be a bonus to convince you of this. I didn't expect that you would kill me."

"You're not so dead as all that," Gilenyia said drolly.

"I couldn't very well shrug off a knife to the gut that filleted me to the breastbone. People might have suspected I wasn't who I appeared to be. Or discovered that I purposely arranged my internal organs a different way than humans."

"So what is your plan now? Wait in cold storage until all are asleep and tiptoe out?"

She did not know that lizards could roll their eyes, but this one did. "I was in hibernation, lady. My plan would have come after I awoke."

Gilenyia tapped the tip of the sword on his sternum. "You are awake now."

"I am a bit preoccupied for planning."

"You are stalling," she said. "I have seen warriors and spies from the Southern Court in action. Not in some hundred years, true, but you cannot have gone so soft in such a short period of time. You could overpower me if you wished. Or turn into a tiny gnat, or a mouse, and disappear before I could stop you."

"All worthy plans. If my goal was to escape."

"Is it not?"

"No, lady, not at all. In fact, my goal is something else entirely."

Gilenyia motioned for him to continue. "Inform me, then. Clearly you wish me to know."

His body split in half and flowed around the sword, then past Gilenyia. She spun, and he was standing behind her in the shape of Hanali. "My dear Gilenyia, I suspect you can put the pieces together yourself."

An instinct to reach for the slab—or anything solid—flooded her, but she did not. No reason to give this spy any indication that he had surprised her, that she had not expected this precise thing. "You wish to take his place."

He even wore clothes like Hanali's. She did not realize the creatures could change their shape to ape the appearance of clothing. The false Hanali studied his gloves as if he could see his fingernails through them. "The Elenil do a fair bit of damage to the world, Cousin. To be the archon would allow a certain amount of bloodless change in the Sunlit Lands, and no one need be the wiser. It would be best for all of us."

"I daresay Hanali might disagree."

"Ha," Trouble said. "Well he might. I need not kill him, you know. I could exile him to the Southern Court."

"I fear he would not like it there," Gilenyia said.

"Well, I can't very well send him to live with the Scim, now can I?"

This could not be good, that the creature was telling her all this. It meant either that he intended to kill her, so a little explanation of his plan wouldn't matter, or that he intended somehow to ensnare her in the plan. "And what is my part in your dangerous charade?"

Hanali blurred, and his face melted away, replaced by her own. "Access," Trouble said. "I need to get near him."

A thousand answers jumped to her mind at once. She knew her cousin well, and in his current role he talked to many people with astonishing regularity. However, the plan made no sense. The creature was lying . . . access to Hanali should be astonishingly easy for a shape-shifter. "He receives messenger birds with some regularity. You could appear as one of them."

Trouble nodded, though it was her face he wore. "A stratagem we have used more than once when we needed the Elenil to know some little fact."

"So why not use that ruse to gain access to him?"

He smiled. "My master said you had a rare ability to suss out the truth."

"You are working hard to deceive me for someone who claims to care only about the truth."

He took on the form of the Scim child Nightfall. The Herald of Mysteries. "The truth can look different from different points of view."

"A nonsensical saying of limited usefulness. I suppose you will tell me that ten blind men would all describe an elephant differently from one another."

Trouble cocked his head to one side. "A useful human example."

"A ludicrous human example that presumes that blind people are idiots. Would they not, upon hearing the different descriptions, immediately know that they were describing an elephant? Or if they had never experienced an elephant before, would they not seek to feel the entire beast, not just the tusk or trunk or tail? It is a simplistic metaphor at best. Specious, ill-formed, and lazy."

"How would you say it, then, lady?"

"The elephant exists," she snapped. "Whether a hundred blind people touch it or not. Whether a thousand sighted people see it or not. There are elephants in Far Seeing. Neither you nor I can see them in this moment. Do they cease to exist because we are not able to point them out?"

"Some philosophers would say yes."

"Sophists and philosophical hobbyists. The truth is the truth, let no one say otherwise."

Trouble hopped up onto the slab and let his form change. It wavered between Gilenyia herself and Hanali, settling at last on her face, her body, her clothing. "So you admit, then, that you are human."

She sniffed. "I do not."

"Ah." Trouble smiled. "Gilenyia, dear woman. You have nothing to fear. Is that not so?"

"Not from the truth."

He reached into his sleeve and pulled out a small vial of liquid. "Wendy juice," he said. "Have you heard of it?"

"A draught of remembrance," she said.

He held it out to her. "Come, let us drink it together. Then we will know what is true."

"No," she said. "Tell me your plan first."

He shrugged. "My first mission is to tell Hanali what I told you."

"That he is human?"

"You misunderstand, Gilenyia. To tell him that *all of the Elenil* are human."

It would be a blow to the very heart of Hanali's plan. It could derail, even, his ascension to archon, if it were played exactly right. It was clearly untrue, but whispered in the right ears, just the rumor could undo him. Not to mention that he was unlikely to take it well. She had nearly asked for addleberry wine herself so she could forget it all, and she knew her cousin to be less equipped for keeping unpleasant truths in his head. "And you wish me to help you."

He shrugged, still wearing Gilenyia's face. "Anything I need you to do, I could do myself."

"Do not think too highly of yourself, Trouble. I am not so easily copied. Your deception would last only a short time before you were found out."

"Perhaps," Trouble said. "I need you for another reason, though. Once Hanali knows this truth, there will be trauma. He will take either the easier route—forgetting it completely—or the harder: holding the pain and reevaluating everything about our entire culture. The Elenil not only not in charge, but nothing special, no different from the humans. No humans to exile, for we are all humans. Those myths are just that, myths. But during that pain and evaluation, there will still need to be a public face." And with that he turned into Hanali again.

"I cannot allow this little plan," Gilenyia said. "It is interesting and there is some merit to it, but to have the Southern Court in charge of the Elenil? To have them ruling the Sunlit Lands? This cannot be."

"But surely you don't understand—"

"On the contrary, Trouble, I understand exactly. Here is what is going to happen. I am going to call my Ricardo in. I am going to tell him to kill you, and he is going to do it. I will decide what to do about Hanali. And I will send your head back to the Southern Court with a sweet messenger bird." The shape-shifter had a look of shock on his face that she could only assume was legitimate. "Ricardo!" she called.

To his credit, the shape-shifter immediately took on Gilenyia's form. A clever ruse. As Ricardo came in the door, Trouble said, "She is a shape-shifter! Kill her at once!"

Without hesitation, Ricardo retrieved his sword from Gilenyia and lopped off Trouble's head. The body fell.

"Thank you," Gilenyia said. "I did not want to be bothered with killing him a second time. Have Day Song deliver the head via courier bird to the Southern Court. Make it a large bird with a beautiful voice. I will give it the message." She paused. "Ricardo, you did not so much as hesitate. You chopped him down immediately. How did you know?"

He blushed. "It was not a perfect copy, lady."

"I never took you to be such an observant man, Ricardo. I am impressed."

He looked down at his feet. "I am observant about some things, lady."

"I see. Very well, Ricardo. Come to me in my quarters when this mess has been cleaned up. And send a message to Hanali that I must speak to him at once."

"Yes, lady. Of course."

She swept past him. Something strange was going on with the young man, but no matter. She had a game to continue with Hanali. For the first time in some months she looked forward to exchanging words with him.

25
THE PEASANT KING

Death is strong, and the curse could not be broken.

FROM "THE TRIUMPH OF THE PEASANT KING," A SCIM LEGEND

✦

arius stood beside the table in mute shock. The council went on for a while and he didn't say a word, didn't even hear what they were saying. How could Cumberland be the Peasant King? Yes, he had said he was old. Very old, even. And he knew a lot about the Sunlit Lands, but according to the Scim, the Peasant King had *made* the Sunlit Lands. It didn't make any sense. His mind drifted back into the conversation. The man with the long locs—Patra Koja—was speaking.

"—the Southern Court, even in Maduvorea. We have seen a few of them in recent months, and they are increasingly . . . strange."

"Strange how?" Cumberland asked.

"Strange is the Southern Court, through and through," Arakam said. "They have been strange since the world was new."

"True enough," Cumberland said. "But let us allow Patra Koja an answer."

Patra Koja cleared his throat. "They have always enjoyed jokes of their kind, and they have always been a fair bit of trouble. But these days many of them wear the same face. They all look to be in the guise of Wu Song."

Darius knew that name. It stirred him further from his numb shock. "Jason?"

"Have you noticed this, Remi, as you've been blowing from place to place?"

The cat didn't even look up from washing her paw. "Didn't notice, don't care," she said.

"The Zhanin are also troubled," Malgwin said. "They have a new ruler, one who rules by force of magic. They are not performing their agreed-upon duties."

"Are we in danger then?" Cumberland asked.

Malgwin looked to Pookie. "He would know better than I."

The rock man tapped his chin thoughtfully. "Yes, in many ways I suspect you are."

Fantok stood and circled the table. "What action should we take? My people tire of standing silently and watching."

Cumberland glanced at Darius, then back to his council. "You are a council. But I am hearing precious little counseling. Just an airing of observations and concerns."

"Give the Sunlit Lands to me," Malgwin said. "Let me bring the Sea Beneath up to cover the earth."

"Surely things are not so dire," Patra Koja said.

"A clean start," Malgwin said.

"Genocide," Patra Koja replied. "Let's not mince words."

Malgwin frowned. "It's not genocide if we kill them all. Only if we target a certain type."

"The suggestion is noted and dismissed," Cumberland said.

"The Elenil contemplate genocide as well," Fantok said. "Hanali has said he will banish or kill all humans to cement his own place of power."

"But he's human," Darius blurted. He had read it in a book that had been given him by King Ian. It was the sayings and secrets of Vivi, Hanali's own Elenil father. Darius knew it, and he knew that Hanali knew it. Darius had told him. Just before Hanali framed him for murder and kicked him out of the Sunlit Lands.

"Is this a play?" Remi, the cat, asked.

"What do you mean?" Cumberland asked.

"You already know all of this, Cumberland. We know you keep an eye on everything and everyone in the Sunlit Lands. You already have a plan, and no doubt one you set in motion a hundred years ago. So why are you asking us for our counsel?"

"Remi, behave."

She gave an unsatisfied half-meow and started working on cleaning her tail.

"Is that true?" Darius asked.

Cumberland sighed. "We start again in five," he said to the assembled people. He stood and put his arm around Darius. "Let's walk."

"Where will we go?"

"Here, above the heavens themselves, what does it even matter?" He guided Darius away from the strange makeshift meeting space. They walked along the top of the crystalline sphere and under the feet of the nearest flying Kharobem. It was covered in eyes of all different colors, and it blinked—not all at once, but like a school of fish turning—all flashing and movement and color. "Don't mind them," Cumberland said. "They won't hurt you." He motioned, and Darius noticed—or maybe they hadn't been there before?—two hay bales. He sat down on one, and Cumberland on the other.

"Now what's bothering you, Darius?"

"What's *not* bothering me? You're the Peasant King? Or are you just sitting in for him? I don't understand."

Cumberland's smile was wide and bright. "I've been called a lot of names, and that's one of them. Why? Who were you expecting?"

"Well, first of all, you're *Black*."

"Never said I wasn't."

"But no one said you were. I mean, I've heard all these stories about the Peasant King, and never once did someone mention that you were Black."

Cumberland leaned forward, his fingertips steepled, looking at Darius closely. "So what did you think I looked like?"

"Well, I pictured a white guy, I guess, with sort of curly reddish-brown hair that came most of the way to his shoulders. A sort of goatee beard thing. And medieval king clothing." Darius shrugged.

Cumberland roared with laughter. "Son, you just described the *Burger King*." He tried to stop laughing, but he couldn't—he was too tickled by the whole thing. He kept laughing so much and for so long that Darius couldn't help a smile sneaking onto his face as well. "Listen, Darius, that's okay. You've been living for a long time in a world where people assume whiteness."

"But I—"

"It's not your fault, I'm saying. You thought the Peasant King was white because no one ever told you otherwise. Because it would be, well, *remarkable* if he was something else. Right?"

Darius frowned. "But Madeline met you, and she never thought to mention—"

"Was Madeline the kind of girl to go around pointing out who was Black and who was not?"

No, she wasn't. "But—"

"But nothing, Darius. It's a hard pill to swallow. You need a glass of water? Or are you going to be okay?"

He was going to be fine. But he hated it when he found these little places. They were like pockets he didn't know were in his clothes. And at some point he put his hand in them and discovered things he didn't realize he had been carrying. Cumberland was right. He thought the Peasant King was white because white was the default. He wasn't disappointed that the Peasant King was Black—though he was still struggling to get his mind around it—but disappointed in himself for never considering that might be a possibility. In all this time, in all the stories he had heard during his time with the Scim, the idea had never occurred to him for a moment.

"If it makes you feel better, the Elenil depict the Majestic One as Elenil."

"What?"

"When you see the Majestic One in Elenil art. He's—well, *I* am—an Elenil. That's a lot of shades lighter than I really am, I'll tell you that much."

Darius shifted on his hay bale as if changing his position would make things clearer somehow. "But you're the Majestic One?"

"The Elenil wouldn't recognize me if I walked through the Court of Far Seeing wearing my crown and sat down on a throne, but yes, I am."

"The Scim, though—they talk about you really differently. They say you're the Peasant King."

"Yes, true, but they also think of me as Scim. If you look at the earlier stories about me, I'm more human, and so are the people I interact with. But as time went by, the stories definitely started to lose my shape. I imagine I could walk through the center of the Wasted Lands without getting much of a parade lining up behind me."

"And then other people call you other things."

"Yeah."

"Like the Kakri call you the Story King."

Cumberland grabbed Darius's knee. "No, not that one. That's not me."

"What do you mean?"

"That's not me, that's all. The Story King. That's someone, well, bigger than me. Older. More powerful. Our stories get confused sometimes, but the Kakri, they never got too wrapped up in the Peasant King or the Majestic One. They've been a little busy what with rebuilding their whole culture after the water dried up in the desert."

Darius knocked his heel against the crystal sphere below him, and it made a clanging sound that reverberated all around them. "So you made this place somehow?"

"Most of it. A long time ago. It took a lot of time and a lot of magic, but I got it up and running."

"So what's that story?"

"It's a story for another time, and you don't need it. Not today. People get all hung up on the beginning and the end and forget that the middle is important too."

"And where are we in the story?"

"Closer to the end than the beginning," Cumberland said. "We don't have to go all the way back to the start. But we do need to have some common history. Some common memory of what happened here. I'll tell you the story of how the people of the Sunlit Lands came to be here, if you want to hear it."

A sudden sadness fell on Darius. The history of the Sunlit Lands—the big-picture history—wasn't what he most cared about. What he cared about was Madeline. And she was gone now. He wasn't sure he wanted to hear the story. He felt like he was in a small space, and bricks of grief and melancholy were being laid around him. He didn't care enough to try to stop the walls from rising. All the questions and the overwhelming strangeness of meeting the Peasant King—well, that didn't seem to matter too much either.

"It started in deep grief," the old man said. "Sorrow so deep you didn't think you could plumb it. So wide that you could never get your arms around it. So high you could never jump it, never climb it, maybe never even fly over it. It's the sort of grief that comes when a person has lost more than he knows how to count, when the loss is so great he can't see it all. Do you know what I mean by that?"

Darius thought he did. He was falling into it, sliding into it. It wasn't just the loss of a single loved one. It wasn't only losing Madeline. That was a grief to sink into. A heavy loss, but one he thought he might be able to carry in time. This was something more.

"It was a weariness to the world," the Peasant King said. "A weight so heavy that if you put it on your back you would sink into the earth, one step at a time. If you tried to carry it all yourself."

"You have to carry it together," Darius said.

"That's right. That's exactly right. I had spent all this time—literally spent it, twisted it around and stretched it out and woven it through here and over there—making the Sunlit Lands, and I realized that it was no good without someone in it. Even in my grief I saw that. So I started to people it. Started to let them in. But careful. Cautious. Studying them. Picking them out. People in pain. People who weren't safe in the world and needed a place to heal. People with hard lives and big sorrows. Because I figured, well, our sorrow was so big we needed people who knew how to carry it. People who knew how to carry it together. So they came. From all over the world they came. And I worked the magic to help them talk to each other. And I worked the magic to help them know one another. And I used the magic to give them the strength to shape themselves, to become something more, if that's what they wanted to do."

"You gave them magic," Darius said.

"That's right."

"And some of them became the Scim."

"Yes, sir. And some the Elenil. And others the Zhanin, the Kakri, and so on. In the first days, there were some who helped me. You met them right here—they're singular people. There's only one Malgwin. Then there were some who came from outside, later, after we had been settled for a while. The Pastisians, I let them in like foreigners from another land. They didn't want any magic, and they wanted to be left alone, so I gave them none of one and a whole lot of the other."

Darius leaned forward and put his head in his hands. "And for the first generation or two, everything was wonderful."

Cumberland's voice sounded like it had a smile in it when he said, "You've always been so cynical, Darius. But yes. A few generations. They remembered what it had been like where they came from. They were mindful about caring for one another. Until they weren't."

"This is always the way of it," Malgwin said, gliding toward them. Her face was calm, serene. "Forty years, fifty, and all is forgotten. Humanity collapses into the same patterns. 'Unprecedented times,' they say, never mentioning that their own grandparents lived through the same, or worse."

Darius stood, unable to keep his seat. He paced around them. "So this whole thing, it was an experiment. And it failed."

"'*Is* failing' might be more accurate," Cumberland said. "There are still parts of it functioning. There are still good things coming from it."

"The Sunlit Lands are dying," Malgwin said. "They have been dying for a long time."

"But they're not dead yet," the old man said, a sad smile on his face.

Darius looked at them. They weren't enemies, he realized. They were in some strange balance. He asked Malgwin, "You think they're done. It's time to wash it all away?"

"There are three things that show you the health of a society," she said. "Three groups of people you look to. If they are thriving, then all is well. If they are suffering, then there is sickness. The whole world is in danger, for it has been corrupted."

"What are the three things?"

"The foreigner is one. The outsider. Like your Madeline. Would you say she was well treated by the Sunlit Lands? She or you or your friend Wu Song?"

"No," he said emphatically.

"Then there is the orphan. You have seen your share of those among the Scim. Yenil. Nightfall and his siblings."

"Living in squalor," Darius said. "On the run from the Elenil. Orphaned by the Elenil."

Malgwin nodded curtly. "And the widow. What of the widows of the Sunlit Lands?"

He had known some, among the Scim. But for some reason he could not explain, the first widow who came into his mind was Hanali's mother. The wife of Vivi. He couldn't even remember her name. He had known it once. No one had mentioned her since Vivi died. Not Hanali, not Darius, not anyone he could think of. She was invisible. Forgotten.

"The Sunlit Lands are dying," Malgwin repeated. "Soon they will be gone."

"We can save them," Cumberland said. "If we can help them remember."

"How?" Darius asked. "Is this why you brought me here? To save them?"

Cumberland put his hand on Darius's arm. "I like that about you, Darius. You always want to know your role in saving the world. But sometimes, the way you save the world is just by saving the people in it. Do you know what I mean?"

"No," Darius said. He had no idea what that meant.

The Peasant King bent down to the ground and breathed on the crystal sphere. It fogged over and then went clear. Darius could see all the way through it, through all the spheres, to the Sunlit Lands beneath them, far, far away. "You know why I filled this place with unicorns and dragons and giant stone statues and so on, Darius?"

"I have no clue."

"It's because the idea of the Sunlit Lands—someplace where the sun will always shine, where we will be safe, where we will be loved the way a human being should be loved—that's always been a fantasy. And I wanted the people to know that. To remember that."

Darius looked up, and the whole council was around him now.

"Enough talk," Malgwin said. "You think telling him stories will give him what he needs? You think the stories will help him decide what is to be done?"

Fantok said, "Do you think something other than a story will do it?"

"I am the guardian of the power of the Sunlit Lands," Malgwin said. "He cannot do what he has come to do without coming to me, to the Sea Beneath." Malgwin's mouth began to grow . . . her whole body stretching and morphing into something bigger. Not a mermaid. A sea monster, a great black beast of a creature. "He must learn to see it for himself, not be told what to see."

Darius fell back from her, and the monster began to undulate, to smash against the crystal sphere at their feet. The Kharobem were floating nearer now, slowly moving toward them, and all their eyes were on Darius. A crack appeared.

"Do something," Darius shouted to Cumberland.

"I fear she's right," he said. The sound of the cracking crystal was so loud, he had to shout to be heard over it. "Go and see the state of the Sunlit Lands, and when you're ready, find the power source that Malgwin guards! You'll know what to do!"

The crack spread, moving from Malgwin toward Darius. The sphere made a snapping sound, like thin ice beneath his feet. It gave way, and Darius fell through, landing with a bone-jarring smack on the next sphere.

Then Fantok dove like a great bird-shaped comet, crashing through the spheres. Not just one or two, but all of them. Through the breach, Darius saw a shower of jagged crystal shards falling away toward the Sunlit Lands, far below. Fantok's dive stopped, and she glided away into the distance. Darius scrambled away from the edge, trying to be careful, but he stumbled.

And then he was falling, arms flailing, toward the distant ground far, far below.

26
THE PRISONER

*Enjoy the good, and experience the pain. Don't try to avoid what is bad
or fear the loss of what is good, but notice what is happening with both.*
FROM *THE WISE SAYINGS OF MOTHER CROW*

✦

I hate you," Jason said. "Like, really hate you."

TJ was walking alongside him in the desert heat. Jason's hands were tied behind his back. "Well, I think you're charming," TJ said. "I have a lot of respect for you."

"I see you talking to my friends, and it makes me really mad. Last night you said something to Break Bones, and he just roared with laughter. I could hear it in my tent, and I could hear him saying my name. What did you say?"

"I don't even remember," TJ said.

Jason mumbled to himself. The Kakri had set out two days ago and started moving south. Try as he might, he couldn't convince anyone that he was himself. He had talked to a few people, but his friends were keeping their distance. He suspected that Baileya Crow had told them he was off-limits. Every once in a while, TJ dropped by just to harass him. "Was it a joke about the Elenil? He really hates the Elenil."

TJ scrunched up his face, as if trying to remember. "I doubt it."

A large bird came trotting alongside them, and for a blessed moment the rider's shadow fell on Jason's face, blocking the sun. It was Bezaed, riding Moriarty. He must have taken the bird back after Jason had been tied up, and he was welcome to the troublesome creature. In fact, that was the best news Jason had heard all day. Bezaed looked down, ignored Jason, and spoke to TJ. "We will travel through the Passage soon, and Mother Crow wants you at her side when we enter the territories of the Southern Court."

"Sounds good," TJ said. "I'll be there in two shakes of a lamb's tail."

Bezaed didn't respond, he just snapped his reins and rode toward the head of the caravan. Jason made a disparaging noise. "I would never say that, you know."

"Two shakes of a lamb's tail?"

"What does it even mean? How long does a lamb's tail shake? Do they shake them all the time or almost never? Do sheep even have tails?"

"Yeah, little fluffy ones," TJ said. "Like a rabbit."

"So is a lamb shake long or short?"

TJ rolled his eyes. "It's just a saying."

"And I'm *just saying*, if you're going to pretend to be me, you need to represent me better." Jason shook his head. "I didn't grow up on a lamb farm." To be honest, he was surprised and relieved that the Southern Court didn't know everything about him. Maybe someone would notice and realize he was the actual Jason? Aw, who was he kidding. Break Bones didn't recognize him, and neither did Baileya. That stung. The thought of TJ chatting it up with his friends, building little inside jokes, or just spending time with them made him mad.

"Mother Crow. Not the most observant, is she? Hasn't even noticed that her lover and her prisoner have changed places. She's a good kisser, though, don't you think?" TJ gave Jason a sly sideways look.

Jason didn't know what volcanoes felt like before they exploded, but he had to imagine it was something like what he was feeling right now:

an intense pressure, a buildup of anger that he tried to stop, tried to slow, but couldn't. And the whole time his face was getting hotter, his muscles were tightening, and then, without his permission, a primal scream tore through his body, and he tackled TJ. Since his arms were tied behind his back, maybe *tackle* wasn't the right word. But he jumped and knocked him over, and was headbutting and biting and yelling and doing his best to kick TJ when the Kakri guards pulled him off, laughing. To the Kakri, that was entertaining theater, a little story for later.

Bezaed reappeared, frowning at TJ. "Why are you still talking to the prisoner, Wu Song? I told you that Mother Crow demanded your presence."

"Yeah, yeah," TJ said, rubbing at the various places Jason had kicked, headbutted, and bitten him. "I got a little distracted."

"Wait until I get these ropes off. Then I'm going to distract you like crazy," Jason said.

"I was just joking, you know," TJ said. "What I said wasn't true."

Jason's eyes practically popped out of his head. "Bezaed, did you hear that? He just admitted that he's not me! I don't tell lies, but he said something that wasn't true!"

Bezaed looked at Jason coolly. "Silence, prisoner. We do not speak to ones such as you. It is shameful that you would take the face of another."

"Don't say that, Bezaed. I thought you of all people would be able to tell who I am because you hate me so much." Jason fell to his knees. So this was the way it was going to be. That was about as close to a confession as Jason could expect, and it hadn't been enough.

The path took them into the Passage, the same place where Break Bones and Bezaed had saved him from the other Jasons. "Should have gotten a tattoo," Jason said to himself. But then again, the shape-shifters could probably get tattoos themselves. There had to be some way to differentiate himself.

He tried thinking back to the one other time he had met people from the Southern Court. It had been during the Festival of the Turning. Jason and his friends had confronted them. He remembered the fine scales on their bodies, which seemed to sparkle in the sun. That's why he'd thought they were lizards.

Well, his doubles didn't have any obvious scales, so maybe the ones posing as Black Skulls had done that on purpose, or maybe the most gifted shape-shifters could smooth out their scales or something. Regardless, these doubles were, apparently, foolproof.

The Kharobem that had surrounded the Kakri camp were following them. Jason looked back at them occasionally. They had six wings each, and they didn't turn when they flew. They just . . . changed directions while still facing forward. He wondered where Clawdia had gotten off to. Maybe she had six wings now and was flying behind them. That baby Kharobem would probably know he was the real Jason, although he had no idea how she would tell anyone since she only spoke in stories.

He remembered that the Southern Court folks he had met at the festival had invited him to come and visit sometime. He had made what he thought was a threatening remark to them . . . something like how he was going to take the shape of their greatest enemy when he came to visit, and they had laughed. They had laughed, and said he was very welcome. Baileya had said at the time—or maybe it was Shula—that they had liked him and that they rarely invited people to their homeland. Apparently he had given them a big compliment by saying he would come in the form of their greatest enemy because that meant he had shown them that he didn't believe they had an enemy that they were frightened of. Jason didn't understand it all. He just knew that they'd genuinely seemed to be fond of him, which was pretty great since almost everyone else in the Sunlit Lands was trying to murder him.

Of course, if they liked him so much, he wasn't sure why they were stealing his shape, trying to kidnap him, and even now taking over his friendships and *kissing Baileya*. Jason struggled against his ropes. No, wait, TJ said he was joking. But it wasn't funny. He was a liar one way or the other, and that was the one thing that Jason manifestly was not.

The path was sloping upward now, and the sun was starting to set. It was that time of day Jason loved, when the desert was starting to cool but there was no need for a fire, and the sun lit the sand and turned anything in the distance to a silhouette.

"It is confusing," Break Bones said. He had snuck up on Jason somehow in the dusk. "Even good friends may not know things about those they are closest to."

"Or even be able to tell who their friend is and who is an imposter," Jason said, sullen.

"Yes. This is what I mean. It is confusing when your friend appears to be one person but you suspect he is another." Break Bones walked in silence for a few steps, and Jason found himself harboring the smallest hope that maybe Break Bones knew the truth. "Wu Song, do you remember when Madeline died, what I said to you?"

He did. Break Bones shared his true name with Jason. "You told me that we were brothers now. That I could see your true face and know your true name."

"Do you remember that name?"

"I kept it safe," Jason said.

"Hmm. I do not like this," Break Bones said. "Marching to the gates of the enemy. I have noticed something about you, Wu Song. I will share it with you today in case we do not see one another again, and in case you are the true Wu Song."

"I really am."

The caravan came to a halt. Torches were being lit. Break Bones sat on a stone and motioned to another nearby. Jason sat too. "My whole life, I have been both Croion and Break Bones," he said. "I say that my true name is Croion, but very few people know this name. Croion is a Scim who longs for peace. He longs to lay aside his ax. To stop fighting. To be safe, to raise a family. But the world we live in does not provide a place for this. Do you understand? So my war skin becomes my true skin more often than not. More people in the world know me by this name. The life of Break Bones—war and violence, the oaths of the warrior, the valorous acts done to protect my people—fills most of my days. I begin to wonder if Croion can be my true self when he is such a small part of my life. Perhaps this war skin, the person I have created to keep Croion safe, has destroyed Croion in an attempt to save him."

Jason raised his eyebrows. That was a pretty insightful and devastating critique. Break Bones had this philosopher streak that went through him, and in moments like this, Jason actually saw the glimmer of Croion beneath the war skin. "You could move away from all this," Jason said. "Go somewhere you could live in peace."

Break Bones smiled, showing off his yellow teeth. "Some of my people have tried it in years past. A small farm somewhere, on land that no one else would think could yield a single potato. They have eked out a life there. But the same thing always happens. An Elenil comes along, and then it all falls apart. There is a misunderstanding, or something the Elenil wants, and then the Scim is in his war skin again, fighting or running." There was a commotion from the front of their party. Break Bones looked that direction, his face tired. "But I said I had an observation about you to share."

"Sure," Jason said. "What is it?"

"You volunteer your true name, Wu Song, to any who ask it of you."

He shrugged. "Mostly true."

"But it seems to me that you do not use it yourself."

"What do you mean?" Jason asked.

"It seems to me that when you think of yourself, you think of yourself as Jason."

Uh. Hmm. He had never considered this. Jason was his English name, the name he used so substitute teachers could get it right. So many of his friends in school "couldn't" say his name, which was just another way to say they didn't want to or didn't think it was worth the work to say his name correctly. Honestly, back on Earth the only people who used his real name were his parents. And his sister, when she was alive. Some family friends, people like that. School had been a place where his real name just got made fun of, with dumb jokes about how it sounded, purposeful mispronunciations, stupid rhymes. And there was no way he could introduce the concept of tones. The fact was, even the people who got the sounds right usually got the tones wrong. Not that he blamed them—they didn't speak a language that used tones. Fine. But the reason his name didn't get learned and used was that it was "foreign." Alien. So he was Jason. Normal Jason. American Jason. He had a name that anyone could say. Nothing tricky, nothing "weird."

Break Bones stood up. "Do not confuse your war skin self for your real self," Break Bones said. "To change who you are can be a kind of dishonesty too." He grabbed Jason by the arm and yanked him painfully to his feet. "Mother Crow desires to see you."

Uh-oh. "Hey, what's going on, Break Bones?"

Break Bones didn't slow his pace. Jason half stumbled, the Scim's hand keeping him mostly upright, then started an awkward jog to keep up. "As I said, Wu Song. If I do not see you again, I wanted to share those words with you. It was an honor to be your friend."

"Oh, hey, don't get all past-tense on me, buddy." They were moving toward the head of the party. Kakri were getting out of their way, seeing the intensity on Break Bones's face. "Did you say all this to the other me?"

Break Bones grinned. "You can always make me smile, Wu Song. What funny paths your mind runs down. Even now you are jealous."

"So you admit that it's me," Jason said.

"I admit that it could be you. But the Southern Court is convincing. It could not be you, also. And as you know, in situations like these my advice would always be to eliminate you both."

"Ha haaaaa," Jason said. "That's terrible advice that I hope you have not mentioned to anyone else."

Break Bones shoved him to the ground at Mother Crow's feet. Baileya Crow, actually. She was wearing her crow cape, and her clothes were bound tight to her body with long black cords, in the way that Kakri dressed for battle. On her head was a helmet that had been made to look like a crow's head, the beak open wide to reveal her face. TJ was standing beside her with a smug expression, his arms folded. Bezaed was there too, grim as always.

Baileya grabbed Jason's arm and dragged him roughly to his feet. She pulled him behind her toward the last rise of the path. As they went over the top, the first thing he saw was a Southern Court city . . . if that's what it was. A giant butte rose in the distance, and on top of it were great towers, similar in appearance to the giant termite mounds he had seen on nature documentaries. People flew between them. People with wings.

But, much more concerning and immediate, a Southern Court army stood directly in front of them and stretched back almost all the way to the butte. A muscular woman dressed in armor was at their head, and she was flanked by entire companies of Jasons. There were other people mixed in, and other magical beings too. A few Black Skulls. Some Scim. Even some Elenil. A few of them wore the faces of Jason's friends. He thought he saw Kekoa there, and Ruth, too.

Baileya grabbed Jason and yanked him forward. "I am Mother Crow," she said. "And you have brought me upon yourselves. I have come for answers."

The woman in armor—she must be their queen—narrowed her eyes. "You have come uninvited into the Southern Court, Mother Crow. You know as well as I that there are penalties for such things."

Baileya grabbed Jason hard by the back of the neck. "I have brought your man," she said. "Now. You are going to tell me a story. You are going to explain what is happening here and why you have invaded Kakri territories, attempted to murder Mother Crow, and kidnapped our Wu Song."

"I will not," the queen said.

"Then it will be war between us," Baileya said. "And the first to die—" here she paused and shook Jason like a rag doll—"will be your man."

"Do I get a say in this?" Jason asked.

"Silence," both women said at once.

Baileya's grip tightened, and she lifted Jason from the ground. "Speak, Majesty. Before I break his neck."

Jason kicked, but there was nothing beneath his feet.

The queen smiled. "Go ahead and kill him."

"Hey," Jason said. "Seriously, last request. Mother Crow, please." Now that his life was literally in Baileya's hands, a sudden, gut-wrenching fear grabbed him. Not because he was afraid to die . . . to his great surprise, he wasn't, not really. But because of what would happen afterward when Baileya realized she had killed him. The real Jason.

"Speak quickly," Baileya Crow said.

"Please, Mother Crow. Please. Have Break Bones do it. Or Bezaed. Just . . . not you." He couldn't bear the thought of Baileya realizing she had been the one to kill her beloved.

"Very well," she said. "It is a small enough request. Wu Song."

"Yes?" Jason said.

She shook him. "Wu Song," she repeated, and TJ stepped forward. "You do it."

TJ smiled. "My pleasure."

"Uh, second request," Jason said. "Not that guy. Actually, third request—it has to be someone on Earth. Just send me to Earth, and I'll point out the guy. He lives really far away and is pretty busy, but we'll schedule an appointment." He wasn't afraid, but he wasn't, like, looking forward to being murdered, either.

TJ had a knife in his hand, and he stepped into range. Baileya held Jason tight so he couldn't fight back.

Jason remembered when Mother Crow—the other Mother Crow—had been shot with an arrow, and she had told him one last story. The story that could change the world, or so she said. He didn't see how it could possibly help him in this moment, but it did give him, somehow, a feeling of peace. He closed his eyes and waited for the blade.

PART 4

THE ARRIVAL OF DEATH

---

*Something stalks me in the house. I know not what it is—
in fact, I thought myself paranoid for a few weeks—yet I
am certain that it is there. It is not, I think, the Story
King's doing. I have not seen a Kharobem since that first
encounter, though I feel their thousand eyes on me at all
moments. No, it feels closer. Less powerful, certainly, than
the Story King, and yet each day there are tiny objects
out of place. A book open to a different page from
where I left it. A crystal moved a hair to the left on its
shelf. The dogs whining at nothing. As an educated
man, I must dismiss my fears. Yet as a magician, I know
there are things beyond mortal comprehension. I fear, in
the end, that my status as mortal is the thing that will
prevent my plan. I know that death comes for all, and*

who knows but this spectral presence may be the cold attention of that skeletal ferryman, come at last. But I have learned certain tricks, certain spells to forestall death's attention. They are dangerous to use, for they call the Story King's attention and ire. He has no patience for those who would use the life force of another to increase their own. So what I do, I must do quickly. Soon I shall have my own world, set aside from his prying eyes, and there I shall do as I wish. There I shall be a god of my own making, and the world—my world—shall tremble.

FROM *THE MAGICIAN'S GRIMOIRE*

27

DETOURS

*Once there was a boy . . . spoiled, rude, and cruel. He was
not a prince, though prince-like in many ways.*

FROM "RANA'S TALE"

✝

Hanali, son of Vivi, paced his quarters alone.

It had been a difficult year, but he was on the verge of triumph. The Palace of a Thousand Years nearly restored, and his own place as archon almost certainly set. Gilenyia as his wife, and the humans exiled or dead. All would be in its proper place. All for the common good, too, as he would be a wise and kindhearted ruler. He had every intention of raising the standard of living for the Scim. And yet . . . why was he so unhappy?

"Big place," Jason said. "Wide doorways, too—must make it easier for you to get all your shoulder pads through, right?"

Hanali's eyes widened, and despite himself, a smile snuck onto his face. "Mr. Wu. How did you possibly get through all the security and into my quarters?"

The boy jumped over the back of a divan—at least a hundred years old—lay down on it, and propped his feet on the backrest. "I heard you were looking for me, that's all."

"And here you are. I don't understand how you got here in the first place. How you tricked me in Madeline's hospital room."

"I just really like pudding, man. That's what you never understood. Pudding makes the world go round."

Hanali sighed. The boy never stopped with the pudding. "Now that I am archon, you could have whatever phantasmagorical feast you desire. Surely ice cream would be of more interest than pudding?"

"You can't eat ice cream for breakfast."

"No," Hanali said. "This isn't working."

Jason raised his eyebrows. "What? Why not? Seems fine to me."

"Mr. Wu is less respectful, less predictable. He would have . . . broken a vase, fallen off the divan. He would have called me a ridiculous name."

"Whatever the problem, magistrate, I'm certain I can—"

"No, no, just get out." Hanali pinched the bridge of his nose. His people had caught several Jason pretenders of late, and one of them had—after some magical persuasion—agreed to play the part as a sort of jester for Hanali. He had found the real Jason Wu endlessly infuriating, but he had to admit the child brought a certain wellspring of life with him. But this pale copy didn't do anything to cheer him.

A gentle knock sounded at the far door. Perhaps it was tea. He had asked for some several minutes ago. "Come."

It took him a moment when she walked in. The sight of her didn't register correctly. She was a human woman. In her early forties, perhaps, with platinum blonde hair and thin worry lines on her face. He knew her, of course. Mrs. Oliver.

"No," he said. "I do not know where you met her to take her shape, but I do not wish to see her. Begone."

She smiled, just a little, and stepped toward him, studying him. She set a backpack on the floor. Her head was cocked to the side, and she seemed uncertain about something. "It is you, isn't it? You look the same around the eyes. Too thin. Too tall. But it's you, right?"

"I do not care for this game."

"You always liked games before."

He raised an eyebrow. "I will say it one more time. Out. I command you as a magistrate of the Elenil."

She looked almost wistful. "Oh, Lee. The Elenil have no power over me. Not anymore. Not now that Madeline is gone."

It was her. He knew it with a sudden, ferocious certainty. "Mrs. Oliver."

"Wendy."

"I am surprised to see you here. How did you come to the Sunlit Lands?"

"Madeline brought me. A monster in the swamp used his magic. In Maduvorea." She sat on a chair and gestured to the one beside her.

He remained where he was. "I meant no harm to your daughter. I truly did not." The girl had been so hardheaded. If she had only done what was laid out for her. If she had just followed the brightly marked path he had made, if she hadn't been so good at finding more and more alternatives to every difficult choice he put in front of her, if she hadn't rejected her healing. He was surprised, as he thought about her, to discover . . . "I miss her."

Mrs. Oliver smiled. "Me too."

He moved to the chair across from her, intentionally choosing a different seat from the one she had indicated. The other was too close to her. "May I?"

She nodded. "You never liked such elaborate clothes when we were kids."

His outfit was a purple silk coat with sleeves so long they dropped past his knees, the interior of the sleeves a pale green. He wore a sunshine-yellow vest beneath it, bright-green pants that only reached his knees, and dual-toned socks, orange and red, that showed from the knees to mid-calf, until they disappeared into his boots. He wore a blue, shapeless hat on his head. He had been experimenting with the strange "prom" outfit that Mr. Wu had worn, once upon a time. It did not feel altogether successful, and it had not lifted his mood.

"When we were kids? My dear, I am surely at least two hundred years older than you."

She produced a small vial. "I've been drinking this," she said. "My memories are back. Almost all of them."

"And what, pray tell, is that?"

"It's called Wendy juice."

"You named it after yourself? How gauche."

She laughed. "Gauche? You never would have said that word back when I knew you."

Just then the tea arrived. He requested another cup and poured for her in the meantime. "I have an appointment, Mrs. Oliver. I need to meet my fiancée at the base of the tower in a short time. It would be the height of rudeness to leave her waiting."

"Lee," she said. "Lee, I want you to drink this. So you'll get your memories back."

He waved a hand at her. "Oh, my dear Mrs. Oliver. Wendy. I have already heard what the Pastisians say about my father in their books. I know the story you will tell, about the poor teenagers who wandered into the Sunlit Lands, but not all of them returned home."

She reached across and took his hands. Hers were surprisingly warm, and softer than he would have expected. "We shouldn't have left you, Lee. We were scared. Allison was dead, and when Vivi and Resca said they would send us home, would make a deal with us, we just wanted out. That was wrong. It was wrong for them to put us in that situation, but it was wrong for us to accept their deal. And we never should have offered them our firstborn children. You were right to say no to them."

His hands trembled, but he stilled them through sheer force of will. There was a door inside of him. He could feel something pushing from the other side. Something large and uncontainable. If he opened that door, he feared he would be flooded, washed away as the ocean burst through the doorframe. Memories were threatening to come in again. Wendy's presence was undoing the Historian's work. He would need to go for his regular visit soon to keep the story stable. "What were their names? The members of our group?"

"Wendy," she said.

"Yes."

"Your girlfriend."

It took him longer to say it this time. "Yes."

"There was Anthony. He had been in a fire, do you remember? He's a priest now."

Ah. The priest. Hanali had met him once, with Jason, and recognized the smell of Elenil magic on him. Then another name came to mind, and he said it with some bitterness. "Kyle."

Wendy squeezed his hand. "My husband now, but your best friend then. Then there was Gabrielle. And . . . Allison, who was killed by the Aluvoreans."

"Plus one more." Hanali's own cup had arrived, and he lifted it for a sip.

"Lee Foster," Wendy said, and a gentle smile came to her face.

Confused for a moment, Hanali lowered his cup and studied the woman. "Yes, but there was still one more. We were seven." His memories pounded on the door. He tried to pull out the name of this seventh while keeping the door shut, but he could not do it.

"Seven," she said. "You know, I think you're right, Lee. But who?"

It didn't matter. He didn't care. It was all so long ago. And if there was one more small memory hole in a great sea of them, what did it matter?

In one sense his friends had betrayed him. But in another he had volunteered. He had offered to stay so they could go. "It was good," he said, "that we all gave up those memories. Do you want to forget them again? I can help you."

"No, Lee, it's not good that we forgot." She sighed. "I remember, before they took me to that cave. I remember being so angry. I told Vivi and Resca that I would come back to the Sunlit Lands and kill them, and I was going to take you home. Do you remember that?" She looked into her cup as if she could see the past there somehow. "In the end I think Tony had it right. He kept his memories. When you don't remember a wound, you can't heal from it. You have to acknowledge it, study it, and then you start to heal."

This conversation was too strange, talking together about a life that Hanali had heard about but did not remember, did not want to remember. "I am Elenil now," he said. "I have always been Elenil."

"That's not true. Lee, oh, Lee, these ridiculous outfits, the way you treat the human children, don't you see this is all you trying to convince yourself that you're something you're not?"

He stiffened and sat up straighter. "I am Elenil. I am."

She deflated, put her tea down. "I'm not saying you aren't. But you used to wear jeans and a baseball cap. All the time. You were on the baseball team, Lee. During the summer we'd drive to the coast in your truck—do you remember?—and we'd dig a big hole, fill it with driftwood and pallets, and Kyle brought gasoline and the fire was so huge! Gaby would play her guitar, and when the moon came out, you always liked to sing "Moon River." I don't know why you loved that song so much, but Gaby couldn't really play it, so you learned it as a surprise, and we all laughed when you picked up the guitar—I didn't even know you could play—and just started this perfect song when we'd never even seen you pick out a note before." She didn't raise her head, just her eyes. "That's the place you told me you loved me the first time. Walking on the beach. The moonlight on the water."

That song. He knew it, could hear this faint echo within himself. "My mother used to sing it to me." What was her name? Not Resca, but another woman, a human one, from so long ago. He couldn't remember. Maybe he didn't know it anymore. Who called their mother by her first name? Not him.

The room seemed to tilt sideways. He couldn't breathe, his heart was pounding too fast.

The cup slipped from his hands and broke. He gripped the arms of his chair as if he were about to fall to the floor himself. "I will let you leave with your life," he said, "because of who you once were to me. But understand, Mrs. Oliver, my intention is to remove every human being from the Sunlit Lands." He had to. Remove them. Kill them if he had to. That would be better than just kicking them out because then they couldn't come back like Wendy. Mrs. Oliver.

"Get out," Hanali said.

She fell to her knees, came close to him. "Lee. Lee, leave this place. Come with me. We'll go home. You don't have to stay here anymore. Madeline broke all the old agreements. You're free now. Come home. Kyle will be so happy to see you, I promise. We'll go find Gaby, too. We'll go to the beach, Lee. We'll have a bonfire and sing."

Hanali tried to speak, but the pain twisted his face into a sneer. He squeezed his eyes shut, hard, until he regained control. "It's too late for me, Wendy. I have gone too far. There is not a path from here to forgiveness. The only way out is through. I have to press on. I have to finish this, have to restore the Elenil to their former glory."

Wendy was still kneeling in front of him, waiting for him to meet her eyes, but he could not. It seemed interminable how long she waited. But at last she stood. "Lee, listen to me. Do you remember the spring? Where we said goodbye all those years ago?"

He winced as more memories forced their way into his head. "It's a fountain now," he said. "A singing fountain."

"I'll wait for you there. Change out of those ridiculous clothes. Come meet me. We'll find the way to forgiveness together, Lee. I swear it's out there. Somewhere."

Then she was gone. Again. He needed a moment to nail down all the doors that were bursting open inside him, and when he was done, he felt the cold certainty of control coming back to him. He would send word to the magistrates, swiftly, and let them know that the plan for the humans must become more severe. More permanent.

And Gilenyia must certainly be here by now. He stood, and his outfit seemed, suddenly, like something ridiculous and strange, something that did not fit even though it was perfectly tailored. As if he had accidentally put on someone else's shoes.

"I am Hanali, son of Vivi," he said out loud to no one in particular. "I am a magistrate and will be archon soon." A small voice inside of him asked, *Are you so sure?* He pushed it down. Gilenyia was coming. He needed to be himself. He took a deep breath. "I am Hanali, son of Vivi. Hanali, son of Vivi." He closed his eyes and saw a bonfire, a field of stars, a wide expanse of dark waves, and people he knew—his friends—singing and laughing there.

"No," he said fiercely.

He stood straighter and composed himself.

He crossed to the closet to choose another style for entertaining Gilenyia. He was an Elenil. A dream maker. He chose the direction for his people, and they went with him.

He said it a fourth time: "I am Hanali, son of Vivi." By the fifth time, he had begun to believe it again.

28
A HUMAN PROBLEM

It's the sort of grief that comes when a person has lost more than he knows how to count, when the loss is so great he can't see it all.

THE PEASANT KING

✢

Gilenyia paced at the base of the Palace of a Thousand Years. She had taken her time this morning coming to the tower. Hanali had gleefully accepted her request for an audience but then had made a variety of transparently false excuses for why he could not meet at this or that time. She had arrived at the Tower at the agreed-upon time only to discover that Hanali did not intend to come greet her at the entrance, but had left word for her to meet him at the top of the tower—the sort of message that a better leaves for his lesser. A good host—and certainly a suitor—would have been waiting for her at the entrance, or maybe even closer. A good suitor would have arrived at her own home with an entourage and princely gifts.

No matter. Gilenyia had never been one to indulge in childish fantasies about the Elenil she would marry. She had always assumed it would be someone with power and wealth, and Hanali, she was forced to admit, had both . . . much to her surprise. Now that her own heritage as an Elenil was in question, she knew that this match was more important than she had originally thought. But then there were the haunting words suggesting that not just she but all Elenil were human. She wasn't sure what to make of that.

If she were truly human—if all the Elenil were truly human—that would have ramifications that she was not prepared to engage with fully. The entire authority structure of the Sunlit Lands was predicated on the understanding that the Majestic One had created a sort of hierarchy based on the different types of people in the Sunlit Lands: Elenil at the top, Scim at the bottom, and humans exiled to a different world. All the others took their places here and there, in a fluid list that changed largely based on the whims and needs of the Elenil, who were, after all, the benevolent rulers of the Sunlit Lands.

"Lady, are you well?"

Ricardo. Always so attentive to her needs. "I am angry, Ricardo."

"He has done you wrong," Ricardo said, an obvious attempt at diplomacy.

"It's not because of him," Gilenyia said. "It is the state of the world."

"Ah. You have discovered something about the Elenil and denied it for as long as you were able. And now you are angry about what you have discovered."

Astonished, she looked at Ricardo more carefully. But there was nothing special to see. He appeared as he always did: carefully dressed, a weapon at his side, eyes roving their surroundings, seeking threats. She had a strange, almost alien desire to take him into her confidence. But he was human and could not be trusted with Elenil business.

She bristled when the thought came to her, *He is human like you.*

Not like me, she told herself.

And then the anger came again, like waves at the ocean. The sea might look calm in the distance, and yet waves came without end. "I am not angry," she said, knowing full well how ridiculous this sounded when she had just told him that she was. But it rankled her to think that he knew her well enough to know things about her without being told. . . . She had spent a long time building her emotional armor, and it was not meant to be pierced so easily. But, it seemed, Ricardo had been studying her all along, unnoticed.

"It is normal, lady," he said.

"Do not presume to tell me what is normal." And still Hanali had not arrived. She had waited here, hoping that he would come to his senses and treat her as an equal. No doubt he was waiting at the top, gleefully anticipating the moment that she would use the magical elevation steps that floated through the center of the tower. But she would not give him that satisfaction. "We climb the stairs," she said at last, and started upward.

"Have you heard of the stages of grief?" Ricardo asked after they had walked up the first several flights. "I could tell you about them while we climb. For your entertainment."

Ah. He was being so careful in how he offered to share this information he clearly wanted to discuss, giving her the authority to decide whether to hear it or not. He had remembered his place. "If it would amuse you," she said.

"When my father was dying, I experienced this," he said simply, though he had never mentioned his father's death before. "My father was shot in the stomach. They told me he would likely die. At first I thought, no, there's no way. Not my dad. He won't die. Not like this. The doctors would be able to save him, I thought. Even when the doctors said they did not think they could. Denial. That's called denial."

"Who shot him?" she asked.

His face went still, and he continued without answering her question. "Then came the anger. Anger at the doctors, at my father, at the world. This is normal, this anger. It comes when mourning the loss of a loved one, and it comes when realizing the world is different from what you thought it to be."

She frowned. He was speaking with an almost alarming familiarity. "And in what way do you assume that my world has changed?"

He shook his head. "Take no offense, lady." He paused, as if weighing his next words carefully. "It's only human."

She pursed her lips. It was a canny comment. Just enough to imply he knew precisely what she was struggling with, which—if true—meant either that he was far more observant than she'd expected or that the fact of Elenil humanity was somehow more obvious than she had known. "What are the other stages you speak of? Denial and then anger. What should the grieving expect after that?"

"Then comes bargaining."

"What does this look like?"

"Trying to make a deal. Like me praying that if God would save my father, I would become a priest. That's bargaining. Then comes depression."

"Natural enough," she said.

"Then, finally, acceptance. Then you can move out of grief. You've learned to carry it, to make peace with it. But these five stages, they can happen together or you can skip one or cycle through them more than once. It's not like climbing a mountain—it's like being caught in a raging river. There are times you are swept back into the water when you thought you were done."

"But my father is not dead," Gilenyia said. "I have lost no one of consequence."

Ricardo said nothing to that.

"Are you suggesting, Ricardo, that grief might come for reasons other than death?"

"Loss of any kind, lady. Discovering that you are something other than what you thought. One must mourn the death of an old identity to take on a new one."

They paused, now about halfway up the tower. Gilenyia studied the distance they had yet to climb. She imagined Hanali at the top, furious at the length of time she was taking. That made her smile at least. Ricardo was not wrong. She was swinging wildly through denial and anger. She didn't think she would come to the bargaining stage, but she didn't understand her own emotions, either.

Gilenyia was struck by the sudden thought that it wasn't the possibility of being a human that was most upsetting. It was unsettling, yes. But more disturbing was the idea that all the decisions she had made, all the things the Elenil had done, might now need to be accounted for. They had treated humans as something a step or two above the Scim. They had offered the humans some little taste of Elenil magic in exchange for their loyalty and service. Not only that, but they had purposely chosen the most vulnerable people available to them. Refugees, orphans, the poor, people on the run, people with terminal illnesses. The Elenil had built enough of their culture around this symbiotic relationship that the thought of Hanali removing the humans filled her with some dread. There would be a vacuum in the place where the Elenil's servants currently stood. Would the Scim race in to fill it? She did not know. Hanali was playing a dangerous game.

They walked the rest of the way in silence, Ricardo clearly noticing her mood and falling in step just behind her. When they reached the top, a tame Scim porter greeted them, looking with some displeasure at the state of their clothing after the long climb.

He bowed. "Lady Gilenyia. May I bring you some fresh clothing?"

"You may not. Take me to Hanali immediately."

The Scim bowed again, but he did nothing to disguise the contempt in his eyes. "This way, lady."

Hanali had, as always, staged the entire space to perfection. He was in the archon's throne room, but he had ordered a full collection of comfortable chairs and small handmade tables and even a divan brought in to one end of the room. Flowers decorated the tables, and Hanali wore a light-cream outfit, the shirt of which buttoned with ties and went past his knees. The pants were loose and the same cream color. He wore no shoes, something that Gilenyia had never known him to do before, but he had been taking fashion risks lately. He wore a diadem that looked suspiciously like something belonging to a king, even though it was thin, small, and had only a tiny purple gem set in the center. All in all, Hanali looked unaccountably Spartan, and the comparative simplicity of his fashion filled Gilenyia with unease. And yet he appeared genuinely delighted to see her. "Gilenyia! My dear! Please come and have a seat."

He didn't stand to greet her. She smoothed her dress and sat on a wingback chair across from him. Ricardo stood at her side. "Hanali. You are looking well."

He beamed at her. "As are you! Aside from your companion."

"He does as I ask," Gilenyia said. "There is nothing more I require of him."

Hanali bounced to his feet. "I, on the other hand, require his absence. Thank you, Mr. Sánchez, but you may leave us now."

Ricardo bowed his head reverentially. "Forgive me, magistrate, but I must stay unless the lady dismisses me."

Hanali laughed at that. "Of course. But she and I have weighty matters to discuss—Elenil matters—that require that only Elenil be present."

Gilenyia was pleased that Ricardo did not leave when Hanali said this. He only shifted his weight for a moment and continued to stand quietly. "I was surprised when you did not greet me at the base of the tower," she said.

"Matters of state kept me from being able to," Hanali said. "Of course I wanted to."

"Which is why you sent one of your servants to escort me."

Hanali raised an eyebrow. "Was he not there to greet you?"

Gilenyia sighed. "Ricardo, please wait for me outside this room."

Her servant bowed. "I will never be too far to hear the sound of your voice," he said, and slowly exited the room.

Hanali watched him go, amused. "He's an intense one. I remember when I first brought him to the Sunlit Lands. Has he told you his story, Gilenyia? It's suitably tragic."

A Scim servant entered with drinks. Gilenyia took hers and sipped. Some mix of fruit juices, the perfect balance of sweet and tart. Hanali had always been a gifted party planner, and in this aspect she knew he would excel as archon. Assuming he became archon. "Cousin," she said. "I want to have words with you about something."

"And I with you. Thus the meeting, lady. Please, have your say."

She set her drink aside and leaned toward him. "You have changed, Cousin. I remember a time when all your words bounced around like a fantastical banquet. The plight of the Scim! The need for a stronger archon! The fashion decisions of the elder Elenil! But now your talk is all of a single color and single topic: more power for yourself."

"Focus is required for achieving one's goals," Hanali said absently.

"It is boring," Gilenyia said. "What of the old Hanali?"

"That fop." He put his drink aside as well. "You never gave him much more than a few party invitations, Gilenyia. Or am I mistaken that you are at least considering my offer of marriage?"

She sighed. "I am tired, Cousin. So tired. And I have learned things that fill my head with such conflict I scarcely know what to do. The world has become more complex than I ever imagined, and I do not see a solution to problems today that I did not know existed three days ago."

"Tell me what ails you, my dear. I will take care of you. All of my other friends are gone, and the most entertaining of my servants dead or disappeared. What do you need, Gilenyia? What troubles you?"

So. Here was her moment. She would tell Hanali the truth. "It is a problem concerning the humans," she said.

Hanali, delighted, clapped his hands in joy. "How wonderful! That's precisely the news I brought you here to discuss. I have a new plan, and whatever your problem, I feel certain that this little plan will take care of it completely. Would you like to hear it?"

He had derailed her confession, but she felt a burning desire to know his plan. "Pray tell me, Cousin."

Hanali leapt onto the divan, standing atop it. "The magistrates are even more concerned about the humans than I could have expected. They've given me permission for a preemptive strike. Tonight at midnight they will make me archon, and before two more nights pass, I will send the Elenil army out to kill every human in the city."

Her heart leapt into her throat. "But you had said before, Hanali, that you would banish some of them, exile them!"

Hanali laughed. "Yes, a good plan to start. But the magistrates pointed out that all of those humans, then, would be loose in the world. Back on Earth, telling people about us. And how long before someone would come back with every intention of overthrowing our people or me?"

"You cannot do this, Hanali." Panic was taking hold of her. "What of the servants . . . people like Ricardo? Will you kill my best servant?"

"We will train you another. Soon a tame young Scim will bring you your tea."

"Hanali, please. I beg of you. Threaten them all, and those who remain behind you can kill. But give them a chance at least. Many of them want to go home, and only their bargain with the Elenil keeps them here in any case . . . for those who have chosen to renew their service since Madeline broke all bonds. Let them free, and they will leave."

He put his hand on his chest, as if he was surprised that she would be so resistant. "My good lady, do you not see the hole in your plan? What is the story then? It is a story of immigration policy. 'We have sent the humans home.' But it does not leave them appropriately vilified for me to rise to power. If the humans are so vile, why would I let them live? They have to be monsters. And one does not settle for chaining a monster up or kicking it out of one's home. Monsters must be destroyed."

"But they are not monsters!" Gilenyia said and, with a jolt, realized that she was bargaining with Hanali. Another one of Ricardo's stages of grief. Bargaining. There was nothing to be gained. Hanali would not be moved, not like this.

"No. They are not monsters, they are just humans," he agreed. "But in the future, if we need them, we can always let some more in. Think of it this way, Gilenyia. With this plan, we put the entire Sunlit Lands back in its rightful order. We send a warning to the other peoples of the Sunlit Lands—if we treated the humans thus, who is to say we wouldn't do it to them as well?—and not a drop of Elenil blood needs be spilled."

She couldn't stop herself, she just blurted it out. "But the Elenil are humans too."

Hanali became very still. "What did you say?"

"The Elenil are human, Hanali. I am human. I was born a human and *made* an Elenil. Someone else decided that's what I am. They changed me, told me I was meant to rule, that I was better than the other humans. But I'm not, and I never was." She crossed to him. His face was stone. "I am a human being," she said. "Not anything better than them. And you know what this means, Hanali . . . you are a human too."

He put his hand over hers, then reached for his drink and took a sip. She did not envy him the process that was about to come. He sat back, a look of pain on his face. "Gilenyia, it hurts me deeply to think that you presumed this would surprise me."

Her mouth fell open in shock. "You already knew—"

"There are humans, and there are *humans*," he said. "Some are worthless, short-lived little balls of clay. *Humans.* Some are glorious, urbane, beautiful. *Elenil.* You may have been human once, but you are Elenil now."

"I could say the same about you," she said, still in shock.

He raised his glass. "And many thanks for the compliment." He drained the glass and set it aside. "In any case, Gilenyia, I have a great deal of work to do for tonight, as you might imagine. Archon ascensions to plan, soldiers to prepare, you know how it is."

"Hanali," she said, and grabbed his hands, desperate to change his mind. "When Madeline healed me, she . . . she *changed* me."

"Whatever do you mean?"

"I mean that . . . Hanali, I think I can have children. Something the Elenil cannot do. Not anymore."

Hanali chuckled. "Oh, my dear. What a vivid imagination you have. Would you like to come to the coronation? Or, well, an archon isn't king— I suppose 'installation' might be the best term. And we've not put in a new archon in centuries. Would you like to come?"

She nodded in mute wonder. How had he done all of this so quickly? "What shall I wear?"

"I shall send a bird with more information." He stood, took her hand, and walked her toward the door. "Do not worry, Gilenyia. Your secret is safe with me." He pecked her on the cheek. Then he said, his voice full of wonder, "Wife of the archon! Did your parents ever think that would be possible? Or did you?"

Then she was out of the room, and Hanali was gone. Ricardo was at her side, and the last two stages of grief hit her simultaneously. Depression. And acceptance. Her legs felt weak, and Ricardo's hand was on her arm, steadying her. She would have to find a way to get Ricardo out of the Sunlit Lands. At least him. "Ricardo," she said. "When someone has gone through all the stages, what happens then?"

"It depends, lady. Some people get stuck. For instance, where I come from, in America, there are certain people like yourself who come from a place of privilege and wealth. When they begin to understand how the rest of the world works, they may become angry or depressed and get stuck there. Never grow past it, just perpetually angry forever."

"And is that wrong?"

"Not necessarily," he said. "Anger can be just. Anger can be powerful, and it can be important. But there is something more important than anger."

"What is that?"

"Doing something about it. About whatever the injustice is. We have to change it. Not just say that we will, not just speak up about it, not just fight the powers that be, but actually change the world. If we don't do that, what use is all the anger and the words?"

Of course. A firm resolve came to her. "Ricardo," she said, "we need to get home quickly. We have a great deal of work ahead of us and not much time. Go at once to the Knight of the Mirror and bring him to my quarters. Do not take no for an answer."

"Yes, lady," he said, and was gone.

Midnight was, perhaps, ten hours away, and Hanali had said it would be two more nights before he killed the humans. Nearly three days, then. A plan was forming in her mind. But was there enough time?

29
THINGS FOUND

The one-word story changes the world, making it better for some, worse for others. It throws down kings and raises up cities. It destroys governments and creates worlds.

FROM *THE WISE SAYINGS OF MOTHER CROW*

✢

arius was pinwheeling, out of control, and the ground was getting closer every moment. He wasn't even thinking about what had happened, about how Malgwin and Fantok had broken the sky—with Cumberland's approval—and caused him to fall through. His mind was racing against gravity. Could he call his Scim owl, Bubo, who had often carried him on its back? But no, even if he could call, Bubo would be too far away.

Fantok swooped back, coasting under Darius, who landed on her back. Now *that* felt like old times. The Sunlit Lands spread beneath him, his legs warm against the feathers of his bird. He looked back at the dome of heaven where he had broken through, and at this height he could still see the hole.

"Where do you want to go?" Fantok asked.

Where *did* he want to go? He wanted to get Hanali in his hands. But he wasn't ready for that, not yet. A pang of regret hit him. He had gone after the archon before, when Madeline had asked him to come to her instead. He'd thought that he had time, but he hadn't. He should have chosen Madeline. The archon could have waited. "I want to see where she died," Darius said. "Take me to Aluvorea."

Fantok replied, "I cannot take you all the way to that place, but I can take you to the forest. It is called Maduvorea now."

"Then to Maduvorea," Darius said.

But then he remembered the Pastisian dirigible that he and Cumberland had seen. It was headed south. Toward the Southern Court. And why was he going to Maduvorea? Out of some maudlin need to see the place where Madeline had died without him? Maybe this was the same type of choice he had faced before, but now he thought . . . why not be with someone familiar? Why not be with his friends? "Fantok," he said.

"I hear you," the bird called.

"Take me to King Ian."

The bird looked over her shoulder at Darius. Then, without a word, she banked south. Darius didn't know if Fantok was somehow aware that Ian was in that dirigible they had passed earlier. Maybe her bird vision was sharp enough to have picked him out. Or maybe, since she was the sovereign of the Kharobem, whatever that meant, she had some special abilities that allowed her to do things like know where everyone was. Or perhaps just important people—who knew?

Darius might have slept for part of the trip. He wasn't sure. He did close his eyes, his hands wrapped deep in Fantok's feathers, and the flight seemed to go quickly. Time was strange in the Sunlit Lands, though. Sometimes things happened faster than it seemed they should. It wasn't like a dream, where you were in one place and then suddenly in another. But trips that seemed like they should transpire over the course of weeks could be completed in days. Sometimes. It wasn't consistent—the same journey could take different amounts of time.

The Scim had told Darius that was the way life was, and they thought it strange that he would expect anything different. He told them that on Earth it always took the same amount of time to go somewhere as to return, and that the same journey on a different day wouldn't vary in length. The Scim laughed and told him a story about two Scim who set off for the same place at the same pace and arrived a week apart from one another.

Darius could see King Ian's dirigible now, docked at a high platform on a wide butte to the south. He also noticed towers, some of which looked like natural formations, and others which appeared to have been built at some point in the distant past. It was a place Darius had never been, the far southern part of the world.

"Many of my people are gathered here," Fantok said.

"What does that mean?"

"Something of import is happening. They are drawn to consequential moments in the history of the Sunlit Lands, to stand as witnesses."

"Why don't they get involved? Do something to help?"

"Who says they do not?"

Six large birds were rising from the butte. They flapped hard to get altitude, then banked toward Darius and Fantok. "Visitors?"

"We are the visitors," Fantok said.

"They don't look friendly," Darius said. "How do you feel about it?"

"I also doubt they are friendly," Fantok said. "They are shape-shifters. You have no weapon, and I will be sorely limited in how I fight with you on my back."

"You could drop me," Darius said with some bitterness.

"It's true," Fantok said. "But you would die, I think."

"So what's our best option?"

"I'll dip low so you can jump off. Then I'll come back for you," Fantok said.

"Makes sense," Darius replied. "Just as long as it's not too high."

The birds were closer now, and Darius realized they weren't birds at all but other large, winged beasts. One looked like a dragon straight out of one of Madeline's books, and two of them were definitely pterodactyls. The fourth was a bat, the fifth something he had never seen . . . some sort of hairy nightmare with lots of teeth. The sixth was changing shape even as it flew and settled on mirroring Fantok.

"When you come back for me," Darius said, "we need some sort of code word so I know it's really you."

"I will say the true name of the Peasant King," Fantok said.

"Fine," Darius said. "That will do."

Fantok folded her wings and descended. "When I say, jump," Fantok yelled.

Darius readied himself. He wished he had his Black Skull outfit on now so he could do things like this with no real danger to himself. When they got closer to the ground, Darius saw that Fantok was headed for a lake. Good thinking. Darius could jump into the water, which would be marginally safer than landing on the ground, and Fantok wouldn't have to slow down much. Fantok flung her wings open, banked hard, and shouted for Darius to jump.

He shoved off hard and put his body in alignment to go in feetfirst. A pencil dive, they called it. He pointed his toes and held his hands at his sides. He hit the water hard and plummeted deep into the lake. When his downward motion stopped, he swam up. He hurt from the fall, but he had experienced worse plenty of times. He knew he'd recover shortly.

Darius surfaced and looked for the closest shore. Grey rocks loomed over the beach, along with plenty of places to hunker down and hide if he needed to. He had always been a natural swimmer—his parents had insisted he take lessons when he was young, as neither of them had ever learned—and he found the regular pull of his arms and kick of his legs familiar and relaxing. No one was around when he got to shore. He peeled off his shirt, kicked off his shoes, and sat to sun himself dry. It was a strange and relaxing moment, made stranger by the thought that Fantok was off fighting dragons and giant bats.

The wind blew across the water, gentle and cool. Something was singing in the long grass on the other side of the lake. Frogs, maybe, though knowing the Sunlit Lands, it could just as easily be fairies or some ridiculous little creatures Darius had never heard of. The breeze carried a sweet smell, some sort of flower. Darius put his hands under his head, leaned back, and looked at the sky. He couldn't see Fantok, only white clouds journeying across the blue dome of the sky above. He could just make out the crystalline crack where he had fallen through, and he wondered what would happen if the sky ever broke completely.

It was a good place, the Sunlit Lands. At least, in places and at moments like this. If he just enjoyed the present and didn't think about the poverty of the Scim, or the misdeeds of the Elenil, or the Kakri eking out an existence in the desert while fountains splashed in every square of the Court of Far Seeing. Not that it was all about the Elenil—there were other issues too. But even the places with the most challenges weren't all bad. Darius had loved his time in the Wasted Lands and had learned to see joy and peace in the faces of those blessed people. The Scim took care of each other—they thought about their community. When someone had no food, it was likely that another Scim would show up with enough food for the day . . . if not the week. And the magic of the Black Skulls, which had given him fighting abilities and protection from harm, had been the direct result of the Scim community lending those things to him.

"I do not mean to startle you," a voice said nearby.

Strangely, Darius was so relaxed that the voice didn't startle him at all. "It's a beautiful day," he said.

"I suppose it is. Though dire deeds are afoot."

"Aren't they always," Darius replied. "Come out and sit with me, whoever you are." It seemed safe to assume that someone who was doing his best not to startle Darius probably didn't have ill intentions.

It was a Maegrom, and one dressed in finer clothes than was typical for the little grey people. He wore rich red attire, including a small red cape with white trim. He carried a glass box in front of him. Where the panes of glass came together, the edges were lined with gold. The frame was decorated in delicately forged rings. "I am called Crukibal," the Maegrom said. "I am a noble among my people."

Darius sat up. "I'm Darius Walker. What are you doing here, Crukibal?"

The Maegrom held up his box, giving Darius a closer look. Darius could see multiple colored shapes dancing inside the glass. Bright, glowing animals—stags and dogs, lions and rabbits, people and sheep, oxen and bears—moved within the glass, as if they were telling stories. "This box told me to meet you here, at this time. Your Peasant King sent instructions."

Of course he did. "Are you meant to give me the box? What is the plan?"

Crukibal's hand moved slowly across the top of the box. "This is not what it appears to be. It is a sort of prison, wrongfully made by my people long ago. Inside there are six Kharobem imprisoned . . . one for each of the peoples of the Sunlit Lands, save the Kakri, whose Kharobem has been released."

"Doesn't seem smart to keep them locked up like that," Darius said. "I've never seen Kharobem do much, but they're powerful. I wouldn't want to get on the wrong side of them."

"Nor I, Darius Walker. But the Heart of Flame—my ruler—does not want to lose the power that he gains from having access to these creatures of story. He can ask any question and the Kharobem will tell him the story he needs to know at that time, for the canny magic of the box binds them to answer true."

"Hmm," Darius said, leaning back again to enjoy the blue sky. He wasn't sure he wanted to enter back into this world of fire and fighting and captive Kharobem. "What question am I supposed to ask it?"

"I do not know," Crukibal said, and he pushed his thumb against the ringed frame so that one of the rings slid into his palm. He handed it to Darius. "Put this on your finger, and you can hear the stories that the Kharobem tell."

He weighed it in his hand. Cumberland had told Darius that he was giving him the final say in what was going to become of the Sunlit Lands. He had also said that the key might be in learning the story of how the Sunlit Lands came to be. But he hadn't told him that story, not really. The Maegrom was watching him intently. He slipped on the ring.

Six Kharobem hovered around him. Each was about twelve feet tall, with four faces—human, eagle, lion, and ox—and many wings, all of which were covered in eyes. They had human torsos and two legs that ended in hooves. To say they were intimidating was an understatement.

"Free us," one of them said, its voice like thunder.

"How?" Darius said. "Break the box?"

"Free us," said a second.

"But I don't know how."

They hovered for a moment, eyes blinking. "Free us," said the third.

"Just tell me how," he said again, but they didn't answer. Maybe they didn't know how?

Then they all asked the same question at once, in an eerie chorus: "What story would you like to hear?"

"I want to know how the Sunlit Lands came to be."

The Kharobems' wings buzzed faster, and their eyes winked and blinked at one another, sending some sort of code that he could not understand or even have the hope of understanding. Something like lightning passed between their wings.

"Whose version of the story would you like to hear? The Elenil's or the Scim's? The humans' or the Maegrom's? We can tell you any version you wish. Any save the Kakri version, which is theirs alone to tell."

"I want to know the true version. The version that really happened."

"We can tell you the human story. The story that Cumberland would tell."

"Is that the true story?"

More buzzing and signaling. One of them finally answered, "It is not untrue. It has all that he knows of the story."

"I want the true story," Darius repeated.

The buzzing went on for a full minute this time. One of them answered, "You are asking for the Kharobem story of the founding of the Sunlit Lands?"

"If that's the one that is true, then yes."

"We are required to tell you that this may break our captivity."

"All the better," Darius said.

"No one has asked for a Kharobem story before."

"I want to hear the Kharobem story about the founding of the Sunlit Lands," Darius said.

"So be it," the Kharobem chorus replied. "Many years ago, there was a magician who lived in the American South—"

Darius felt the ring on his hand grow hot, and the Kharobem slowly disappeared, and then it was as if they had hacked his eyes. He didn't see the lake or Crukibal, or the stones or sky around him. He saw a white mansion with ivy growing up around it. It was night, and warm lights came from the windows. He saw a long, white gravel driveway and a stable off to the right, where horses neighed softly. The grass was perfect, and bright flowers grew beneath the windows on the ground floor. The cicadas were singing, filling the air with their rhythmic buzz.

"—and his life was one of deep study of magics, both bright and dark, and he had built a world of considerable ease to inhabit."

Darius knew what was coming before the picture changed to show a long house, a sort of cabin. It was clean enough. Not a hovel, not a shack. There were rows of bunk beds. And on the beds were people. All of them Black, all of them men. In every bed but one the men were asleep. And in that one bed—the picture moved toward it—a man lay on his back, wearing only a pair of homespun pants. His eyes were open, and he stared at the bunk of the man above him.

Though he had no beard, Darius recognized him at once. It was Cumberland.

30

THE STORY
OF THE SUNLIT LANDS

Sometimes the way you save the world is just by saving the people in it.

THE PEASANT KING

✦

Cumberland Armstrong Walker lay on his back in the bunkhouse—the master called it the servant quarters—and thought about power and freedom. He had to earn his freedom, that's what they said. But his "master" had been born to freedom. His master had power, and Cumberland did not. In fact, his master had power not only over himself but over Cumberland and the other folks who had been enslaved too. He could, with a flick of a pen, decide who was free. So they had to be careful, and they had to be deferential, and that was how they stayed safe. Cumberland thought about parents and time and circumstance and how he had been born into slavery and the master had been born free. But he couldn't stop thinking that freedom and power, they came together somehow, and if he could understand how that worked, well, that would be power, and that would mean he was free.

He tried to discuss this with the others, but they were afraid the master would overhear, and it was the kind of talk he did not like, talk about power, talk about freedom. *Why would they want freedom, anyway? Didn't he give them food and a roof over their heads? Didn't they have clothes free of charge and beds, too? It was the master who had to worry about all these things. They had real freedom. They didn't have to worry about where their next meal would come from. They didn't have to take care of each other or themselves—they just needed to do what the master said. There was a kind of freedom in that, too.*

Even though it was his fellow captives who said this, these were the master's words. Not even their words were free, Cumberland said to himself. The master had somehow put his words in their mouths. The master had that kind of power. The master had built a world of considerable ease to inhabit, and his life was one of deep study of magics, both bright and dark. His master had learned the secrets to the universe, that if one could find the right words, one could bend the world, shape it to one's own preference. Sometimes his master would use the phrase "words of power."

These thoughts had come to Cumberland over the course of years, not moments. In that time he had made friends and lost them. He thought sometimes of the friends and family he had left behind who still lived—he hoped—in other homes and at other plantations. (For the master kept only male slaves, and all had been bought using some mysterious calculus of his own invention. Cumberland had been brought here when he was thirteen.) In the arena of friendship, Cumberland counted himself a man of wealth in comparison to the magician, who had, it seemed, neither friend nor family, but only long days and longer nights of study, and two large, vicious dogs who loved neither man nor woman, but only their master. On the magician's property were those who worked the fields and the overseers of those who worked the fields, and in the house all those who cared for the master and his needs directly. The master did as little of this work as possible, entrusting his slaves with a great deal of responsibility.

So it was with some surprise that Cumberland saw the master one bright summer day, riding a horse through the field and watching his people do their work. It was harvest time, which meant that the months of weeding were past, the buds had all been topped, and any hornworms snatched off and killed. Cumberland had snapped the juice out of a thousand or more himself, though he didn't know his numbers to count so high. Now it was late July, which meant walking through the rows of tobacco, leaning low to get the bottom leaves, holding them under his arm until he had a good load, then back to the sled that the donkey pulled. When the sled was full, it was off to the curing barn, where others would tie the leaves to sticks and hang them in the barn, and the fires must be kept at just the right temperature to cure the leaves over the course of five or seven days. But Cumberland, he'd be in the fields for the next five to seven weeks.

He had known the master was coming because the singing had stopped. The master didn't mind the singing most of the time, but he didn't like it when he was out among the men. Sing when he was gone, but if he came too close, he wanted you quiet so you could hear what he had to say. He must have surprised everyone, though, because the song had been in full swing and stopped abruptly. Maybe he had used his magic, so no one saw him until he was near. But the song had been a favorite of Cumberland's, about the heavenly home they would find when they met the good Lord in heaven, and the crown and robe he would give to his faithful servants at that time.

Cumberland had noticed the sharp eyes of the magician on him more than once in recent months, as if weighing him carefully for some task, or, as the foreman in his bunkhouse had said, "sizing you up for the stew." Which Cumberland did not like to think about, not only because he did not want to be in the stew but also because he did not want to eat any stew if his fellows were in it.

"And what is so fair about that heavenly home?" the master asked. "Is this not as close to heaven as you can get on this side of life? Food and bed and clothes and every need taken care of by a loving master?"

There was a great deal of "Yes, master" and head nods and "Thank you, master" from the others.

Cumberland did not begrudge them this, and he knew he was supposed to say those things too—and had for many years. But today, whether from the heat or the weight of the tobacco leaves he did not know, he found himself standing straight and speaking to the master. "The heavenly home is bright and fair, master, and there every man will wear a crown, not just one."

The master did not look angry at this, but Cumberland knew that the man's emotions ran deep and did not always reach his face. "Cumberland! Of all here, you are the only one to answer your master's question."

"It seemed only right, sir," he said, now a little nervous. "To treat you like a human being, I mean, sir. To answer you when you asked a question."

Now the master laughed. He slid down from his horse, the riding crop in his hand. Why a man would need a riding crop when only coming out to the field, Cumberland did not know, and it struck him for the first time that although the master knew how to use certain tools that Cumberland did not—magic and reading and so on—Cumberland, too, knew things the master did not, like how to use a hoe, and the best way to deal with an infected blister on your hand, and the songs that would help ease a man new to the bunkhouse who longed for home.

"Tell me," the master said. "If you could be anyone in the whole world, Cumberland, who would you be?"

"Oh, I would be myself, master."

The master whipped the crop against his gloved hand. "Just so. And if you could do anything, Cumberland, what would you do? Would you be baker or barber? Blacksmith, brewer? Bricklayer or butcher?" He looked at Cumberland as if studying him.

Cumberland did not know this at the time, but in years to come he would realize that the master was testing him, seeing if he had learned to read somehow. The master was afraid the slaves would learn to read, and he had purposely used only words beginning with *b* and in alphabetical order. The man watched Cumberland carefully for any sign that the words struck him as strange. But Cumberland could not read at that time, and he did not know what the master meant.

"A pilot on a riverboat might be nice, master," he said. "I've thought of that before." He had been brought here on a riverboat and had enjoyed the way the men called to one another as they did their work and the way the pilot had kept the boat and passengers safe and made the most important decisions.

The master had not responded to this revelation, nor had he ordered Cumberland whipped, which had seemed most likely. Instead he had simply mounted his horse and ridden back to the house. But the next day Cumberland was told that he would not be working in the fields but in the kitchen. Which was not a better job, not really, as there were meals to make for the master and those in the house, and meals to make for those in the fields and in the barns, and as he was the new boy, he got the lowest and worst of the jobs. But it kept him busy and kept him from thinking, and it made him tired in a new and different way. Often he would lie in his bunk and fall asleep within a few minutes.

So it was a few months before he realized that the answer he had given to his master was not true. He did not want to be a riverboat pilot. He didn't want to be a cook or a woodworker, a hostler or a carpenter. He wanted to be a magician. He wanted to know the secret words that would let him build a new and different world.

There were many moments along the way that matter to this story. But the most important one was this: one Sunday Cumberland was sent to take the master his supper. It was chicken and dumplings and a glass of milk, a simpler meal for Sundays. And he had been told the way through the house, which was still new to him. He had not wandered far from the kitchen before this day. He wondered at the soft carpets beneath his feet and the beautiful but foreign art in different places and finally arrived at the master's workshop and learned, at last, the key to the magician's power: he could read. Floor to ceiling were books. Books on shelves, books on tables, books piled on the floor or broken open on chairs. There was paper covered with scribbled notes and a sign with gold lettering on the wall. And there were strange crystals, too, of all sizes, some on pedestals and some thrown on the ground, and even a few discarded on the bookshelves. And the magician himself sat at his desk, head bowed over a book, and so deeply immersed in it that Cumberland thought he might be in a trance.

The master's dogs saw him at the door, and one of them growled, "That's far enough."

The master's dogs could talk, of course. That was one of the things the magician had learned to do. He'd told the men that the dogs had been human once too, but he had thought they would serve better as dogs—faster runners and sharper teeth—and they were terrible and cruel animals. Two months earlier a man had tried to escape in the middle of the night, and the master had only released the dogs to deal with it. They had brought back pieces of him to make it clear that he had not escaped, and the dogs had not eaten any food offered them for three days but would slink away toward the woods come mealtimes.

In any case, Cumberland knew not to take another step when the dogs said something like that. So he stood with his tray and waited for the master to notice him, but the book held his whole attention. When the master became aware of Cumberland some half hour later, he waved him in. The dogs snarled but said nothing. The master tried the soup and grumbled that it was not hot. On some days, that would earn the whip, and Cumberland had his share of raised scars on his back. But today the master seemed preoccupied with something else. On the paper in front of him were words, but also a series of diagrams and pictures—a sort of map with mountains and oceans and deserts and so on, and when Cumberland had been staring at it too long, the magician looked at him sharply.

So Cumberland bowed his head like he had been taught and walked backward out of the room . . . not because that was required, but because he did not want to turn his back on the dogs who had once been men.

"We're watching you," one of the dogs growled, and Cumberland stole a look at the magician to see if he was also watching, but he had returned to his books and notations. That was the day when Cumberland had come to understand something of what the master was doing. For Cumberland was a natural magician, unbeknownst to him or his master.

The master was building another world. Just as Cumberland was not satisfied with his place and lot in life, the magician, too, evidently wanted something more. Cumberland knew that any world this man built was not one that would be kind to his servants. Not unkind, either, maybe. But a man who could make men into dogs could surely also use magic to make the tobacco harvest easier or make the roof of the bunkhouse leak less, and he had not done those things. An idea came to Cumberland that if he could just learn magic himself, he could steal the magician's plans and make them his own or maybe turn those plans on their head in some way.

This was not the work of days. First he learned to read, and it was hard work done in secret. A young white boy who sometimes wandered through their field had been convinced to "lose" his primer to Cumberland in exchange for a pie from the kitchen. So it was that Cumberland learned to read the alphabet and "In Adam's fall, We sinned all" and "The Cat doth play, And after slay." Sometimes he felt the book could read him, too. For when his plan to steal the master's papers came to a head, he could only think of the primer's words "A dog will bite, A thief at night."

The master had grown frustrated in the years it took Cumberland to read and prepare and think and pray about his exit from the plantation. There was something in his magic that was too complicated, and the magician could not figure it out. But Cumberland had become a fixture in the house now, and the master thought nothing of seeing him wandering in the upstairs halls. The magician had put no alarms or warnings on his secret books because who but he could read them? So it was that Cumberland learned the times of day when he could sneak in unannounced, "looking for master," and snatch a few moments alone with the books.

The night he planned his escape, he fed the dogs special. The greedy one died in less than an hour from the special tincture of herbs that had been rubbed on the hock of meat. The other was dead before bedtime had come. Cumberland buried both beneath the back porch. The master knew something was wrong. He called and called for the dogs, but they did not come. The master flew into a rage, and that night the bunkhouse door was locked from the outside. The lock was a simple and elegant solution, and Cumberland felt both defeated and foolish. Of course the master would not leave the men free to run. But, Cumberland thought, perhaps the next day he could slip away.

But the next day there were two new great dogs at the master's side come dinnertime. Cumberland sweat buckets in fear that these dogs would tell him about how the other two had been buried under the porch, but when he slipped away to check, the dirt beneath the porch was undisturbed. Cumberland couldn't help but notice that two beds were empty that night when it came time to turn in.

The master's eye was turned toward him after that. He was sent back to the fields, and in truth he didn't mind that simply because it gave him some distance from the oppressive presence of the master. One day the master called Cumberland to the front porch, where the old magician was reading a book and sipping lemonade. He offered Cumberland a glass, but he refused, uncertain what the man might have mixed into the drink and thinking of the two dogs he had poisoned not so long ago.

"Stay here and keep an eye on my book," the magician said.

Then he left Cumberland alone with the book and the lemonade and no one about. He'd taken the dogs with him too. Cumberland waited until he could sing a whole song twice through in his head, then took a chance to read the title. *CURSES* was the first word, *AND* was the second, and the third word he had to work his way through. It was *IMPRECATIONS*, a word he did not know. He thought of picking it up—it could be that a curse was exactly what he needed to get the magician out of his way.

But as he reached for it, he heard a whisper coming from the pages of the book. *In me you will find freedom,* it said. *Read me.* And if he had not been able to read the title, maybe he would have picked it up. But his mother had told him when he was just a child, *Bless and do not curse* and *A hen's curses have never killed an eagle* and *The one who digs a pit falls into it.* So he stayed his hand, and when the magician returned he looked surprised and asked Cumberland to send another man, a man named Peter, to come and see him at the porch.

Cumberland did not see Peter again after that. So far as he knew the man could not read, but that night some of the others said that they had been called to clean up a mess on the porch and that it had taken sixteen buckets of water to wash the porch clear.

"There was a book that wept blood," one of them whispered, and Cumberland knew it had eaten Peter. So he was more cautious and set aside his plans for a while so that he would not shake in his bed at night or reveal his fear when the master saw him in the daylight.

Still, he learned his little spells. His mother had said to bless, not curse, and that is what he did. The hookworms were few that season. The tobacco practically fell from the stalk. There seemed to be a scoop more of the best food for every man, even as the master was complaining that his plate seemed light. One time when the master came at night, intent on taking away one of the men for his dark spells, he found that the lock was stuck. He worked on it for a good while, then gave up and came back in the morning when it opened smooth and easy. Cumberland stayed vigilant and learned small things from observing the master. Words of power, dropped because the magician could not imagine someone near him could wield them. Scraps of paper around the house. He even learned that some things could be discovered just in the way he traveled in his own thoughts at night. True magic could be unraveled in places other than books.

It was a Sunday when he discovered among his own people a magic that the master did not know. On Sundays no work was allowed at the house, and the men gathered to sing hymns and to pray. Sometimes the master would come and read a Scripture to them. Sometimes one of the brothers would stand and preach from remembered verses and well-worn Bible stories. It was one of those days when the master had joined them. His sermon, short and pointed, was about the need to obey authority. No one liked when he came, except that they sometimes heard a new scrap of Scripture. The master sat in the front of the chapel—a chapel they had built with their own hands—his clothes pressed and cleaned and laid out by the men around him. He gave his little message, then sat uncomfortably as they stretched the service out and sang and prayed well into the late morning.

"One more song only," he said at some point, clearly tired of being in their presence in something like a social setting.

And they said, "Yes, master, yes," and looped into a half-hour rendition of "Swing Low, Sweet Chariot," complete with new verses that they made up themselves. There was joy there, and they even began to sing about their life on his property, a daring and insulting thing to do, for then they again launched into, "Swing low, sweet chariot, coming for to carry me home!" It was well past the lunch hour when they released him.

When *they* released *him*. There was a relationship to time that the men had and the master did not. They could bend it, make a two-minute song last a half hour. Cumberland began to experiment with this power, to try it in other places. When the master said, "Come here, Cumberland," he could immediately obey but do it slow and easy, and the master would have no excuse to punish him. He and the others, they could control how long it took to bring in the tobacco. When the master sent them to mend fences, it could take a week or two months. Not only couldn't the master control time like they could, but he did not know how they did it, did not know when they did it.

With some practice, Cumberland could make time stop. Could shape it, mold it, make it flow like water. He could lengthen the nice parts of the day. A water break could go on for hours. He made unpleasant tasks pass in moments. Eventually, he could freeze other people in the moment they were in, and that was how he accessed the library at last. He walked past the master, past the snarling dogs, and spent whole afternoons there. Days, sometimes.

The magician felt the change in the magic in his home. He felt it and searched for Cumberland with a restless anger. But how could he catch a man who could disappear between the movements of the second hand on a watch?

Cumberland became certain of himself. Prideful. Careless.

One day he stepped into the library, having evaded the master and the dogs once again, and magic chains clapped on his wrists and ankles, and another clapped shut around his mouth. He could speak no word of power, could perform no magic.

"Cumberland Walker," the magician said. "I should have known it was you." He sneered. "There will be a price to pay, Cumberland. I hope you realize that."

Then came the whipping, while he was still in chains. The master healed him with his magic and did it again. Forty days and forty nights he whipped him. Cumberland would have wept and pleaded for an end if he could speak, but his voice had been taken from him. Nothing could be done. He was starved and beaten. Insulted and berated. Paraded in front of his old companions. A stake was driven in the field, and he was left chained to it, naked, as an example.

He had been in the field a long time. He did not know how long. Without his voice he could not stop time, or so he believed. But he turned his attention to the world around him and began to wonder. The seasons changed without a voice. The sun rose and set every day without a voice, unless the song of the birds was magic. Could it be that he could change time without words?

And so he did. He stopped time completely. Then he let time move forward on his chains—years, decades, centuries—and when at last time wore them down he broke free of the bonds on his arms. He tore off the shackles on his feet. He crumpled the iron clamped on his mouth. In the centuries of his captivity he had grown both weary and wise, and his anger burned like a coal in a furnace. Though centuries had passed in Cumberland's mind, only a handful of days had passed at the magician's house.

Was the magician surprised when Cumberland Armstrong Walker burst into the house, naked and full of power? Was he astonished when Cumberland dressed himself with a few authoritative words of magic, or when he gestured to the house and it fell like matchsticks? Did he drop to his knees and beg for mercy?

In the ruins of the house stood a single room. The library. Cumberland commanded one of the men to bring a sheaf of paper and a pen, and he stood over the master as he wrote letters granting each man his freedom. They ran from that place, each of them singing and praising God. The last letter was Cumberland's, and he took it from the magician when it was dry, folded it, and placed it near his heart.

"I will chase you," the magician said, "to the ends of the earth."

"Then I will go farther still, and a simple magician like yourself will not find me."

"I will find you," the magician said, "and your punishment will be much worse than you can imagine. My words of power will rend your flesh from your muscles. I will take everything you hold dear and strip it from you."

So it was that Cumberland took the magician's voice forever so that he could never use his magic again. A simple magician like this man could not use the magic that came without words, the magic of Being. "I will not kill you," Cumberland said. "For it seems to me the best revenge would be for you to come to recognize your evil ways and repent of them and spend what remains of your life in horror at your past self. May God have mercy on you."

With a flick of his wrist, Cumberland set the library aflame, and the bunkhouses fell, and even the little chapel trembled. And perhaps it was a final cruelty, though some say it was a parting gift, but the man known as Cumberland Walker showed the magician how he had mastered his plan to make a new world. The magician had never been able to achieve the final necessary step to make this magical place. He had worked out the main bits, and Cumberland used those plans: the sea and the Sea Beneath. The crystal spheres. The land and the islands and the desert.

But the magician could not do what Cumberland could do: take a small amount of time and twist it, change it, use it so that he could grow trees and mountains and rivers and create a land infused with magic in the spaces between this world and another. It was a place of great beauty, pristine and unsullied by the petty hatreds of this world.

Cumberland placed the land in a crystal sphere to keep it safe and filled the bottom of the sphere with a great expanse of water, which came to be called the Sea Beneath, so the whole world would be balanced. And he spoke more spheres—sun and moon, stars and planets—into being. He shaped mountains and scooped out lakes and filled mountains and lakes and plains with fantastical creatures the like of which had never walked the earth.

The master had made a plan for how to power this world, and there were two necessary elements: something to make it all spin, and something to keep it going. For the core of power the magician needed something effective but simple, something to define the heart of the world. And he had chosen the chains of a slave, for he had plans to use this world to keep still more slaves and increase his dominance. Cumberland threw out that part of the plan and replaced the master's chains with two simple objects of his own, and he placed them in a cave in the Sea Beneath.

The second key component was a collection of living things to keep the world vibrant. The magician had cleverly designed the crystal spheres to contain them. They were spiritual creatures. Cumberland would have called them angels at that time. In all the stories he knew, they protected the Garden of Eden or served at God's leisure, flying in God's presence. And Cumberland saw how they could be called inside the magical world and how, with the crystals, they could be forced to stay. So he followed the magician's plans in this.

Now the magician watched it all in bitter wonder and made his own plans of how he would come to this place, the Sunlit Lands, and would in time retake it for himself. He would replace Cumberland's source of power with his own—the chains—and kill Cumberland, and then this magical pocket world would be his. And Cumberland could see all this in the magician's eyes.

So Cumberland put a gate on the world with a magic word that would let no one pass it unless they had experienced great trouble in their lives, and this trouble not of their own choosing. Though the magician had lost all, he could not enter, for his loss was his own doing. But any person who had been enslaved, or child who had been orphaned, or spouse who had been widowed . . . the sick or dying, the poor, the oppressed, could walk into the land without so much as knocking on a door.

Then Cumberland said farewell to the magician and stepped into his new kingdom. And the magician wept bitter tears and gnashed his teeth, and he died unremarked and alone and was buried in a pauper's grave.

31
SHAPE-SHIFTERS
AND NECROMANCERS

*Our sorrow was so big we needed people who knew how
to carry it. People who knew how to carry it together.
So they came. From all over the world they came.*

THE PEASANT KING

✛

Shula was glad she had taken David's hand. The path through the ivy wasn't a path at all—it was an unending experience of leaves slapping you in the face, over and over. It was more than unpleasant, but at least David's hand made her feel anchored, connected to something. She gasped in relief when they finally burst through on the other side, only to find themselves standing in a wide square packed with people and other things . . . strangely shaped creatures of all kinds. And standing right in front of them was Jason.

"Jason!" she shouted, and wrapped him in her arms. "We were so worried about you!"

Jason backed away sheepishly. "I'm not Jason. I'm from the Southern Court. I just have his shape. Hello!"

"What?"

"Shape-shifters," David said. "Did you notice how Dee didn't react to Jason at all?"

It was true. The little rhino hadn't so much as snorted when she saw Jason. Shula filed that away for later. David put Yenil on the ground, and the girl shook her head as if clearing ivy from her face. Rana was nowhere to be seen.

Shula crossed her arms. "Take Jason's face off. Now."

He looked at her guiltily. "But lots of people are wearing it. Who do you want me to look like?"

"Like yourself," she said.

"It's not that simple," he mumbled. His face and body shifted into that of a young woman with blonde hair and a dimpled chin.

"That's a famous singer," Shula said. It was a pop star from the US. "Do you not have a face that is someone I won't recognize so I can at least pretend it's your face?"

"Fine," he grumbled, and took on another shape, that of an elderly man with long white hair, half of it dyed blue. "You know him?"

"No," Shula said.

"Great," the old man replied, and shuffled toward a nearby tower. The towers almost looked like enormous stalagmites that had been hollowed out so that people could live within them. "All three of you, come with me."

"Four," Yenil said, stroking Dee's nose and letting her down to run.

"We don't have time for this," Shula said to the old man. "We need to find the real Jason."

"I'm taking you to Lelise, ruler of the Southern Court. They sent me to get you. The—what do you call it—the king knows where your friend is."

The man led them into a tower and down a long hall. A Jason ran past and dipped his head in greeting. "Looking old," he shouted at their guide.

"Kids these days," he mumbled. He pushed through a pair of double doors, and it opened into a wide, airy space that must be in the center of the tower but was much, much larger than Shula had expected. It might be magic, of course. At least a thousand people were in there, each running to do some specific errand. And nearly every single one of them wore Jason's face.

She grabbed Yenil's hand and pulled her to her side. "Stay close."

"The king is on the other side of the hall here," their guide said. "We'll have to go across together. Stay close to me. Maybe it will help that I look like this now," he said, glancing down at his body in disgust.

He pushed into the crowd, and Shula followed him, Yenil's hand in hers, David taking up the back and, Shula was glad to see, keeping a close eye on the people they passed. As they moved through the crowd, a solid 90 percent of the Southern Courtiers wore Jason's face, or something close to it. Their bodies might be slightly off, or the faces not quite correct—a nose too crooked or the hair the wrong color or cut—but they were all recognizably Jason.

She stared too long at one Jason, apparently, who was about a foot taller than the real one, because he turned to look at her, and his face quickly shifted to mirror Shula's. She gasped and looked away, but it was like it set something off, and a cascade of Shula faces moved through the crowd now. She glanced to the right and saw that the same thing was happening to Yenil, as well. They were following behind the old man, but they left a wake of Shulas and Yenils and Davids behind them. It was a strange, overwhelming feeling.

Yenil seemed more interested than frightened. She was slowing down, laughing at all the faces that were so close to her own, and the Southern Courtiers were responding to her, smiling and laughing and making goofy faces, some of them faces that Yenil herself couldn't make. She crowed with delight, and Shula had to pull on her arm to keep her moving.

The old man saw what was happening and grumbled, "Oh, everyone else is allowed to take your faces, no problem. But I can't even take the shape of your friends. It's not fair, I say."

"Does your personality change with your shape?" Shula asked. It might be a rude question, but he seemed different since he'd shed Jason's shape.

"Some, of course. Different bodies fit differently. The size, the gender, the shape. It changes the way you feel sometimes. Like this body—the knees hurt. Makes me cranky when I walk. And Jason's body is full of strange energy surges. His brain is moving too fast all the time. Impulse control is harder. Sometimes, though, it's only the outer body that changes. I mean, some of us just alter our appearance, not our insides. It's not the best way of doing things, it seems to me, but kids today have no respect." He cackled and threw his hand over his mouth. "That's the old man in me talking. And, of course, if we're in war or danger, it only makes sense to move some internal organs around so we're less likely to be hurt or killed."

The old man finally got them across the floor, and two Jasons stood guard on either side of an enormous door. "Go on, then, open it up and be quick about it!" their guide said.

"Aw, change your shape, old man," one of the guards said.

"Show some respect," the old man snapped. He turned to Shula. "That's a big insult in the Southern Court, saying to change your shape."

The door opened, and the old man led them inside. "The royal ante-chamber," he said. "One more door and we'll be in the presence of the king of the Southern Court."

"How do I know they're not just more of you shape-changers?"

"The king has pronounced that all members of the Southern Court must wear their true forms today if they are in the presence of the king. Perhaps the king will change this later in the day, but the desire was that you and your friends feel at peace and be comfortable in this first meeting."

The door opened, revealing a strikingly handsome woman on the throne, her long hair curled and oiled, her skin dark and luminous, her eyes large and brown. She wore a gold crown—a series of stars welded together in a circle—and a long, heavy-looking purple robe.

"I will leave you here," the old man said.

"Who is that?" Shula asked.

"The king!"

"The king is a woman?"

The old man threw his head back as if suddenly remembering some-thing. "Ohhhhh, I forgot to mention. The king is a shape-shifter, like all of us. We use the term 'king' to make things easier for you humans. Our term is different. Her name is Lelise. She has been king for several months now. I think you will find King Lelise both fair and kind."

Shula shook her head. The whole thing made very little sense. They stepped into the room, and the king stood, a bright smile on her face. "Come in, Shula Bishara, David Glenn, and Yenil. Welcome! I am King Lelise," she said, extending her hand.

Shula wasn't sure if she was meant to bow or what, but she took the hand and shook it. The king's face lit with delight. "We have less time than I had intended," she said. "For it seems the necromancer king has just arrived, and I must welcome her, as well."

"Him," David said. "The necromancer king is a him."

"Ah, thank you," King Lelise said. "Getting the *he*s and *she*s right is a challenge for us here in the Southern Court. Come, let us all go and greet him. *His* dirigible has just docked."

Shula had never met the Pastisian necromancers. They had invaded Far Seeing a year ago, but they had only been there a handful of days, agreeing to leave after Hanali had been installed by the magistrates and the city seemed under control. She had been told a wide variety of stories about them, though. How they spoke to the dead and how they used this evil power to learn secret knowledge. There were rumors now that Darius had been working for the Pastisians when he killed the archon and had taken the archon's spirit to them. It didn't make much sense since Hanali claimed he had immediately exiled Darius when he found him crouched over the archon's lifeless body.

King Lelise led the way, her entourage of Southern Court officials hovering around her (a few of them literally hovering with large wings). They appeared in a lot of different shapes, and Shula realized that many of the strange, unique creatures she had seen in the Sunlit Lands must have been members of the Southern Court. She didn't understand how their shapes could be so different, yet they could still all be one people. How did they have children? How did they recognize each other? It was a mystery to her. The king led them outside, past the wall of ivy, and headed south.

"Our friend Jason—" she started to say, but King Lelise just waved her to silence.

"We're keeping close tabs on him," the king said.

The buildings in the Southern Court were very strange. Some of them had no doors on the ground floor. Others had doors, but they were mouse-sized. Every once in a while there was a house standing alone that looked like it had been lifted directly from Earth, right next to something that looked like it had come from Dr. Seuss. Meanwhile, all around her were people with wings, strange yak-like men who stood on their hind legs, cats which may have actually been cats, lizard people, carnival-version caricatures of famous people in the Sunlit Lands, and, around every corner, another Jason Wu.

They came to the top of a street that looked down on the edge of the butte where there was, apparently, an airship dock. The blimp was nearly in place.

When they got to the port of entry, there wasn't a gate or a locked fence or anything ("Wouldn't stop a shape-shifter," David said), and they followed the king up a wide, flat surface that connected to a walkway that extended to the cab of the aircraft.

King Lelise moved that direction, when Shula noticed two figures standing there whom she immediately recognized. "David, do you see?"

David was already running, and he wrapped the taller one in a monster hug. "Kekoa!"

"Hey, brah!" They embraced again, laughing. "Together again after all this time!"

"I'm so sorry I didn't get to you in time—"

"No worries," Kekoa said, grinning. "Ruth managed to save us all on her own. It's a long story, and don't worry, I'm gonna tell you alllll about it."

The small girl with the blindfold smiled at that, and she reached out for Shula. They squeezed hands. "I'm the one who told the king you were on your way here," Ruth said. "I saw you on the Green Road."

Shula didn't know how Ruth had seen her, but she was thankful.

"They're coming out!" Yenil shouted. "The necromancers!"

The king of the necromancers was the first to exit. He wore all black—a deep black that seemed to swallow the light—a fitted shirt and pants, gloves, and boots, along with a black robe with a hood. His face was covered by a gold mask with a stern expression.

Some of the Courtiers in the crowd began to shake, changing shapes with alarming speed and assuming ever more threatening shapes: bears and wolves and predators of various kinds, and then strange, frightening combinations of those and many other creatures. Kekoa shrugged. "Don't worry, that happens sometimes when they're frightened. They can't hold their shape, especially when they feel uncertain about what the threat is."

Behind the necromancer king came a woman wearing a simple,

no-nonsense dress in a dusty-blue color. Shula's eyes almost glanced right over her to the honor guards who followed, but something about the woman caught her attention. The regal way she held her head, maybe, or the fact that she didn't seem to be the least bit scared to be so close to the king of the necromancers. "Wait," Shula said. "David, do you see that woman?"

He gripped her shoulder. "Yeah . . . I think that's . . ."

"It's Mrs. Raymond!" Shula said. She pushed forward through the crowd until she was standing next to King Lelise. "I know that woman," she said.

"Who, Queen Mary Patricia?" Lelise asked.

What? Shula's mind flew through a vortex of confusion. She felt dizzy. The king knew Mrs. Raymond? She was the woman who had run Transition House, the first place most humans in the Sunlit Lands stayed. She and Shula had a somewhat antagonistic relationship, but Shula had never taken her to be someone who was talking to the dead. The two kings stood facing one another.

King Lelise spoke first. "King Ian. It is as much pleasure as surprise to see you here."

"King Lelise," he said, and his voice was deep and rich. "I am pleased to see you well. I have news of some importance. News that could not be sent in our traditional ways. We need a place to speak privately, you and I and those we trust."

"There are a few humans here you may not know," Lelise said.

The gold-faced mask turned slowly, taking them in. "If they are human, let them come. This news concerns them."

Lelise blinked in surprise. "You are not one to trust so quickly, my royal cousin."

"Time is in short supply these days, which is rare in the Sunlit Lands. And as you know, my own wife is a human."

Wow, Shula thought. So he wasn't a human? It was strange that they were letting them all come together to the meeting.

A winged Courtier dropped from the sky and took on a humanoid shape. He leaned over and spoke to the king. Shula was close enough to hear him say, "Majesty, the Kakri delegation has arrived at the northern entrance. They have our spy with them, and the Wu boy."

Jason.

King Lelise, pleased, turned to the nearest Courtiers. "Who will be King Lelise at the north entrance, and welcome the Kakri? It may be a delicate negotiation, so no one looking to make jokes. No, not you, Svindelig. I know you are trying to make it as a comedian. Who? Ah yes, Jendileen. Excellent. Meet us at the Conjunction."

One of the Courtiers took King Lelise's shape and headed out immediately, the large crowd they were in splitting so that half stayed and half followed.

"Your Majesty," Shula said quietly. "Did you say Jason Wu is with them? I'm his friend and worried about his safety. Could I go with them?"

The king raised her voice. "Shula Bishara wishes to go, but I have need of her here. Who will go in her place?"

Three different Courtiers volunteered, and the king nodded her assent. "All of you may go if you wish." They immediately took on Shula's shape and dashed off without so much as a nod to her.

"Well, that was weird," Shula said to David.

"You'll get used to it," Kekoa said.

They were ushered behind the kings, who appeared to be in close conference as they walked. Mrs. Raymond fell into step beside Shula. "Miss Bishara," she said.

"Mrs. Raymond." Shula didn't know what else to say. "I knew you were close to Hanali, but I had no idea you knew the king of the necro—"

The older woman patted her hand. "No doubt there are many things you do not know about me, Miss Bishara, as you never gave me much of a chance. But yes, I know King Lelise, and have in fact known her since she was quite young. When we were both children, I found her wounded in the Wasted Lands and nursed her back to health. King Ian, king of the 'necromancers' as you so colorfully put it, is my husband."

David said to Yenil, "Stay close."

Mrs. Raymond noticed the Scim girl, holding Dee tightly in her arms. "Is that Mr. Wu's unicorn? Hello, Mr. Glenn. Mr. Kahananui. And is that Miss Mbewe? From the Knight of the Mirror's household?"

"Mrs. Raymond," David said. "I'm glad you're here."

"Thank you, young man. I hope I can help shed some light on the current situation."

They entered a large indoor amphitheater. It was shaped like the concentric inner rings of some seashells, the whorls doubling as benches rising to different heights depending on where in the whorl you sat. The two kings moved to the center, and the rest of them quickly filled the benches. Ruth Mbewe joined them on the stage.

"I stand for the Southern Court," King Lelise proclaimed, loud enough for all to hear, and sat in a chair that was provided to her. She smiled when some of the Courtiers cheered, and others laughed.

"Southern Court humor is pretty hard to follow," Kekoa said. "But that was funny because she said she stood for the court and sat down. Apparently that's super funny to these guys." Yenil sat close to Shula, and David on Yenil's other side. Then Kekoa. Yenil cuddled in beside Shula, then grabbed David and pulled him closer to them.

King Ian stood and addressed them all. "It is said that the Southern Court has ears among all the people of the Sunlit Lands." Apparently this was funny, too, because he paused for a laugh and got one. "We Pastisians also have ears. Our two peoples have never had trouble, not even when there might have been cause for it in years past. It is time, friends, for us to go a step closer than even that." He reached up a gloved hand and removed his hood, then took off his gold mask. He was a handsome man, dark-skinned, regal, his hair cut short, his face angular. "It is time for our people to set aside our secrets and build a true alliance. The Elenil have sent word to me, as the archon Hanali has been my recent ally. He wanted to assure me that in days to come, he would not consider the Pastisians to be humans, but rather a people of the Sunlit Lands . . . on one condition."

"What does that mean?" Shula asked.

"Shh," Mrs. Raymond said.

"On the third night hence, Hanali plans to kill every human he can find, and in the weeks to come will hunt them to extinction. Not the Pastisians . . . so long as we do not shelter the humans or raise a hand in their defense."

"They can't do that!" Shula shouted. She wasn't the only one. Other humans in the hall, and human-shaped Courtiers, also called out. David was silent but clearly disturbed. Kekoa must have already known. He said nothing.

Yenil started to cry. Dee, not sure what was going on, began to let out plaintive wails. David put his arm around Yenil and Shula. "Don't worry," he said. "We'll be safe. It will be okay." But the way he said it . . . as if he knew that it was not always true, that there was not always a place to hide, not always a way to escape the enemy.

The king held his palm out, a call for quiet. "I have sent word to Hanali that I need time to consult my advisers. I have reminded him that my wife is human. He told me that time was of the essence, and that my wife could be exempt, so long as she promised to remain in Pastisian territories all the rest of the days of her life."

"A generous offer," Mrs. Raymond said to herself. "From an old friend. And he wonders why I don't let him call me by my Christian name."

"I have told him," the king said, "that I will send my answer shortly. No doubt he has seen my airship headed south by now and suspects what it means. So I imagine that he will be ready for us when the time comes."

"Could it be a bluff?" This was from David.

"It's possible," the king admitted. "It would make more sense to let the humans go home if he wishes to be rid of them. Many of them are waiting to go. But there would be a considerable magical cost to pay out all the promises that have been made to the humans and none at all for the dead."

King Lelise said, "Hanali always wears another shape beneath the one he presents. I suspect there are other shapes we do not yet see. And they have killed one of ours, one who took the shape of a Jason in Far Seeing. We cannot sit idly by while he murders the humans. I speak for the Southern Court when I say, if such a massacre comes, the Southern Court will stand with the humans."

"And I say the same for the Pastisians," Ian said.

Ruth Mbewe stood. "And I speak for the Zhanin. Kekoa and I have recently brokered an agreement with the shark people, an alliance between them and the humans. There is great trouble in the sea kingdom now, and though we cannot send an army, we will do what we can to limit the magical advantages of the Elenil should a battle come. This may be of little use if the Elenil themselves fight, but so be it."

"A representative of the Kakri should join us soon," King Lelise said. "And perhaps one of the Scim—"

Yenil leapt onto her bench, and her war skin flowed over her, her teeth protruding from her mouth now, her skin thickening, muscles layering on. "I speak for the Scim!" she shouted. "We have been crushed beneath the heel of the Elenil for too long. We will stand with you, and die with you if we must!"

The people of the Southern Court roared their approval of the young Scim.

King Lelise smiled at Yenil. "Very well. But I fear you may be too young. We shall appoint you our envoy to the Scim to bear the message."

"She can't go alone," Shula said. Although it was possible it would be safer for Yenil than going with Shula . . . trying to help Jason and then heading to Far Seeing to find her brother.

"I will send some of my finest warriors with Yenil," King Lelise said. "She will be safe." She turned her attention to Yenil again. "When will you go, lady?"

"Now," Yenil said. "Now and with all haste." She hugged Shula so fiercely she thought her ribs would break. The Scim girl kissed her on the cheek. "Dee will stay with you, to keep you safe," she said, and before Shula could object, she had pushed Dee's embiggenator into Shula's hands and had leapt off to go with two members of the Southern Court, one of whom looked like Shula, and the other appearing as a large, intimidating Scim warrior.

"It will be okay," David said, and squeezed Shula's shoulders. "Do you want me to go with her?"

Shula frowned. She wasn't sure.

"It was a year ago that the Pastisians attacked the Court of Far Seeing," King Ian said. "We removed the head of the Elenil, but it did not change what was corrupt. It is not the head alone that is sick. It is the heart, and it is pumping poison into the whole body, and where our societies overlap, it is pumping poison into us, as well."

Someone called, "The Elenil are killing us!"

"Yes," King Lelise said.

"Then we have to kill them!"

The two kings looked to Ruth Mbewe. She stood. She was still so small, shorter than everyone around her. She didn't look weak, though she undoubtedly was weaker physically than anyone else in the room. The blindfold over her eyes gave her a strange, almost hypnotic presence as she turned her face up toward them all to speak.

"When I was young," she began, and no one laughed at that, though she was still a child. "When I was young, some men came to my village and said they would kill everyone who lived there. I do not know why. Perhaps they needed food. Or perhaps they hated us because we were of another ethnicity. Or perhaps the men of my village had killed one of them, or stolen something of theirs. I do not know. But it was the Elenil who saved me." Ruth let that settle in. She let the crowd sit with that, and it created a sense of unease. People shifted in their seats. "Do you understand? I owe my life to them."

"What are you suggesting?" someone yelled. "That we let them kill all the humans?"

"I am only saying we must remember that I am here today because of a young Elenil named Hanali, who reached into my world and gave me another home here. Fear and hatred are things we learn." She lifted her hands, making a sort of helpless gesture. "We are in danger of learning them now. If we kill the Elenil, it will be because we have become their students, instead of them becoming ours."

"Are you saying that it would be better for all the humans to die than for the humans to kill all the Elenil? Better dead than a killer?"

"I am not." She breathed out a deep, world-weary sigh. "You are shapeshifters. Maybe you will understand this: What if there is a way that we can teach the Elenil a new shape?"

King Lelise stood and raised her hands at the fervor that broke out among her people at this suggestion. "When the Kakri join us, we have a plan to discuss. Perhaps if all our people unite—"

A Courtier burst into the amphitheater, shouting for the king. "Majesty! The Kakri are here and threatening to kill one of your subjects! The king-who-is-there goads them to action. And a great bird approaches, a man riding upon his back."

Shouts began to rise from the assembled Courtiers so that they could scarcely hear the king's command. She ordered six of them to greet the bird, and announced that she herself would race to stop the Kakri from murdering her subject if she was fast enough. David, Shula, and Kekoa watched it all and debated whether to follow.

"We're not fast enough," David said. "And either way they'll come back here."

"This is why we came here," Shula said, and ran for the door.

David and Kekoa exchanged glances, and then they were running too.

32
DANGER AT THE FEAST

The one-word story cannot be mastered, only learned anew.

FROM *THE WISE SAYINGS OF MOTHER CROW*

✛

In grade school, Jason had drawn a—let's say *unflattering*—picture of his teacher during class. He had a cone head and big protruding eyes and a word bubble that said, "YOU KIDS BETTER SETTLE DOWN." It was the sort of picture that was perfectly in touch with its audience. As the kids passed it around the class, a muted wave of riotous laughter followed, and it didn't help that his teacher turned around and shouted, "You kids better settle down!" Which of course set off a class-stopping roar of tear-inducing laughter. One kid fell out of his seat he was laughing so hard.

When the teacher grabbed hold of the piece of art, it happened to be in the hands of Jay Hightower, a nice enough kid who also got in trouble all the time. Jay was sent to the principal's office, the assumption being that he had drawn the picture. Also, Jason had signed the picture with his Chinese name, and their teacher couldn't read Chinese. So he assumed it was Jay's name because he was the only other Chinese kid in the class. Jay didn't rat Jason out, though. He took the punishment. Jason had been surprised but also, let's admit it, delighted.

Now that he was in Baileya's grip, about to be murdered because she thought he was a Southern Court spy, Jason couldn't help but feel that it was time for him to take an undeserved punishment. "I'd just like to take this moment to apologize to Jay Hightower, wherever he is," Jason said. "As well as my parents, all my classmates, and the all-you-can-eat buffet in Vancouver, Washington." He had a lot of buffet rules, but the most important ones were "Don't fill up on bread" and "Eat the most expensive things first." When they had given him his lifetime ban, he had stood outside every day for a week handing out flyers about how to get your money's worth at a buffet. They had called the cops, but Jason wasn't doing anything wrong, and he had given the policemen a big stack of flyers to hand out to the rest of the force. Anyway, *Sorry, Golden Bucket!*

He didn't have a lot of time to explore his feelings since the fake Jason was coming toward him with a knife and Baileya was holding him by the nape of the neck. He'd be dead in a minute. Maybe less! But he couldn't help that thoughts of his parents were flooding his head. And he never got a chance to tell Baileya how he felt. Well, he thought she knew, but he had never really laid it all out—or he felt like he hadn't. He had told her that he loved her, but that just seemed like . . . not enough. He would need something big. Something grand and life-altering. And he didn't know how to do that. Definitely not when he was about to be gutted.

The people of the Southern Court were watching, the queen with her arms crossed and a smug look on her face. She probably knew that Baileya had him and TJ backward. There were also multiple copies of his friends out there. He gave a little half wave to one of the Shulas. *Hiiiii.* Where was Dee? Well, he knew Yenil would take care of her. In the distance he could see more of the Southern Court folks flying toward them, in a great big hurry. He wondered what that was all about and realized he might never know. He just hoped that Third Jason made it quick. He had never killed anyone himself, so he hoped TJ was better at it than he was.

"Any last words, spy?" Baileya asked.

"I love you," Jason said. "And also I hope that one day you get the internet here in the Sunlit Lands. It's really great."

TJ lunged forward with the knife, and in a sudden frenzy of movement Jason found himself on the ground at Baileya's feet, and Baileya had snatched TJ by the neck instead. Baileya had a fierce grin on her face, and it only grew wider when TJ turned himself into a bird, then a giant snake, then some sort of thick-necked warthog. Still, she didn't let go of him, and as he struggled and shifted, he dropped the knife, which she plucked from the air and set at his throat.

Baileya held the squirming creature as it flashed through more forms, and her voice was both triumphant and on the verge of laughter when she called out, "Should I kill him?"

"I'm going to faint now," Jason said. "Wake me when this is all over."

The booming laughter of Break Bones crashed through the crowd. "We could not tell you, Wu Song, that we knew the truth. We feared the spy would run home and give warning."

"I thought I was dead for sure," Jason said.

Baileya stole a glance at him. "I must keep my attention on the spy," she said. "But surely, Wu Song, after my speech in the tent you realized that I knew it was you?"

"Uh, no."

"I said you were my heart's blood? Do you recall this?"

He blushed. "I mean, yes, I understood that part, but I didn't realize you knew it was me. I thought you thought you were talking to TJ!"

"TJ?"

"Third Jason," he said. Then, when Baileya looked at him blankly. "It's an alphabet thing, don't worry about it."

As they spoke, the distant group of flying shape-shifters landed in front of them, and one of them took the shape of the king. There were two kings now. "You are dismissed," the new one said, and the first one, looking disappointed, shifted into the shape of a man with a lion's head.

"I am King Lelise," the new king said.

"Queen Lelise," Jason said. He could never stop words from coming out of his mouth. Now was probably not the time to correct someone in power about such things, but he couldn't help himself.

Lelise paused and had a quick sidebar conversation with a few of her Courtiers. "*Queen* Lelise," she said. "Yes. Gendered language is difficult for us."

"No problem," Jason said. "Did you know that in spoken Chinese there's no *he* or *she* pronouns? Just *ta*. My cousins—they're in China—have a really hard time when they're speaking English. It's always 'My boyfriend, she is coming over.'"

Everyone stared at him. "What point are you making?" Break Bones asked.

Jason shrugged. "I don't know. Gendered pronouns are hard if you didn't grow up with them? I'm glad to call you king if you want."

"Ah," Lelise said. She looked out over the crowd, and Jason was surprised to see that a good number of people out there were changing shapes. More of them were taking on *his* shape. Well, that was weird.

"We do not wish you to kill our Jason," Lelise said. "I must apologize for the aggressive greeting you have received from Queen Lelise."

Baileya gave a small shake to TJ, who had taken on Jason's form again. "I am told that I should not have come to the Southern Court without permission," she said. "But I am Mother Crow, who flies where she will, and does what she will, in all of the Sunlit Lands."

Queen Lelise shook her head. "It was poorly said, for we reached out to you and wished you to come to us. Even more so to Jason Wu, whom we desired to come to us some time ago. Indeed, some of his friends are here as well. Kekoa. Shula Bishara. David Glenn. Ruth Mbewe. And even now the necromancers have arrived, and I have left them in a great hurry."

Jason perked up. His friends were actually here somewhere?

"We have many issues to discuss, not least of which is the attack upon my predecessor," Baileya said. "An attack that this person was involved in. I fear that the Southern Court's . . . differences . . . related to individuality will make it difficult for me to find him again should I release him."

"A fair concern," the queen said. "We will give you our word that he will be turned over to you . . . if there is an agreement that wrongdoing was committed."

Baileya seemed to consider this. She took the knife and cut a long gash down TJ's arm. He shouted in pain, and she released him. He quickly shifted forms several times, and Jason was astonished to see that in each form he carried some equivalent wound. "I will be able to find him now, should there be a disagreement."

The queen raised an eyebrow. "Was there ever any doubt that you would, Mother Crow? I have heard stories of your adventures even here."

"Those stories are mine to tell," Baileya said, and she held out her hand to Jason, who gladly took it and jumped to his feet.

"Mother Crow, it seems there are many things our people must discuss together," Queen Lelise said. "But there is an issue of some delicacy that requires a swift agreement. Would you care to join me and representatives of the Pastisians and the Zhanin to discuss together what we might do?"

"These are perilous times," Baileya Crow said. "I will discuss it with you. I trust you will be more hospitable to me and my people than what I have experienced from your spies?"

"Indeed," Queen Lelise said. "Hear me, my people: the Kakri and their guests are to be treated with full respect, as if they were citizens of the Southern Court. Any who break this command will face the consequences, up to and including the Stilling, exile, or death."

As she finished saying these words, a small group of humans shoved their way to the front of the crowd.

Jason jumped to them, full of joy. "Shula! David! Kekoa!" He wrapped his arms around the three of them and hugged them tight.

Shula pushed him away. "Are you the real Jason or some Southern Court copy?"

"Are you the real Shula or are you going to tie me up and frame me for attempted murder?"

Shula smiled. "Sure sounds like you."

Then there was a squawking, hooting, bellowing sort of sound that came from the crowd, and people fell back to make way for a furious little bundle of energy who was not going to let anyone get between her and Jason. It was Delightful Glitter Lady, kitten-sized but sprinting full steam. Jason got down on his knees and shouted, "DEE!" and then she slammed into his chest, knocking him backward and covering his face with tiny rhinoceros kisses. "Aw, who's the best unicorn of them all? Huh? Who's the greatest? You're such a good girl!"

David grinned. "That's him all right."

There was a great deal of hugging and backslapping and friendly banter. "It's all of us, together again!" David said, and that was true, but it also gave Jason a momentary sharp pain, remembering Madeline. He couldn't help it. He still thought of her at moments like this.

On the long walk to the meeting place, Jason tried to take in the Kingdom of the Southern Court. The houses and everything were fine, but he was most interested in the people. All different shapes and sizes, and it was like all the people of the Sunlit Lands lived here. There were Maegrom and Elenil, Pastisians and humans and Scim. Sure, there were other creatures—unique and odd creatures. But all the people—Maduvoreans and Kakri, too!—were represented. But of course most striking of all was the fact that an awful lot of the Southern Courtiers looked like Jason. Not always perfect copies . . . there were little inconsistencies. But when they saw him, when he walked by, they would shift closer. Their hair would grow a bit or get shorter. Their clothes would change to look more like his.

"What's the story here?" Jason asked. Baileya had been asked to walk with the queen, so he was with David and Shula and Kekoa . . . and Break Bones. Of course Dee was in his arms. "Why do they all look like me?"

Break Bones grinned, his long yellow teeth sticking out of his mouth. "Oh, Wu Song. So humble. So blind to his own value. The Southern Court has always prized truthfulness. I think they are trying to learn from you. To incorporate your honesty into their culture."

"That's weird," Jason said. "And it also seems like there might be easier ways to do it."

"The Southern Court catches interest in someone or something, and it spreads like a virus," Kekoa said. "It's not bad—it's how they study something, see what it means, how it works. It's a pretty big compliment."

Jason snorted. "It might have been if they hadn't tried to kill Mother Crow and hadn't kidnapped me."

They made it to the meeting place, where the Southern Court had set out a long table of food for the Kakri. Jason and Break Bones decided to see who could demolish the most food. David tried to keep pace but gave up after three plates. Kekoa just watched and egged them on, laughing.

Jason was glad Baileya wasn't there—she was still in a meeting—because he knew she could eat twice as much as he could. But he thought he had a chance at beating the old Scim.

Jason was piling his plate with another round of roasted bird and some sort of mashed tuber when he almost dropped it. Bezaed stood at the end of the table, watching him. "Let there be no mistake, brother," he said. "I would not have knowingly allowed you to be murdered in the place of a spy."

"Aw, thanks, Bezaed."

"Mother Crow had forbidden us from making it clear to you how many of us knew that it was you in captivity and not the spy."

"Man, did everyone figure it out?"

"I knew it would take a colossal misstep and enormous stupidity to be alone with the prisoner and be tricked into switching places, so of course I suspected from the first that is what had happened."

"Oh," Jason said. "Okay, thanks."

Bezaed grabbed his wrist. "To be painfully clear, Wu Song, I would not allow another to kill you, and certainly not someone who was not a Kakri."

"Got it. It's sort of sweet in a way."

"We begin to understand one another at last."

Break Bones appeared on the other side of the table, chewing loudly. "However, Bezaed, I have what Wu Song calls 'dibs.' I promised to kill him on his first day in the Sunlit Lands."

"Second day," Jason said. "And I thought we were past that."

Break Bones shrugged and piled some stir-fried green weeds onto his plate. "If someone else was going to kill you and there was no escape, why not keep my oath and kill you before they do? And I am certain it was the first day."

"Lovely," Jason said. "You know, when Mother Crow—old Mother Crow—thought she was dying, she told me a story that was only one word long. I think you both should hear that story."

Bezaed's eyes went wide. "Mother Crow told you the one-word story?"

"Oh, you know it? She said it was common, but also really special."

"She *did* tell you! But that means . . . Wu Song, that is the final story we learn when we go into the desert to become Kakri."

"Wait, what?"

Bezaed pulled out his sword. "It means you are Kakri now."

"Hey now, just a second."

"And that means I can stay true to my vows and kill you, a suitor to my sister, at last."

"Think fast," Jason said, and threw his mashed tubers in Bezaed's face. He didn't see how Bezaed responded to that because he was already running full speed toward the meeting place to find Baileya Crow.

Then he had another thought, and, cackling maniacally, he disappeared into a crowd. There were only about forty-seven Jason Wus just within shouting distance. Let Bezaed try to find him now!

The Kakri warrior's lip curled as he scanned the crowd. But then an idea seemed to occur to him, and he bent down and picked up Delightful Glitter Lady. "Where's Jason?" he asked. "Can you find him, girl?"

He released the tiny rhino, who charged straight toward Jason, trumpeting in pleasure. "Uh-oh," Jason said. "Why does this always happen to me?"

33
REUNIONS

The whole world is in danger, for it has been corrupted.

MALGWIN

✢

arius was still turning Cumberland's story over in his head when Fantok returned. Her wings were torn in places, but she didn't look badly wounded. "We have a short window in which I can fly you all the way there," she said.

"You had better come with me," Darius said to Crukibal.

"Very well," the Maegrom prince replied, and Darius took his hand to help him mount the great bird.

No sentries met them this time, though the city below seemed to buzz with activity as if preparing for some great event. "War," Crukibal said.

"Do you think so? With whom?"

Crukibal pointed to the airships. "Not the necromancers, it appears. Unless those are stolen."

"That's King Ian's airship," Darius said. "Set us near there, Fantok."

Fantok banked to take them in that direction. Darius could see the

Pastisian honor guard standing near the dock. "There are other things I must do," Fantok said. "I will not stay once I drop you here."

"No problem," Darius said. The great bird landed easily, and when her passengers had their feet on solid ground, she leapt into the sky again.

"Farewell, Darius Walker," she said. "I will see you again soon."

Crukibal was carrying the glass box, and he seemed nervous now that they were around other people. He hefted it in his arms and tried to tuck it more inconspicuously under his cape.

"Jason!" Darius called. He couldn't believe it. His old classmate was here, in the Southern Court?

Jason turned and looked at him. "Oh, hey, man." He didn't seem particularly surprised or excited.

"What are you doing here?"

Jason frowned. "The same as you—I live here. Is that you, Gortbul?"

"Gortbul? What are you talking about? It's me, Darius Walker."

"Oh, man, you've gone deep. There aren't any other humans around. Who is that really?"

"What are you—?" Darius squinted at Jason. No, it definitely looked like him. He had met a few Southern Courtiers in his time. He had never found their shapes particularly convincing because they usually wanted you to know they were taking your shape. They were usually either slightly exaggerated in appearance or, sometimes, sort of scaly. "Are you a shape-shifter?" Darius asked. "How did you get Jason's face?"

"He's a Courtier," Crukibal said.

"Ooh, a Maegrom prince," Jason said. "Those are rare! Where did you meet him? Was he at Far Seeing? You must have gotten very close to take his shape so well. I met Hanali once. He's going to be archon, you know. I'll show you!"

Jason twisted in a strange way, and now he was definitely Hanali, wearing a sharply tailored suit with a long red-and-black cape that dragged on the ground. Darius said, "That's impressive. You look just like him."

"As if you have ever had the honor of meeting the archon, Gortbul. Though your compliment is received as intended."

That was weird. Even the way the guy talked had changed. "What's going on here, anyway?"

"Ah, Gortbul. You really have internalized the shape of your character. Do you need some Wendy concentrate, friend, so you can remember your true shape?"

Darius cocked his head to the side. "Some *what*?"

Hanali rolled his eyes. "My dear boy. Gortbul. Try to keep up. We use addleberry in our magic to help us forget who we are, so we can change forms. We've always had to be careful not to take on another shape too perfectly, so we don't completely forget who we are and become unable to return to our former selves. But now that Wendy juice exists—a juice that helps us remember—we can go as deep as we want! Concentrated Wendy juice brings all our memories back. Even if, like you, we've gone so deep that we don't even know we're from the Southern Court anymore!"

The Maegrom prince turned to Darius. "Are you from the Southern Court?"

"No!" Darius said. "Of course not."

"That's what they always say before they take a sip," Hanali replied. He pulled a small vial from his jacket. "Just drink a bit of this."

"No, thanks," Darius said. "I'm perfectly happy with the memories I have."

Crukibal took a look at the flask and shook his head. "I don't drink with Elenil. I hope you understand."

"Bah. The Maegrom are the ones who betrayed the Elenil at the Festival of the Turning!" Hanali's face shifted to Jason's for a moment. "I hope that's not taking things too far, but I'm certain that's what Hanali would say. Don't you agree?"

"Probably," Darius said. "You never told us, Hanali—what's going on here?"

Hanali sniffed. "If you insist on this charade so that I have to do the hard work of explaining everything that is happening, then so be it." (Then, in Jason's voice, "I sound just like him, don't I? Hahahaha!")

"Wonderful," Darius said. "But tell us quickly. We have things to do in the city."

"Oh, *of course* you do. The Elenil have threatened to kill all the humans in the Sunlit Lands and—"

"They *what*?"

"Indeed. Led by yours truly." Hanali gave a little bow.

Darius frowned. Once upon a time he would have doubted this news. But he had seen Hanali kill Archon Thenody. He had felt Hanali's hand on him as he was pushed out of this world and back to Earth. He knew Hanali was devious. But the scale of it . . . he hoped it wasn't true.

"Hanali told King Ian himself. It's true and it's happening. But not if the Southern Court can do anything about it! King Lelise is preparing our armies to go to battle right now."

"Take me to the king," Darius said.

Hanali raised his eyebrows. "Am I your servant?"

"I do not have time for games," Darius said. "If Hanali is killing all humans in a matter of days, there's no time to stand around chatting. Lead the way."

"You badly need some Wendy concentrate," Hanali said, but he led the way to a large amphitheater.

As they entered, another Jason raced past them, a tiny rhinoceros close behind him and a murderous-looking Kakri on his heels. Jason was yelling, "MOTHER CROW!" and the rhino was honking with delight.

"Everyone needs some Wendy concentrate," the fake Hanali said. "It's a madhouse here today."

"Now *that* looked like the real Jason."

Inside the amphitheater they found Jason holding Dee, the Kakri warrior standing eight feet away, and Baileya in between them, as well as someone Darius assumed was the leader of the Southern Court, standing near Baileya. Baileya was speaking, and she did not look happy. ". . . all the childish and infantile things to do at this time. I am deeply disappointed in you."

"Sorry," Jason said.

"Oh, I'm not talking to you," Baileya said gently, and whirled on the Kakri man. "I am speaking to you, Brother. Bezaed, we are in the midst of war, and if you opened your eyes you would see that Wu Song is an important piece of the story. Look around you, Brother. Do you see how many from the Southern Court take his shape? What do you think will happen if you kill him?"

"Baileya—"

Before the man could speak any more than that, Baileya cut him off. "You are to call me Mother Crow. We are at war, Bezaed, and now—in direct defiance of my order to keep Wu Song safe—you are trying to kill him."

Her brother fell to his knees. "Sister, listen to me. Mother Crow—your predecessor—told him the one-word story. He is Kakri now. Does this not change all of your commands? Does this not alter what must be done?"

Her face softened, and she looked at Jason. "Is this so?"

"Uh, well, yes it's true."

She turned back to Bezaed. "I see why this confused you, Brother. The short answer is that it does not change the story we are in. You are trying to tell some different story, and the whole world will struggle against your narrative. I say this to you as your sister, not as your Mother Crow: perhaps you would be well served by reflecting on the one-word story. I fear you have forgotten it."

Bezaed dropped his head in shame. "I will take your words to heart," he said. "And when next you have need of me, Mother Crow, only say my name and I will be there to do whatever task you require." He glared at Jason. "No matter how distasteful."

He quickly left the amphitheater. Jason put his hand on Baileya's shoulder. "Distasteful? Do you think that was a dig at my cooking?"

She smiled at him and took his forearms in her grip. "Wu Song, you are Kakri now. It grieves me that we have not had time to welcome you properly. But know this: though I am consumed with the business of saving the humans, you are never far from my thoughts. I look forward to talking with you once all of this trouble has passed."

He grinned. "Same same."

Darius clapped Jason on the shoulder. "Hey, man." It was strange. They'd never been close, not really. But they had both been friends to Madeline. Not in a way that made Darius jealous at all—it had never been like that. And Darius and Jason's friendship had mostly grown in the Sunlit Lands, where Darius had scarcely spent any time with Madeline. Then there was the fact that they were from the same town, the same part of the world. Had attended the same high school, had common memories of epic moments in their community. Not least of which, of course, had been the time when Jason had taken the principal's toupee and the football team had run it up the flagpole. Darius had a sort of distant affection for Jason . . . someone he didn't feel a need to hide much with, felt like they could be real friends given the chance. Like maybe if they worked together in the same business, or if they were roommates in college, they could be friends for life.

"Darius!" Jason cocked his head to the side. "That's you, right? Not some shape-shifting dude?"

"Nah, it's me."

"Oh, hey! And that's Crukibal! How's it going?"

"You two know each other?"

"Sure, we met when I was living in the desert."

Jason had a strange way of knowing everyone. Darius had gotten in deep with the Scim, yes, and he was respected by them. Jason had somehow made friends with Break Bones while trying to avoid being killed by him. It was an odd talent.

King Ian was here, too, and Mrs. Raymond. Darius embraced them both warmly. "What news?" King Ian asked. "And whither in the world are you headed, Darius Walker? We feared you lost when Hanali said you had been banished. I thought he had surely killed you."

"Banished," Darius said. "Trapped on Earth, and I finally got back."

"How?" Mrs. Raymond asked. "I was banished from the Sunlit Lands myself once upon a time. There's no easy road back here."

Darius debated whether to give them the full and true answer. These were his allies, surely. "Hanali killed Archon Thenody right before my eyes. Then he kicked me out of the Sunlit Lands. As for how I got back . . . the short version is that the Peasant King himself walked me in."

"And have you decided *why* you are here?" King Ian asked this with real concern.

Darius rubbed his jaw with his hand. Had he? The first time he had come, it had been to be with Madeline. He had stayed to try to bring justice for the Scim, and had been so wrapped up in that seemingly impossible mission that he had lost sight of the people he loved. He had come back again for . . . for what? Revenge, partly. And a feeling of unfinished business. But something in the story of Cumberland Walker had broken out something new. He wasn't just here for revenge or justice, not really. "I'm here to save the Sunlit Lands," he said at last. "People won't recognize it as that, not at first. But I'm going to save them."

"Hey!" Jason said. "I've got to save the world, too, so I can marry Baileya!" He blushed immediately after the words came out of his mouth. "Uh, I hadn't told her that's what I was planning yet."

King Ian and Mrs. Raymond exchanged glances. "Darius," he said. "People throughout history have done terrible things claiming they were going to save the world. No doubt Hanali believes *he* is saving the world."

"I get that. But this time it's true. The Sunlit Lands are dying, Ian. Do you deny it?"

The king smiled. "Ah, Darius Walker. I see that you no longer call me king. Could it be that you are embracing your own birthright?"

"The Sunlit Lands are so full of royalty, it's surprising they can hold up under their own weight," Darius said. "I have no interest in a crown, but it's time for me to embrace my role here. As much as I respect you, Ian, I don't report to you. Not to Hanali, either, or the queen of the Southern Court, or anyone else in this whole place. When I decide what needs to be done, I'll do it, and no one here can stop me."

"Brave words," Break Bones said. "And the Scim know better than any others the brokenness of the Sunlit Lands. How will you save them, Darius? What is your plan?"

"I need to go to the Zhanin," he said. "The caretakers of magic in this world. It's time to get to the source of this whole place, and that means going to the Sea Beneath. I have this feeling . . ." He shook his head. It was more than a feeling, but how could he explain it? There was a certainty, a sort of clear direction that lit its way in his mind. It had come to him when he was listening to the story of the Kharobem. He knew exactly what needed to be done, but he also knew for a fact that no one here would understand. "I need to get to the source of the magic of the Sunlit Lands. Not the Elenil magic. All the magic. Everything that makes this place what it is."

And when he got there, he was going to destroy it. Burn it. Smash it. Break it. Whatever it took. No matter what the people here said, no matter the cost. Because it was the magic that was destroying these people, whether they realized it or not. There was something dangerous at the core of it, something destructive. He was going to find it and snuff it out.

"Good plan," Jason said. "Save the world. I mean, that's my plan too. I had it first, I'm saying."

Darius clapped him on the back. "I'll be happy to do it together."

34
THE ONE-WORD STORY

The Warbird must abandon lover and parent
and brother and sister and cousin.
Her every thought must be for her people.

FROM *THE WISE SAYINGS OF MOTHER CROW*

other Crow told me the story that can change the world," Jason said. "The old Mother Crow, I mean. I wasn't sure what it meant at first, but it's starting to make sense to me."

Baileya had been given a small room to rest, and she had invited him to come sit with her so they could have a few moments alone. Baileya had been meeting nonstop with the leaders of other peoples, and she was exhausted. It was strange to see her lying back on a pile of pillows, eyes half-open, because Jason had been with her in so many places where a normal person would be about to collapse, and she had just kept going. Their first time in the desert, for instance, when they had run forever, and she had been badly wounded, but she didn't stop running.

"It is the central lesson of our people," Baileya said, a smile inching onto her face. "We are all learning it forever. Before we are taught the word and after. Children and elders. Men and women. Warriors and those who tend the cooking fires."

"And that's . . . I mean, when you called off our engagement, really, part of what you were saying was that you wanted me to grow in this story."

Her face clouded. "Yes. In your story, Wu Song, but yes, the one-word story, too."

"It's, uh, I'm guessing it's a weird time to talk about whether we're in the place to get re-engaged."

She smiled at him. "Not because I do not wish to talk about it. But yes, I am Mother Crow now. Other concerns must come to the forefront. The Kakri must be my first thought, not my beloved."

He warmed at that. It still didn't make complete sense to him how you could call someone your beloved but not be dating him. Of course, Baileya didn't even understand the concept of dating—it wasn't something the Kakri did. For them, when a couple was considering marriage, one of them told the other a story they had never told anyone else. This was a gift of great value. The receiver of the gift would consider it for a year.

Baileya hadn't needed that long. Jason's story had been about the loss of his sister, and his part in it. She had considered the story for some time and then rejected it. She hadn't rejected Jason . . . she had rejected the story. She told him when he had learned to tell it correctly—when he had learned to love himself—he should come back to her. But until then she could not accept his proposal.

Jason felt like he was finding the edges of what she meant. It was a strange blind spot, and he only knew it was there because of Baileya. Trying to find it was a process of groping in the dark, but he was starting to get the shape of it. He had thought through the way he'd told his story . . . how his sister, Jenny, was dead because of him. And he could see that part of the problem was centering himself, making it all his fault. Because his dad and mom had a part to play in the story, and so did Jenny herself.

But he couldn't come up with another answer to the part that had really upset Baileya: when he had found Jenny, bloody and dying, upside down in the wrecked car, and she had said, "Didi, I was waiting for you." Those words burned in him, and he didn't know how to take them other than the way he *did* take them: that she had been dying, hanging there alone, wishing that he would come faster and get there sooner—that he knew where she was and no one else did, and she was waiting for him to save her. So he hadn't found all the pieces yet. Which meant Baileya wasn't going to accept his story. Which meant they couldn't be engaged, but apparently didn't mean that she didn't love him. The whole thing ran a little contrary to how he thought about relationships.

"Knives," Baileya said.

"What?"

"Is that the first thing Mother Crow taught you in the desert? How to fight with knives?"

Yes, actually. Not just how to fight with them, but how to survive with them. If you were going to make a mash of the fat, cactus-like thumbtree, you were going to need a knife. You could cut poles and cloth to construct a shelter. Defend yourself against a wylna. "Yes, of course."

"She could have taught you the spear or bow and arrow or any number of other weapons."

"Laser guns would be nice."

"But she taught you the knife. Did she tell you why?"

"I don't think I even asked," Jason said.

She smiled. "Because the knife is about getting close to your problems. With a bow, you can stand far away. One skilled with the bow can destroy an enemy without ever seeing his face. But with the knife you must get close enough to touch, to grapple, to know the enemy. Those who know the enemy best are the greatest with the knife. The Kakri believe that we must know ourselves—and know our enemies. Because the greatest stories require knowledge of what is true."

Jason reflected on that. "Which takes us back to the one-word story."

"Yes, in many ways it does."

There was a knock at the door, and Jason leapt up to answer it so Baileya wouldn't have to move. On the other side of the door was another Jason. "Oh, hi," he said.

"Hi yourself," the other Jason said.

"Literally," Jason said, and they both started laughing.

"Good one," the other Jason said.

"I know, right! Okay, but what can I do for you, Jason?"

"Well, Jason," the other Jason said, grinning, "Queen Lelise wants Mother Crow to come as quickly as possible because an emissary from the Elenil has arrived. We are meeting in the Garden of Shapes."

Baileya didn't need much warning to get back on her feet and look as if she had never been tired. They made it to the garden in a matter of minutes. It was a strange place with thousands of plants: tropical and desert, forest and mountain, creeping vines and towering trees. There were hedges as well, which had been cleverly trimmed into shapes of all kinds . . . different people and places in the Sunlit Lands. There were also hedges cut to look like a Courtier mid-transformation—half one creature and half another.

The fake Jason said, "We bring our children here to stretch their imaginations about what shapes there are in the world and what forms they could take. And we often invite foreign dignitaries to meet with us here because it sets their minds at ease to see themselves represented in this garden."

Jason didn't know about that. He suspected it would worry them that the Courtiers might have already infiltrated their people. Or would just generally creep them out. He was leaning toward creeping them out.

Queen Lelise stood in the center of a clearing, where towering hedges formed Kharobem touching wing to wing, setting aside a sort of meeting space in the center of their wings. King Ian and Mrs. Raymond were there, as well as Ruth Mbewe representing the Zhanin, Break Bones as a stand-in for the Scim, and a familiar Elenil who stood with a tiger lounging at his feet. Off to the side, arms crossed and a scowl on his face, stood Darius Walker, with Crukibal nearby for the Maegrom.

Jason immediately understood why Darius would be angry. The Elenil was familiar because he had been part of an Elenil party that had captured Jason and Darius when they were on the run on the edges of the Wasted Lands. His name was Sochar, and he had skewered a Scim child named Nightfall right in front of them. Darius and Jason both had vowed vengeance.

"Greetings," Sochar said, "from Hanali, son of Vivi, highest-ranking of the Elenil."

"Is he truly archon then?" King Ian asked.

Sochar gave a little half bow. "He surely will be before the day is through. The magistrates meet this very night to confirm it."

"So he is not highest-ranking of the Elenil," Mrs. Raymond said. "And he has sent a careless speaker to be his mouthpiece."

Sochar smiled politely. "These are the words he gave me to bring to you."

"We knew Hanali was a liar already," Darius said.

The Elenil regarded him coolly. "I had been given to understand that you had been banished."

"I do not recognize his authority," Darius said. "Or the Elenil's authority, for that matter."

Sochar looked as if he had accidentally swallowed a bug. "You always were more Scim than human."

Break Bones threw his arm around Darius. "It is a high compliment, little brother."

Darius cracked a smile for the first time since they had all arrived together. "Say your piece, Elenil lackey, and then begone before Jason and I follow through on our vows concerning you."

Jason gave Darius a weird look. He had a habit of falling into Scim-like turns of phrase when he was in situations like this.

Sochar folded his hands behind his back. "Hanali is . . . concerned . . . to see so many representatives of various peoples gathering in the Southern Court. He has sent me to remind you that the Elenil have been placed in charge of the Sunlit Lands by the Majestic One himself and that any action against our people will be punished. Severely punished." He looked around at them. "While certain of the representatives present are—how should I say this?—untraditional, it concerns the archon—"

"He's not the archon," Ruth Mbewe reminded him.

"It concerns Hanali to see nearly all the people groups represented here, and he himself not invited. He has sent me here to stand in his place and to speak for the Elenil in whatever meetings you may hold."

"Excellent," Queen Lelise said. "The Elenil are welcome here."

"They *are*?" Jason asked.

"We are missing only the Maduvoreans," King Ian said. "An historic meeting, to be sure."

There was a rustling from one of the great hedges, and a woman stepped out of it. She was dressed in the lightest of greens, her dress fluttering like leaves in a gentle breeze. Flowers were braided into her hair, and when Jason saw her, his mind went blank. His chest felt hollow. It couldn't be, and yet it was. Madeline! Jason burst across the gathering of people and hugged her. She gave an involuntary laugh but was not displeased.

"Madeline!"

She smiled and pushed him back so he could see her face. It wasn't her. Not exactly. Her eyes were a deep, emerald green, and her skin had a slightly green tint to it also. "Not so, my boy, but thank you for saying it. Your Maddie called me the Garden Lady, and when she took the Heartwood Crown into herself and planted the Queen Seed, I was patterned after her. I'm the new lady of the wood." She stroked his face. "So not her, but I know much of what she knew. She loved you, you know."

Jason burst into tears, something that came as suddenly as an unexpected storm. "You look almost like her."

"I don't mean to cause you pain," she said. "Think of me like an echo. A recording of her voice, perhaps."

"Well, you sure don't sound like her," Jason said, wiping his eyes. He thought, suddenly, of Darius and turned to see him standing on the other side of the crowd, distraught and clearly in pain. "Darius," he said.

"It's not her," Darius said.

The Garden Lady looked respectfully away from Darius. "When you are ready, Darius, I hope you will come to Maduvorea and walk a few hours in the cool of the evening with me. There are things between you and Madeline that were left unsaid. There are tendrils that should be unspooled."

"I'll think about it," Darius said, but Jason could tell by the look on his face that the thought made him sick.

"So now we are gathered," the Garden Lady said. "Or at least, now we are all represented. What words and wisdom shall we share?"

"I believe," Sochar said, "that the proposal on the table is that all people here acknowledge the centuries-held right of the Elenil to rule, given them by the Majestic One and reinforced over the centuries time and time again. The Elenil vote aye."

Break Bones growled. "The Scim vote nay, with one voice. I need not speak to our elders to know that. What of the Kakri, Mother Crow?"

Baileya shocked Jason in that she did not speak immediately but seemed to be thinking it over. "The Kakri do not desire war. We do not wish to spill a single drop of Kakri blood. But we do not feel that the proposal as currently stated is one we can agree to."

"Open to conversation, then," Sochar said.

"Perhaps."

"Bai, what? Are you serious?"

Baileya gave him a warning look. "You are Kakri, and I am Mother Crow. I speak for all my people, not myself. You can speak to Baileya in the way that you have done, but not to Mother Crow."

"Uhhh," Jason said. "Okay. But me and Baileya are going to need to talk about this later."

King Ian cleared his throat. "The Pastisians have never owed fealty to the Elenil. We have been left to our own devices. We fear this has changed over the last year. We are satisfied to stay out of the way of the Elenil so long as the Pastisians are left in peace. Or such would be our position if the Elenil agreed to leave the humans in peace as well. We cannot stand idly by and watch a genocide."

"You're all saying you want peace no matter the cost," Jason said. "How is that right or just? You'll leave the Scim or someone else to suffer so long as you're not directly being impacted, is that what you're saying? I don't understand."

"Leaders must make complicated calculations," Ruth Mbewe said. "I fear, Jason, that you are right. But in the many months of my time among the Zhanin, I have been accepted as one of them . . . and though I do not know them as well as I could, I know I can speak for them in this: the Zhanin cannot go to war and still fulfill their function as stewards of magic. We must keep the peace. We will not rise up against the Elenil."

"Well, first of all you are literally a little girl," Jason said. "Second of all, you're in charge of magic. Just cut the Elenil off!"

"Then the Zhanin would be the rulers of the Sunlit Lands. Such is not our role. We keep the balance—we do not use our powers to alter the world to our liking."

"Crukibal, tell this maniac that the Maegrom will fight," Jason said.

The Maegrom bowed deeply. "Wu Song, my new friend. I cannot say this. The Maegrom have been of two minds in recent years. We have allied with the Scim and with the Elenil, and I cannot pretend to know the mind of our ruler, the Heart of Flame. I cannot say with any certainty what he will do. I can only say, friend, that I stand with you."

"Well, that's something at least," Jason said. "What about the Southern Court and the Maduvoreans?"

The Garden Lady bowed her head as if in deep thought or maybe even in prayer. At last she said, "Madeline has given you a great weapon, Wu Song, though I fear you do not see it. This is our greatest and only contribution."

"A great weapon? What are you talking about? The Sword of Years?" But the Garden Lady had finished speaking and said nothing more. He filed this away for later reflection. What weapon could Madeline have possibly left behind?

"That leaves us, then, with the Southern Court," Sochar said.

Queen Lelise folded her hands calmly against her stomach and said, "We will infiltrate Elenil society, take your shapes and forms, and help move you in the right direction. We will not stand idly by and let the Elenil destroy all for their own gain."

"I feared you would say that," Sochar said. "So the Scim and the Southern Court against us, and all the others against us in spirit but too afraid to stand."

"Not afraid," King Ian said.

Sochar moved so fast they were all taken off guard. He grabbed Lelise and slipped a bracelet on her arm, one which constricted in a moment, then gave a familiar, bright flash as the magic took hold. At the same moment, Sochar's tiger leapt on Break Bones, knocking him backward. The Scim warrior gave a shout of surprise, followed by a delighted laugh, because he loved a good fight.

"You have crippled me," Lelise shouted in horror. "I cannot change my shape!"

Baileya advanced on the Elenil, while everyone else stepped back, trying to make room. Sochar had pulled a long, vicious-looking dagger from his coat. "A necrotic blade," he said. "The smallest scrape of its blade will bring death."

"You were safe here under the auspices of being an ambassador," Baileya said. "Do not think I will spare your life now."

The Elenil, after many centuries of practice, were the most fearsome warriors of the Sunlit Lands. They were significantly longer-lived, and they used this difference to their advantage at every turn. Baileya was little more than a small child to them, an infant. Still, she had greater reach with her double-bladed spear. Jason couldn't figure why Sochar would agree to fight. Even if he managed to defeat several of them in battle, the Southern Court would surely overwhelm him with numbers.

Sochar lunged for Baileya, who just managed to slide away from the knife. She bashed him in the nose with the handle of her spear and danced backward. Sochar snarled, then spotted Jason. A devilish glint came into his eye, and he moved toward Jason instead of toward Baileya.

"Wu Song!" she shouted, and disconnected the center groove of her spear, tossing him half.

He caught it. He knew to stay out of Sochar's range, and this half spear would give him an advantage there. And he knew that the Kakri way was to know your enemy—and to use that knowledge to find weaknesses. What he knew about Sochar was this: he had a deep, even irrational, hatred of the Scim. He saw them as inferior, poorly made copies of the Elenil. He was cocky, overconfident, and believed to the core of his being that he was an authority figure whom other people should respect and obey. He had attacked an unarmed Scim child because he knew he could get away with it.

Jason swiped his spear in a long horizontal arc, keeping Sochar at bay. Baileya was approaching from behind, and Jason knew the two of them could take care of the guy if he had to deal with both of them. From the sounds behind him, where Break Bones was fighting the tiger, he suspected the Scim would soon be bounding to their rescue as well.

"I'm not a defenseless Scim child," Jason said.

Sochar sneered and shifted his grip on the poisonous dagger. "They are serpents, every one of them. None of them are defenseless."

Unseen and unnoticed by Sochar, Crukibal had slipped up behind him. He had a small dagger of his own, and with a quick cut he sliced across the back of the Elenil's thigh, then tumbled out of the way. As the Elenil fell,

Jason kicked the necrotic blade from his hand. Baileya sprang forward and put her spear at Sochar's throat.

"Traitor," Sochar spit at Crukibal.

"It is the Elenil who have betrayed the Sunlit Lands," Crukibal said, dusting off his clothes.

"Do not harm him," Lelise cried. "He has Stilled me, and the Southern Court will have our revenge."

"Fools," Sochar said. "When I do not return, Hanali will know what has happened here, and he will raze the Southern Court." He slipped a blade—barely more than a straight razor—from his sleeve.

"Another necrotic blade," Baileya shouted. She went to knock it from Sochar's hand, but he had already released it. It flew, straight and fast as an angry hornet, and sped past Crukibal.

Break Bones was on Sochar in a moment, and with a furious roar he broke the Elenil's hand. The Elenil fell to the ground, nursing his hand, but with a triumphant grin on his face. Sochar wouldn't be holding another blade for a while, that much was certain. And yet why did he smile?

"Are all safe?" Baileya asked. "No one touch the knives, for there may be poison on more than just the blade. The Elenil are not to be trusted in a situation such as this."

Crukibal walked to the small necrotic blade and picked it up, then did the same with the dagger. He slipped both into a pocket in his cape. "No need to worry, Mother Crow." He held out his hand, and they could see a bright gash across the palm. "It clipped me as it passed."

Sochar laughed, and Break Bones struck him twice. "Silence, Elenil."

"No!" Jason said, and he dropped to his knees beside the dying Maegrom, who stood calm and regal and seemingly unconcerned.

"Wu Song," Crukibal said. He turned to see all who were gathered. Even Lelise—still in shock from her own wound—watched in horror and wonder as the Maegrom addressed them. "I hope you will forgive me for speaking my advice all at once. I fear I have no time to hear your wise counsel." He stumbled, and Jason helped him to sit. "To Darius Walker I leave this box. It is of some import. Held within it are all the stories of the world, save those of the Kakri. Use it wisely, sir. I have never seen another ask for the type of story you did, and this makes you, to my way of thinking, particularly well-disposed to decide its fate." His skin, which was naturally a greyish hue, was starting to turn white, like a stone being slowly bleached from within. "Queen Lelise. I can only suggest what you surely must have already considered: send your best shifters to take the place of this ambassador and his tiger. Surely it will buy us a day or maybe even two." He was breathing raggedly. "Where is the Scim?"

Break Bones knelt beside him. "I am here, brave warrior. What need do you have of me, a stranger?"

"Make me a promise, sir. Take my body to the Heart of Flame. Tell him of this day. Hold nothing back. Should he join the Scim in rising up against the Elenil, my sacrifice today will have done what I could not do when living, and thus I rejoice. Should the Heart of Flame even then not be stirred to action, I hope, sir, you at least will make him feel shame."

When Break Bones spoke, his voice was thick with emotion. "I swear this, sir. Nothing will prevent me."

Crukibal's eyes closed. "What I would not give to see you rage against the Heart of Flame." His last words were spoken aloud, but so quiet that all fell silent to hear them. "And so my spirit is gathered to my fathers. I have shaped stone, and been shaped by it. Now, to dust I return."

"He has departed," Break Bones said, and then, quieter, to the body: "May the Peasant King welcome you into his court in a seat of honor."

Darius had a strange reaction to this phrase . . . he seemed troubled rather than grieved, and looked away, out of the garden.

"Good riddance," Sochar said.

"Show some respect," Jason said.

Queen Lelise stood, flanked now by a full twenty Courtiers. "Sit the villain up so he can see me clearly," she said.

Jason and Baileya lifted Sochar, and Baileya quickly checked him for other weapons. The tiger was dead, its blood mingled with Break Bones's. The queen's fingers searched for the edges of the bracelet Sochar had put on her arm, but—as was common with Elenil magic—it had disappeared, leaving only a complicated network of magical tattoos. Jason had never seen magic like that applied against someone's will.

"It's permanent," Sochar said. "Even now my compatriots are pretending to be Courtiers, and slipping these on the arms of your people."

"Your master is afraid," Lelise said.

"Not of you."

"No," she said. "Of him." She pointed at Jason.

"I, uh . . . hey, wait a minute," Jason said.

Queen Lelise put her hand on Jason's arm. "It is my prerogative as ruler of the Southern Court to give power to whomever I please. Did you know that? It is why I can tell another Courtier to take my shape and go do this or that thing. It is why I can sleep a full night and wake and discover that I—the sovereign ruler of the Southern Court—have done much work in the night." She turned to Jason. "My people are quite taken with you."

Jason's heart was beating so hard against his chest, he thought it might be trying to get out. "I noticed."

"I wish to make you king of the Southern Court."

There was a sort of gasp from the other Courtiers, followed by what could only be described as a cheer, though it was full of the brays and roars and crows of inhuman shapes as well.

"Do not be foolish," Sochar gasped. "You would give your power to a human? He is too unpredictable. He does not respond to authority, and you would offer him your own? He is no member of the Southern Court. He cannot even change his shape."

"Nor can I," the queen spat.

Jason felt light-headed. "Do I have to change shapes?"

"If you wish to, you may. We can teach you. It takes addleberry wine—to help you forget your own shape—and then the magic of the Southern Court."

He looked up, found Baileya's eyes. "Bai, any advice?"

"Be true to your own heart," she said, but she was smiling.

"Don't be a fool," Sochar said.

"Every time I'm being true to my own heart," Jason said, "someone calls me a fool." He shrugged. "Thanks, Sochar—that clinches it. Sure, Your Majesty, I accept."

Lelise stood and cried out in a booming voice, "I, King of the Southern Court, give all my authority and power to Jason Wu, sometimes called Wu Song. Long may he reign!"

There were cheers and chants of "Long may he reign!" and "All hail His Majesty King Jason of the Southern Court!"

Jason raised his hands for quiet. Courtiers had begun crowding into the garden as the news spread, appearing as birds and other fast-moving creatures, pushing in to get a better view and to hear him better.

When they had all fallen silent, he said, "Thanks, everybody. It's an honor just to be nominated." He looked at Sochar for a moment, who had undisguised hatred on his face. "I need two volunteers. One to be Sochar, and the other his tiger." He got them, quickly, and he gave them instructions to return to Far Seeing and tell Hanali that all of the other people of the Sunlit Lands were either neutral or coming to destroy the Elenil.

"No lies," Jason said, and it was as if he had invented a new slogan, an oath for the people of the Southern Court. They shouted it back to him.

Break Bones came to him, a wide grin on his face. "Your Majesty," he said, and could barely keep the smile from his voice.

"Break Bones," Jason said, grinning back.

"With your permission I will take Crukibal and return him to his people."

Jason embraced him. "Meet us two days from now at the gate of Far Seeing, with or without the Maegrom."

"So be it," Break Bones said, and he lifted the small corpse with gentle care. Jason watched his friend disappear before returning to the issue at hand.

"People of the Southern Court," Jason said. "Prepare yourselves for war."

Jason didn't give them any more instruction than that, and the Courtiers sprang into action, preparing themselves for what was to come. Loud cries echoed throughout the city as they called to one another . . . instructions, announcements, questions, plans.

He ordered Sochar bound and imprisoned. He debated what should be done. Many things were suggested, but the only one Jason considered carefully was when someone said they should use the new fruits of Maduvorea. One of them, called pudding fruit, caused people to tell the truth for the rest of the day whether they wished to or not. Jason felt a small, fierce fire of happiness. Clearly Madeline had left this fruit for him and in his honor. He didn't see the need to use it on Sochar, as he knew that Sochar saw no value in lies—he shared his repulsive ideas and ideologies willingly with anyone who asked.

Lelise suggested they retire to the receiving room. "Your royal receiving room," she said, with a bow of her head. It was a fascinating and complicated room, with spaces designed for the various peoples of the Sunlit Lands. There were, Jason noted, more than seven spaces . . . the Southern Court must count people groups differently than the Elenil had taught Jason to count them. Which wasn't surprising since the Elenil never had much to say about the Southern Court. They settled into the "human" part of the room—a couch and several chairs making one of the more comfortable setups Jason had seen in the Sunlit Lands—and settled in to make plans.

Baileya was with him, and Darius. Shula had found them too. David and Kekoa stood nearby, talking to one another. Jason held Delightful Glitter Lady in his lap, stroking her as they chatted. "I need to understand how the magic works," he said. "I feel an idea forming, and it's connected somehow to this."

"Very well," Lelise said. She had been crippled by the Elenil, no longer able to change her shape. Nevertheless, she had remained focused and clear thinking. "This first rule of magic is—"

"Poop has to go somewhere," Jason said. "I know."

Lelise looked startled. "No. At least, not in the Southern Court. The first rule of magic is that memory makes us."

"Memory makes us."

"What does that mean?" Shula asked, and there was a hint of desperation in her voice.

"Just as I said. What we say and believe and remember about the past changes who we are. There is a need for honesty about the past, not only honest talk in the present."

"I get it," Jason said, and realized that he did. The way you told your story changed what was happening to you today. And suddenly he understood what Baileya had been trying to say to him. When he told his story about Jenny, it went like this: Jenny and his parents had been fighting, and she went out with a boy they didn't approve of. She asked Jason to lie about where she was going, and he did. They were in a terrible car accident, and when she didn't return, Jason's parents kept asking where she was, and he said he didn't know, though he sort of did. By the time they found her, she was crushed in an overturned car, dying, and she had said, "I was waiting for you," meaning "Where were you? Why didn't you save me?"

Except she *hadn't* said, "Where were you?"

She had said, "I was waiting for you."

Baileya thought maybe what she meant was "I knew you were coming." It could even be, Jason realized, that she was saying, "I stayed alive because I knew you'd be here, and I wanted to say goodbye." Depending on how you told the story, Jason's sister might think he was a good brother or a bad one. She might be angry at him or understanding or even thankful. He was afraid to interrogate the story further because he didn't want to know which version was true. He had settled on "bad brother" and worked hard never to tell a lie again. Baileya thought he had been telling himself a false story. *Memory makes us.*

"That's the first rule. What's next?" Jason said.

Lelise spoke softly. "It is simple enough. If memory makes us, then we must realize that *memory also makes other people.* We can become like them—take on their shape—if we learn to see things in the past and present as they did."

Darius cleared his throat. "Seems like your ability to copy others has only increased in the last year, though."

"Yes. In times past, there were Courtiers who so fully embraced other memories that they could never become themselves again. We drink addleberry juice to forget ourselves, and even our shapes. But the new Wendy fruit brings memory back. We can take on any shape, alter ourselves completely, and one drink of concentrated Wendy juice brings us back to ourselves. We have more effectively seeded our people through all the other peoples of the Sunlit Lands since making this discovery."

Darius paced the room. "The Elenil . . . I read a book that said Hanali was human once, that the Elenil kidnapped him or made a bargain with him, and they turned him into an Elenil. But he certainly didn't seem aware of it when I told him that story."

Lelise nodded slowly. "Yes. The Elenil take individuals—it doesn't matter from which people—and teach them to become like Elenil. They tame the Scim, for instance, or bring the humans in as servants. And some of them, in a secret ceremony, are given addleberry juice until they forget their shapes, and they are remolded into Elenil. Such was Hanali. Such were all of them, once."

"So all we need is—" Jason jumped up. "What if we took all the Wendy juice we could, and we made the Elenil drink it? They'd remember everything?"

"Yes, but to what end?"

"You said it yourself, 'Memory makes us.' If they don't remember being human, then we remind them. When they're human again, they won't be in such a rush to destroy us."

Shula laughed, but it sounded cynical. "No, Jason, it doesn't work like that. Maybe for some of them, but not all."

"We have to try something," he said.

"It is worth an attempt," Baileya said. "And we have two armies ready—yours and mine—should we fail."

"I have to go to the Zhanin," Darius said. "I need their help to get to the Sea Beneath. I'm going to figure out how to end this once and for all."

"And I need to get to Far Seeing," Shula said. "My brother is there. We were told you were in danger, Jason, but . . . well, it seems like you're okay for now."

"So we all have a plan," Jason said. "There's just one thing that's bothering me." He looked to the former ruler of the Southern Court. "So many of the Courtiers are pretending to be me. . . . Why did you send them to kidnap me? Why not just send word that we needed to meet?"

Lelise looked at him, pity in her eyes. "That was our original plan. But as more and more of us took on your shape, it changed our story."

"How?" Jason was baffled.

"Because we learned that you didn't believe people would come if you just asked them. As more of us took on your characteristics, we came to believe the same thing."

Jason was stunned. "You kidnapped me because . . ."

"Because in your heart of hearts, you believe that if you call for help, no one will answer. We came to believe the same. Not just generally, but about you personally."

Jason sat back in the couch, a little in shock. Lelise wasn't wrong, but it wasn't something he would usually volunteer. "I—" How could he explain it? It wasn't so much that he didn't believe other people would come to his rescue—it was that he didn't think it was worth their trouble. That they shouldn't bother to come when he called. "I did think that. That no one would come to help me if I called. That's true."

Baileya reached out and took his hand. "You were wrong, Wu Song."

Shula threw her arm over his shoulder. "You're a big dummy, you know that?"

Darius just shook his head. "Honestly, Wu, you should know us better than that."

"Hey," Kekoa called from the side of the room. "You should have known us roomies would show up."

David laughed. "Eventually. We didn't really help Kekoa when he asked for help."

Kekoa punched him in the arm. "Next time, brah."

Jason felt something crack inside him. It was a wall of belief that said, *You aren't worth enough that people will come if you ask them to.* He had never noticed it before, but now it was crumbling. He wanted to make a joke. He wanted to laugh it away, say it wasn't true—but it was true, and he didn't lie, not anymore. He wanted to patch up the wall and pretend this conversation had never happened. *Memory shapes us.*

"Thank you," he said instead, and they all embraced, and he wished they could stay there, stay like that—but there was work to be done, and too soon the moment was over. "Lelise, get our Wendy juice stores, all of them. Have the army pack it for us. We leave for Far Seeing in an hour."

"Yes, Your Majesty," she said, and was gone.

35

THE TRAITOR

Is this why you brought me here? To save them?

DARIUS WALKER

+

The installation of the next archon should be a glorious affair, worthy of all the largesse and beauty that the Elenil have to offer," Hanali said, patting Gilenyia's arm as they climbed toward a certain place she knew well and that Hanali had clearly picked with dreadful purpose. "Unfortunately, the current situation demands speed more than luxury." He smiled at her. "We shall save the largesse and beauty for the wedding!"

Gilenyia smiled back. She knew how to hide her emotions far below the level of her face. No doubt he could not see the fear, the terror, the horror in her heart . . . and the sorrow at how things had changed between them. "Hanali, who could have imagined when we were young that such a thing could come to pass."

"Who indeed," he said. They had entered the warren of strange rooms that made up the archon's living quarters, a maze that took up the entire top of the Tower of a Thousand Years. "Isn't it lovely to have my ascension take place in the archon's own living space? It is here that Madeline Oliver first struck against the Elenil, in the garden. And it is here that Darius Walker killed Archon Thenody. There is some poetic justice in me—the one who will bring the Elenil back to our full glory—being crowned here."

Gilenyia made appreciative, appropriate noises. "I am surprised you did not choose the Meadow at World's End," she said. The Bidding, a ceremony where humans were assigned to their Elenil caretakers, happened in the building which held the meadow . . . a place where a copse of thick trees was said to lead back to Earth.

"When the Majestic One first cursed the humans to a life without magic, it is said they were banished there, in that meadow," Hanali mused. "I should have consulted you. That would have been resonant tonight, indeed."

Gilenyia noticed that he now said the humans had been "banished." It was not so long before that she had heard him say that the humans had chosen to leave, and the Elenil stories about it could be read either way, she supposed. It was strange, the malleable nature of the past, and the lessons such tales brought into the present.

Not that it was strange to hear Hanali changing opinion midsentence. It was ludicrous, for instance, that he'd suggested that luxury would not be a part of things, for he wore a purple robe that billowed as he walked, and a collar made of golden feathers that fluffed out on his chest and also burst up toward his face, completely covering his neck. He had at least two rings on every gloved finger, and he was in high spirits. "The good I will do," he said. He patted her hand again. "There are sacrifices to be made along the way, Gilenyia, that is true. But if we can stomach them, we shall bring lasting change to the Sunlit Lands and make it what is meant to be . . . a land of plenty for all, with the wise Elenil overseeing it."

"I am disappointed the ceremony will be so small," she said. The magistrates would be there, of course. Hanali's mother, Resca. Many in Gilenyia's family had been invited, yet another indication of the seriousness of his marriage offers. He thought it was a decision that had been made already. Some of the more interesting of the younger Elenil had been invited too. She suspected, for instance, that Rondelo would be there with his white stag, perhaps as some sort of honor guard.

"Will you do the ceremony in the garden itself, then?" she asked.

"I had a better idea," he said, pleased. "There are only a few of us, so we will do the ceremony in private. Then I will send someone out to the garden, where there will be thousands of messenger birds waiting. He—or she—will announce my new position and send the birds out to tell all the others." He looked at her slyly. "I have yet to decide to whom this honor should go."

She nearly blushed. Nothing could be further from her desires than to be the one to announce to the Sunlit Lands that Hanali was now Archon Hanali. "It should be, perhaps, one of the magistrates."

Hanali said nothing to that, he only smiled. He had a plan. Something she could not see.

Gilenyia was surprised to see the Scim boy known as the Herald of Mysteries present. She mentioned it to Hanali, who laughed and said, "I would not be myself if there were not a few surprises."

She exchanged pleasantries with a few of the other Elenil. Rondelo stood beside her when it came time for the ceremony. "Something strange is happening," he said.

Surely he was not reaching out to her to see if she was in opposition to Hanali? "What do you mean, my young friend?" She mentioned their age difference to remind him of her superior position and relative importance. To his credit, he did not bristle. Whatever his intention, it was not to harm her . . . not that she could see.

"I have not witnessed the installation of an archon before," he said, "though I have seen magistrates celebrated as they entered service." When the Scim had attacked the festival some time ago, more than one magistrate had been killed. "I have never seen it done so simply or so small, and never in private."

"Hanali is humble," Gilenyia answered and was rewarded with a quick, genuine laugh from Rondelo. So he was truly sharing his mind, it seemed.

"My lady Gilenyia, it has been said more than once that I might be considered a candidate for the magistracy myself." He blushed. "I am young, I know, but influential among the fighting Elenil and among the humans who are in our army."

"I have heard this too," she said, encouraging him.

He leaned close to her, his eyes roving the crowd. "Why am I the only martial Elenil here, lady?"

It was true! All the Elenil who were given to war or patrols were missing. It could be a message from Hanali that he did not consider such things to be of value for the Elenil, but far more likely it meant something else. Especially because not to have them here was to leave himself and the magistrates unguarded. She gasped. "No human guards, either."

"No humans at all." He shook his head. "Lady Gilenyia, I do not know what is happening, but I do not like it."

The ceremony itself was boring, stuffy, and quick. Rondelo stood near her throughout. Each of the magistrates said a few words about Hanali and what qualities of his they most appreciated. Then, in a strange and unprecedented moment, the Scim Herald of Mysteries was invited to speak.

The Scim boy stood, the shortest among them by any measure, and bowed low to Hanali. "Archon Hanali," he said, and he was the first to use the title. "I thank you all for the honor of attending this historic moment. It does not pass unnoticed that no other Scim is here, and none other invited."

"It is a great pleasure to have you," Hanali said in his most charming voice.

"I have been asked to contribute a small insight, and then our new archon will share a few words." There was a smattering of applause. The herald launched into a long recitation of the Elenil creation story, how Ele and Nala obeyed the Majestic One when no one else did, and how they were put in charge of the whole of the Sunlit Lands. "And my people, the Scim, banished to darkness," the herald said. "Does it seem unfair? No, for we rebelled against our truest authority. Does it seem too heavy a punishment? Perhaps. But who are we to question the decisions of the Majestic One?" He clapped his hands together, and several of the Elenil startled as if someone had woken them from a dream. "I believe the Majestic One has brought us Archon Hanali for a time such as this. He, of all of us, remembers that the behavior of the Elenil toward the Scim should not be characterized by hatred or animosity, but rather should reflect the loving care between a parent and a child. There are Scim, too, who hate the Elenil, and this should not be. Instead, let the Scim embrace their work and their lot in life, and worry not about what they will eat or drink or where they will live or what they will wear, for the Elenil will care for them and meet all their needs."

"Powerfully spoken," Hanali said, applauding.

"When the Majestic One returns," the herald said, "he will come with fire. He will judge those—human or Scim or Elenil—who have not obeyed the laws which he set forth. And for those who have obeyed—human or Scim or Elenil—great rewards await." He lowered himself to one knee, facing Hanali. "Which is why I pledge my service to Archon Hanali. Long may he reign."

Long may he reign? Gilenyia bristled at the words. The archon was not a king—he was not royalty. She had no doubt the speech was a rehearsed one and that Hanali had been the director. The archon did not reign—he was a caretaker. He was a magistrate, and in theory all the other magistrates had the same amount of power that he did, though the archon had come to be seen as "first among equals" over the decades, largely through Thenody's work. But Hanali had scorned Thenody, had despised him. She had seen this before: sometimes those with distance from power critiqued it less when their own proximity to power altered.

"I will not speak long," Hanali said. "I am overwhelmed with gratitude that you have seen fit to make me archon." He smiled at the magistrates. "I know I have caused you enough pain over the years with my constant campaign to make life better for the Scim. Our dear herald is correct, though. To improve life for the Scim is not a matter of providing them more resources, but rather of making sure that Scim people are participating in the work they are meant to do, according to the Majestic One.

"One of the first priorities in my leadership will be making sure that all the people of the Sunlit Lands remember their ancient callings. On that note, I have two announcements to make, which I think will please all who are gathered here. The first concerns the humans. As you know, I have been the staunchest proponent of importing humans here to the Sunlit Lands. I have come to see that this was a dire error. The Majestic One gave them Earth and gave us magic, and I have been too sloppy with the many whom I have invited in. All of our recent challenges—the incursion at the Festival of the Turning, the attack upon the Crescent Stone, the resetting of magic with the Heartwood Crown—these are all problems which can be traced back to the *humans*.

"I spoke about this with Gilenyia, and I realized this was no mere error, but a transgression against the Majestic One himself. I said to Gilenyia, 'Perhaps we should send all the humans home,' and she replied, 'Do you think the Majestic One so easily dismissed? You have brought punishments upon our people by bringing in the humans, and now you will send them home? Send them home with magical gifts, which you promised them? The Majestic One said they would be a people bereft of magic, and you wish to disobey him.' I was deeply troubled by these words."

Gilenyia stood in shocked horror. He had lied. Lied in public, and *about her*. A rage rose in the center of her soul.

"I do not understand the direction of his speech," Rondelo said.

But Gilenyia did. He was telling everyone here how wise and wonderful she was, and then pinning his plan in her mouth, so that if it all went poorly in the future, the most influential Elenil would think it had come from her. He was lifting her up to protect himself. She felt betrayed, and then disappointed in herself for feeling betrayed. Of course he would do such a thing—this was the way of it among the Elenil. But she had thought their relationship something outside such petty machinations.

"As most of us know," Hanali said, "the Elenil are . . . dependent . . . on the humans in certain ways. We require them when we wish to expand the numbers of our fair people. Yet I led us astray in the past when I made them so integral to our society. Serving our food, guarding our walls. No more. In my own heart, if I were alone responsible for this decision, I would send the humans home, to Earth. But in discussions with the magistrates and my dear, insightful Gilenyia, it has been clear that there must also be a punishment. There must be a public denouncing of the harm the humans have brought to our people in these last years. So it has been decided to purge them."

"To purge them," Rondelo repeated to himself. Then, to Gilenyia, "To purge them? What does he mean?"

"To kill them," Gilenyia said, her voice cold, and she could see from the complicated emotions flitting across Rondelo's face that he opposed this scheme with an immediate vehemence, and also that he believed Hanali, who said it had been her idea.

"You jest," Rondelo said, loud, and Gilenyia was surprised by his strength.

Hanali placed a hand to his chest, a look of mock surprise on his face. "My dear Rondelo. I may have lobbed a humorous canard or two when I was a private citizen, but I am archon now. My word is law. I assure you that I do not jest. In point of fact, Gilenyia and I had discussed the extermination of the humans to take place two nights hence. But I decided, as a surprise, and with the magistrates' approval, to send our soldiers out today. Even now they are searching for the humans, gathering them, and showing them what happens when a person stands against the Majestic One."

No, Gilenyia thought. *No, no, no.* Of course he moved the timeline up. She had been working to prepare for two days from now, and he had already started to act. A sudden panic gripped her. What of Ricardo? She had other human servants too. Would Hanali's forces find them swiftly? How long until the humans discerned what was happening and began to hide? She did not know. She gripped Rondelo's forearm, feeling lightheaded. She needed to get away from here, back to her rooms where she could work, where she could plan, where she could move things faster and give her humans a chance. Her humans. And herself. For was she not one of them?

"Rondelo," she said, nearly whispering. "Listen well and closely. I am not of a single mind with the archon on this point. It seems to me that we must move the humans with all speed to the Meadow at World's End. We can send them home from there. There will not be much time, and we will need as many Elenil and human soldiers as we can muster to protect the humans as they retreat."

"You must think me a fool," Rondelo said. "It is your plan to kill them, and now you ask me to bring all the humans and any Elenil who would stand in your way, and gather them all in one place? I am young, lady, but not so young as that." Then, his voice raised again toward Hanali, "You are archon, sir, and thus owed my honor and respect. Your actions, however, turn my stomach, and I will have no part in them."

"Arrest him," Hanali said, simply.

But there were no true soldiers in the small crowd, and Rondelo leapt upon his white stag and disappeared before anyone could stop him. Gilenyia thought she might weep. Not only had her closest thing to an ally disappeared, he was hunted now and believed her to be his enemy. The best plan she had—to move the refugee humans out of the Sunlit Lands—would be near impossible if he spread the word that the meadow was a killing field.

"Do not despair, Lady Gilenyia," Hanali said, a gentle smile on his face. "I brought Rondelo here knowing the truth would be difficult, and I wanted him to hear it from my own mouth. He will come around in time. In five decades or ten, who will remember what is done to the humans today? Who will speak their names? Perhaps a few of us here, who recognize their sacrifice in supporting the return of the Elenil to glory."

One of the magistrates said, "I still think, Archon Hanali, that you are moving too quickly. The humans form the core of our army, and there are more of them than us. And there is unrest among the other peoples of the Sunlit Lands. The Elenil are not as popular as we once were."

"True enough," Hanali said. "But the Elenil are better fighters, and many of the humans are useless without magic. The greatest threats are the Knight of the Mirror and his followers, and I have sent the strongest of my forces there to deal with him and his." He paused, waiting for more objections, but there were none. He threw his hands up as if in celebration. "My second announcement is of much greater cheer, gentle friends, so do not despair! I have asked my lady Gilenyia to marry me, and she has agreed."

Which she had not. She should have known this moment was coming. The eyes of every Elenil turned toward her. Many faces were lit with excitement, but a few looked confused or concerned. She took note of those. Perhaps they were deeper thinkers who could be more useful in the difficult days to come.

The Elenil raised their voices in congratulations, and Gilenyia, feeling pinned beneath Hanali's plan, smiled and raised her hand in reply. If she denied his announcement, this meeting would only drag longer, and the sooner she was able to leave here, the sooner she could race to help Ricardo and the others.

"One last surprise, a small one," Hanali said. "Thousands of messenger birds await in the garden, perched in every tree and on every railing. As you know, I have repaired the gardens, at considerable expense to myself. If it pleases all of you, I would like to invite my lady Gilenyia to announce to the birds and thus the Sunlit Lands the good news about my new position as your archon, and to share in her own voice her excitement about our matrimonial plans."

There was a general murmur of assent, and Hanali thanked them all for coming. The herald said, "All hail Hanali, archon of the Elenil," and Hanali smiled sheepishly as all the assembled people came to congratulate him. Hanali caught her eye, and his smile widened. He motioned toward the garden balcony, shooing her out to the messenger birds.

Gilenyia moved toward the balcony, brushing aside the congratulations of the Elenil who reached out to her as she passed them. The gardens at the top of the tower were considered a jewel of Elenil culture. Acres of gardens, magically disguised so they did not ruin the palace's appearance from below, ringed the tower. Stone balustrades lined the outer edge. She came to the precise place where Madeline Oliver had defeated Archon Thenody. He had given Madeline two choices, and she had created her own, a third.

Hanali had been far ahead of Gilenyia's every move. She did not know anymore whether he thought she had been won over or whether he knew that she was against his plans. Was letting her make this announcement a sign of trust or a power play to humiliate her? She did not know. He had been playing this game for years before she even knew it had begun.

As she stepped onto the very place where Archon Thenody had his hand cut off by a Scim girl, an idea came to her. Thousands of birds filled the trees, stood on the ground, perched on the balustrades. Small brown sparrows, great purple birds she did not recognize, hawks and eagles, flamingos and robins.

Hanali was not near her. He had told her what he wanted announced— or had made his wishes clear enough, anyway. She was to announce their engagement and proclaim that he was now archon. He knew that, and she knew that, and the few people who were gathered here knew that. But the other Elenil did not know what she was meant to say. She had an open door, an exhilarating, impossible moment to shape what was happening in the Sunlit Lands. It would sow confusion, yes, but confusion would slow things, and that was what she needed to save the humans. The only problem was that she would have to disobey the archon, something she had not done in her long life. She had always been the most Elenil of the Elenil.

But she was something else now. Someone else now. She was Elenil still, yes. But was she not also human? Were not the people Hanali was about to kill in some sense her people? Her own heart shied away from that truth still, but truth it was. She stood before the birds, straightened her spine, and began to speak.

"People of the Sunlit Lands, we are bursting with news. I am pleased to say that we have, at last, by the wisdom of the magistrates, been blessed with a new archon . . . Hanali, son of Vivi!" She paused. The birds would do their best to follow her natural rhythm of speech when they delivered her words. "May his reign be one of wisdom and great compassion." She paused again and looked back to Hanali, who was basking in the congratulations of the magistrates. No doubt he intended to hear her message later, via messenger bird.

She leaned closer to the birds, which shuffled their feet, craned their heads, flapped, and jostled to get better views. "His first proclamation as archon is one both shocking and wonderful. He has revealed that by the power of Elenil magic, any human can now become an Elenil should they so desire. 'We wish to expand the numbers of our fair race,' he said, just a few moments ago. And so, from this moment, all humans are to be considered as Elenil until such a time as it can be determined which he will choose to ascend to become a permanent part of our race.'"

A great chorus of squawks and honks, chirps and cries came from the birds. This was shocking news indeed. "Any who harms a human from this moment forth," Gilenyia added, "must consider themselves under the wrath of Archon Hanali." Hanali was moving toward her now, a smile on his face, no doubt wondering what all the commotion was from the messenger birds. "What are you waiting for, messengers? You have your message, now fly!" She pointed at one bird—a small one, a sparrow. "As for you, fly with all speed to the Knight of the Mirror and tell him to meet me at the Meadow at World's End with all the might he can muster. Can you do this?"

"Of course, lady," the bird chirped, and leapt into the air.

Gilenyia opened her arms to her fiancé as he approached. She did not show her anger or her fear. She held Hanali for a moment and felt regret. Her bones ached as if she had purposely skipped sleep for a night, even two. The weariness was such that she could scarcely keep her head up, and she rested her cheek upon his shoulder. This, she felt certain, was the last time that she would embrace her old friend, her cousin, her childhood playmate, Hanali, son of Vivi. He was archon now, and she . . . she was a traitor.

36

MALGWIN'S STORY

There are three groups of people who show you the health of a society.
If they are thriving, then all is well. If they are suffering, then there is sickness.
They are the foreigners and widows and orphans.

MALGWIN

✜

arius had never been at sea before, and despite the situation, he loved it. The sun on his face, the spray of the salt water, the sound of the waves crashing into them, even the movement of the boat—well, if it could be called a boat—charmed him. Kekoa had immediately volunteered the "boats" of the Zhanin to take Darius to the Sea Beneath . . . or, at least, to the sunset of World's End. It was unclear to him how to make the journey the rest of the way.

The boats were living creatures, similar to enormous turtles. There was a depressed shell on each boat's back that functioned as a sort of deck, and there was precious little required as far as navigation because the boats knew the way. Kekoa stood at the bow, a wide grin on his face, talking to one of the Zhanin. A few of the boats, Darius knew, did not belong to the

Zhanin at all, but were members of the Southern Court who had taken on the shape of boats. While Jason had wanted most of the Southern Courtiers to stick with him for the assault on Far Seeing, he didn't want Darius to go alone, either.

The planned attack on the Elenil was one that seemed desperate to Darius. He knew the strength of their armies—had fought them many times—though in the past, the Elenil themselves had never deigned to join the battle. He suspected this time they would, especially if the humans were being removed from the equation in some way. He had told Jason that maybe if the humans knew what was happening, they would join forces with the Scim and the Southern Court. Jason agreed it was worth a shot.

"Hey, Darius."

He looked up, startled. It was Kekoa. He didn't know the guy, had never really met him. He knew Kekoa was friends, close friends, with David and Jason. "Hey, man," Darius said.

Kekoa stepped across the deck, barefoot. "You're going to go fight Malgwin, eh?"

"Not fight her. Not if I don't have to."

"I've seen her before, you know," Kekoa said, looking out over the sea. "When I was with the Zhanin this year. I was trying to find the source of magic. I was using the Robe of Ascension to control the Zhanin and . . . well, that's another story. But we took a boat, one of the living ones, and headed due west, toward the crystal sun. Where the sphere meets the sea, the water gets warmer, and there's a churn. It's dangerous. I wouldn't try to surf it, you know, if it were closer to shore. And I saw her. A great beast of a thing."

Sometimes. Darius knew she only appeared that way sometimes. "I've seen her too. I don't know enough about her." He felt the box . . . the story box from Crukibal. He set it in his lap. The breeze was warm and fair. The other boats—most of them living boats, but there were a handful of wooden ones—moving easily through the water, toward Malgwin's territory. Darius felt a sudden premonition of dread. He snapped a ring from the box and slipped it on his finger. He offered one to Kekoa. "You want to learn more?"

Kekoa took the ring and slid it on. "All right, brah. Never hurts to know more." A towering Kharobem floated above them. Kekoa fell backward, steadying himself on the living ship. "Okay, maybe it hurts a little sometimes."

"Tell me about Malgwin," Darius said. "The Kharobem version. What do you know of her?"

The many eyes of the Kharobem fluttered closed, then opened again. "What does a name matter, if the one who held it was taken from you?"

"What?" Kekoa sat forward. "What does that mean?"

"Shh," Darius said, and he leaned forward. "Let the story answer our questions."

✛

What did a name matter, if the one who held it was taken from you?

Her name had been Aarvi once, but that was many years ago, and she scarcely remembered it. She remembered the man her parents had chosen for her, and he was a good man. They had learned to love one another in no time at all. As her husband had said, "If we are to be married, then we shall be gloriously in love." And so it had been.

He had been taller than she, his hair lustrous and black, and on the days that he was paid he brought not only fresh meat from the market but also in the summer he loved to bring her marigolds, for he said she was an explosion of color in his grey heart when they had wed. And they were happy.

She had heard many stories of unhappy marriages, of poor matches and evil husbands, but this was not her story. And they were more than happy when they were blessed with a daughter, and they named her Jyotika, for she was a brilliant flame in their tiny apartment. Even her cries in the middle of the night were met with good humor by Aarvi's husband, who would scoop the baby into his arms and say, "Who has lit this brilliant flame? I cannot sleep she is so bright!"

It had been a traffic accident that killed him—and not only him, but ten others, too. The rains had been heavy the night before, the road was slick, and a Toyota driven by a family on their way back from praying at the temple lost control, went sideways on the highway. A bus swerved to miss the Toyota, so she was told, and it was the bus that hit his truck, full of workers on their way home. Seven dead on the truck, and three from cars that had hit the bus afterward. And her dear husband.

She and Jyotika had moved in with his mother, for her own parents had passed in the last several years. They had very little money, though Aarvi worked hard to bring home more than scraps. She came home one day to find both her mother-in-law and Jyotika gone, and her mother-in-law's possessions (and any of Aarvi's that held any value) gone too.

From there the story began to follow a path that would be familiar to too many of Aarvi's peers: being taken advantage of, offering favors, incurring debts, increasing in desperation, and ending in something just this side of captivity. Or perhaps it was captivity. She roamed the streets looking for her daughter, called for her, but in a city of more than six million it was no use. She found that she could not work, could not concentrate, could only think of her daughter.

A man offered her a bed one night, and when he had fed her and showed her the rolled-up mat on which she could sleep, he locked the door and pocketed the key. He had a knife, and for three days kept her locked in his apartment. She tore at him like a wild animal whenever he came near, tried to take his eyes with her fingernails. He couldn't touch her, couldn't overpower her, for she was like some force of nature. She would not let him sleep, but screamed and broke things if he left her unattended for a moment. After three days, exhausted, he finally managed a few minutes of sleep and woke to find his knife in her hand. She was leaving, and taking anything from his apartment that she fancied. She told him that if he crossed her path again she would take more than valuables, and if he called the police she would find him and eat him. She left him sobbing in his cramped kitchen, begging for mercy.

Aarvi discovered a certain freedom in shedding the rules that had been put upon her. She had been told that she could not survive this world without a man or a parent or an authority figure to guard her, provide for her, but she discovered this was not true. She began to collect children who had been taken advantage of on the streets. She feared and half hoped she would find Jyotika in this way. She cornered certain men when they were alone and made passionate and detailed threats against them for the way they treated vulnerable children. She gained a certain reputation. She did not let them know her name or where she lived, only how they could make donations to the children.

Those who feared her called her Makara—the water monster of myth, the vehicle of the gods who rose up from the depths and swallowed men whole. And so she was. *Don't mistreat a child*, they said, *or Makara will find you*. And so she did.

She grew bitter, and her heart hard. Her only tenderness was for her children, though she had compassion for widowed mothers and women in hard times, too. She didn't hide her name anymore, for it was now Makara. She did not hide where she lived any longer, for the sea monster could not hide its home. What man would be brave enough to approach her in the depths of the sea beneath? None.

In time a certain man came to her, a foreigner. He appeared in her home unannounced. He was dark-skinned, bearded, and she was surprised to discover that he spoke Gujarati perfectly. When she asked him about it, he said, "Magic. No special skill of my own."

She knew at once that a man with this much power could only be there to destroy her, for she had become a monster. She had heard that name given to her more than once. "Beware," she said. "I will fight until the last breath to protect my offspring, and even the little ones have teeth."

"I do not come to fight," said he, "but to offer you and yours a home. A place that is safe, and far from those who hurt you. It is called the Sunlit Lands, and there it is always pleasant, and children are always cared for, and so long as I live you will be welcome there."

But Makara knew the way of these things. A good man in power may cease to be good. A bad man without power may seek to take it from another. This Cumberland Walker might be kind and generous now, but what of the future? Yet his offer seemed sincere. She wondered if she could ask for more.

So she asked him for power of her own, and he offered that to her. She asked him to know the secret of his own power, and he told her. She asked him to give her the ability to protect his power or destroy it, so that if he ceased to be what he appeared, she could destroy him forever. Even this he did not withhold from her but told her of a secret cave beneath his world where the core of his power was kept.

Then she asked one last boon: to know where her beloved Jyotika might be, and to be reunited with her if such a thing were possible.

And he took her far away, to another land, where she did not speak the language. Jyotika was there, and though she was fully grown, Makara recognized her at once. She stood in front of a small house with a tidy yard and pots of marigolds on her porch. On her hip was a child, no older than two, and smiles were on both of their faces. Makara's heart flared with both sorrow and joy. Her mother-in-law was nowhere to be seen, but Makara felt the piercing knife of forgiveness . . . for perhaps she and her mother-in-law were not so different. Her mother-in-law had seen a way to save the child, a way that required leaving Makara—leaving Aarvi—behind, and she had taken it. Monstrous? Yes. But sometimes monsters were necessary to protect the children.

"Take me to your Sunlit Lands," she said to Cumberland. She could not bear the thought that reuniting with her daughter might bring Jyotika some measure of unhappiness, and she dreaded what the girl would say to see her dear mother transformed into the thing she had become. There were the children to consider, too. Who would care for them if she came here, to this foreign land? "Take me to your Sunlit Lands, and my children, too," she said again, "Quickly, before my will fails me." And so he did.

The two became good friends over time, though they often disagreed. She protected his power, and he protected her and her children. Through many years, the people of the Sunlit Lands struggled to say her name. Magara, some said, or Makra. She had been called Nalgva for a time. But in recent years, as the Sunlit Lands slipped toward their motherland's own failings in morality and safety, as the children grew to be ever more at risk, the name whispered by those who feared monsters became Malgwin.

She accepted this name along with all the others. For what did a name matter to a monster? And in the deep waters of the Sea Beneath, she whispered a word in her mother tongue: "Jyotika!" And the deep darkness lit with brilliant flame.

✛

Kekoa let out a low whistle. "That was intense."

"She knows where the power is," Darius said. "She protects it."

"A monster now, though, brah."

Darius didn't know what to say to that. Was she truly a monster? Just for abandoning the societal expectations put on her? For protecting children from being exploited? "Maybe," he said. But then again, maybe monsters were something different from what he had been taught.

"When we get near the world's edge," Kekoa said, "the sea changes. The Zhanin boats may panic. We might have to take dead boats—wooden ones—to go farther."

"She'll find us," Darius said.

"The real question," Kekoa said, "is what we're trying to do once we get there."

Darius showed him the story box. "This thing has captive Kharobem in it," Darius said.

"That seems . . . really stupid," Kekoa said.

"Indeed." Darius showed him the crystal sides and the ornate gold framing that marked the box's corners and boundaries. "Something about the crystals. They can't get out. I don't know how. If what the Kharobem say is true, the Zhanin have kept the balance of magic for many years in the Sunlit Lands, or tried to. I want to go to the source and see if there's something more to be done." He turned the box over, looked at it more carefully. "I wish it were something simple, like a key."

"A key?" Kekoa looked troubled, then gazed back out to sea.

"What is it?" Darius asked.

Kekoa squatted down next to him. "I messed up, Darius. Like, really messed up. I had the Robe of Ascension, and the Knight of the Mirror sent me to deliver it to the Zhanin. But they tried to kill us—me and Ruth—and I kept the robe on. So I could control them, you know? That's what it does with its magic. And then . . . I was too afraid to take it off. Couldn't figure out how to get it off without the Zhanin killing us."

"Where is it now?"

"Ruth burned it. But here's the thing, brah. I was doing . . . I did the same thing the haoles did to the Hawaiians. I needed the Zhanin to act a certain way, so I *made* them act that way. I had the power, and I did the wrong thing. I feel horrible about it, and if it weren't for Ruth . . . either I'd still be there, or I'd be dead."

Darius didn't give him any platitudes. He had messed up plenty of times, and he knew that to tell Kekoa he hadn't done anything wrong would be empty, not to mention dishonest. "It's hard when you realize you've made a mistake like that," he said at last.

"Yeah, well. David—I'm not sure how well you know him—David gave me something. Another magical little something. Told me it was a second chance. He said I'd know when to use it."

"That's a good friend," Darius said.

"I thought of it when you mentioned the key," Kekoa said. "Because that's what it is." He held it up. It looked like a skeleton key. Unremarkable. "It's another of the Scim artifacts—the Disenthraller."

Darius shrugged. "Well, this thing doesn't have a keyhole."

"Yeah," Kekoa said slowly. "Like I said, just made me think of it."

Their boat made a sound, a sort of high-pitched bleating. Kekoa looked ahead, and suddenly the Zhanin were calling to one another from boat to boat. "Rough waters ahead," Kekoa said.

Darius could see it now, where the sun's crystalline sphere lowered into the water. Steam rose as the crystal cooled itself in the ocean, and there was a roar greater than any waterfall Darius had ever heard.

As their boat entered the roiling waters of the world's end, it started panicking. The water seemed to be pulling it, tugging it down.

"Steady," Kekoa said to the boat, patting the boat on the neck. It squealed but swam forward.

One of the Zhanin came alongside them. "The boats are too frightened. Come up on the barge." That was the "dead" boat—a thing of wood, not flesh. The Zhanin tossed Kekoa a line, and he tied it tight so they could come in close. There were a couple more wooden boats, too, though the Zhanin didn't prefer them.

Kekoa jumped first and held a hand out to Darius. The way the waves were roiling, Darius definitely didn't want to land in the water. "What will the living boats do?" Darius asked, leaping across the gap, but just then a monstrous black coil looped over the boat and dragged it beneath the churning waves. Darius leapt to the bow and hacked at the rope that connected them. The entire barge tipped forward, and Darius just managed to cut through the rope before they could go under.

The Zhanin were all shouting now. One of the other boats turned away, trying to get back to the calmer waters. Another sinewy loop of sea monster smashed a smaller craft into so many toothpicks, Zhanin warriors screaming in terror and disappearing into a vortex of swirling water.

The Zhanin warriors leapt back and forth between the various boats, keeping an eye on the churning water, weapons at the ready. Darius wasn't sure what was to be done.

"I hope you can swim, brah!" Kekoa shouted, but Darius didn't have time to answer, for a great shadow rose from beneath them, and a monstrous blunt head, all teeth and eyes, erupted from the center of the barge, lumber spinning away like chaff, spray coming from the wide-open maw. He smelled rotten fish and flesh on its breath, and Kekoa was knocked overboard.

Darius held on to the remains of the barge for a moment longer—not that it mattered, because when the beast resurfaced, it took one Zhanin boat, capsized another, and then barreled straight for Darius's own little island of wood.

The water crashed over him. He tried to see, but the water was in too much chaos. Yards of lumber swirled around him, knocked into him, pushed him deeper. He had taken barely half a breath before he had been pushed under, and his lungs burned. His head pounded, and he kicked for the surface. Something muscular and much too large glided past him and brushed against him, as if feeling for where it would strike next.

Darius was almost to the surface, couldn't hold his breath anymore, was exhaling as hard as he could so he'd be ready to take a deep breath the moment air touched his lips—and then he was breathing again, gasping in great gulps of oxygen.

He was alone amid the wreckage. Kekoa was gone. The Zhanin, gone. He swam to a spar of lumber and grabbed on to it. He called for Kekoa but heard no reply, only the roar of the water as it tumbled over the edge of the world.

PART 5

A GLIMMER OF LIGHT

I have read all the notes. I have learned all the spells. I have studied the schematics over and over again. I see how it can be done, how it can be crafted. A beautiful clockwork world, wheels within wheels, and all I need is something to turn the spheres. The Kharobem will do nicely for that, I know. I feel a tinge of dismay over that, I do, but it's for the greater good. I have to stay focused on the poor and lowly folk who will find liberty and hope in this place. They have seen a glimmer of light in their unseasonable darkness, but there is a greater light to come. A land that is not drowning in sorrow and darkness, but rather soaked in sunlight.

A HANDWRITTEN NOTE SCRAWLED IN THE MARGINS OF *THE MAGICIAN'S GRIMOIRE*

37

THE COUNCIL OF WU

Why is there only one word in some stories? Because some stories must be lived, not spoken.

FROM *THE WISE SAYINGS OF MOTHER CROW*

✦

Jason Wu, king of the Southern Court, looked out at ten thousand of his subjects. They were a motley collection of monsters, strange creatures, familiar faces, and—in increasing numbers—a whole bunch of Jason Wus. He stood on a stage that jutted from the palace of the Southern Court and watched them, spread throughout the city, waiting to hear his magically amplified voice. Baileya—Mother Crow—stood at his side.

"I want to start by thanking you all for coming here. Unless you were born here, in which case you were here before me. Or if anyone was, for instance, kidnapped like me—in which case, sorry about that. My bad."

There was an enormous rolling wave of laughter. He didn't understand their sense of humor, but the people of the Southern Court found him extremely funny.

"We've had a council," Jason said. "A war council, actually, about what should be done about the Elenil. There are a lot of thoughts out there, and a lot of opinions. Some people said we should leave well enough alone. The Elenil don't bother the Southern Court much, and if we stay quiet, either they will keep not bothering us, or it might be a lot of years before they do. I get that. I understand it. To be honest, for a long time I lived my life like that. Keep your head down, keep quiet, try not to be noticed. But the problem is, sooner or later 'being quiet' means picking a side. Do you know what I mean?"

Of course he had no way for them to tell him whether they knew what he meant. Lelise was beside him, too, and he turned to her. "Do you think they know what I mean?"

She rubbed her arm where Sochar had put on the bracelet that Stilled her. "It is best when speaking to a large crowd to assume that some may not," she said.

He nodded. That made sense. "Okay, it's like this. In my world, there's a lot of, uh, animosity between human beings about the color of our skin. Do you know what I mean?" he asked again. No, of course they didn't. As if in answer, a group in the crowd changed their skin color, which set off a momentary wave of rainbows chasing themselves through the crowd as Courtiers showed off their shape-shifting powers. "Of course you don't—you're shape-shifters. You change your colors all the time. Okay, well, it's sort of like being Elenil or Scim or from the Southern Court. So imagine that there's an Elenil who is—how do I explain this—"

Baileya put her hand on his arm. "You are Kakri, Wu Song. Tell them a story."

Right. Jason had a sudden unpleasant memory of a Scim child who tried to pickpocket him. Mud was his name. And how an Elenil guard had heard about it and harmed the kid. He could use that, maybe.

"Once upon a time," Jason said, "there was a kid from the Southern Court who loved people and loved justice. He lived in Far Seeing, and when he was old enough, he volunteered to work for the palace guard." He could see that those in the front of the audience were following along—they understood what he was saying. "And he thought to himself, *I'll just keep my head down and keep to myself, and I'll get promoted higher into the ranks.* He was partnered with another guard, an Elenil named Sochar who hated the Scim."

There were actual hisses from the audience. Oh yeah. Some of them knew about Sochar, knew what he had done to Lelise.

"So one day this kid was with Sochar, and they caught a Scim who had been stealing fruit. And the Elenil grabbed him and said, 'I know you are a traitor and have done far more than just steal fruit, and I am going to kill you!'" There were gasps from the crowd. "I know, right! It's terrible. And if the Courtier kept his head down and didn't say anything, there would be no worries for him. But that wouldn't be much help for the Scim kid, would it? And I think that's where we are right now. Because the Elenil are talking about killing all the humans, and you know their plans for the Scim can't be great, either. Which means that if we just sit here and do nothing, well, we're working for Sochar, and all of the Elenil like him. And I don't know about you, but I don't want to be like Sochar."

There was a powerful, resonant cheer that engulfed the city. They started to chant his name: "Wu Song! Wu Song!" and even more of them took on his shape. The crowd had to be coming up on 80 percent Wu.

"This is weird," Jason said, and his voice echoed out among them. He turned to Lelise. "Oh, I didn't mean to say that to everyone." But that echoed out to them too. "Okay, I'll just say it to everyone. So where I live, back on Earth, my ancestors are from this country called China. But I live in a country sort of like the Sunlit Lands . . . we're all mixed together. And people will sometimes say that they can't tell one person from another if they're from China or Thailand or Japan or a whole bunch of other places. Which is not true—it's just that instead of remembering us, instead of looking at our unique features, in their heads they're just saying, *That kid came from somewhere in Asia.*"

He shook his head, realizing that the Southern Court had no idea what all these countries and areas of the world were. "Here's what I'm saying: pretend you made terrible copies of me. Wrong color hair, nose too wide or narrow, eyes the wrong color or too far apart, a foot taller than me or six inches shorter . . . You could go to my school and no one would know you weren't me. And that really wears on you after a while, right?" He grabbed Baileya's hand. "It makes you thankful for the people who recognize you even if there's a pretty close copy out there. Which is such a low bar for your friends. 'Wow, you could look at me and know who I am.' Unless, you know, your friend has face blindness or something." Uh-oh. Tangent again.

Baileya spoke gently to him. "Why have you called the Southern Court together, Wu Song? What will you ask of them?"

"Right. So I had all these counselors, and some of them said, 'Let's keep our heads down and do nothing,' and some others said, 'If the Elenil are going to try to wipe all the humans out and kill them, then it is right and just for us to kill all the Elenil instead.' And I don't know, that might be right, but it doesn't feel right to me. So I have another plan. It might be more dangerous than the other. It might be harder. And it all comes down to this." He held up a gourd of concentrated Wendy juice. "My plan is, let's make them remember."

There was murmuring among the crowd, and someone shouted, "Remember what?"

Another voice: "Do the Elenil change shape?"

And a third: "Are they of the Southern Court? Is that why they need help to remember? Have they lost their shape?"

"In a way, yes," Jason said, and there was another explosive round of comments from the audience. "But they only change their shape once. Mother Crow told me a story in the desert this year. She said that a long time ago the Elenil were humans. That they traded all their future children for long life and power. They drank addleberry wine and forgot their human shapes, and they re-formed themselves as the Elenil. So I'm thinking they've forgotten. They don't remember that they're the same as me, as my friends." He was quiet for a moment, not sure if he should say this next bit. "And I'm guessing you already know this. Because what I'm thinking is that you in the Southern Court are pretty secretive about marriage and pregnancy and everything else, and I'm thinking it's because when a baby Courtier is born, the little cutie is human."

Baileya gasped this time, but the Southern Court was silent.

"Right. Because Lelise said everyone had to take their true forms in her presence, and she was a human, wasn't she? And when Sochar used the bracelet to Still her, she got trapped in that form . . . her true form. And

I'm guessing that maybe you start changing shapes young, but now that you have the Wendy concentrate, you realize that you're human too. So now that the Elenil are threatening all humans, you know that if your secret got out, you'd be on the list." Lelise's face was so torn, so full of sorrow, that he stopped for just a moment and put his hand on her shoulder. She patted his arm, thanked him, told him to go on.

He held the gourd high, turned it so everyone in the city could see. The Wendy juice. Liquified remembrance. "So I'm thinking, what if we made all the Elenil have a drink? Maybe some of them already know they're humans. Maybe it won't change anything—maybe they'll all deny it. Or maybe, just maybe . . . they'll embrace us like long-lost family. Maybe they'll realize that we are more alike than we are different, despite the magic and our cultures and our history. That we're all human."

The Courtiers were in fierce conversation now, and many started shouting. Lelise said, "You will lose them, Majesty, if you do not use a strong hand now."

Jason shouted, "This is not Maduvorea! This is not the Sunlit Lands! This is not the Southern Court!" He had learned these statements from Mother Crow, in a rather long and protracted discussion of humor in the Southern Court. "This is not the Southern Court" was nearly a rebel battle cry. Only the Elenil called them Southern. They called themselves something else. Jason should probably learn what that was now that he was their king. To say "This is not the Southern Court" was to suggest that maybe their entire existence wasn't dependent on the Elenil.

Someone shouted, "Your plan is madness! More of us will die doing this than bringing violence against the Elenil!"

Jason pointed at the Courtier, one of the few who was still in some form other than Jason Wu—a lumbering bear. "Are the words I said true or false?" The Courtier didn't answer. Jason turned back to the audience. "Are you humans? Is it true?"

They shouted back, "It is true!"

"I have heard that the Southern Court cares about truth. *This is not the Southern Court!*"

A good number in the crowd echoed it back to him. "This is not the Southern Court!"

"I don't want a single one of you to die," he said. "I mean, look at you. You're the most handsome army I've ever seen."

This got an appreciative laugh from the crowd, and Baileya shouted, "I agree!" which got Jason turning red and the audience roaring with laughter.

"I don't want any of you—any of *us*—to die. I want you to take care of yourselves. I want you to take care of one another. And if none of you are with me, I'll hand over the kingship right now to whoever you want, and I'll march to Far Seeing by myself with as much Wendy juice as I can carry."

"Not by yourself!" Baileya shouted, holding her spear in the air. "For Mother Crow and the Kakri will march with you!"

There was a roar from the Kakri, a roar that was soon overpowered by the Southern Court, as nearly every person in the crowd took on Jason's shape and began to chant, "This is not the Southern Court!"

"Gather the Wendy juice," Jason shouted. "Gather your weapons and supplies. Take whatever form you please, but I would really like at least one battalion of flying Jasons with wings. Bat wings, bird wings, even flying squirrels, I don't care—but flying Jasons are the best Jasons."

"We will not do that," Lelise said quietly. "We take pride in making our forms as exact as possible. It would be disrespectful not to take your true shape. It is a rude thing for you to request."

"Ah," Jason said. He addressed the crowd again. "Just heard that was rude. Sorry. No flying Jasons, got it." He raised his hands over his head. "Prepare yourselves and meet me at the city gates! We ride for the Court of Far Seeing!"

They roared their approval, and at once the crowd dissipated as if it were a beehive that Jason had whacked with a stick. He and Baileya made swift plans. The Kakri could move faster than the larger army of the Southern Court, and they would leave soon after him and head for the northern side of Far Seeing. Jason would bring his people from the south, and they would meet in the center of the city.

"I can't believe they're all following me," he said to Baileya.

"They are all trying to be like you," she said. "Of course they will follow."

Bezaed came toward them, his head bowed. "May I approach?" he asked.

"Of course, dude," Jason said.

"Mother Crow," he said, his voice shaking with emotion. "I did wrong in disobeying you before, and I ask your permission to join Wu Song and the Southern Court in the battle to come, that I might keep him safe."

Baileya raised an eyebrow to Jason. He wasn't sure how he should feel, but he wasn't really afraid of Bezaed, not anymore. He shrugged, leaving it up to Baileya. She took Bezaed by the shoulders and said, "Brother, you have always been a Kakri of great honor. Maybe too much honor. It would be a great service to Mother Crow and to the people of the Southern Court if you would keep Wu Song safe and bring him home to me at battle's end."

"Thank you, Sister," he said, and from that moment refused to leave Jason's side while he was getting ready. Which, yes, Jason was glad for that in one sense, but Bezaed was very literal. Jason felt like he should use the bathroom before going to war, and put some other clothes on, and, well, it turned out Bezaed was nearby the entire time. Keeping him safe.

After everything else was ready, Jason dialed Delightful Glitter Lady up to BATTLE UNICORN BEAST MODE, and the Courtiers helped him find a light sword and a breastplate. He wouldn't take any more armor than that because his first experience with armor wasn't great. If his plan worked, he wouldn't need a weapon anyway.

He rode at the head of a column of thousands of warriors. Delightful Glitter Lady pranced with joy beneath him, and he lifted his sword. A cheer rose behind him. He looked, and there on a high part of the wall, looking down at him, was Baileya. His heart swelled. He loved her. That was not a new discovery. He had loved her, he thought, from the first moment he had seen her throw an ax. But seeing her there on the wall, her feathered cape hanging from her golden shoulders, her hair pulled back, and her clothing tied with cords in the Kakri way, he realized it wasn't love like anything he had known before. He had heard people say before that their girlfriend was "everything they ever wanted," but Baileya was so much more than he ever could have invented. She was kind and loyal, loving and wise, strong and swift. He wanted to follow her around like a puppy dog. He wanted to cook her meals. Like, good ones, not the kind he made now. He wanted to lay beside her underneath the stars, tell her stories, and listen to hers. He wanted to be Father Crow. If that was allowed.

And when Jason looked up at her and shouted, "I love you, Baileya!" he tried to put all of that in his words somehow and send it across the space between them. He didn't know if he had succeeded, but he knew that he would spend the rest of his life trying to tell her.

He told Dee to start moving forward, and they passed through the gate. He never took his eyes from Baileya. He kept his head turned toward her and lifted his sword, the point high, a salute in her honor. Bezaed, beside him on Moriarty, raised his weapon to Mother Crow as well. And then each of the thousands of Jasons behind him raised their weapons, and the entire procession shouted pronouncements of Jason's love to her as they left the city. Ten thousand times, the Jasons shouted his love to Baileya, and he knew that even so, it was nowhere near enough. Not even close.

38
GILENYIA'S PLAN

Will you die to save these people who have rejected and despised you?

FROM "THE TRIUMPH OF THE PEASANT KING," A SCIM LEGEND

✦

Gilenyia swept through her home, barking orders at the servants. "No," she commanded one. "Do not pack anything of mine, not from the kitchen or anywhere else. Only your own belongings, and do it quickly. Any who are not in the courtyard in three minutes' time will be removed from service."

She had not told them the truth about what had happened when Hanali became archon, and she had not told them her plan. Ricardo never left her side, but he had a way of helping the other servants move a step quicker than they would have otherwise. On the way from the Palace of a Thousand Years, they had seen two human bodies in the street. Rumors had already begun to fly. Gilenyia was not sure if Hanali's military forces had set to work before her messenger birds flew. She had hurriedly laid out her improvised plan to Ricardo on the short journey home, and he had set it in motion.

So much depended on everything going just as she hoped. A single missed message, or a recipient who was less friendly toward humans than she expected, and the whole plan could collapse. The loss of Rondelo as an ally was grievous. Not only was he a formidable warrior but he was also well respected and better connected to the younger Elenil than she.

When the servants had all gathered in the courtyard, she spoke to them simply and briskly. "Archon Hanali plans to murder any human being he finds in the Sunlit Lands. This is regardless of previous promises or service you have done us." A thrill of fear went through the crowd . . . thirty-six humans under her care, plus Ricardo. "I have no intention of following his direction. I am, as of this moment, releasing you from your terms of service to the Elenil. I cannot guarantee you will receive your agreed-upon payment, but I will escort you safely back to your homes on Earth should you choose to go. If you choose to stay for whatever reason, I will not stop you. I suspect you will be safest among the Scim, who have no little animosity toward the Elenil—and also have centuries of experience living under the oppressive thumb of a powerful adversary."

Ricardo stood beside her and addressed the group of humans. "We are forty." He was including Gilenyia herself and her two closest Scim servants, Day Song and New Dawn, in the number. "There is considerable confusion among the Elenil about what is being asked of them, thanks in large part to our lady. We will make a conspicuous group, but it seems to me better that we go together and quickly rather than in small, less defensible groups."

"Go where?" someone called.

"To the Meadow at World's End," Gilenyia said. "In the forest there, portals will open to take you back to the homes you left. For some, I know, this will be a joy, and for others a dire danger. Yet no more dangerous than here. Again, if you choose to go your own way, so be it."

She wondered if Hanali had already discovered the message she had sent via the birds. It was not hard to imagine that an Elenil somewhere, having received the orders of genocide, might be confused upon hearing her message, which promised the archon's wrath on any who harmed a human. They would certainly send a messenger back asking for clarification. No doubt Hanali would send another message correcting hers as soon as he learned of it. It was entirely possible they would meet Elenil soldiers waiting for them in the street.

"I don't understand," one of the kitchen boys said.

"There is not time to bring understanding to all of you," Gilenyia snapped. "Gather your meager belongings and either join us on the path to the meadow or find your own way to some other presumed safety." She could not help that she was perceived as cold and uncaring sometimes. There were times for questions and endless conversation, and times for action. "Come," she ordered.

She stepped into the street. There were no Elenil within sight. The street was strangely deserted. No doubt the people were quick to lock themselves indoors after the fright of the Scim attack not so long ago, followed by the Pastisian incursion a year back. When they sensed change and disaster on the wind, it made sense to put themselves out of harm's way, especially if there was a question about the state of magic. Healers such as Gilenyia wouldn't be able to do much to help a wounded Elenil if magic had been crippled again. Twice in recent history something unpredictable had happened to their magic, after centuries of consistency.

Day Song and New Dawn stepped out beside her, thick woven bags thrown over their shoulders. They looked rough, not presenting the sharp, clean, civilized appearance she required of her Scim servants. "Here we take our leave of you," New Dawn said. Gilenyia noticed at once that she did not call her lady or mistress.

"I have need of your services yet," Gilenyia said. "We will require your protection as we help the humans escape."

"We are thankful for your newfound conscience," Day Song said. His words pierced her, and she recoiled. "We have only ever served you here because we were prisoners of war. We did not run because you have always given us some modest pay, which allowed us to care for our families in the Wasted Lands. Now that fortunes are shifting, we must make another way for ourselves in the world."

"You have served me faithfully for years," she said, still shocked.

"You have paid us faithfully for years," New Dawn replied. She was already walking away.

"No farewell then? No quick embrace or kind words before we part?"

New Dawn stopped and turned back, her face like stone. "Did we become friends and I was unaware of it? Were we ever treated as anything more than horses to pull a carriage?"

Gilenyia could not hide her distress. She felt her face flush. "You have cared for me—"

"Say 'taken care of' you and be more precise and more honest," Day Song said. "We have not cared for you, nor you for us. You have paid us some little amount for our hard work. For this we do not thank you. It was no more than we were due."

They both bowed their heads politely and trotted away, neither looking back at her. Gilenyia was dumbfounded. Ricardo, always at her side, said nothing. The thought that her servants saw her as little more than a salary stung more than she would have expected. She had thought, at least, that they cared for her somewhat. "Did you hear that?" she asked Ricardo. "Did you hear how they treated me? As if I were no more than an employer."

Ricardo pursed his lips. "Or less than that, lady. Remember, for the Scim it is a hard life to turn oneself over to the Elenil."

She began to answer him, then realized with an unpleasant jolt that neither Day Song nor New Dawn *had* "turned themselves over" to the Elenil. They had been captured on the field of battle. Reeducated. Civilized. Assigned to her when she chose them from among the prisoners. And she had been so certain that she was providing a better life for them, she had never once asked herself if that life was the one they wanted.

"There is little time to reflect on it now," Ricardo said. "We must move quickly, lady."

She heard the *lady* and appreciated it. He was right—now was not a time to sit and wallow in emotion. But her own facade had been cracking. For so long she had kept her emotions in check easily, but she found it more and more difficult. Should not Day Song and New Dawn be proud of her? Should they not thank her for releasing them and the humans from their terms of service? Instead they walked away with words bordering on cruelty, without so much as a goodbye.

"Lady," Ricardo said again.

"Yes, yes, let us make haste."

Ricardo led the way, and the rest of them followed. She walked behind him, the others two and three abreast. He led them through quiet lanes until they reached the wider, more bustling streets. A woman lay on the ground in their path, a wound in her stomach. She was gasping heavily, and Gilenyia had seen enough wounds to know this one would end in death, though it may take as long as ten or even fifteen hours. One of Gilenyia's own servants cried out and could not pass the dying woman. Others moved around her, following Ricardo.

Gilenyia took her servant's hand. "There is nothing to be done," she said. "Come."

The woman did not move. "She's dying."

Gilenyia searched her memory for the servant's name, but it would not come to her. She had met her, of course, at the Bidding if nowhere else. She looked to be perhaps sixteen years old. "What is your name?"

"I—I'm Eloise," she said, shaking with fear.

Gilenyia put an arm around her. "Eloise, I do not know who has harmed this woman. But it may be that they are still nearby, and we are so close to an escape for you and your friends. But I need you to walk away from this woman. Can you do that?" Gilenyia steered Eloise—down the street. She *was* a friend to her servants, Gilenyia told herself. She showed them care in diverse ways.

"But lady, she was *dying*," Eloise said again, and her voice nearly broke.

"True," Gilenyia said. "Let us not be added to the list of the dead today."

"You're a healer," Eloise said, but clearly couldn't bring herself to say more.

Gilenyia was a healer, yes, but according to the laws of Elenil magic, she couldn't heal a random woman without someone else to take the wounds. If it were some smaller, more manageable wound, Gilenyia could take it on herself. But to accept a fatal wound meant that she would die. She had no intention of doing that today. "Once you have passed through the meadow," she said, "I will return and see if there is anything to be done for her." She did not know, even as she said it, if these words were true.

Eloise nodded and wiped her nose on her own sleeve. "Thank you, lady."

"But we must move quickly so that there is a chance she will still be living when I return. Can you do that, Eloise?"

"Of course, lady," she said, and began to move faster, catching up with the tail end of the line.

Ricardo had slowed when Gilenyia had fallen behind, but now he moved the group faster again. They were in sight of the building where the meadow was housed. A long, wide stairway led to the entry, a large door surrounded by white columns. It looked almost Greek, like someone had been building the Parthenon from memory and hadn't quite gotten it right. Compared to the buildings around it, though, this place appeared somewhat plain.

She knew that, once they entered the building, they would think they were still outside, in an enormous wood. When they entered the room where the meadow was, they would encounter a thick copse of trees, and as they walked through the trees, each human would be returned to the place on Earth they had come from. It was said that the meadow was the same place that the Majestic One had sent the humans when he divided them and gave each their blessing or curse.

"Elenil," Ricardo said, his voice low but intense.

Five of them stood at the base of the stairs. Perhaps Hanali had sent them, or perhaps it was coincidence. "Is there a way to tell with whom they stand?"

"I can ask them," Ricardo said gently, but of course this was ludicrous. Why would Gilenyia herself not ask them?

"Prepare the others to run," she said. "I will ask."

"We could wait for the knight, lady. If he is coming, and if he brings even a handful of his warriors, that would be more than distraction enough to get these to safety."

She shook her head. "Has he sent word that he is coming?"

The look on his face told her no. So it had come to this. There were to be no allies today, no one to help them. "I will approach them with you," Ricardo said. "You have no sword."

Gilenyia raised herself to her full height. "Surely we have not reached the day where an Elenil would think to strike me, one of the highest ranking of our people."

"I am not sure that is true, lady."

She gathered the servants near her. "If those Elenil come toward you here, you must run. Into the meadow if you can. Or if you cannot get past them, then flee into the city and return here when you are able. If you are scattered and in danger, look for me. I will help as I am able. If I speak to the Elenil and they turn away from you, then move with speed and a gentle demeanor. Do not speak to them or me, but follow Ricardo into the meadow." She paused. "Do not forget to destroy the gems in your tattoos, the agreement of service to the Elenil. And . . . thank you for your service."

"Thank you, lady," they whispered.

"Ricardo," she said. "If the worst comes, do not hold back with your sword."

He nodded, grim. "Yes, lady."

She recognized the five Elenil. The three younger ones had fought against the Scim. They were not as well known or regarded as Rondelo, however. They would still have better fighting skills than most any human, but in the world of the Elenil, they were a lower class of fighter. The older two she knew as well, hangers-on who had tried to become magistrates and failed, and had settled for the life of endless balls and parties and social climbing. Both of them had requested attendance at balls she had thrown in the last five years, an eyeblink for an Elenil.

She greeted them.

"Congratulations on your engagement," one of them said, a good indication he had heard from the archon, because she had been careful not to mention the supposed engagement to the birds she had sent.

She thanked him demurely. "It is, of course, of less import than Archon Hanali's announcement that he will make all the humans into Elenil."

"Ah," the oldest of them replied. "But, lady, surely you heard that the archon has already corrected that misinformation. He said all humans are to be killed on sight." He pulled his sword from his scabbard, and the blade was sticky with blood. He looked over her shoulder at her people. "It appears I have sighted a few."

He went to brush past her, but she grabbed him by the collar and yanked him backward. She was no fighter, but it startled him enough that he let out a roar and turned his sword point toward her.

"Run!" Ricardo shouted as he pulled his own sword, and the humans bounded toward them like deer escaping a flock of wolves, headed for the stairs.

She tried to hold the Elenil back, but they shook her off and waded into the crowd of humans. Two of her servants fell in a moment, and then the Elenil bounded up the stairs after more. She followed, scratching and dragging at them.

Ricardo stood at the top of the stairs, his sword solid and sure, a look of determination on his face. "I am not a gifted swordsman," he said. "But I do have the high ground, and I am not slow."

"We are under orders of the archon," an Elenil said. "We must pass you, and we will do so with ease."

There was a clattering on the steps behind them, and Gilenyia turned in time to see a great white stag leap and soar over her head, landing on the stairs above them. Rondelo slid from his stag, Evernu, sword in his hand. "I know you all well," he said. "And you know me. Believe me when I say that we three—this human, Evernu, and I—will hold this stair. And if you are mortally wounded, it is not Gilenyia's gentle hand that will heal you."

"Rondelo," one of the youth shouted. "The archon told us to do this. He commanded it."

"Let him come and say it to my face," Rondelo said. "Or is the coward sitting in a tower? Let him bloody his own hands and not ours."

"We must pass," one of the soldiers said.

Rondelo frowned. "And I must not allow it."

Then the battle was joined. Though Rondelo and Ricardo and Evernu had the high ground, they were outnumbered. It was a clash of moments, and left one Elenil dead, Evernu chasing another into the street, a third still in conflict with Rondelo, and Ricardo on the ground, bleeding. Two Elenil had managed to get past them and even now were seeking humans, trying to prevent them from entering the meadow.

Gilenyia knelt beside Ricardo, who was bleeding heavily from his shoulder. "Help me up, lady. We must make sure the others got through safely."

She ignored him, took hold of his Elenil tattoo, and closed her eyes, letting her magic flow from her arm into his, as she had done thousands of times when she healed others. She explored his wound. It would not kill him, but he could lose his arm if it became infected.

She had warned her students many times not to go too deeply into their patients, not to push into their private worlds while exploring their wounds. She found that Ricardo was open in a way she had never experienced before. He had no walls. At least, not against her. There was an ocean of affection there, and she saw herself, standing like a golden statue in the center of it. Her heart clutched within her, and tears sprang into her eyes, something that had not happened in a decade. After the stinging loss of Day Song and New Dawn, it spoke to her deeply.

She took Ricardo's wounds into herself. She felt him wrestle against it, but she had been doing this for a long time. She gasped as the pain blossomed in her shoulder, and when she opened her eyes again, it was she lying on the ground and Ricardo sitting up, his shirt torn but his flesh mended.

"Lady!" he said, and there was reproof in his voice.

"The servants," she said. "Quickly."

She heard a clattering below and managed to raise herself enough to see the Knight of the Mirror arriving, complete with a small force of soldiers. "Gilenyia," he said.

A few quick words from Rondelo and the knight was up to speed. He rode his silver horse, Rayo, into the building, flanked by his best warriors. The sound of battle rang out, and a few minutes later he returned, one Elenil dead and two under guard. He carried a corpse in his arms.

He set her body gently beside Gilenyia.

"I am sorry, lady," he said. "My men will bring the others out. Six are dead, and several more wounded."

Eloise's still, unmoving eyes stared into Gilenyia's.

For the second time that day Gilenyia felt tears fall. This time she could not stop them, and a sob came from her. "Bring me one of the captives," she said.

Ricardo touched her hand gingerly. "Lady, she is dead. There is nothing to be done."

"I know that," she snapped.

Ricardo brought over one of the Elenil, Rondelo keeping a close eye on him. She snatched his forearm in her hand and shoved her wounds across the link into his body. He gasped in shock from the sudden pain, and for good measure she pushed her own grief and fatigue into him as well, and noted with some satisfaction when he began to sob.

She stood, smoothed her dress, and turned to her people. "Go out into the city, and bring all the humans you can find," she said. "If Elenil oppose you, cut them down. If Hanali opposes you, put the knife in my hand."

When they did not move, she gave them her iciest stare, and they jumped to obey.

39

THE HISTORIAN

Lies and half-truths always become the tools of men with evil intent.

THE PEASANT KING

✛

You're distracted," David said. They were standing in front of the wall of ivy in the Southern Court. Now that they had reconnected with Jason, Shula was eager to search for her brother.

"I can't stop thinking about Yenil. I should have gone with her."

"She has two Southern Court warriors with her, and the Scim are her people. She'll be safe."

"Still." She put her hand in the ivy. "I wish I had gone with her."

"Do you want me to go to her?" David asked. "They're only a few hours ahead of me, and unless they're carrying her, I can move faster. I can ask for a Courtier to fly me so I can get there quickly."

Relief washed through her. She did. "Yes, David, please."

He hugged her, and she pressed into his lean arms. "I'll meet you in Far Seeing," he said, and then he was gone, trotting away to find the path to the Wasted Lands.

She only watched him for a moment, then checked her supplies. She had two gourds of Wendy juice. A new knife. Her knapsack. "Rana," she said. "I need to go to Far Seeing."

"Then come," a voice said from the ivy, and Shula pushed in. The experience this time was less pleasant. She would have liked to have David's hand in her own as she pushed through the leaves.

When she exited at last, it wasn't through the wall in the storyteller's room. She was at the base of the Palace of a Thousand Years, in the sprawling garden that surrounded it. Past the guards. Humans weren't supposed to be here without an Elenil guide. And yet no alarm was raised. In fact, no one seemed to be around at all. A unicorn (an actual one) grazed nearby, its foal standing a few feet away.

"Oh, Shula, you're back," said the unicorn.

"I . . . excuse me?"

The unicorn trotted over to her. "Don't you remember me?"

She reached up tentatively and touched his soft mane. "No?"

"Frank," he said, as if that should clear everything up.

"Frank." Frank the unicorn. It seemed like if she had met him before, that should ring a bell.

"You come here . . . oh, every six months or so?"

"No," Shula said. "That's not true."

The unicorn shook his head as if he were getting rid of a rather pesky fly. "Oh yeah. I forget how forgetful you are. I suppose I need to show you the way to go. Even though I've warned you a hundred times, nothing good comes from going into that place."

She put it together pretty fast. "The Historian's cave."

Frank snorted. "Sure, if that's what you want to call it." He trotted over to the foal. "Hey, Gary, you remember Shula."

"Hello, Ms. Bishara," he said, his high voice full of affection. "Need us to show you the way again?"

"I . . . I guess I do."

"'kay. Dad, I can take her."

"Are you sure, Gary?"

"Yeah, I'm sure." The little unicorn posed, chest full, nose pointed upward in a noble direction. "I'm not scared."

He trotted westward, toward the side of the tower. "Thanks," Shula said to Frank.

"See ya later," Frank said, and bent for a mouthful of grass.

Shula ran to catch up with Gary, who fell into a trot beside her. "I used to be scared," he said. "But then I learned that guy can't even come out of the cave. So long as I stay out here, he can't get me."

"The Historian?"

"Sure," Gary said. "If that's what you want to call him. So this is the place."

At the base of the tower there was a . . . she didn't even want to call it a hole. A crack. Cool, dank air wafted out of it. "In there?"

"Sure. The crack's bigger sometimes. But if you ignore it, it goes away."

"Okay." Shula knelt down and put her hand near the crack. It widened like a mouth. She snatched her hand back and exhaled, hard. "Okay."

"Do you need me to go with you?" Gary asked, and he sounded concerned.

"No, thank you," she said, and rubbed his head.

Gary hopped around happily, then came back to her. "I'll wait here, and if you need help, just shout. I'll get Dad to come."

"Thank you, Gary. Truly." She took a deep breath and swung her legs into the crack, and it pried open, revealing mossy stairs. She stepped onto the first one, then the second, and descended into the earth.

"Bye, Ms. Bishara!" Gary called, but his voice seemed a long way off now. With a resounding clap, the crack closed over her head, and she was in pitch darkness. It took her eyes a minute to adjust before she saw the pale light coming from below. She carefully put her feet on the next step and made her way downward.

Shula had no memory of this place. None. It didn't even feel familiar. Of course, she hadn't remembered Vasya, either—that strange woman who suddenly appeared in memories of her brother. Until she drank the Wendy juice. She quickly searched her pockets and found the gourds. She still had them.

She heard a loud *gong*, like the reverberation of an enormous bell in a clock, or a church. She touched the wall for balance and felt it vibrating with the sound. Then another *gong*, and when it had died away, a third.

She was having trouble walking. Her hands had begun to shake. An involuntary whimper came from her mouth. As if her body remembered this place, even though her mind didn't. "It's going to be okay," she told herself.

When she came to the bottom of the stairs, the light seemed brighter, and she could see the looming shadows of what she thought were trees. Trees growing underground. She remembered Madeline and Jason's story about their entrance to the Sunlit Lands. There had been a sort of underground forest for them, too. It was a dark wood. She could just make out the trees, but within a few feet there was only darkness. A figure stood at the edge of the trees in a long, dark robe, and his face floated above it like a white, overexposed smear on a photograph.

"Who is that?" Shula asked herself, and at the same time a voice in her head said, *Turn back, we need to go back.* She pushed against the voice. "I've seen worse things than this."

She managed to take more steps toward the woods.

The man at the edge of the woods was so pale as to appear sickly, and he had no hair on him at all. His face was long, and his chin was pointed. So were his ears. His eyes were too small, black, unreadable. He was terribly thin, and his fingers were too long. He was tall, and when he turned his eyes toward her, the act of bending his face forward made it seem as if he was hunching over like a buzzard.

"Shula Bishara," he said, and his voice sounded like it had come from the bottom of a cold and dark cave. "You have returned."

"Who are you?" she managed to ask.

"You said you would not return. Yet here you are," he said, and it seemed that he meant it in the sense of, *What's to be done? You made a promise, and yet . . .*

"My brother," Shula managed to say. A bird—or something—called from the wood, and she flinched. She wanted to run, to hide.

This man, the creature, whatever he was, had no weapons. He made no threats. But Shula kept seeing images of him standing over broken bodies, his long fingers covered in blood. In her mind she saw him smile, and all of his teeth were needle-sharp. And yet he stood in front of her, completely still, not moving, except that his eyes watched her, unblinking.

"Your brother is dead," he said, and there was such certainty, such finality to his voice. "Burned to death in your home in Aleppo." That's right. She remembered it. She had been in the apartment, seen her parents' and her little sister's bodies.

"No," she said. "No, I never saw his body. That's not what happened."

"Why do you say this?" he asked.

It was the Wendy juice, of course. "Vasilisa Markova," she said. "Who is she? Vasya. I remember her."

The Historian smirked. "You never even liked her. Is that really the stick that has broken the spell? You scarcely know her. How stupid that you would remember her and not your brother."

Right. She didn't know Vasya, did she? Except that she did. When she had taken the Wendy juice, some memories of her had come back. She had seen her—she struggled to remember—sitting at their dinner table? Eating her mother's riz a'djaj, and laughing at something Boulos had said. Her mother liked Vasya, she remembered that. Had she come to church with them? Listened to her father preach? Boulos tried to translate, but his Russian was terrible, and they had laughed at that, too.

"You have partaken of the fruit of the new plants of Maduvorea," the man said, terrible contempt in his voice. He turned and stepped into the darkness of the woods. "You have broken the agreement we made," he said as he walked away. "The memories we wove for you are coming unraveled."

Shula was panting and had begun to sweat, as if waking from a terrible nightmare. The creature's power seemed to lessen as it moved away from her. *I have to follow him. I don't want to, but I have to follow.*

His voice floated back. "I will take you to your brother if you wish." He turned back, from the deeper darkness, and Shula felt a terrible, convulsive nausea at the sight of his paleness floating in that pitch blackness. "Come," he said, and turned on his way again.

And Shula, shaking, stepped into the dark.

40

THE SEA BENEATH

What man would be brave enough to approach
her in the depths of the sea beneath?

FROM "MALGWIN'S STORY," A TALE OF THE KHAROBEM

✦

Night had fallen. Somehow in the last several hours, Darius had drifted out of the troubled water near the world's end and was in a relatively peaceful part of the sea. Both his arms were draped over a waterlogged spar of wood. He hadn't seen Kekoa or the Zhanin since Malgwin's attack. There had been more than one monster, though. One large one, and many smaller ones. Malgwin's children, maybe.

As the crystal sphere of stars pulled itself overhead, and the bright light of the moon turned to meet them, the sea gained a soft and eerie blue glow. He needed to get to the Sea Beneath, but he wasn't sure how. His only thought was that perhaps he could find a way to weight himself and just . . . ride the weights to the bottom? It seemed like a significant risk to take because if he was wrong, he would just drown.

Darius couldn't even see the shore. There were no boats in sight, no islands. He had called out to the Peasant King, and Fantok, and the Garden Lady, and every other person or being in the Sunlit Lands whom he thought might possibly hear him, but none of them answered. He was completely alone. Lost at sea. And he had no idea how to get to the power core of the Sunlit Lands.

"Well, Mads," he said. "I guess this is the end. And I'm doing the same thing all over again. Trying to fix the world and avoiding everything I care about in the world in the meantime. Adrift and alone." He laid his head down on the wood. He was thirsty, and hungry, and tired. He knew he shouldn't sleep, should focus on a direction and head there, but he felt an honest certainty that it would be pointless. He had gone as far as his strength could take him. There was nothing else to do, and it was time to be honest about that. He closed his eyes.

He wasn't sure how long it had been when he heard the fluttering. Like someone whipping a feather duster around in the air. "Hello," a voice said.

It was a bird. A robin. Standing on the far end of his spar of lumber, its head cocked to one side. "Hi there," Darius said.

"Are you in distress?"

"Distress. I guess you could say that."

The bird hopped a few steps closer. "Do you remember me?"

He had seen a few thousand robins in his life. He didn't remember one that stood out—at least, not here in the Sunlit Lands. Maybe it had been a messenger for him once? "Did you fly a message for me?"

The robin gave a little trill of delight. "No, no. You saved me."

"I did?"

"From a cat! I was wrapped in twine and couldn't get away, and you set me free."

"Oh! In Madeline's backyard. Of course." Could birds travel back and forth between Earth and the Sunlit Lands so easily?

"You need wings," the bird said. "It seems to me."

"I'm not sure," Darius said. "I'm trying to get to the Sea Beneath."

As soon as he said the words, the bird leapt into the air and flew away, panicked. It came back in a minute, flew around but didn't land. "I see a shadow," it said. "Darker than the sea, swimming in circles under you."

"That doesn't seem good," Darius said.

"I can take you to the Sea Beneath," the robin said. "But I need some friends. Can you wait here?"

"I can't do anything but wait here," Darius said to the bird, and it immediately flew away.

It seemed like a long time later that the bird returned and hopped onto the log again. It carried a long piece of string in its mouth. It dropped the string in Darius's hand. "Keep hold of that," it said, and flew away again.

Another bird, a seagull, brought him a second length of string, then flew away. The robin came back, gave him another string. "What are you waiting for? Start braiding them together!"

For the next several hours, birds of all shapes and sizes brought him string, and Darius dutifully braided them until he had a rope of decent thickness, about ten feet long. "That should do it," the robin said. "Now center yourself and put the rope under your arms with the ends coming out behind you. Good!" The robin frayed the end of the makeshift rope and grabbed a few strings in its mouth before jumping in the air, flapping its wings desperately.

"You'll never get me out of—" Darius started to say, but then a huge flock of birds descended, all of them grabbing some strings from the rope end, and they lifted him into the air. Not smoothly. Not easily. But he was definitely rising, up and out of the water, and now a few feet above. He could see the shadow the robin had mentioned now, and it stirred as if it had been guarding him and was only now realizing he had gotten away. "The sea monster," he said, and the birds flapped harder and lifted him higher, just as the great shiny black maw lifted from the water and snapped where he had been.

The birds were flying toward the world's end now. Darius called a question, asking if they knew the way to the Sea Beneath, then remembered that they all needed to keep their beaks closed if he hoped to stay airborne. The black shadow in the water kept pace with them easily, breaching every half a minute and rolling over so its wide eye could spy on him.

As they came nearer the crystal stars, the water became more turgid, roiling and crashing with waves. He couldn't see the monster anymore, except when it surfaced to take a look at him. Twice, when the exhausted birds had dipped closer to the water, the monster had risen out of the depths and tried to take a bite out of Darius, but both times the birds managed to move just enough to prevent him from becoming a snack.

When they came to the end of the water, the waves smashed and reverberated against the crystal wall of the world. The sound was enormous, the roaring so loud that Darius could scarcely hear his own voice when he shouted to the birds, "What now?"

The robin flew down and perched on his shoulder, the other birds struggling to keep him aloft. "We drop you," the robin shouted. "Into the space between the world and the crystal sky, where the water falls into the Sea Beneath."

"That seems like it might be a long fall?"

"It would be better if you had wings," the bird shouted back. "We could take you back to shore . . ."

But no, that was the opposite of where he wanted to go. "No," he said. "Drop me! And thank you!"

"Stay close to the wall," the bird said. "Stay touching it if you can! Good luck!"

He watched the robin as it chirped to the others, and then, all at once, they released the strings and flew their separate ways.

It was like the sudden jolt of a ride at an amusement park. The kind that goes straight up in the air, clicks into place, then drops you multiple stories. He felt the blood in his feet rising up into his body. His arms flew out as if they might be wings. The churning water below was rising toward him at an alarming rate. Then he saw the sea monster rise, slapping the water as it propelled itself toward Darius's rapidly falling form.

He hit the water, and it was like striking the edge of a waterfall. It immediately threw him backward, toward the crystal. He slammed against the wall and slid down, following and being followed by water. He gasped for air when his face wasn't covered in water, and saw that there was a sort of glass wall, a bowl that kept the upper sea from the Sea Beneath. The monster leapt for him just as he slid past the lip, crashing into the crystal sphere of the sky where it met the water. The monster couldn't fit down the crack but roared after him on the other side of the glass as he sped under the world in a roiling waterfall.

It got brighter as Darius raced downward. The sensation was like being on a wide crystal waterslide. The brightness, he realized, was coming from the sun sphere, which he was following under the world. He could only see darkness above because the bowl of the sea and the Sunlit Lands themselves blocked light from coming down. He wasn't sure it would all make sense in a science book, but this was a land built on magic and words of power.

There was no way to control his speed, and yet the water seemed to slow as it sloped toward a new, second ocean below. He could see the whole thing from here: the Sunlit Lands above, like a dark shadow continent in the sky, held up in an enormous bowl, sea monsters and whales and fish swimming all around in it. Below was the second sea, and a great island in the middle of it, with beautiful, colorful buildings and a tree like a sky-scraper standing straight in the center, pushing upward and through the world above. No doubt its crown was in Maduvorea somewhere.

Darius curved off the sphere and hit the ocean below, skipping across the waves before finally tumbling over himself and coming to a stop in the water. It was warm and full of light. He swam toward the island. A sea monster surfaced beside him, at least twice as long as Darius, with wet black eyes and a wide mouth. When Darius shouted, it submerged and reemerged a few yards to his left. Several more joined the first, and they kept their distance, swimming alongside him all the way. Though they made him nervous, they didn't seem threatening.

A dolphin popped up beside him and laughed in dolphin language, throwing its head back in glee. It kept jumping over him, dancing on its tail, swimming in circles around him, and he finally realized it wanted him to grab hold of its dorsal fin. It carried him to shore, and he lay on his back, panting and exhausted, clutching the Maegrom's glass box, still tucked inside his shirt, to his chest.

Malgwin came to him on the beach, not as a monster but as a woman, wearing the same sari as before. "So," she said. "You've come at last."

"No thanks to you," he said.

She smiled, and he thought for a moment that he saw the needlelike teeth of the sea monster in her mouth. "Too often there are those like you who claim to want to come to the Sea Beneath. They want to help us, they say. They want to join us in our work. But when they arrive, we discover they are liars. Cowards. Self-centered, self-focused. I find it helps to weed out the less serious ones if they see a sea monster before they reach the ocean's edge." She motioned for him to stand. "Come. Let's get you dried and fed. Your friend is waiting." Kekoa? Had he managed to get here too?

Malgwin led him to a room that looked like it had been carved from mother-of-pearl, and there was a regal suit in white and gold laid out for him. After she left, he stripped and dried and put on the perfectly tailored clothes. There was a gold circlet beside the clothing, a sort of simple crown. That he did not take. There was nowhere to put the Maegrom story box, so he carried it with him.

A short walk brought him to a wide marble patio built so it hung over the water. A long table was piled with lobster, steamed fish, yellow spiced shrimp on rice, a curry with what looked like salmon in it, salads made with seaweed, brined eel, roasted duck, and more. Malgwin did not wait for him to dish up—she loaded a plate and set it before him with a pile of steaming-hot flatbread.

Kekoa was there, also in new, fancy clothes . . . though his were not quite as fine as Darius's, and his shirt was black with a print of large red tropical flowers. "Darius!" he said. "You made it. I was worried, brah. You gotta try this food, it's ono."

Malgwin sat across from Darius, and they all began to eat as if it were the first dish they'd had in months. When the others were finished, Darius's plate wasn't even half-empty—Malgwin had given him a mountain of food—and Malgwin called for two children to take it all away. As they bent over him for his plate, he saw that they had gills on their necks.

"So you have come to see the center of power in the Sunlit Lands," she said. "Or come to take it for yourself?"

Darius put his hands on the table. "Something is wrong with it, I think, Malgwin. Maybe it can be repaired. I don't know. But I've come to see what can be done."

"You think we haven't tried over all these years?"

"It's the children who inherit the world who have to decide what to do with it."

She grinned at him, and she did, indeed, still have her monstrous teeth. "Well said, young man. Come, walk with me."

"No offense, but I'm coming too," Kekoa said.

She nodded once but didn't take her eyes off Darius. She led them down to the beach. They walked awhile on the edge of the surf. Sea monsters peeked out at them occasionally. "Children," she said. "Broken and harmed by the world. I bring them here, teach them how to survive. Make them stronger, sharper, fiercer."

"I don't understand why you've been trying to stop me. Throwing me out of the crystal spheres. Destroying my ship, trying to drown me and my friends."

"None of you drowned." She shook her head. "If you are too weak to get to the Sea Beneath when I oppose you, then you are too weak to be of help. Too often we have heard these words: *Oh, it's terrible what happened to you. Try helping yourself this other way. Don't be so angry, we are trying to help.* Your kind always want me to do things a certain way."

"My kind?"

"Men," she said, simply. "And what magical item do you carry with you, Darius Walker?"

He wasn't surprised she recognized it. "It's from the Maegrom. There are Kharobem trapped inside. They tell stories."

"Canny craftsmen, the Maegrom." She held out her hands for it, and he gave it to her. She turned it over, studying the way the gold held the glass walls in place. "They learned to do this by looking at the Sunlit Lands itself. Do you understand?"

"No," Darius said. He didn't know what she meant, not at all.

"Does this not remind you of another magical item you know well?"

He thought about it. The Sword of Years. The Crescent Stone. The Heartwood Crown. The Robe of Ascension. Even the Scim artifact that opened doors, the key Kekoa had. The Disenthraller. "No," he said honestly. "I don't know what you mean."

She sighed. "And you?" She held out her hand to Kekoa. "What do you carry?"

He put the key in her palm. "It's called the Disenthraller."

"Scim work," she said. "They are rightfully concerned about liberty and captivity. Much of their magic bends toward those two things." She put it back in his hand. She pointed out a dark gash in the rocks ahead. A cave.

She walked toward it. "Do you know the story of how the Sunlit Lands were made?"

"Yes," Darius said. "More or less. Cumberland stole the plans from his owner, and he built the Sunlit Lands as a place for people to go, to be safe from people who would oppress them."

"Who's Cumberland?" Kekoa asked.

"My . . ." He was going to say *grandfather*. "My relative."

Malgwin laughed at him. "But *how did he make it*, Darius Walker? What power did he use?"

"Magic," Darius said.

"Magic," she said, mocking him.

Darius scowled. "If we could describe it or replicate it, it wouldn't be magic, would it?"

Malgwin stopped. "In this cave you will find the source of the power that made the Sunlit Lands. Two simple things, common and old, are the source of magic here. The battery that stores the power. Everything else in the Sunlit Lands is built around the power that comes from them. But Cumberland also called on a greater power. Do you know what it is? Do you know its name, or the name of its servants?"

"No," he said. "I don't know what you are talking about."

The story box lit up in her hands, colors flaring against the glass. Animals made of light bashed against the walls: stags and sea monsters, apes and great birds, humans and oxen and massive hounds. "Take this with you," she said, "into the cave. When you know the answer to these questions, you will know what to do. And if you do not discover the answer . . ." She shrugged. "Then what does it matter? I will destroy the Sunlit Lands one day. Perhaps it will be today."

He took the box from her, confused and uncertain what she was saying. The air grew cooler as he walked into the darkness. The walls were black and wet and slick, looking a great deal like Malgwin's skin when she was a sea monster. She was saying that he didn't know the whole story of how the Sunlit Lands came to be. He had no doubt that was true. The box was practically vibrating in his hands, the Kharobem inside desperate to explain to him.

Kekoa hurried to walk beside him, but then Malgwin's voice came to them. "He must go into the cave alone, Kekoa. You must wait for him here."

They exchanged a look. "We can't fight her," Kekoa said. He looked over his shoulder, then back at Darius. "Here." He put the key—the Disenthraller—in Darius's palm. "I don't know why David gave it to me, but better that you have it in that cave than me sitting around on the beach. Be safe, brah."

"You, too," Darius said, studying the key. His jacket had a small pocket. He slipped the key inside and moved forward.

There was an island in the middle of a pond within the deepness of the cave. A hole in the cave ceiling let in a shaft of light, illuminating a table of stone on the island. Darius waded over to the island, the water coming almost to his neck. Malgwin slid past him in the water, her great black eyes watching him without blinking. So. Alone meant alone with Malgwin. Okay.

He set the story box down and looked at the two items on the table. One was a book, small and very old. On the cover it said *The New England Primer*. He recognized it from the story the Kharobem had told him about Cumberland. This was the book that had taught him to read. The book had given him access to power, to the world in the study where he had taught himself magic. Darius flipped it open. There were lists of vowels and consonants, little rhymes to show off the different letters of the alphabet ("As runs the Glass, Man's life doth pass"), and small lessons to attend to and memorize.

The second thing on the table was a single piece of paper. On the top was written *Deed of Manumission for Cumberland Armstrong Walker*, and the next line was a date. Darius read on. It was a legal document, saying that Cumberland was no longer a slave. He had been freed, "discharged of all duties and claims of servitude whatsoever" with "all the rights and privileges of a freedman."

Darius set it back on the table, looked at the primer, the letter, the box of Kharobem. "Malgwin," he said.

She came up from the water, in human form again, dripping. "Darius."

"Tell me what he did. How he did it."

"There is power in words," she said. "It is words that make the world.

And even more power in story, for what is a story but a collection of words, arranged to bring order to the world, to change the world, to make the world."

"The Kharobem," Darius said. "They are made of story. I've heard that said more than once."

She nodded slyly. "Cumberland needed more than words. And remember, the original plans for this place were not his. The blueprints came from his *master*."

Darius rapped his knuckles on the box. "They're trapped because of the glass."

She nodded once, slowly, a wide smile coming onto her face. "Yes, Darius. Yes."

"Cumberland trapped the Kharobem in the Sunlit Lands. This whole thing is a terrarium."

She clapped her hands in delight. "You figured it out. I knew you would."

"The Kharobem aren't servants of the Peasant King."

"No. They are his prisoners. Trapped here by the crystal spheres that keep the boundaries of this magic land separate from the world around it. He has twisted time in strange ways, and the Kharobem cannot find a way out. They are servants of the Story King, not of Cumberland."

"Servants of the Story King," he said. He looked at the box again, a prison within a prison for the Kharobem. He looked at the primer, at the writ of manumission for a slave.

He pulled the Disenthraller from his pocket and studied the box. There was no keyhole. But he moved the key close, and a tiny opening appeared in the gold workings of the edges. He wasn't surprised, but he was reminded once again of the strange magics of this place. He turned the key. The box started to open, like a flower, and the strange, colored presences inside began to swirl around, to escape the box like fog. There was a cracking, a horrific sound as if someone had broken the Earth itself, and glass shrapnel exploded at him. Darius covered his face with his arms.

Six towering presences surrounded him, blazing with fire, their wings full of eyes and whipping up a stinging wind. They had the faces of oxen and lions and eagles and human beings, and they were furious. The box had collapsed, broken into so many tiny shards of glass.

Darius stood straight, the hot wind buffeting his face, the flames crackling between the Kharobem like lightning. The sound of their wings was like the waterfall pounding against the edge of the world. "Now," Darius shouted over the noise, "now we break the crystal spheres and set you truly free." And the Kharobem blared their approval.

41

THE FINAL BATTLE

In the day they climb free, they will destroy
all things. And none can stop them.

FROM "THE TRIUMPH OF THE PEASANT KING," A SCIM LEGEND

✦

Jason Wu had first seen the Court of Far Seeing from a high cliff overlooking the plain, fresh from a day's long journey through mud, muck, and a strange forest inside a cave. It had seemed distant and beautiful and wonderful and strange. Today, as he looked down at the city, he couldn't help but feel a melancholy sadness. Madeline had been so committed to making this world a better place. She had given her life to provide the Sunlit Lands with a chance at making changes, and he couldn't help but feel that the city looked pretty much like it had the first time he had seen it, so long ago.

Delightful Glitter Lady was almost twice the size of an actual rhinoceros. She snorted with joy when she saw the city and shifted under Jason, eager to run down the rise and attack. She had always been a war unicorn.

But Jason pulled her to a stop and stood on her back, facing his Southern Court soldiers.

"Okay, guys, listen up. We're not here to destroy the Elenil," Jason said. The assembled Courtiers, nearly all of them Jasons now, moved restlessly. "We're not here to kill Archon Hanali. We're not here to break down the walls or tear down the towers."

Bezaed settled his giant bird, stroking its feathers. "Tell them why we are here, Wu Song. Do not confuse them before we go into battle."

"Right. So the Kakri have this story. It's a story that changes the world, and it's only one word. If you inject this word into any story, it changes it. Makes it better. Changes the way the ending goes, and changes the way you get to the ending. It's not a riddle or anything—it's the exact word you think it might be. This word you've known since you were a child, that you've always known."

Jason waved at the city behind him. "Some people might think the story we're in, it's about vengeance, but that's not true. We're not here for revenge. Sure, we want to protect people, but that includes the Elenil. Because what they're doing in the world, it's not just destroying everyone else, it's destroying them, too." He held up a gourd of the concentrated Wendy juice. He had two straps across his chest, each weighted down with a generous number of gourds. He looked like a runaway fruit tree. "So I want you to understand . . . this is a kindness. We are doing them a favor. Will we have to fight? Yeah, probably. But I don't want any of you to get hurt. And if we can help it, I don't want you to hurt them, either. So we offer them a drink. And if they won't take it, we give it to them anyway."

"Will that change anything?" someone shouted.

Jason shrugged. "It's the truth. It's the truth as a liquid. And we gotta believe that the truth is going to set them free."

Bezaed's steed tromped its feet nervously. "We need a war cry, brother," Bezaed said.

"Right," Jason bent down so they could speak more privately. "I'd like to say, 'Avengers assemble,' but I just gave a big speech about how this isn't about vengeance."

Bezaed sighed. "It is merely a way for us to show our solidarity. Have them say, 'Liquid truth.' Or 'Set them free.' Whatever you please."

"Oh. Those seem a little stodgy. I need something that makes sense for an army of me." He hefted the Wendy juice in his hand. "I guess we're basically here to give them a drink? I wish it was chocolate pudding. That would make a great war cry. 'Chocolate pudding!' Hmm."

Jason straightened back up and addressed his army. "Thank you for your patience as we worked on a war cry." He thrust his fist in the air, holding the Wendy juice over his head. "It's snack time!"

The Jasons let loose with a full-throated roar. Jason let Delightful Glitter Lady race top speed for the city, juice over his head, his army thundering behind him, all of them as if in one voice, shouting, "SNACK TIME!"

✛

Gilenyia hurried the latest group of humans into the meadow. She watched them disappear into the woods, headed for home. She envied them that, because she didn't believe she had a home anymore, not really.

A flurry of messenger birds passed overhead. One peeled off and came to her. "All Elenil are warned that an army from the Southern Court has appeared. They do not appear to come peacefully. All Elenil must report to the magistrates to receive orders. We require you in battle."

Gilenyia clucked her tongue and threw the bird into the air.

"Do you need to go?" Ricardo asked.

"Don't be ridiculous. Let the other Elenil take care of that. We must get the humans away safely."

The Knight of the Mirror came up, riding his silver stallion. "Another thirty humans are on their way. Most of the nearby locations have been contacted, now, lady. We will need to ride farther afield to bring in more of them."

"What of you, Sir Knight? You are human and not immune to Hanali's order. Perhaps you should ride through the meadow."

A dark cloud crossed his face. "Think not that Hanali could enforce a death sentence on me, lady. Nor can I leave my true lady, for she is still locked in the mirror realm. If I could undo that magic, I would. But I cannot, so I must stay."

For the first time in her life, the knight's story struck Gilenyia as unbelievably sorrowful. In the past she had always seen it as a necessary evil: the Elenil had need of him, so he must be controlled. The easiest way to control him was his lady. She had a rare magical ability to enter the mirror realm, but it was Elenil magic that had trapped her there. Could Gilenyia unwind it? She had never wondered such a thing before.

"Sir Knight. It could be that if you take me to the place where this magic first was wrought, I may be able to undo it. What say you?"

He looked down on her from his horse. "Nothing would please me more. But let us get these humans to safety first, and then I shall take you to her."

Gilenyia reached up and placed her hand on his forearm. "Have you not waited long enough? Today is a day that we discover an end to captivities. It is a fool who remains in chains when the master seeks to murder him."

The knight shook his head. "You have precious little experience with chains. Unless you were snapping them onto someone else. I wish to be free, yes, but not if it prevents the freedom of my fellows."

"At least take me to the place," she said, "so I can see if my magic can effect an escape for her and for you."

He considered this, then extended her a hand. He pulled her onto the saddle behind him. "No doubt there are more humans near Westwind," he said, "though everyone in the castle should have already come here."

"Ricardo," she called. "Rondelo. If Elenil come and you are in need, send a bird to Westwind."

Rondelo bowed low in acknowledgment, and Ricardo waved his hand and shouted, "Yes, lady." Then they were off, the knight's horse, Rayo, flashing across the paved streets.

✦

The darkness got deeper, if such a thing were possible, as Shula followed the spectral form into the woods. The trees loomed closer, their skeletal branches scraping her skin. "What is your name?" she asked, trying to find something to fill the darkness. Her voice was dampened, falling away to almost nothing.

He stopped and turned with a slow inevitability that made her shiver. "You know my name. You have but to remember it."

She clutched the gourd of juice. "Should I drink this?"

He frowned, shook his head, and started forward again.

"You said you would take me to my brother!"

"So I am. But first you must walk through the mists."

"The mists?" But even as she asked the question, she saw the tendrils of thick grey fog, like wool, coming up over his feet. He walked forward, unconcerned, but she felt her pulse quicken. Her throat tightened, her eyes watered.

Still, she stepped forward, and memories swept over her.

✚

"I have someone I want you to meet," Boulos said, and he smiled that smile, the one that always got him out of trouble with their parents.

"Ugh," Shula said. "You're not trying to set me up with someone again, are you?"

"Ha!" Boulos punched her playfully in the arm. "Who would be good enough for my sister anyway?"

"So who is it?"

"A woman I met the other day."

"What, an old lady? Does she need help from the church or something?"

Boulos rolled his eyes. "Not an old lady. A *woman*."

Shula's eyes widened. "Wait, like your age? A girl? Are you dating someone?"

"Not dating, exactly. I just want you to meet her."

"Because they say '*girl*friend,' not '*woman*friend.'" She said that in English. They had been practicing together. Neither of them was very good so far, but she liked this word in English. It made her laugh, the way the words were pushed together, but it had to be those two words. You couldn't replace *girl* with *woman*.

"Shut up," he said, also in English.

They met her at a café. She was nervous, sitting and sipping a Turkish coffee. The woman lit up when she saw Boulos and gave him a big smile. She wasn't wearing a head covering, but they were in a Christian part of town, so there were plenty of women who weren't. She also wasn't wearing her uniform, but Shula knew immediately that she was a Russian soldier.

The way she held herself. The nervous way she looked at Shula. It wasn't "I'm meeting your sister" nervous, it was "Will she hate me because I'm Russian?" nervous.

The woman wasn't wrong to be nervous. Shula had particularly strong feelings about the Russians. Enough that her pastor father had pulled her aside, tried to remind her, "Russians are children of God too." But Shula wouldn't have any of that, and she hated when her dad tried to get all pastoral with her.

Her name, her familiar name, was Vasya, and she invited Shula to call her that. Shula didn't see that as an invitation to friendship—it just made her wonder how she had become close to Boulos so quickly. She was a nice enough girl. Clever. Funny. Polite. But what did she want with Shula's brother? What was she trying to do?

"I come from a town in Siberia," she said. "It's called Ulan-Ude. A wonderful place."

"Tell her what you do for fun there," Boulos said, his eyes sparkling.

"We love to dance," she said. "And in the summer we go to Lake Baikal. In the winter there is—"

"You know what I'm getting at," Boulos said.

Vasya blushed. "We have the largest statue of Lenin's head in the world," she said sheepishly.

Boulos roared with laughter. "When I asked her about her hometown, that's the first thing she said!"

"It's very famous for it! We're in the book of world records! You didn't say anything better about Aleppo."

"Ha!" He pointed at her. "Not true! I said pistachios, wheat fields, orchards, fortresses, museums."

She grinned slyly. "But how big is your biggest Lenin head?"

"We're one of the oldest cities in the world! History! Covered bazaars!"

"That's what I thought! You don't even have one, do you?"

Shula hated this. Hated the whole conversation, hated the way her brother was looking at the Russian girl, despised the way Vasya reflected the look on her own face. She was the enemy. The reason they were scrambling around like refugees in their own city, the reason so many of her friends had left for another city or another country. She stood up, knocking her chair back. "If we had one," she said, raising her voice, "I suppose the Russians would have already bombed it by now."

She stormed out while Boulos yelled after her, "Vasya's a medic, not a pilot!"

✛

Shula came back to herself, gasping for breath.

The tall, thin, creepy stranger watched her, like a spider studying the vibrations of its web. "Shall we continue," he said as if it were a suggestion, not a question.

"This happened to me before," she said, still shaking. "In Aluvorea. There was a fire, and I . . . I saw my father in the fire."

"Interesting. Our work was already fraying then. Your mind is fighting against the false memories again."

"I had another memory," she said. "Of the way I treated Vasya. I didn't give her a chance. I was rude. Unkind."

"We rarely remove happy memories," the creature said, and bent down to continue on the narrow trail.

Shula took a deep breath and followed.

✛

Wendy Oliver had searched every room at the top of the Tower of a Thousand Years, until at last she found her. Resca. Wife of Vivi. Mother of Hanali. She was sitting in a chair, looking out a tower window. She glanced at Wendy, then out again.

"After all these years," she said. "Little Wendy, come back to keep her promise. There's a knife there on the table if you want it."

"I begged you not to take Lee. I begged," Wendy said.

"I remember, child."

"I don't think you do," Wendy said, and she squeezed the vial in her palm. "My daughter is dead because of what happened that day, Resca."

Her eyes tracked back to Wendy for a moment. "So kill me, dear. End this suffering for me. My own Vivi is gone, and Hanali changed beyond all recognition. Your dear daughter did those things." Her face softened. "You always were passionate and couldn't stand to see a wrong left standing.

Madeline reminded me of you in that way. I told Vivi we should take you, not Lee. I always wanted a daughter."

Wendy closed her eyes, breathed in deep through her nose. "Resca. You weren't always Elenil, do you know that?"

"Of course, child. I drank the addleberry juice, I went through the rituals. I left the human bits of me behind."

Wendy pressed the vial into Resca's hand. "In case you want to be human again." She moved for the door, didn't even hesitate as she passed by the knife.

"Where are you going?"

"I promised Lee I would wait for him."

✛

"Yes," Malgwin hissed. "Destroy the land. Destroy it all."

Darius leaned against the stone table. The electric fire of the Kharobem burned over his head. "I'm not sure you're wrong."

Darius held up the two sources of power of the Sunlit Lands. Cumberland's primer, the way he had learned to read, to access the magic. And the contract of freedom from his master, which had released him from his chains. "It makes sense," Darius said. "He went to build a new place, where they could be safe from slavery and safe from people trying to control them because they were Black." He looked at Malgwin. "Cumberland said it fell apart pretty quickly. Just a few generations, right?"

"One," she said. "Maybe two. Cumberland had to let more people in."

"That's one of the problems, isn't it? Because to make a world that's safe, you have to keep some people out. You have to build it so you can control it, which means you need to be on the top. And you have to put locks on the doors that you control." He sighed, put his hand on his forehead. "Cumberland built a little clockwork version of the world he was already in."

"He started with making a place that was good," Malgwin said. "A place that was safe."

"Yeah, but he built it by saying, 'These are the only people who are welcome here.' If you make paradise but keep other people out—if your paradise *relies* on keeping people out—what have you made?"

"Heaven," Malgwin said.

"Nah. This is just another gated community. It shouldn't be a big surprise that the Elenil went all neighborhood watch and put themselves in charge." He held up the writ of manumission. "And I think it's because of this."

"His papers that made him free?"

Darius shook his head. "These papers didn't make him free. These papers were a promise from a kidnapper to let him go. Cumberland was already free. And by putting these papers at the center of the magic, he's built them into the story of this place. He's giving his 'master' power because he's saying his master had the authority to free him. The only power his master had was to stop abusing him, stop stealing from him, stop harming him. This paper puts the wrong spin on it all." He stared at it, thinking about it. "This is the heart of the imperfection in Elenil magic. It's that belief that power is limited. That if I'm going to live a good life, someone else has to live in squalor. And it's not true." He tore the writ of manumission in half, tore it again, kept going until it was confetti. A shock wave of light and sound broke out of it when he made the last tear, and shook the Sea Beneath.

"What have you done?" Malgwin asked, her voice torn between excitement and fear.

"What? You think he's suddenly gonna be a slave again because I tore up a piece of paper? Cumberland is free. Still free. He doesn't have to prove it to anyone, doesn't have to show some cop or judge a piece of paper. He's free. And now the Sunlit Lands are free, too, of that broken bit of things." Darius laughed. His hands were glowing. "I can see how he did it now," he said. "He needed the Kharobem's power for part of it. I can see how time is all bent, tied up in knots."

"There are giant statues in the desert," one of the Kharobem said. "We set them in motion at the beginning of the world, to try to break the sky so we could escape. Cumberland stopped them by slowing time around them."

"Yeah, well, no more." Darius could see the magic like great, enormous ropes of different colors surrounding him. It took him a moment, but he figured out how to untie them, how to unkink the lines, make time flow correctly again. If he was right about this—and he was almost certain he was—the Sunlit Lands and Earth would run alongside one another now. No more two weeks in the Sunlit Lands meaning a year on Earth or vice versa. No more statues frozen in the desert.

"Why is Fantok working with Cumberland?" he asked. "If he trapped you here?"

One of the Kharobem buzzed its wings, then said, "We serve the Story King. So long as we are trapped here, we must still do what we believe the king desires. He is one who requires good to be done to others. We have found that though Cumberland's methods have done us harm, his intentions are good. But we long for our own freedoms. We long for the walls to come down between this world and ours."

Darius thought of Cumberland and his spirituals, and he couldn't help himself. A tune had come into his head, and he started humming it as he moved magic around, retrofitted the system. "Joshua fit the battle at Jericho," he sang to himself, "and the walls came a-tumblin' down."

✦

Far out in the Kakri territories, the enormous stone statues shifted. At last, at long last they could move the speed they were designed for. They lifted themselves from the sand, shook it off. They looked to one another, proud of their glorious appearance. If a mortal saw these giants, that mortal would tremble. They dug into the sand from which they came and pulled forth their hammers. Long, two-handed hammers, the kind that would be used for heavy labor. Driving a stake. Or breaking a wall. The kind of hammers that could crush even the strongest barrier . . . stone or steel or crystal. Satisfied, they strode toward the crystal walls that rose to the east, swinging their ponderous arms and massive hammers as they went.

✦

The Elenil were too strong for Jason's army. Too accomplished in battle. Too powerful. "It takes ten of us to bring down one of them," Bezaed yelled.

It was true. Since Jason kept insisting on at least trying to keep from hurting anyone, his army had to overwhelm the enemy instead: disarm them, surround them, pin them down, try to get them to drink. And it was a disaster. It wasn't working. Not only that, it appeared that many human soldiers hadn't gotten the memo that the Elenil were planning to kill them all. There were more than a few humans on the other side.

"Don't you want to know the truth?" Jason yelled at an Elenil warrior who was holding off five of Jason's people with a single spear.

"I know the truth already," he yelled back, and he speared a fake Jason through the heart. "The truth is that you don't know your proper place. If you'd just do what you're told, everything would be fine."

Jason's blood boiled as he watched the other Jason fall to the ground, mortally wounded. "Bezaed, get in there!"

Bezaed ran his brucok into the fray, and without getting off it, he took a swipe at the Elenil's helm. The Elenil ducked to the side, and one of the Jasons caught hold of his spear. Bezaed leapt onto him, knocking him backward, and the other Jasons piled on.

Jason ran to them, uncorking a gourd as he went. He jumped on the Elenil's chest. "Get his mouth open!"

The Elenil fought them, but they managed to open his mouth wide. "Man, we should have taken the time to make funnels," Jason said, pouring the liquid into the guy's mouth. He struggled, so it splashed all over the place, soaking his face and chest. "Hey, stop moving! I'm getting your battle armor all wet," Jason said.

"Now swallow," Bezaed snarled, and they pushed the Elenil's jaw closed, and Bezaed pinned his nose shut.

You could tell when the concentrate took effect because the Elenil's pupils went wide, and his body went limp. "No," he said. "That can't be true. I don't believe it."

The other thing that Jason hadn't counted on: the truth didn't necessarily make them all suddenly switch sides. In fact, some of them got angry and fought harder. Jason had seen one guy get his dose, then stand up and kill four more Courtiers before they took him down again and gave him another dose. But it didn't affect him that time. He already knew the truth—he just refused to live by it.

"Let him up," Jason said. "Take his spear, but let him up."

"Are you sure—?"

"What else are we going to do? Tie them all up?"

"Yes!" Bezaed said. "Or kill them. Cripple them, at least."

Jason heard a horn, a familiar horn blowing on the wind. The Scim were here! "Hooray!" Jason shouted. The Scim poured into the battle, wearing their war skins. Some of them rode giant possums or rats. There were oversize spiders, and above them flew bats and owls and other winged creatures.

The Scim set to work on the Elenil, cutting them down when they could, fighting with a ferocity born of centuries of pain. The ancient Elenil were stronger warriors, but Jason saw more than one fall beneath the blades of the Scim. Two Black Skulls strode into battle. Their scythes struck down the human allies of the Elenil.

"Uh," Jason said. "I don't think they got the memo about us trying not to kill the Elenil."

Bezaed leapt back into battle, and the Jasons followed. Jason went to get on Dee, but she had apparently run off to tromp around and flatten things. "Have fun, little lady," he said to himself. Well. He didn't love battles. He thought he would try to get in the city gate, inspire his folks to break in too.

He turned just in time to see an Elenil, a blade in his hand.

"I know you," the Elenil said. "You're Hanali's pet."

"Pet? Now that's just rude." He pointed at the knife. "And unless you're planning to make me a sandwich, that knife seems a little rude, too."

"This is a necrotic blade," the Elenil said. "It's a knife that—"

"Good grief, I know what a necrotic blade is," Jason said, pulling his own blade. "As if the name isn't enough to let you know."

"Then you know that one cut—"

"I said I knew what it was. Man!"

Then Elenil's face went red. "Do not call me that! I am not a human!"

"Okay," Jason said, stepping slowly backward. "I can see that you need a quick crash course on human slang. And I can provide that. Just put down the psychotic blade—"

"Necrotic."

"Uh-huh, that's what I said, necrotic."

Look, there was no way he was going to beat an Elenil in hand-to-hand combat. He had learned through long periods of trial and error on Hanali that his best weapon against the Elenil was to make them angry by talking a lot.

He had put some good space between him and the Elenil, but the guy suddenly charged him. Jason scrambled backward. A giant possum darted between them, and when it passed to the other side, the Elenil was on his knees, holding one arm and moaning in pain. The possum turned back around, and a young girl hopped from the saddle. She held a bloody sword in her hand.

"Yenil!"

"Wu Song!" she shouted, and gave him a huge hug. "Wait, you are Wu Song, right? Not one of the fakes?"

"Yes!" He looked at the Elenil, cradling the stump of his arm. "What is it with you and cutting off hands, anyway?"

She shrugged. "He had a necrotic blade. If he had cut you with—"

"For the eight hundredth time, I know what a necrotic blade is! Does it come with instructions that include explaining what it is to everyone?"

"I thought you would be thankful."

"I am so thankful. Thank you." He looked back at the Elenil. "But honestly, Yen, I think you might need counseling when this is all over. I mean, did your parents let you watch Star Wars too young or something?"

She was about to reply when there was an enormous, reverberating *GONG* that shook the battlefield. People dropped their weapons to cover their ears. Some fell to their knees. *GONG*. It happened again. A third time. *GONG*.

Jason looked up. The whole sky was shaking. He pointed at it, and Yenil moved closer to him. "What's happening?"

"Well, I hate to get all Chicken Little, but it looks to me like the sky is falling."

"What should we do?"

Jason looked to the city walls. He didn't see how this changed the plans. And if the sky really was falling, better to be inside than out in a field. He pointed to the walls. "Let's go!"

David came riding up on a second possum. "Yenil!" he shouted. "I told you, no running off and *no swords*." He held out his hand, and she reluctantly gave him the sword, pouting.

"I said she might need counseling," Jason said.

"Come on," David said. Jason swung up behind him.

The three of them rode toward the wall.

✚

The first swing of the hammer on crystal made a satisfying sound that the stone giants could feel. This was why they had been made. A second giant swung, and a gratifying crack traveled out from the place where it struck. A third, and a piece the size of a house broke off, careened into the space between the spheres, shattered as it fell into the gears of the world.

One of the giants grabbed the edges with stone fingers and cracked off another piece. And another. Until it was large enough for one of them to try to climb through. The first one through smashed at the next sphere with a hammer. The whole structure wobbled.

✚

Gilenyia studied the mirror. It was the original mirror, the knight said—the one the Elenil had used to trap the lady of Westwind, Fernanda Isabela Flores de Castilla. It was tall, oval, with an ornate gold frame. It had been before Gilenyia's time that the Elenil had done this. Most of the humans did not know how long-lived the Knight of the Mirror was. He had been given a variety of gifts by the Elenil, and one of them was his long life. He would have traded all his gifts, he often said, to be reunited with his love.

She did not know if every Elenil could undo this curse, but as she traced the lines of the spell, she saw how similar it was to her healing magic. It was strange—the spell had kept Fernanda in the mirror, held against her will, but the language of the spell said that she had been lost so that something else could be found.

"What is this?" she said to herself. "I don't understand the spell."

The lady stood on one side of the mirror, clearly trying to keep hope from her eyes. The knight stood behind Gilenyia, looking only at his beloved. "It is an old one," the knight said. "From the early days. An Elenil noble had lost his horse . . ."

Gilenyia whirled on him. "He had lost his horse? And he used the lady to find it?"

The knight nodded. "It was a purposeful cruelty. I had . . . crossed him. The archon refused to undo it. He said it was between this Elenil and me."

Gilenyia's skin flushed hot. The fury that came over her tightened every muscle in her body. Would this have angered her a month ago? She wasn't sure. She had a vague memory that maybe she knew this story already. That she had heard it at an Elenil party and laughed.

She put her hands on the mirror frame, probed for the place to attach her magic. She found it, spread her magic into the frame. "Stand back," she said, and *pushed*.

The mirror exploded, the shrapnel of the glass cutting her face and arms. She didn't let go of the frame to cover herself, knew that she couldn't. Only when the sound of falling glass had faded did she dare to lift her face and look. The lady of Westwind stood in the room, whole and solid, staring at her hands in wonder.

The knight ran to her and they embraced, their hands running over one another as if to make sure the other was real. They kissed, released one another, embraced again, then wept.

The knight fell at Gilenyia's feet. "Lady Gilenyia. You have done us a great service that can never be repaid. We are free at last to leave the Elenil. But, lady, if there be some final task you require of me, honor demands that I meet your request, no matter how great."

She raised him to his feet, thinking only: *I could have done that fifty years ago. A hundred. More.* It was simply done, a moment's concentration, a few minutes' study. *This man and that woman, people who are known to me, and I could have given this gift to them decades ago.* She did not feel that she had done any great service—rather, she felt sick. She noticed the stinging cuts from the glass and was glad for them, glad that she had been punished in some small way.

Gilenyia took both of their hands in hers. "My friends—I hope I can call you friends now—I do have one act of service to request, but it will require both of you to accomplish it."

"But say it," the knight said.

"Anything," Fernanda said. "You have reunited me with my love. I will fly to the moon if you desire it."

Gilenyia took a deep breath. "Take the knight's horse, Rayo, and ride him as quickly as you are able to the Meadow at World's End. Do not stop to fight an Elenil nor to save a human. Ride, and do not stop until you have passed out of the Sunlit Lands and back to your home on Earth. You have done too much service for others and not enough for yourselves."

"There are many others who require help," the knight said.

"And I will give it them," Gilenyia said, the familiar cold front moving back into her voice. "But as for you, I was promised a task, no matter how difficult, and this one is simple as cracking an egg. Am I to be denied?"

BOOM. The sky shook. They raced to the window. Two more great rolls of thunder shook them, greater than any noise that had ever been heard in the Sunlit Lands. They raced down the stairs and to the knight's waiting horse.

Gilenyia raised her face to the sky. It did not look right. It was listing to one side as if the crystal sphere had somehow come off its track. The knight also watched it with some concern.

"Come," Gilenyia said. "I have asked this simple task, and I demand to be satisfied."

Fernanda embraced Gilenyia and kissed her cheek. "So it will be," she said. "And if you come home to Earth, lady, and find there is no home for you, then come live with us in Westwind."

The knight also kissed Gilenyia's cheek. "This may be the first kindness I have received from an Elenil."

"I am an Elenil no longer," she said. "I am a human, like you."

The knight nodded, as if this was no surprise to him. "Lady, when I leave the Sunlit Lands, Westwind will follow. You would be wise to be gone from here before we ride through that magical wood."

There were more embraces, another kiss from each of them, and then the knight boosted his lady onto Rayo, mounted behind her, and raced for the meadow that would lead them home.

✚

It seemed that every few steps held new memories, each one terrible in its way. Nearly all of them centered on Vasya. On how much Shula hated her. On how many times the poor woman had tried to make a connection but Shula had denied her. She now had memories of Vasya coming to her home, eating with them, watching television with Boulos, and always, always, receiving a cruel comment from Shula. A cold look. An angry slam of the door as Shula went somewhere else.

In the memory she was currently reliving, though, Shula was lying on the floor drawing with Amira. Sweet little Amira. She didn't know why she would have given this memory up.

"What are you drawing?" Shula asked her sister.

"A horse that lives on the sun," Amira said. "That's why it's yellow and has orange hair."

"It's very beautiful," Shula said. "I like it very much."

"Well, you can't have it," Amira said, not looking up. "It's for Vasya."

Anger, hot and overwhelming, shut Shula off completely. "Amira, I need to tell you something."

BOOM.

"You can't trust Vasya."

BOOM.

"If she says anything to you, remember that she's not part of our family. You don't listen to her, Amira. Don't you ever listen to her."

BOOM.

Her eyes opened, unfocused. The thin white creature was there still, his head turned toward the sky—or where the sky would be if there wasn't so much darkness—a curious expression on his face.

"What was that?" Shula asked groggily. Still more memories were flooding into her. She couldn't see them all, but she could feel them, filling the cracks inside her head.

"The end of the world," he said. "But here in this cave we are concerned with the past, not the future. Come, Shula Bishara. We are getting close to your brother now."

✢

When the first three shaking blows hit the crystal sphere, the entire Sea Beneath sloshed in its bowl, and all the creatures and beasts and monsters cried out as if in one voice.

"And now you must release us for a time," Malgwin said. "There will be terror upon the seas and upon the land. For justice must come, and if it cannot come through the Elenil, then it must come through the creatures and beasts and monsters beneath."

"Why are you asking my permission?" Darius said.

"Because," she said, "the power is yours now. You have taken hold of it. The Sunlit Lands is yours to control, to punish or reward."

He shook his head. "That's the whole problem. I don't want to control it. I want to set it free."

"They must be punished," Malgwin repeated.

"My friends are up there," Darius said. "Maybe they will bring justice."

"For hundreds of years nothing has changed," Malgwin said. "Let us wash it clean in blood."

Darius set the primer down and looked at the Kharobem around him. "What do you say? It was you who were imprisoned."

"Set us free," they said, "and let the Story King do as the Story King pleases."

"You are not the Story King," Malgwin said.

"I know that," Darius said. "But where is he?"

"When the sphere is destroyed, he will return," they said.

"The Sea Beneath will rise," Malgwin said.

✛

The gates were locked, with no clear way to get in. Jason hoped that things were going better for Baileya and the Kakri on the other side of the city. Dee had caught up to them, so now it was him and David, Yenil, Dee, and the possums. Yenil had named hers Murder Mouse.

The tide of the battle was turning, and in favor of the Elenil. Even the arrival of the Scim had only given them a momentary advantage. This whole thing . . . it wasn't working the way Jason had hoped. "I thought if they drank the Wendy juice, it would make them switch sides," Jason said, watching with dismay as a trio of Elenil cut down a crowd of Jasons, then started in on a small company of Scim.

"They have to drink it willingly," Yenil said.

She said it so simply, like it was obvious. And maybe it was. When the Elenil were forced to drink it, it seemed to have the opposite effect of what

Jason had hoped for. They were doubling down, more furious, more committed to their cause than before.

"How do you know?"

"Mrs. Oliver drank some. She cried and cried, and then she said she had to go find Hanali. She said she had to talk to him."

"*Mrs. Oliver* is in there? How did she get in?"

Yenil looked at the wall. "She's stronger than people think, you know. She's Madeline's *mom*."

A messenger bird landed beside them and squawked at the top of its lungs, "The humans and the Scim have a magic potion that gives Elenil fake memories! They are trying to deceive you!"

"Hey!" Jason said. "I know you. You're that bird who sat on my head and said I couldn't go with Madeline to see the Elenil."

"And you're the lying kid who didn't listen to what I said."

"What? That's not true," Jason shouted. "Hey, I don't even tell lies. And the potion doesn't give fake memories—it helps people remember the truth. Who sent you?"

"Hanali, son of Vivi, archon of the Elenil and true ruler of the Sunlit Lands."

"Why, you—," Jason said, and went running for the bird, which, of course, flew away to spread its lies to other corners of the battlefield. Jason sighed. "Well, I can't imagine that's helping anything."

"So what do we do?" Yenil asked. "If the concentrated Wendy juice doesn't work, how do we do this? Should we just try to beat them now, to kill them all?"

"Seriously," Jason said. "You need professional help. You can't just kill everyone."

"They killed my parents," she said seriously. "And Madeline, too."

Oh yeah. He knelt down, put his hand on her shoulder. "You're right, Yen. I'm sorry. I take back what I said about professional help. I mean, it actually would probably be good, but I shouldn't have said it that way."

And David said, "Yenil, Shula doesn't want you fighting. You know that."

There was shouting from the wall above. A young Scim kid was up there, dressed in a weird outfit. He had been "civilized" by the Elenil, obviously, and they were setting up some sort of magical apparatus that looked like a megaphone. "Wait a minute." Jason squinted, trying to get a better view. Could that be? It looked like . . . Nightfall? But he was dead! Killed by Sochar in the Wasted Lands.

"Nightfall!" he shouted. "Nightfall!" He looked at Yenil. He had promised to keep Nightfall's true name safe. But if he could get him to hear, maybe Nightfall could help them somehow. He debated a moment more, then shouted, "NOLA!"

For a moment it looked like the Scim kid had heard him. Nightfall looked around, disoriented. But then he stepped up to the megaphone and began to speak.

✦

Wendy located the fountain, but it took her a while with the changes in the topography since she had been here all those years ago. But she found it and sat on the stone edge. Here is where she had said goodbye to Lee. They had all been weeping. She had thought that Kyle might never stop. And Vivi, standing by so coldly, waiting for them to keep their parts of the bargain.

"Come back to us," she whispered. "Come back to us, Lee."

✦

The Herald of Mysteries arrived at the wall. The archon had ordered he be given whatever he needed, and he had requested only that his people be able to hear him. Human servants set up the megaphone. In time, they would all be removed from the Sunlit Lands, as was only right. Whether by death or exile, it did not matter to the Herald of Mysteries. He was merely the mouthpiece of the Majestic One, as the great Archon Thenody had taught him. He had not known it once, for he was only an ignorant Scim. But at the feet of the archon he had learned his true nature and his true message.

As he was about to speak, he thought he heard someone cry his name. His old name, his Scim name. Nightfall. But that couldn't be. Who here in Far Seeing knew him by that name? Then he heard his true name, Nola, a name that only his closest family knew. No, there was one other. The human. Wu Song. He looked around, disoriented. But he was not Nola any longer. He was not Nightfall. He was the Herald of Mysteries.

"Brethren and sistren," he said, his voice booming out over the battle-field. "Stop this foolish fighting. For the Majestic One—or as our people say, the Peasant King—comes soon. Did you not hear the booming sound of his great fist knocking upon the door of our world? Do you think he will be gentle with those who have disobeyed his word? And as it is said:

Zhanin on the western waters,
    Aluvoreans in forests dispersed.
To the east, the Kakri wanders,
    the Scim in deep darkness accursed.
Humans from magic are fleeing,
    Maegrom in dark earth beneath.
Elenil rule from Far Seeing,
    in lands by our master bequeathed.
The Majestic One keeps all in his sight,
    Elenil first in the warmth of his light.

"The Elenil must rule from this city, for that is the lot the Majestic One has given them. Do you not see how they suffer today? And why? Because they care for us, keep us safe. The humans should not be here. That is the Elenil's fault and their shame. But neither, brethren and sistren, should be in rebellion against those who have been put over us in authority. This is why we first received this curse, when the Peasant King fought to bring peace to our lands, and we fought against him. How much more will our punishment be when he returns if we show we have not learned our lesson? And how much greater our reward if we humbly bow our heads and take our rightful place until he returns? It won't be long now."

A grating noise, like the sound of an earthquake—two great plates of mineral being crushed together—came from above, and both the ground and the crystalline sky shook. "Do you not see? Can you not hear? The Peasant King, the Majestic One is coming. Do not tempt his anger again!"

The herald peered down on the battlefield. Joy filled his heart, for first one, then several, then many of the Scim laid down their weapons, fell to their knees, and cried out for the Elenil to be merciful.

✢

"No," Jason said. The Scim were laying down their weapons, surrendering to the Elenil. "What is going on?"

"They're afraid," Yenil said, simply. "Don't worry. We just need to figure out how to get over this wall."

"If only we could fly," Jason said.

✢

Archon Hanali paced in his quarters. From the garden he could see the conflict in front of the city gates, and he smiled to himself as the Scim herald convinced the Scim to drop their weapons. He had gifted the boy with a small magical token that made words more influential, made people more likely to do as you suggested. The boy refused to use it on any but his own people, but so be it.

The herald understood what others did not: Hanali was doing this for the good of the Scim. He wasn't trying to enslave them, push them back into the dark the way that Thenody had done. He was a friend, a compatriot, a savior. If they didn't understand that, well, he would make them understand through force of arms. If they would just stand back and let him be in control, he could get this whole thing sorted and running in an orderly fashion.

It would all make sense. Except the sky breaking. That concerned him. It must be some sort of natural phenomenon. And the army of Jasons—how was that child so influential and so infuriating?—meant that the Southern Court was here.

The humans were dying or fleeing. Hanali had hoped to catch them all unawares, but reports came to him now that someone had been helping them escape through the Meadow at World's End. No matter. Extermination or elimination—either one would get the vermin clear of one's home. Not that he hated humans—it was just that they were small, and weak, and convenient scapegoats at this moment.

But he felt a nagging doubt. He remembered Mrs. Oliver's words. Wendy's words. Something inside him trembled, and the vaguest of memories knocked on the door of his mind. But he knew that to open that door meant it would be taken off the hinges, that Lee would tear down the house that Hanali had built. This could not be.

Had he made the wrong decision? But no, this was for the greater good. A few must suffer that many might thrive. The Elenil might need more humans in the future, but when that time came, Hanali would carefully lead the charge. Hanali, not Lee.

Two Elenil approached, led by a Scim servant. "You called for us, archon?"

"Indeed. I need you to scour the battlefield and bring me the one called Wu Song. Sometimes called Jason."

The Elenil exchanged looks. "Sir, the whole battlefield is full of them. Which one do you want?"

"The one with the unicorn," Hanali said, exasperated. "And if you can't find that one, find the one that gives you the most heartburn and bring him here. It will almost certainly be the true Wu Song."

✦

Jason was about ten feet off the ground, trying to scale the wall.

"You're doing great," Yenil said, sitting on Delightful Glitter Lady. That put her at about his eye level. He had jumped off Dee's back onto the wall and hadn't moved up a bit. David had told him not to do it. He had said Jason would fall.

He sighed and slid from the wall onto Dee's back. "I would definitely fall." There was a rumbling sound. The whole earth started to shake. "First the sky and now this," Jason said.

Out in the thick of the battle, the Jasons and the few Scim who still fought fell back. Jason's people were losing now, badly, and had retreated to almost the place they had started. Bezaed stood at their head, doing his best to slow their flight and keep the army together.

Just behind the enemy lines, the earth burst upward, and a gaping maw of open tunnel appeared. Pouring from it was the great army of the Maegrom. Their armor was beautiful, handmade of the finest metals and lovingly polished. Many of them had crimson capes or helmets with red crests rising above them. Some of them rode stone war machines, mon-strous things the size of buses, with Maegrom hanging on the sides or shooting arrows from the windows. Others rode on creatures of living stone. Break Bones strode from the midst of them. He pointed his great ax toward the walls of Far Seeing. "FOR CRUKIBAL!" he cried, and the Maegrom shouted it in response, and the walls reverberated with the sound.

The first of the Maegrom hit the walls, and the walls crumbled beneath their stone magic. To the Maegrom, the hardest stone could be treated like clay, or even sand. The walls shifted and melted beneath their magic, and the stones became fine and small, crashing to the ground and sifting past them like a wave. Delightful Glitter Lady shook herself to get the dust off and pulled her feet from what remained of the wall.

Break Bones lifted his ax in greeting and stepped into the city. "Oh," Jason said. "I don't think they got the memo, either."

"For Crukibal!" they shouted again.

And then, from high up on the hill, the sound of what remained of his own army. "SNACK TIME!" they cried, and the Elenil began to fall back . . . toward the waiting Maegrom.

"Come on," Jason said, and Delightful Glitter Lady trotted into the city. Yenil's possum, Murder Mouse, followed close behind, and David brought up the rear, keeping an eye on the battle as it moved ever closer.

✛

Gilenyia stood outside of Westwind, across the moat, watching it intently. It had been about fifteen minutes since the knight and his lady had left. She wanted to make sure that the castle disappeared—meaning they had successfully made it to Earth—before she went to look for Hanali.

Ricardo found her there. "Gilenyia," he said. He was exhausted, covered in dirt and blood. He had a wound in his left arm. "Lady, the Elenil are beginning to choke out the paths to the meadow."

"I see." It wasn't her preference, but they might have to kill some Elenil to keep the paths clear. "Are there many humans still coming?"

He shook his head. "The Knight of the Mirror was fighting his way through the thickest part of them."

Gilenyia laughed. Of course he was. Still being true to his word, but also doing it in such a way that he could be as helpful as possible. "So. What shall we do, Ricardo?"

"Lady," he said gently. "The Southern Court is here. They are asking the Elenil to drink these." He pulled a gourd from his belt. "It is a potion that restores memories."

She took the gourd, sniffed it. It had a floral scent, not unpleasant. "Are you suggesting I drink it?"

"I am."

She thought about it, looked at the drink. "What if they mean to poison the Elenil?"

"Word is that no one has died from drinking it. The effects are unclear. I spoke to a human friend from the battlefield who said an Elenil he knew drank from it and regained memories of his life as a human."

She frowned. Then she tipped it back and drank it in one draught.

The memories hit her like a wall. They came together without any order to them.

A little door she had found in the living room, under a rug. She had been a child, maybe fifteen. A door that led into another world.

Her name came back to her: Jillian Arnott.

Her mother and father, they loved her. So kind. She remembered a thunderstorm, leaping into their bed, her mother tucking her close and singing to her. Her father making pancakes every Saturday. He always burned them. "Pancakes and whipped cream!" he would say. "Just a spoonful of sugar makes the burnt taste go down."

Her father had been sick. Getting worse. The Elenil promised to teach her how to heal people. They would send her back, they said, whenever she wanted to go. She remembered her Elenil "parents." They had struck the deal with her, Jillian. Only a child.

Then they had given her the addleberry juice, and she had forgotten a little bit. They gave her more, until she forgot her deal, her parents, herself. They had reshaped her. Made her Gilenyia. Taught her to heal people. They had kept their promise.

They had taught her that humans didn't matter. Taught her she was Elenil. When she first woke up, after the worst of the forgetting, they called her Gilenyia. Said she was just young—that was why her memories were fuzzy. These things happened. Even now, thinking back on it, it made no sense. The Elenil were never pregnant, but they had children—and everyone thought nothing of it, never mentioned it. Never remembered how it happened.

And yet the Elenil had given her a good life. A life based on a lie.

The gourd fell from her hand.

"Gilenyia?"

"Jillian," she said. "My name is Jillian."

"Are you okay?"

She knew how to control her emotions. She might appear cold to others, but her emotions were bigger than theirs. She knew she had to keep them in check now or be consumed in a tidal wave of grief that was threatening her. How many years since she had been taken away? Was her father still living? Her mother?

"I have to go home," she said. Hanali didn't matter. Saying goodbye to her Elenil parents didn't matter. The end of her story in the Sunlit Lands was rapidly approaching. Gilenyia had been an oppressor—she realized that now. But Jillian had been a victim.

"It's going to be okay," Ricardo said. He reached for her, tentatively, then pulled her into his arms. Jillian wrapped herself around him and sobbed.

✤

There was a story Shula told herself about the night she was attacked, the night her apartment was firebombed. She had followed a homeless family, wanting to bring them some food, when someone had attacked her, tried to hurt her, cut her face with a knife. All of this was true.

Then, on the way back to her apartment, Hanali had stopped her and stopped time and invited her to the Sunlit Lands. She had said no. Or that she would think about it. Arrived at her home to find it on fire. She went upstairs with Hanali, who paused time again so she wouldn't be burned. Had found the bodies of her parents and sister. Hanali had told her not to go into her brother's room, that it was too horrible to see. She had come outside, angry, and agreed to five years in the Sunlit Lands in exchange for the power to light on fire, and the deaths of the person who assaulted her and the person who had started the fire. Hanali had agreed. He had put a knife in her attacker while she watched, and she had climbed through a bombed-out building to get to the Sunlit Lands.

But now, her memories told her that story wasn't true.

She had returned home after she was attacked, but Hanali had not come to her yet. She got there and found only Vasya in the apartment. Vasya had been horrified. "Shula, what happened to your face? Are you okay?"

"It's nothing. What are you doing here alone?"

Vasya hurried to the kitchen, got a cold, wet washcloth. She stroked Shula's hair, put the cloth to her face. "We should get you to the hospital."

"My parents?"

"They were getting groceries. They took your sister with them. Boulos should be home soon."

And they were. Her parents, putting away the groceries, until her mother saw her face. Horrified and clucking over it, telling her father they had to go to the hospital. Amira, crying because it looked like it hurt. Her father, her gentle father, angry and ready to search the city for the man who'd dared lay hands on Shula.

Reliving the memory now, Shula cringed. She knew it ended with her parents and Amira dead, and what was this new story that was unfolding? Who was this strange and unreasonable self at the center of it?

Angry, she lashed out at Vasya. *Why was she here? Where was Boulos?* Furious, screaming. Mother sent Vasya to Boulos's room, told her to wait there. Shula stormed out of the apartment, walked the city, her anger stronger than her fear. She felt some satisfaction when she saw the blood from her face drip onto her shoes as she walked. It seemed fitting.

Hanali had met her when, two hours later, she rounded the corner for home. She had ignored texts and calls. Just let her anger dwindle until all that was left was the smoke.

Her apartment complex was on fire. Hanali had said to her, "Your family is in there, and they can still be saved."

She asked for immunity to fire, and got it, in exchange for a year of service in the Sunlit Lands. She bolted up the stairs. Her parents were dead. Amira was dead. There was still Boulos's door, but it was closed, just like when she left. Just Vasya in there. Should she check on her?

No.

She could not bear the thought of Vasya alive and her family dead.

So she went outside and milled in the crowd, and it was there that she saw Vasya, tears making a trail through the ashes on her face. "Where are they?" she shouted. "Where?"

Shula told her. Dead. But where was Boulos?

"In the apartment," Vasya said. "He came home right after you left. Your parents forgot the rice. Amira and I went down to buy some. When we came back, Amira ran up the stairs, but I saw someone setting a fire in the stairwell. I called to her, *Tell your parents there is a fire,* and I chased that person. Chased them until I lost them and came back to find the apartment on fire, burning down—" She burst into tears.

Tears that Shula could not share, because her own words to Amira were echoing in her head, haunting her. *Don't trust Vasya, and don't do anything she says.* And Amira, wanting Shula to be happy, agreeing. Even if it meant that she didn't tell them there was a fire.

Vasya grabbed her arms. "You saw them? They're dead, all of them?"

"Yes," Shula said, numb.

"Amira and Boulos and your parents, all dead?"

Why did she keep repeating herself?

"I didn't see Boulos . . . his door was closed." *I thought it was you in there.*

The fire was worse now. Things were starting to collapse. "We have to see," Vasya said.

Shula grabbed her arm. "It's too late!" She could feel the heat of the fire from here.

But Vasya had already run into the flames, her arms across her face.

Shula followed, her new power keeping her safe. By the time she caught up, Vasya was in Boulos's room, trying to put out the flames on him with her hands. Shula wrapped him a blanket, threw another over Vasya, and led her down the stairs, carrying her brother over her shoulder. She didn't know how she had the strength to carry him in that moment, but she barely noticed his weight.

Hanali had come to her again when they were all still smoking and lying on the pavement. "Are you ready?" he had asked.

"You said I could save my family!" she shouted.

"And so you did. He was the only one still alive." He held out his hand. "Come now, there are debts to be paid."

"No," she said. "They come too. Both of them. And they get the fire immunity. And I want whoever did this dead, and I want them to know why. And the man who attacked me, I want him dead too."

"You ask for so much," Hanali said. "Why not ask for a new story, and new memories? Wouldn't you rather have that?"

Shula frowned. "I'll take that, too."

Hanali watched her for a long time, thoughtful. "Five years' service for you," he said. "And a year each for them."

"Fine," she said. Hanali introduced himself to Boulos and Vasya. Her hands were badly burned. His chest and face were, too.

"Ah," Hanali said to Boulos, looking off into the crowd. "There's the man who attacked your sister." He was right. There he was.

Hanali pressed a knife into Boulos's hand, and he walked up to the man and put the knife in, no questions asked, no pause, no noticeable emotion, even. He dropped the knife and said, "Let's go."

Then time washed in around them again, and they started the long climb through the dark, ending in the Sunlit Lands. A visit to the tower—to hear a story, that's what she remembered—and then no memories of Boulos or Vasya after that, no accurate recollections of that night.

She was curled on her knees, arms across her stomach. Her throat felt thick, and it hurt, as if from smoke or crying.

She was the villain in her own story. Her petty hatred had harmed Vasya, yes, but had come back and harmed her and her family worse. Far worse.

The Historian smiled, his long white hands clasped in front of him. He leaned over her eagerly. "You remember?"

"Yes," she said.

He grinned to hear it. "I can take the pain away," he said. "For a price."

✛

The giants had climbed to the third heaven. There were cracks—significant cracks—in the first and second spheres now. If they could break the third, they knew it would wobble, and the closer levels would be affected. If they could break the third, it would all start to crash down, would come apart, would shatter like a glass that had been stomped on. Could they break the third heaven? Yes, as easily as moving. They pulled back with their great hammers and began to swing.

✦

The Peasant King had arrived. He entered the cave, Kekoa beside him.

"Darius," he said. "So you've decided."

"It's a beautiful place," Darius said. "It really is. There is so much good in it. But we have to start over, pull out the broken pieces. And to make the new thing, we're going to have to break the old. The bad parts. Tear them out."

Cumberland sighed. "I know, son, I know. But it was a beautiful dream, for a while."

"And it helped some people," Darius said.

"It did."

The Kharobem shivered with outrage.

"They didn't like it so much," Darius said.

"I guess I should have destroyed it when I first found out the price," Cumberland admitted. "But I thought maybe, just maybe, I could turn it into something good."

"The sky is almost broken," Malgwin said. "It is time to release the waters above and below."

"So be it," the Peasant King said.

Malgwin shouted with joy and transformed to her fiercest form. She swam to the bottom of the Sea Beneath, and the whole world shook. Water burst forth in geysers, and the sea began to rise.

"Oh, boy," Kekoa said. "So this is it. The end. The actual end."

The Peasant King looked at Kekoa. "Whom do you wish to be with? When the end comes?"

Kekoa thought about it. "David," he said. "David or Jason."

The man nodded. "There is a door there, near the entrance to the cave. Walk through it, and it will take you where you wish to be."

Kekoa gave Darius a hug, which surprised him. He barely knew the guy. "Be careful, brah."

"You too."

Then Kekoa was gone, headed through the magical door.

The Peasant King stepped onto the air, as if walking up an invisible stairway, and motioned for Darius to follow. "Come," he said. "We have business at Far Seeing. As do the Kharobem."

Darius stepped up and found the air—strangely—to be as solid as the ground itself. The Kharobem lifted alongside him, and he could feel the electrical field tingling on his face when they came too close.

✛

Hanali had been searching for Jason, and Jason for Hanali, so it was no surprise they found one another quickly, in one of Hanali's several banquet rooms with a huge balcony overlooking the city. Yenil stood at Jason's side. He had shrunk both Dee and Murder Mouse to the size of kittens. Yenil hugged Murder Mouse so tight his eyes stuck out. Break Bones stood behind them, ax at the ready, a prodigious frown on his face, with David next to him.

"Wu Song," Hanali said.

Jason inclined his head. "Hamburger."

Hanali made a sour face. "You know I dislike it when you do that."

"I'm not a big fan of you genociding all the humans."

"Ha. Fair enough. It was all for the common good."

"Correct me if I'm wrong, but it doesn't seem great for the humans and their common good."

"Touché."

"It's easy to make points in an argument when someone is lying to themselves," Jason said. Was it Jason's imagination, or did a flicker of uncertainty cross Hanali's face?

Hanali motioned to a large banquet table. "Please. We might as well sit and enjoy ourselves while we talk."

Jason unhooked a gourd from his bandolier. "I brought drinks."

The archon studied the gourd carefully. "I do not think I will try it. Not today." He studied Jason and his little crew. He frowned at Yenil. "Do not think I will allow you to cut off my hand."

"I told you," Jason said to Yenil. "You have a reputation."

Hanali sniffed. "Not that there is much danger of it. I am significantly more powerful than when we last spoke."

"I'm a Kakri now," Jason said offhandedly. "And king of the Southern Court."

Hanali raised an eyebrow. "You never fail to surprise."

"And I'm still the number one pudding importer in the Sunlit Lands."

Hanali fingered a small choker he wore. There was a tiny crescent-shaped stone on it. "So. My dear Jason. Have you come to broker peace? Surely two reasonable sovereigns such as you and I can come to an agreement. We'll 'evacuate' the humans instead of killing them. Return the Scim to their hovels in the Wasted Lands?"

Yenil growled, and Break Bones put a warning hand on her shoulder.

"Nah," said Jason. "I've come to accept your unconditional surrender. My people are already in your city. I'm guessing the Kakri have broken through the northern wall and will be here shortly."

The whole city shook. Dust rained from the ceiling, covering the lavish meal.

Break Bones crossed to the window. "Great geysers break through the city streets. And rain pours from the sky though there are no clouds, as if the storehouses of heaven have come undone."

"Sounds like the end of days," Hanali said calmly.

"Welp," Jason said. "Sounds like you should take off your gloves and give me a big high five. End of the road, Hanali."

Another earthquake, and they all scrambled for cover as chunks of the ceiling fell. All except Hanali, who grabbed Jason by the nape of the neck, crossed to the balcony, and flung him over the side.

✝

Westwind did not fade gradually from sight—it disappeared completely and without warning. A crack of thunder accompanied its departure, and Jillian and Ricardo leapt away from one another, startled and then embarrassed.

Ricardo led them back to the meadow, dodging Elenil patrols with relative ease. They came across a family crouched near the entrance to the meadow, looking for a way past the Elenil guards.

There were five in the family: three adults and two children. All five had tan skin and unkempt blond hair. The man wore only a pair of shorts, and the women shorts and loose, sleeveless shirts. Only one of them wore shoes. The girl's hair hung over her face, covering it completely, and the boy wore a mask made of tree bark.

The boy looked at Jillian, his eyes moving behind the bark mask. "Jillian?"

She knelt down, removed the mask. She remembered this boy vaguely, that the Elenil had tried to turn him into one of them on the same day Jillian had been transformed. He had fought it, said he had family to remember. His face looked like that of an Elenil even though he was still in a human body.

"We heard that humans are fleeing through the meadow," the boy said. "And knew this could be our chance to leave together, after all these years."

She exchanged a look with Ricardo. "We will make a distraction."

The boy nodded in thanks. His small hands reached out and took hers. "Take care," he said, and the way he said it, she knew he meant it from the bottom of his heart.

She drew herself up to her regal Elenil height and marched over to the guards. "The archon is in danger and demands your help," she said. "Bring every Elenil you see along the way. Archon Hanali commands this!"

The guards jumped into immediate action, loping toward the Palace of a Thousand Years. The family ran past her as soon as the guards were out of sight, and one of the women called back, "Our thanks, sister!"

The ground shook, and great geysers of water broke through the pavement in front of the building. In the distance, one of the towers of Far Seeing listed to the side, then fell, crashing into another. "It was my home," she said. "For a long time."

Ricardo touched her arm gently. "It's time to go, lady."

She nodded. A bird flew past, and she called it over. It landed on her finger. "Take this message to my cousin, Hanali, son of Vivi. Tell him I am leaving. And tell him . . . tell him he should drink of the juice." Her eyes watered. "Tell him I am sorry." She threw her hand forward, and the bird circled once, then headed toward the Tower.

Ricardo wiped the tears from Jillian's eyes with the corner of his sleeve. He brushed her hair from her face. "Are you okay?"

She took a deep breath, stood taller. "Ricardo, you have been my servant for some time. But that is no longer appropriate. You have always paid close attention to my needs. Before we leave this place, I have to ask you, sir. Are you in love with me?"

Ricardo smiled and squeezed her arm. "No, Jillian. I am not your lover, and not your servant. Simply your friend. Have you had one of those?"

She searched her newfound memories, reflected on her years of service to the Elenil. "I do not believe I have," she said.

"Then I'm the first," he said. "And it's an honor."

He held out his hand, and she took it, and they walked together into the woods, out of the Sunlit Lands. She did not look back, not even briefly—she just held her friend's hand and walked forward, out of that world and back into her own. Jillian Arnott was never seen in the Sunlit Lands again, nor mentioned in another story, and that was just the way she wanted it.

So ends the story of Jillian Arnott, sometimes called Gilenyia of the Elenil. She lived a full life and made many friends in the years to come, though she had come to it late. It was said she lived in a castle with an old man and his wife, and it was often said that she was the man's sister, or perhaps the woman's sister. No one was sure, but it was clear there was great affection between them, and they were well loved by the children in the nearby village. And she was renowned as a healer. Whether you had a scrape or a fever, if you were sick you could trust that the knock at the door was Jillian with a bowl of hot stew, a kind word, and a cool hand for your forehead. And it was said that in time she fell in love, and married, and had a daughter. She named the girl Madeline, and all who knew her loved her. But none so much as her mother.

✦

The Historian led Shula down the path, which did not seem so dark now. Was sunrise coming? The earth shook, and the Historian paused. "Do not be troubled," he said. "That does not concern those within this cave."

"Are we almost—"

The Historian pointed with his long white finger, the nail sharp, to a small hut in a clearing. "He is there," the Historian said. "When you came to us, we were meant to change your memories, your brother's, and Vasya's. Yours took easily. Your brother fought it. He did not like the new story. He did not want to forget Vasya. Hanali said that you were the priority, so when your new memories were solid, we let you go and kept them." He grimaced. "Your brother, though . . . still he fights my memories. He has thirteen versions of that night in his head. We cannot add another or remove them. He will not give us access, has learned to block us."

Shula started to run before those last words were out of his mouth. She threw open the door. Boulos was stripped to the waist, mumbling in a feverish dream, the burns on his face and chest little more than scars now. She fell beside him and pulled the gourd of concentrated Wendy juice from her belt. She was so thankful she hadn't drunk it now. She put it to his lips, dribbled a bit in at first, then tilted it back, held his head so it could get into his mouth.

He swallowed, groaned, and opened his eyes. When he saw her, he frowned. "Shula? You're back."

She moved away from him. "Boulos."

"Where's Vasya?"

"She's nearby, I think," Shula said quickly. "Not far if you want to see her. Can you walk?"

She helped him to his feet. He was unsteady at first, but strength was returning quickly. She handed him his shirt, and he pulled it on. "I remember . . . everything." He looked at Shula.

Her shoes suddenly seemed interesting. "Me too," she said.

He stepped closer to her. "Shula—"

"Oh, Boulos! It's all my fault. I was terrible, terrible! The way I treated Vasya was . . . was hateful. She's wonderful, and I treated her like garbage, and that's why—" She couldn't finish the sentence. That's why their parents were dead. And little Amira. Why Boulos was covered in scars, and Vasya, too.

"You didn't cut your own face," he said softly. "You didn't light the fire."

"I'm trying to say I'm sorry!" she shouted.

"And I'm trying to say . . . all is forgiven."

"I've broken everything," she said.

"We are family," he said, and he sounded just like their father. "We are family, little sister. When something is broken, well, we fix it if we can. And if not . . . still, we are family."

Shula hugged him again. "Let's go find Vasya."

✚

Jason was falling to his death, which, all things considered, was not the worst thing that had ever happened to him in the Sunlit Lands. He had heard that dying was clarifying. Like, your life flashed in front of your eyes. He was not experiencing that, and he wasn't sure if that meant it was a myth or just meant his body didn't realize he was about to die. Or maybe it was because he had died once already, more or less, on the battlefield. Oh, hey, he could see it over there.

In any case, the only thing flashing in front of his eyes was the pavement really far below, which had become a sort of fountain that was shooting water into the air. Hey, maybe he could land in one of those and be let down to the ground in a gentle spray of water. Well, that seemed unlikely, but it was a comforting thought as he was dying. A sort of cartoon thought, and he hadn't seen any cartoons in a really long time.

His biggest regret, of course, was sweet Baileya. He wished he could see her one last time. He looked in the direction he thought was north, and there was a crowd there. Probably the Kakri, but he wasn't sure if Baileya was there or not.

He looked to the south, where his army should be, and knew he was about to die because he saw angels. Two kinds of angels, actually. There were the ones that looked like Kharobem, but they were on fire and moving toward Far Seeing, surrounding it. And there were the ones that looked like the angels in cartoons. The kind that would get on your shoulder and tell you to do good things: you know, like himself, but with wings.

There was a whole flock of them. Winged Jasons.

Just like . . .

Just like he had requested from the Southern Court. But they had said it wasn't authentic enough!

"You guys!" he shouted. "You guys are the greatest!"

Then ten winged Jasons swept in and lifted him into the air. Jason crowed with delight. "I knew you guys would come! I was *waiting* for you guys to come!"

One of the Jason angels said, "We wanted to be authentic, Your Majesty, but then we realized . . . if you had our powers, you would definitely grow wings."

"Wings, gills, a tail, and maybe an extra hand or two," Jason shouted, still giddy. "Okay, take me up there to where that really dumbfounded archon is standing. Thanks, guys!"

And it wasn't until they dropped him on the balcony that it hit him . . . he had said the same thing to them that Jenny had said to him on the night she had died. *I knew you would come, I was waiting for you to come.* And of course she hadn't been blaming him. She had been happy to see him, thrilled to see him. And he couldn't help it—he knew he should be getting ready to fight Hanali or something, but instead he burst into tears.

He had figured it out. He understood the story. He shouted off the balcony to all the winged Jasons, "I love you guys!" and they shouted back, "We love you too, Your Majesty!"

✢

"Enough," Cumberland said, his voice rough, and the battle stopped.

Darius and Cumberland strode across the battlefield, the Kharobem floating behind them like a fiery honor guard. Everyone put down their weapons as they passed: Scim and Elenil, human and Southern Court. They fell in behind the two men, a strange gravity pulling them in. There were expressions of wonder and fear in the crowd. "The Majestic One," some said, and others "the Peasant King," but some doubted and said, "Isn't the Majestic One an Elenil?" or "Isn't the Peasant King a Scim?"

When they came to the wall, the Peasant King craned his neck to see the top of the wall where it was still intact. "Is my herald still there?" he asked. "The Herald of Mysteries, he's sometimes called."

"I am here," the herald called. "Have you come at last to bring justice to the Sunlit Lands?"

"Indeed," the Peasant King called. "Come down here, that we may have words." To the assembled crowd he said, "Have a seat. We'll be here a minute." And so the warriors took their seats, Scim beside Elenil. And those who had only moments before been trying to murder one another helped one another to sit, and bandaged the wounds of their enemies.

When the herald arrived, Darius greeted him first. "Nightfall! I am so glad to see you well. Hanali told me you were alive, but I'm glad to see it with my own eyes."

"I am the Herald of Mysteries now," he said, and when he said it a great *CRACK* came from the sky. A fissure had formed in the lowest sphere of heaven, and it was not moving straight anymore.

The Peasant King watched it for a moment, half a smile on his face. Then he turned toward the herald. "I know you've been working hard for me," he said. "But, friend, you've been lied to about me. You've got some mistaken ideas. I didn't leave the Elenil in charge. And I would never want the Scim to be slaves."

"Say servants, rather," the herald replied.

The Peasant King gave him a stern look then. "Come aside with me for a moment," the Peasant King said, and the words he spoke then to the Herald of Mysteries were never repeated, but when they returned, the boy looked both chastened and relieved.

"My name is Nola," he said to the assembled armies. The Peasant King put his hand on the boy's shoulder, lending him strength. "I am the Herald of the Majestic One, sometimes called the Peasant King. He has sent me to say to you, he is never one who asks us to do what is unjust. He is never one who asks us to hold another in low esteem, that we may have more power. He has sent me to say that there is neither Scim nor Elenil, Kakri nor Maegrom, for all are precious in his sight. All peoples, and every person. Any who say otherwise speak not for the Peasant King, nor for the Majestic One. And he has told me that even he is only herald of one who is greater yet, called the Story King."

"Nola is a brave soul," the Peasant King said. "And in years to come, he will be a hero well known in the Sunlit Lands."

It was then that the sky began to fall in earnest.

✢

"Why?" Shula asked. "Why would you do this to us?"

The Historian watched her dispassionately. "You wanted freedom from pain, did you not? And Hanali felt that your brother had certain . . . pacifying effects . . . on you that prevented you from fighting the Scim as well as he desired."

"You took my memories, imprisoned my brother, so I would *fight harder*?"

Boulos put his hand on her arm. "Vasya, little sister. We need to get Vasya."

"Take her if you want," the Historian said. "This age comes to an end. All who are imprisoned will be set free. I will find a new place to practice my arts."

"Not if I have anything to say about it," Shula said.

"Where is she?" Boulos didn't seem to care about the Historian, didn't seem to want revenge or even to speak to him.

The Historian gave them directions and dismissed them. They were halfway down a passage, headed the other direction, when Shula pounded back over to him. "Why are you so important? Why does Hanali keep you hidden away down here?"

"My dear, you have it all backward. The Elenil built their settlement around me, not the other way. The Elenil never could have built their empire without me here to wash away the blood and turn their atrocities into heroic sagas. I am the foundation of the Elenil empire, not its servant."

"I hope when it all comes crumbling down you'll be buried in the rubble."

He laughed at that. "I am always forgotten until I am needed." With that he turned and disappeared into the darkness.

They found Vasya easily enough, in a dank cell carved out of the rock. She was lying on the ground, staring at the wall. Boulos held her up, and Shula poured a sip of Wendy juice into her mouth. Color came back into her face, and her eyes focused. She gave a small cry of delight to see them. She embraced Boulos, and Shula fell to her knees and hugged her. "I'm sorry," she said. "I shouldn't have treated you the way that I did."

Vasya kissed her on each cheek. "That is forgiven," she said. "And so long as you remember me, you need not remember any of that."

The whole place shook again, and Boulos said they needed to go. They helped Vasya to her feet. Shula remembered the way, and when they came up the stairs, the crack widened for them again, then closed behind them.

Gary was waiting for them. "Ms. Bishara! This way, quick!" And he led them to a covered portico. Frank came trotting up as well.

Chunks, huge chunks of the sky were falling, crashing toward the Sunlit Lands.

"What's happening, Dad?" Gary asked.

"The old walls are breaking," the unicorn said. "Wild magic will come in now, and we will be able to travel to other places, strange and wonderful places."

Shula put an arm around Boulos, and the other around Vasya. They were together again. A family, of sorts. It made the end of the world seem like small news in comparison.

✦

The whole sky was coming down, and it wasn't small pieces, either. It was like icebergs were falling toward them. Jason leaned over the balcony, amazed. There was some sort of half dome keeping them safe, but sometimes a big piece broke into smaller ones, and those got through. There weren't holes in the domes, but it was like rocks below a certain size had a password or something. The domes were all over, protecting people, and in a few places Jason saw larger domes where, he assumed, more people were gathered. They were transparent but shining, almost like soap bubbles but obviously a lot stronger.

Hanali tried to slip away while everyone's attention was on the falling sky.

"Where do you think you're going?" Break Bones said, and grabbed Hanali by the arm.

"Let's get him downstairs," Jason said. "Something's happening over at the wall, and I think I saw the Kakri coming through town the other way."

By the time they reached the base of the tower, the Kakri had just arrived.

"Mother Crow!" Jason shouted.

"King Wu!" she shouted back, delighted.

He grabbed her hands. "I have a story to tell you," he said, "when this is all over. A story I've never told anyone."

Baileya's eyes filled with tears. "I would like that very much, and I promise I will be very attentive."

He kissed her, and the Kakri cheered. Break Bones let loose with a booming laugh, and the Kakri began one of their whirling, hopping, joyful dances. David clapped him on the shoulder, a wide grin on his face.

"You fools," Hanali said. "Can't you see the whole world is coming apart? And you're dancing."

"Not our world," Yenil said. Her possum struggled out of her arms and scampered away. She and Delightful Glitter Lady ran after him. "Murder Mouse, get back here!"

✦

Jason led the others to the city gates.

The sky fell for nearly four hours. Not only great chunks of sky—parts of every sphere above—but also huge pieces of statues fell, the remnants of the giants, their work now done. Above where the spheres of the sky had been, they could just make out the distant color of another sky, a true sky . . . much like the world back home.

During those hours, many things happened.

Shula, her brother, and their friend showed up, coming from somewhere beneath Far Seeing, with a strange tale of a being called the Historian, who could remove or change memories.

Darius somehow had magic now? He was working together with another man, whom Break Bones called the Peasant King, to keep people safe from the falling sky and the broken fountains of the deep. Between the floods and the crumbling sky, there were a lot of things that were washed away or broken. Darius had left them a few times when there was trouble somewhere else, but the Peasant King had taken care of them in the meantime. Apparently one or both of them were powering the shields, too.

There was a lengthy and significant argument among the Jasons about who got to arrest Hanali.

Gilenyia was nowhere to be found, and they couldn't find Mrs. Oliver, either.

Clawdia showed up out of nowhere, and she told Jason a story. A story about saying goodbye, and captives being released.

Jason and Baileya didn't let each other out of their sight, and they mostly preferred to stay within arm's reach of each other.

When the sky stopped falling, and the magical shields were lowered, the Peasant King stood to speak to them all. "A long time ago," he said, "I peopled this land. I tried to repurpose it when really I should have remade it. That's been fixed now. The Sunlit Lands isn't a terrarium anymore . . . Darius has opened it up to a wider world. It's a wild land of magic, and strange creatures, and big adventures. And if you want to stay here, you can. But if you want to go back to Earth . . . you can do that, too."

Darius stood up, and he seemed, well, different. He had on clothes that looked like something a king would wear. (Hey! Jason was a king now, too. They should have, like, king get-togethers.) And he spoke with an authority that was new.

Darius said, "There are still punishments to be handed out. We can't just remake the world and pretend the past hasn't happened." He crossed his arms. "I'm told that in prior years there was a Kakri city named Ezerbin." The Kakri fell silent and still at the mention of their city, their story. Baileya grabbed Jason's bicep and clutched it. "It was a city that became corrupted, that forgot what it was for. Although it was the greatest city in the Sunlit Lands, it had become a place where orphans were abused and widows taken advantage of. The poor were used to make the rich more money. The weak were food for the powerful. And so it was that the Kharobem came, and they destroyed the city. The ruins still stand today."

The Kharobem had floated away from the group now, were moving into the city limits, spreading around its walls, hovering near its gates. Clawdia smiled at Jason, then transformed into her Kharobem shape. She looked just like the other Kharobem—lion face, human face, ox face, and eagle face, each pointed in a different direction, and a whole lot of wings covered with even more eyes. One of her feet was tucked in a little higher than the other, but it was barely noticeable. She was maybe half the size of the full-grown Kharobem. After a moment, she left to join her people in the ring forming around the city.

"No," Hanali cried. "Mercy, mercy!"

"To those who have shown no mercy, we can give only judgment," Darius said. He cried out, "Fantok, show the people of the Sunlit Lands what happens when the mighty and powerful forget their place."

There was an ominous sound, like rolling water, like thunder, that came from the wings of the creatures, and fire and lightning burst between them, shooting first to this one and then to that. A scorching wind blasted everyone in the assembly, and there were many people who cried out in fear, and many who shouted in terror, and still more who wept.

Then there was silence.

Not a stone stood upon a stone.

The great walls, fallen.

The beautiful towers, rubble.

The once-babbling fountains, silent.

Every statue broken, every home laid bare.

And where the Palace of a Thousand Years had been, the rubble lay higher than in other places, as if there were something there that had been buried. Something that should be left untouched.

"And so Far Seeing has been blinded," Darius said. "No water will spring in this city until such a time as the Kharobem deem the punishment finished. And no one will seek to live in these ruins or seek to dig beneath the ruins of the tower—on pain of death—until springs of running water return."

And then there was silence again. It stretched on and on, and if Jason had to guess, he would have said it was nine full minutes of silence. Hanali put his hand to the choker where the Crescent Stone had been, and his glove came away with only a fine powder that had once been the stone.

It was then that Mother Crow—Baileya—walked to the front of the assembly. "We know your pain," she said. "When Ezerbin fell, we wept. Every year we weep for it. But it was then that a crow came to us and said, 'The desert has claimed your city, so you, you must claim the desert. Come and learn how to live.' So I say to you today, my friends. My brothers. My sisters. If you wish to learn to live, abandon all, and come to the desert."

Then there was silence for a time again. In the sky above, a flaming figure appeared, so bright that no one could look at it directly.

"The Story King!" Cumberland cried, and fell to one knee, his head bowed.

And all the others did the same, save the Kharobem, who rose joyously into the air to greet their king.

A great voice spoke to every heart, and they all heard a different phrase.

And Jason heard only the one-word story, the word he had learned to cherish, the word that changed every story, the word that had changed his life.

PART 6

A CELEBRATION FOR ALL THE PEOPLE

There are not a thousand stories, there is only one,
and we are all heroes or villains.
It is the hero who speaks against injustice.
It is the hero who stands for the oppressed.
It is the hero who protects the weak.
It is the hero who loves.

FROM *THE WISDOM OF WU SONG*

42

FUNCTION
AT THE JUNCTION

Tell me about the Sunlit Lands. Tell me about my friends.
Tell me a story about them.

MADELINE OLIVER

✦

arius had spent the last three months hiking. He had never felt comfortable doing it on Earth—who knew what sort of person you'd meet out in the backwoods—but here in the Sunlit Lands it felt just fine, even though that bright-green hummingbird kept showing up. He knew now it had some sort of message for him, and he couldn't help thinking it was from Madeline. But the bird didn't get in his way, really. He had been to Pastisia and visited with Ian and Mary. Had paid his respects to Crukibal in the underground kingdom of the Maegrom. Had visited Baileya and Jason out in the Kakri desert. Jason kept saying, "Are you sure you don't want to stay?" when Darius was packing his knapsack. Then he kept wandering by, as if he were thinking aloud, saying things like "I'm gonna need *someone* to be my best man."

Darius had two more destinations in mind, and he'd been putting this one off long enough. The trees were beautiful and strange, and when he arrived, Patra Koja was sitting at the entrance, as if he'd been waiting for Darius all along. "She's near the Heartwood Throne," the plant man had said, and gave Darius directions about how to get there.

It was too soon to tell, but he thought the Sunlit Lands was going to get back on its feet. Hanali had managed to escape somehow, to no one's surprise. Well, Jason had been surprised. "Who was in charge of that guy?" he shouted, and twenty-three identical Jasons had pointed at each other.

Maduvorea was beautiful, and it reminded him of Madeline at every turn. She would have loved the flowers. The green light as it filtered down through the leaves. The little faeries who raced hummingbirds through the trees. Sometimes Darius heard them shouting at each other. The return of the faeries' voices was a side effect, he understood, of burning that writ of manumission. Magic didn't require someone to lose for someone else to gain. Not anymore.

He came to a small river and had to wade across it, holding his backpack over his head. A young woman was standing near a tree shaped like a throne. She wore a flowing green gown and a crown of white flowers woven together.

"You're not her," he said, and his voice caught when he said it.

"Darius," she said. "I hoped you would come."

It wasn't her. But she sure looked like Madeline. Sounded like her. "I didn't get a chance to say goodbye," he said.

"She knew, you know." The Garden Lady set a hand on his arm, and her touch was so gentle, so soft. Like a leaf. Like a rose petal.

"Knew what?"

She smiled, and it was Madeline smiling at him. "That you loved her."

He took a deep, sudden breath through his nose. "How do you know?"

"She told me, Darius. She told me before she left us."

"That's good," he said, and he could barely get the words out. "That's really good." He rubbed his eyes with the heels of his hands.

They walked for a while around the island. She showed him the new flowers and fruits that Madeline had left behind. The ivy that undid curses. The pudding fruit that made people tell the truth. The bush with wide yellow berries that made you remember. He took one of those, ate it, felt a flash of bright memories with Madeline.

"She left something for you, too," the Garden Lady said. She reached into a cleft in a tree and pulled out a book. A first-edition copy, signed, of *The Gryphon under the Stairs* by Mary Patricia Wall. Madeline's favorite book. The one he had given to her.

"How?"

The Garden Lady smiled. "Magic, of course."

He turned the book over in his hands. "She loved me too," he said. Not that he doubted it. He just liked to remind himself.

"She loved you very much," the Garden Lady said. The hummingbird zipped around him, circled him several times, then burst upward toward the trees, chirping as it went.

Darius stayed with the Garden Lady in Maduvorea for a few days, until he felt refreshed and strong in a way that he had not for a long, long time.

✛

When it was time for Darius to leave, the Garden Lady opened a way from her garden to Cumberland's, and he found himself walking up a tall hill, his backpack hanging from one shoulder, toward the house that opened to the Sunlit Lands upstairs and Earth downstairs.

His father waved to him from the balcony, and when Darius came in the door, there was his mother, smothering him with kisses and near strangling him with hugs. Cumberland was cooking. There was fried chicken, noodles, mashed potatoes, waffles, steak, hamburgers, and mac and cheese. Really anything you might want. "Leftovers night," Cumberland said with a wink.

His dad put some Shorty Long on the record player—Cumberland hadn't upgraded his technology beyond that—and said, "You gotta update your music, old man!"

"You tell me one thing wrong with Shorty Long," he said.

Mama said, "Well, he hasn't put out a new song in a while," and they all had a laugh at that.

They were halfway through the meal before Cumberland started talking about dessert. Darius pushed back from the table. "I was afraid," he said.

"Of what, baby?" his mom asked. "The Sunlit Lands?"

"No. Not that. I was afraid of being home. Of Earth. That's why I kept staying in the Sunlit Lands. Seems like in the real world, knowing how to save it or break it . . . it's harder. More work. Less magic."

"That's true," his dad said.

"We worked hard," Mama said. "Trying to make a space for you where you never had to steal a pack of cigarettes, never had to put yourself in the kind of danger where someone might kill you over a fake twenty-dollar bill." And he knew what she meant. *Kill you because you're Black.*

"You did good, Mama. You've kept me safe, and I know it hasn't been easy. And I know I don't have to fight to be free."

"You got to fight the ones that don't know you're free," Cumberland said. "That's what."

"So what you gonna do?" his dad asked. "Come home to America and break this place down so we can rebuild it? Become the new Peasant King and babysit the Sunlit Lands? You gonna be the next president of the United States or start a nonprofit or go to college or what?"

"Yeah," Darius said, a smile spreading on his face. "Yeah. One of those things."

43

THE REBUILDING
OF EZERBIN

*Keep your eyes shut, kid, because I'm about
to give Baileya the biggest kiss ever.*

FROM "THE BALLAD OF WU SONG," A KAKRI TALE

✦

The water flowed in Ezerbin again.

When the Kakri found out, there was a party like nothing Jason had ever seen before, and the Kakri moved in immediately. Carting out the sand, fixing up the fountains, rebuilding the houses.

And they were making something new. People took Mother Crow seriously when she invited them to come to the desert, and there were people from every part of the Sunlit Lands with them now.

There had been some conflict at first about whom to let in, mostly because some Elenil had shown up. But Jason had come up with a new custom. A welcoming ritual. Once you did it, you were part of the community, no questions asked.

There was this beverage made out of the concentrated Wendy juice.

And there was this pastry made out of pudding fruit. The drink gave you back all your memories, reminded you of things. Who you were. What had been done for you. Mistakes that had been made and forgiveness that had been extended. And the pudding fruit pastry (or, as Jason called it, the pu-fru pastry) made you tell the truth. Each person had to drink and eat before entering the community in order to remember who they were and share that with complete honesty.

Today, the community was gathered for an especially important moment. An announcement of marriage was about to be made for two very influential and beloved people in the community.

Jason and Baileya were there, of course, and it looked like word had gotten out to practically everyone. Break Bones was present, but that was no surprise because he lived here in Ezerbin. He didn't wear his war skin much anymore, so he was this tall, beautiful-looking man with dusky skin and a network of black tattoos across his muscular arms. His long black hair was pulled back and plaited. (Did he do that himself? Was he going to be a hairdresser now that the war was done? Jason had *questions*.) Everyone called him Croion, his true name.

Other old friends were there too: Yenil and Shula and her boyfriend (duh), David. Boulos and Vasya. The former queen, Lelise. Kekoa was there, and Ruth, too. Even King Ian and Queen Mary Patricia had come. There were some folks from Maduvorea, including faeries named Diwdrap and Thastle, and Lin and Lamisap. And, of course, all the Scim kids who liked to torment Jason had arrived: Eclipse and Shadow and Nightfall (though he went by his true name now, too . . . everyone called him Nola). Rondelo was there with his stag, Evernu. Old Mother Crow and her family and basically every Kakri ever had come. Clawdia had shown up, hanging around on the outskirts of the crowd. The Kharobem could come and go freely now, and Jason felt like . . . maybe there were more of them here now that the walls were down? Even Remi the flying cat had dropped in and acted like it was an accident.

"Well," Jason said, taking the stage. He was a little overwhelmed by the number of people. There were an awful lot of Jasons in the audience too. "I want to start by saying I don't really want to be king of the Southern Court." There was a groan from the crowd. "I know, I know. But I've got other things I need to focus on. And I've been talking to Lelise about it, and we think—this is going to be a little bit different—we think it should be Yenil."

There was a shocked silence, followed by an enormous cheer from the Jasons. Yenil was very, very popular among the Southern Court for her no-nonsense frankness and her devil-may-care bravery. She was beaming. It would be largely ceremonial for a few years, giving her time to learn from Lelise. But they thought it would be good, and would bind the Scim and the Southern Court together in a way that would bring the Courtiers more firmly into the life of the Sunlit Lands.

"Hey!" Shula shouted from the front of the crowd. "She's too young! We want her to live a normal life for a while." (Shula had insisted she be allowed to say this. She didn't want Yenil thinking she'd be sitting on pillows eating chocolates all day.)

"Come on!" Yenil shouted. "Let me be queen!" She turned to Vasya. "Auntie Vasya, what do you think?"

She grinned, her arm around Boulos. "Aw, let her be queen, Shula."

Shula threw her hands up, smiling at Vasya. "Fine, fine, who am I to say? I'm only her mother."

Yenil hugged her fiercely and leapt onto the stage. "As queen, I promise you that I and King Murder Mouse will rule you with wisdom and a lot of free candy."

An enormous roar of approval swept the audience, and she bowed extravagantly before leaping down into David's arms.

"There's another reason we are here," Baileya said. "To announce a wedding that many of you have been waiting to hear about."

Another roar from the crowd, and Jason tried to calm them with his hands. "Hold on, hold on!"

"Wait," someone shouted. "One moment! I'm sorry, but before you do that."

"I know that voice," Jason said. "Mrs. Oliver?"

It *was* Mrs. Oliver. She had disappeared on the day that Far Seeing had fallen. She came onto the stage, guiding a man bent over in a ratty coat, a hood covering his head.

"Who is that with you?" Baileya Crow asked.

He pulled his hood back. Jason recognized him immediately, though his face was haggard and worn. He raised his hands as if expecting a blow.

Baileya crossed her arms. "Why have you come to Ezerbin, Hanali, son of Vivi?"

He shivered. "To face your justice, Baileya. Mother Crow."

The crowd shifted. There was some jeering, a few boos. Jason held up his hand for silence. "Mrs. Oliver?"

She faced the crowds. "Years ago, I came here with a group of my friends, to the Sunlit Lands. Horrible things happened to us in those days. Some of us died. A few of us escaped. It was me. Kyle. Allison. Tony. Gabrielle." She gestured to Hanali. "And Lee. Vivi had taken an interest in him. Lee agreed to stay so the few of us who left could go home. I'm not saying he's innocent. I'm not saying he shouldn't be punished. I'm just saying . . ." She shrugged. "Kill him, put him in prison, exile him. He can't keep living without justice. It's eating him alive."

Jason looked at Baileya, and she nodded. "Bring me the Wendy juice and the pu-fru pastry," Jason said.

Croion brought it over. He looked down on the pitiful Hanali. He handed Jason the juice and the pastry, then bent over to lift the Elenil up. "Be brave," he whispered to Hanali, just loud enough that only Jason could hear it.

Jason held up the drink. "When you drink this, Hanali, it will be to remember who you are, and what you have done, and what has been done for you." He handed him the cup, and Hanali took it in both hands and drank it down greedily, the juice spilling onto his chest. His eyes widened, and he dropped the drink. He began to weep. Croion held the sobbing Elenil up.

Then Jason took the pastry. "And this pu-fru pastry will help you speak truthfully on the day that you eat it." He handed it to Hanali, who shoved it in his mouth, ate it whole. Jason waited until he had swallowed and caught his breath again. "Do you have anything you wish to say to these people?"

Hanali took a deep breath and stepped forward. He started to speak, but his voice caught. He looked down at the ground, took another breath, and spoke. "I have many regrets. I have wronged many people, including most of you here. Perhaps all of you here. I do not ask for mercy. The wrongs that I have done are too great for that. But I do ask that you please accept my apology. My sorrow is deep and true." He bowed his head.

Jason stepped between Hanali and the crowd. "You heard him, friends. He has done great harm to you. He has killed and stolen, lied and cheated. And all this to preserve his own power. What do you say?"

There was murmuring, a growing unease in the crowd. Hanali stared straight ahead, stoic. Cries of "Kill him!" began to gain strength in the crowd.

"He killed my parents," Yenil shouted.

"Let the queen speak," someone replied, and soon people throughout the crowd were shouting it. "Let the queen speak!"

Yenil jumped back onto the stage. "He didn't hold the sword, but it was he who connected me to Madeline, so I couldn't breathe. It was because of him that the Elenil came to my house that night. It was because of him that the sword found my father's heart, because of him that my mother no longer sings to me of bright stars at night. I lived my life in darkness." The crowd was surging forward now, and she shouted at them to stop, to listen. She pointed at the bedraggled, sad-looking man. "And yet did he not drink the juice and eat the bread?" She looked at Jason. "Doesn't that make him part of our community? Isn't that what you said?"

"Yeah," Jason admitted. "That's what I said."

"Then he's already one of us," she said. "And we just gotta figure out what to do about that." It was like she had sung a lullaby to the crowd. They quieted, reflecting on her words. "And it seems to me that Mother Crow is about the smartest and kindest person I know, except maybe my Shula mom. So I say, let Mother Crow decide what to do." The crowd approved, cheering again.

Mother Crow stepped forward. She turned to Hanali. "Your crimes are vile and loathsome. Many of them you did with malice and for your own gain. But I believe your words of sorrow. Among the Kakri, we do not have prisons. There is life, and there is the end of life. There is growth and the end of growth. To me, it looks as if you are still growing, Hanali, son of Vivi. So it seems to me that we should not end your life. Instead, you will spend every day of the rest of your long life—every day—as a servant to those in the Sunlit Lands who are the least. You will walk the land and take care of the poor and the widow and the orphan. And when I, or any ruler in the Sunlit Lands, calls upon you, then you will give account for your deeds. And each year we will decide whether you are still growing." She turned to the audience. "And who will be his guardian? Who will walk the lands with him and help him grow?"

Croion stepped forward immediately and knelt at Baileya's feet. "I, Mother Crow. I, too, have much to atone for. And I will watch over him until such a time as you and Wu Song release me from this duty."

"So be it," Mother Crow said.

"So be it," Jason said.

"So be it!" the crowd shouted back.

Hanali was weeping now, and Croion and Mrs. Oliver helped him from the stage.

"Hey!" Kekoa shouted from the crowd. "I thought you were about to announce a wedding that many of us were waiting to hear about!"

The crowd stomped and cheered.

"Oh yeah," Jason said. "You still want to know about that?"

You would have thought he had poured gasoline out and lit a match. The crowd was screaming at him to get on with it.

Baileya smiled. "I was once engaged to Wu Song."

"It was an accident."

She grinned. "Was it?"

"But Baileya broke up with me!"

The crowd shouted, *"Awwwwwww."*

"He didn't love himself enough," she said. "So I knew he couldn't receive my love."

"Hey, that's personal," Jason said.

"But he has told me a new story," Baileya said, putting her arm around him. "A wonderful story."

"And she has given me this lovely gold arm bracelet," Jason said, pulling up his sleeve. Everyone went wild.

She pointed at all the Jasons in the audience. "I have you to thank for this! He learned to love himself by spending time with you!"

"Anyway," Jason said, "since we're Kakri and all . . . we're going to have a big party, and I mean a *huge* party tonight, and then me and Mother Crow are gonna go hide for a year while her brothers try to kill us!"

"Well, just you, technically," Baileya said. "No one wants to kill me."

"You got that right," David yelled, and everyone laughed.

"It's gonna be fun!" Jason said. There was riotous cheering now. "I learned something," Jason said, "during my time in the desert. Where I come from, we like to end a story by saying, 'They all lived happily ever after.' That's how we know a story has a happy ending. *They all lived happily ever after.* I've been thinking about that. It's not '*I* lived happily ever after.' It's all of us. You and me. Us. And if one of us has something terrible going on—if there's one person that the Sunlit Land is unjust toward—well, how can we all live happily ever after? I guess what I'm saying is, we're not free unless we're all free. You and me, together. To say we all lived happily ever after is just to say we have each other's backs. That when terrible things come, it means we're going to stand together, and I'm not going to say, 'No, it's okay, I'm happy' if you're being harmed by someone. That's what this place, what Ezerbin could be, if we can figure out how to build it. 'Happily ever after' means whatever comes, we're going to fight for each other."

"Shut up and kiss her," Kekoa shouted, and Baileya shouted back, "Thank you!"

Everyone laughed and cheered and Jason reached for her—

"NO!"

Jason stopped. "Are you kidding me? What now?"

Baileya's brother Bezaed leapt upon the stage. Oh, great. Of course. This guy had literally chased him all over the Sunlit Lands. Well, maybe he was going to give him a head start or something.

To his surprise, Bezaed knelt in front of them and set his knives between them, the blades toward himself. "Mother Crow," he said. "Wu Song. I come to you speaking for the Kakri, and also for our new people, the people of Ezerbin."

"Go on," Mother Crow said, her voice even.

"I have hunted this man across the Sunlit Lands, and he has avoided my blade at every turn. How? Because the people love him. Maybe not all the people. But he has friends among the Scim, the Kakri, the Maegrom. Even a flying cat—"

"Not a cat," Remi said.

"And the reason for our tradition—a tradition which I love—is to give our people time to be sure that the suitor is worth the bride. And it seems to me, as I have hunted this man and fought beside him, and as I have lived beside Baileya my whole life . . . who could object to this match? And so I ask, humbly, Mother Crow, Wu Song . . . why must we wait a year to be blessed by your marriage? We ask you, please, my sister Baileya, my friend Wu Song . . . why could we not have this wedding tonight?"

"Yes," the audience shouted. "Yes, yes!"

Jason started to say something again, but Kekoa shouted "Kiss her!" again, and the crowd began chanting for them to kiss.

And Jason kissed Baileya for the longest time, and everyone who loved someone in the audience kissed them, and the music began, and they sang and leapt together, and told old stories and made new ones, and they ate and danced some more, and there was laughter and there were a few tears, but it was a night they never forgot.

And they all lived happily ever after.

EPILOGUE

On the shore of the Ginian Sea, there is a small village on a cliff overlooking the water. It's only a few cottages, a pen of goats, a garden, and some chickens. But the most influential people in the world come to visit this humble place with its thatched roofs and open doors.

Mother Crow visits, it is said, and the Heart of Flame, and even the king of the necromancers from time to time. There is a queen there who likes to show royalty "*Here is how to milk a goat*," and she loves to eat fresh bread from the oven and frolic and play with the animals. Famous warriors and poets and philosophers from the recent past come to visit, and the queen calls them all auntie and uncle.

She has a tragic story, or so we are told, a young life of relentless darkness, for she lost her parents in a brutal war. But to see her with the women she lives with—Shula Mom she calls the one, and Mama Wendy the other—to see her ride upon her Uncle Boulos's shoulders or make drawings with her Aunt Vasya or race her Papa Kyle to the beach for their morning swim or to hear her telling stories with Uncle David, one might be forgiven for wondering aloud why she is called the Orphan Queen.

And she will smile and tell you, "For I am the queen of orphans, and every orphan I find must be blessed with mother and father, grandmother, and aunt and uncle, just like me." And if they are lucky, she says, perhaps they may even be given a unicorn, like her Uncle Jason has Delightful Glitter Lady, or a good possum, like she has Murder Mouse.

Then the little Scim girl is off to collect the eggs or pick the daisies or to sing at the top of her lungs and dance in the bright, bright sunlight.

THE END

THE BITTAR

The most famous and beloved Kakri musical instrument is a six-stringed instrument called the bittar. The Kakri consider music to be a type of story. In the Kakri language, there is no distinction made between stories and songs, and even instrumental music is considered a form of storytelling.

The bittar has six strings, each of which has a name. They are, in ascending order:

The Beginning

The Mountain Which Must Be Climbed

The Sound of a Voice, Like Many Birds

The Shadow String (or the Arrival of Death)

A Glimmer of Light

A Celebration for All the People

These strings, when played in certain orders and chords, form recognizable stories to the Kakri people. There are, of course, various ways to make chords, some of which have their own names. For instance, a common chord used in tragic stories is formed by playing The Sound of a Voice/The Shadow String/A Celebration for All the People—a chord that is informally called The Hero's Funeral. A common chord in stories of love, Mountain/Sound/Light is also called The Lover Worth Any Sacrifice.

ACKNOWLEDGMENTS

First and foremost, three friends who read an early edition of *The Story King* and have been cheering this whole series on: Sienna Emery, Jenna McComas, and Joshua Chapman. Thank you!

Special thanks, too, to Dr. Michelle Reyes who spent hours on the phone with me talking about fairy tales and the Sunlit Lands. She brought so many incredible insights that ended up in the final book.

The Story King wouldn't be in your hands right now if it weren't for a wonderful team of amazing folks who helped at different points along the way, including Wes Yoder, agent extraordinaire; Linda Howard, Empress of the Sunlit Lands; Sarah Atkinson, Keeper of Bullet; Sarah Rubio, the Not-So-Secret Architect of Continuity and Consistency; Danika King, who jumped in mid-project and did an astounding job as editor; and copyeditors Debbie King and Debbie MacPherson. I am not exaggerating one bit when I say one of my favorite moments of any book production is seeing the incredible design work of Dean Renninger. And of course you almost certainly heard about this book because of the hard work of Kristi Gravemann and Mariah León.

The whole *Fascinating Podcast* team is responsible for so many good things in my life, and it's often reflected in my books—either in the things I'm learning through them or the ways their friendship shapes me. You all know who you are, but for the rest of the world, that's Aaron Kretzmann, Elliott and Lauren Dodge, Clay Morgan, Jen Cho, Kathy Khang, Peter Chang, and JR. and Amanda Forasteros.

I would have never reached out to Tyndale about this series if not for my buddy Jesse Doogan, so you get part of the blame here too!

Jermayne Chapman, so thankful for your friendship and all the time you've spent giving me feedback.

To my parents, who always help me make space in life to be a functioning member of society and my family and still get my writing done!

And of course, as always, my beloved wife, Krista, and my three daughters, Myca, Allie, and Zoey. Myca is the inventor of a certain not-a-cat in this book, and Allie and Zoey have been the constant voice of deadly threats if I did wrong by Jason and Baileya. Much, much love to all of you, and I am so thankful for your patience when I am spending so much time writing!

I am deeply thankful to all the Sunlit Lands fans who keep reading, spreading the word, sending me notes or art (or board games you've created!) or book reports about the Sunlit Lands. I enjoy it so much. Thank you for letting the Sunlit Lands take root in the world.

Lastly, a big shout-out to Bruce the Rabbit. Someone read this to him, because he is still a baby and can't even read or anything.

ABOUT THE AUTHOR

MATT MIKALATOS entered Middle-earth in third grade and quickly went from there to Narnia, kindling a lifelong love of fantasy novels that are rich in adventure and explore deep questions about life and the world we live in. He believes in the hopeful vision of those two fantasy worlds in particular: the Stone Table will always be broken; the King will always return; love and friendship empower us and change the world.

For the last two decades Matt has worked in a nonprofit organization committed to creating a safer, more loving world by teaching people how to love one another, accept love themselves, and live good lives. He has lived in East Asia and served all over the world.

Matt's science fiction and fantasy short stories have been published in a variety of places, including *Nature*'s "Futures" page, *Daily Science Fiction*, and the Unidentified Funny Objects anthologies. His nonfiction work has appeared on Time.com, on the *Today* show website, and in *Relevant* magazine, among others. He also cohosts *The Fascinating Podcast* at norvillerogers.com /podcast/fascinating/.

Matt lives in the Portland, Oregon, area with his wife and three daughters. You can connect with him on Twitter (@MattMikalatos), Facebook (facebook.com/mikalatosbooks), or via his website (thesunlitlands.com).